P9-DEU-895

Close to the Bone

CLOSE
TO THE
BONE

David Wiltse

G. P. PUTNAM'S SONS   NEW YORK

G. P. Putnam's Sons
Publishers Since 1838
200 Madison Avenue
New York, NY 10016

Library of Congress Cataloging-in-Publication Data

Wiltse, David.
Close to the bone / David Wiltse.
p.   cm.
ISBN 0-399-13718-1 (acid-free paper)
I.   Title.
PS3573.I478C5   1992
813'.54—dc20   92-18848 CIP

Printed in the United States of America
1   2   3   4   5   6   7   8   9   10

This book is printed on acid-free paper.
∞

TO ANNIE
WITH LOVE

Close to the Bone

PROLOGUE

His grandmother could no longer negotiate the stairs, so Leon Brade took his victims to the basement. Her hearing was failing along with her wits, so when she heard the moans at all she confused them with the television noises. There had been a scream or two before Brade had perfected his techniques, but that had been several years before now and his grandmother had long since forgotten.

Brade also preferred the basement because of the large drain in the floor that had once served the old-fashioned, multi-tubbed washing machine and wringer arrangement. The drain now served Brade well. He could dispose of all the messy by-products of his work with a hose. He worked in the nude so he could spray himself off as well. The drain was quite large and had never clogged except for the time early on when a mass of hair had obstructed the pipe. Brade learned his lesson and thereafter used the hair to stuff the handsewn and embroidered throw pillows that made such a nice, casual decoration throughout the living room. He first washed the hair thoroughly, of course. Some of the victims had put the most disgusting oils and lotions, sprays, and mousses on it, and others were, frankly, unclean in their personal habits. Brade was revolted by bad hygiene.

The greatest thing about the basement, however, was not its inaccessibility to his grandmother, nor its drain, nor even the exposed overhead pipes, which were so convenient for suspending the victims. The greatest feature of the basement was the escape pipe.

Brade had discovered it after noticing his cat emerging from behind the furnace with one of the endless supply of mice she liked to drop on Brade's workbench beside the drain. Sometimes Brade wondered if Tiger wasn't competing with Brade himself on her own small feline scale.

There was a dirt-floored crawl space behind the furnace, accessible through a small gap in the brick retaining wall. Brade had removed some more bricks and slithered into the space under the house until he found Tiger's source of victims. The house had been built by Brade's grandfather in what had been a cornfield at the time. The old man had visions of suburbia sweeping out from the city to engulf his property and enrich his pocketbook, and in preparation he had marked off his one hundred twenty acres in city blocks and building lots, part of a development that finally came long after the old man had died. As part of his preparations for civilization, the old man had begun to install a sewer system that was to have emptied into Brade's creek, which in turn, and in time, poured itself into the Niobrara River. Nothing had happened as he'd envisioned, but the wide mouth of the first storm drain still lay under Brade's house, gaping with promise.

Brade had tested the huge pipe, crawling its length until he emerged on the bank of the creek, out of sight and several hundred yards from the house. It was dark and frightening in the pipe and in some stretches Brade had to slide on his belly to squeeze over mounds of dirt and droppings, but the way was passable and nearly straight. Even the few jogs in the line could serve a purpose by providing him a space in which to turn around and face whatever was behind him.

If they came for him—and Brade knew that eventually they would come—only a fool would be bold enough to follow him into the sheer blackness of the hole. A prudent man would call for help, delay, try to find the egress of the pipe, all of which would give Brade the time he would need to get away. But if it happened that they sent a fool after him, Brade was ready for that, too. Around the second bend in the pipe where he could turn around and where his pursuer would be totally blind and unsuspecting, Brade had secreted his favorite knife, the one used for filleting. Long, narrow, and sharpened to a lethal edge on both sides, it was an exact duplicate of the one Brade kept on his workbench by the drain.

Brade had wired the doorbell to ring in the basement. He didn't want any solicitous neighbor, bearing fruit and comfort for his grandmother, hearing no response to the bell, to wander in unannounced. When it rang, Brade looked up from his work, startled. He was expecting no one; he had sent the officers away convinced of his innocence, he was sure of it.

Hurriedly he stripped off his surgical gloves, pulled on his mechanic's uniform, thrust his feet into his boots, and then checked that

the tape across the victim's mouth was secure before he started up
the hazardous wooden stairs to the main floor. The victim's eyes were
closed, but Brade had learned long ago that his victims were not to
be trusted. They liked to trick him if they could; they were not always
as dead as they looked.

Brade recognized the man at the door. He had been with the police
earlier but had said nothing during the interview.

"Hello, Leon," the man said. "I'm John Becker."

"Did you forget something?" Brade asked politely. He stepped
back, allowing the man to come into the house. He must maintain the
appearance of someone who had nothing to hide. The police were
welcome in his home.

The man named Becker walked into the living room with a familiarity that Brade found annoying.

"I think *you* forgot something," Becker said.

"I don't think so."

"Yes, you di-id, Leon," Becker said. His tone was sing-songy,
taunting, as if he were speaking to a child.

"What did I forget?"

"You forgot to tell the tru-uth."

Becker wagged his finger at Brade, playfully scolding a naughty
boy.

Brade sat on the sofa and folded one of his special pillows across
his chest.

"I don't understand what you mean," Brade said. "I told you
everything I know."

"Oh, no, Leon. No, no, no."

"You were here before and you didn't say anything."

"But I watched you. I saw what you di-id."

"Are you really a policeman? I don't believe you are."

"Oh, I'm worse than a policeman, Leon. Much worse than that."
Becker picked up one of the throw pillows and tossed it lightly from
hand to hand. Brade thought it was the pillow from the redhead—
such a glorious cascade of hair.

"You know who I am, don't you, Leon? You knew I'd pay a visit
eventually."

"I don't know what you mean," Leon said.

"Sure you do." Becker leaned close to Brade and smiled. It was a
frightening smile. "I'm your conscience."

Brade tried to chuckle, to turn it into a joke, but he could tell the man was not being funny.

Becker sat beside Brade on the sofa and put his arm around Brade's shoulders. He spoke in the whisper of horror movies.

"Leon," he whispered. "I know about you."

Brade started up, but Becker's arm held him firmly on the sofa.

"I know what you do," he hissed. "I know what you do when you think you're alone." Brade struggled, but Becker pushed him harder against the sofa.

"I know how it feels, Leon. I know how you feel when you do it," Becker said into his ear.

Brade broke away and leaped to his feet.

"You're not a cop! A cop wouldn't act like this!"

"I'm a special cop. I'm a cop just for you. This is just between us. No one else knows what goes on between you and your conscience."

Brade backed across the room, clinging to the pillow with one arm.

"Don't you need a warrant? You need a warrant or something."

Brade was close to the kitchen. From there it was but a few feet to the basement door.

"You have blood on your hands, Leon. You forgot to wash."

Involuntarily, Brade glanced at his hands. The man was lying. He'd worn gloves; he always wore gloves in the basement.

"I don't know anything about those women, my grandmother can tell you that, I'm going to get my grandmother, she'll tell you."

Brade stepped into the kitchen and ran for the basement. He was behind the furnace before the man could have seen him, he was sure of it. He crawled to the pipe in the dark. He had no need of the light; he knew the way, he had practiced. He felt the emptiness of the hole with his hands, then arched into it and slid into the pipe without hesitation.

Halfway to the first bend in the pipe Brade realized he was not alone. Someone was behind him in the dark, coming fast. There was no way to turn around where he was, nothing to see in the blackness if he did. But the man behind him was not a fool, as he had thought he would have to be to follow him. He was something much worse. Becker had called himself Brade's conscience. Brade prayed that his conscience was the only thing gaining on him.

At the first turn in the pipe Brade glanced back just long enough to see the darkness move. It seemed to shift and surge, coming at him.

Brade crawled faster than he thought he could toward the second bend and the knife.

Still, the man was gaining on him as if he could see in the dark, as if he were more comfortable going into the unknown than Brade was in a stretch he knew well. Brade was ahead by only a few yards when he rounded the second turn and groped for the knife. He found the handle just as Becker caught him by the ankle and yanked. The knife fell and clanked dully against the cement pipe. Brade clawed desperately for it, ripping his fingernails, squirming against the grip on his ankle. The flesh on his fingers tore as he sought a grip in the concrete, but still Brade was drawn inexorably backwards into the dark. For a second Brade had the feeling that he was being swallowed whole by a giant snake in whose gaping mouth lay all the inky dark of the world.

He kicked back with his free leg, felt the boot strike bone and the grip on his ankle loosen. Surging forward, he grabbed the knife and turned to face his tormentor. He stabbed into the black. The blade struck flesh, then Becker had his wrist and his throat and Brade felt the knife being slowly turned back toward himself. He heard Becker sigh, a sound of deep relief. Brade knew the sound well. He made it himself when he first touched each of the victims.

1

1989

Palaces were built for splendor, castles for defense, an historical distinction Holzer was reminded of as he entered Pelovo castle and passed through an opening framed with the three-foot-thick stones that formed the walls of the scarp. The air in the barbican was so thick and oppressive that he turned involuntarily for one last look at the outside, and his eye caught a glint of the Danube coiling its romanticized way through the valley below. At this point in its journey seaward, the Danube passed through the industrial dumps of Romania. Any reflection Holzer saw was as apt to come from pollutants as from the water itself.

At one point several centuries ago, Pelovo castle had withstood a siege by the Ottoman Turks for sixteen weeks before the inhabitants, starved and mad from thirst, had surrendered on the condition that there would be no reprisals and that their women and children would be well treated. Upon raising the portcullis and allowing the Turks to enter, the defenders of the castle were saluted for their courage and obstinacy and gallantry in battle. Then they were slaughtered to a man by their conquerors. The women were raped and then killed in keeping with the custom of the day. Little girls were taken to serve as concubines wherever they could be afforded throughout the empire, and the stronger, more promising boys were shipped off to be trained as mercenaries to serve with the janissary or the Mamluks of Egypt where, given time and good fortune, they would grow up to besiege and sack and massacre a few castles or towns of their own—perhaps right back in their native land of Bulgaria. The Ottoman Turks were democratic in that way.

Holzer knew none of the history of this particular castle, nor of Bulgaria nor the Ottomans and their two-century grip on southern Europe and the Middle East, but he did know a forbidding prison when he saw one. He was something of an expert in that line, having had more first-hand experience than he cared to remember but couldn't forget. He was a man with a good deal of experience he hadn't wished for.

They led Holzer below ground and he hesitated instinctively. Even in his current position as messenger/recruiter, the abrupt drop in temperature and rise in humidity as they descended made him cringe as if he himself was a prisoner once more. The warder turned and looked back at Holzer inquiringly.

"Cold?" the warder asked in Bulgarian.

Holzer spoke Russian, English, French, and a bit of Arabic, as well as his native German, but not Bulgarian.

The warder grinned knowingly as Holzer indicated his incomprehension by shrugging his shoulders. There was a hint of a sneer in the grin, a trace of condescension in his tone.

"You get used to it," he said, again in Bulgarian. Like many of his race, the Bulgarian warder felt a mixture of inferiority and contempt for his taller, fairer northern cousins. The Ottomans were long since gone from Pelovo, but their blood, their stature, and Turkic features remained behind as well as an inborn distaste for the infidel. Even ideologically correct infidels like Holzer.

The dungeon had been carved out of the rocky hillside overlooking the Danube. Given the terrain, there had been little need for elaborate walls. The sixteenth century was not a time for humanitarian concern or the aesthetic niceties of architecture when it came to making prisons. That was reserved for cathedrals and those were all farther north in any event. The dungeon of Pelovo castle was not a place for penal rehabilitation; it was a junk heap, an underground midden for the refuse of the society that the leaders, for a variety of reasons, chose not to destroy but to get more or less permanently out of sight. Rather more permanently than less. The inhabitants were assumed to be recidivists of a rather determined nature, men beyond redemption.

There had been an attempt many years back to cover the stone walls with concrete, but the constant seepage had long since rendered the cement and sand a crumbling mass, almost as soft and impressionable a writing surface as when it was first poured. Once in the cell, Holzer could see names and messages scrawled in a polyglot of languages. Pelovo, after all, was a dumping ground for undesirables from all over the Soviet system. Of course, by the time his eyes adjusted to the dim light in the cell, Holzer was not concerned with reading graffiti. His attention was taken entirely by the man he had come to see.

"You don't look comfortable," Bahoud said. He was standing in the corner, leaning against the walls of the cell, his hands clasped at his waist.

He looks like a man holding up a lamp post, waiting for a bus, Holzer thought. He remembered his own state after six months in a cell. He had been more like a man sitting atop an anthill, all tics and twitches with a nervous system that was as busy as if the ants were already crawling over his skin.

"You do," said Holzer.

"One adjusts," said Bahoud, his lips twisting into the slightest sardonic grimace.

"Some do," Holzer agreed. They were speaking English. Holzer spoke the language fluently. Bahoud spoke it like a native. "And some do better than others. You are a man who adjusts very well, indeed."

"Do I?"

"According to what I hear," said Holzer. "Or I did not speak correctly. You do not adjust yourself to fit your surroundings, perhaps. Perhaps you adjust your environment to fit you."

Bahoud shrugged. "The result is the same."

"Not necessarily for the environment," said Holzer. He studied Bahoud carefully as they spoke, trying to reconcile the man's dossier with the man himself. Terror came often enough in pleasant packages as Holzer knew very well. He himself did not appear the type of man who would have planted bombs in airports or murdered American soldiers on the streets of Europe. Had he looked that way, of course, he would have spent many more years in confinement than he already had.

Bahoud stuck his finger in a gouge in the cement and tugged until a few flecks of sand dislodged and landed on the floor. For the first time, Holzer realized the floor was covered in sand.

"This environment is a little tough to adjust," Bahoud said. "It takes a lot of digging, especially if you have no tools."

"Perhaps there is an easier way for you to get out," said Holzer.

"I assumed you had something like that in mind," said Bahoud.

"Why?"

"Because I'm too valuable to allow to molder in this sewer for very long."

"Do you understand why you are here?" Holzer asked.

"Of course."

"Would you tell me?"

"I'm being punished because they say I broke their rules."

"What rules?"

"You know perfectly well. If you didn't, you wouldn't be here."
Holzer took out a notebook and pencil.

"Explain to me, please," he said.

Bahoud stared evenly at Holzer for a moment, then smiled broadly.
It was a smile of such warmth that the German was startled.

"You haf your orderz," said Bahoud, in a burlesque of a German
accent.

"Actually, I do," said Holzer, who was accustomed to but not
reconciled with mocking parodies. "And I also have a good deal of
leeway in deciding what to do with you." He tapped the pencil on
the notebook. "I think you want to be my friend."

Bahoud laughed. "Well, that's subtle enough. What do you want
to know?"

"Tell me about the Master Camp."

"It's a finishing school," said Bahoud. "Ever been there?"

"I wasn't invited," said Holzer. "I wasn't good enough. I was
good, but not good enough." In fact, I was very good, Holzer thought
to himself. It made him wonder just how much better someone like
Bahoud must be. "Only the very best are invited to the Master
Camp."

Bahoud shrugged but without any trace of humility. *He obviously
accepts himself as the best,* Holzer thought. That kind of confidence
seemed a prerequisite for selection. No one with self-doubts could be
among the best; self-doubt would slow him down.

"There are classes, lots of classes, basically just refinements of
what they taught you in—wherever you were."

"Ostrova."

Bahoud nodded. "The Czechs are good."

Not as good as the Russians was the implied criticism, but Holzer
could not argue; it was the truth.

"I'm not interested in the classes—or only academically, you understand. Perhaps you could tell me about them another time. Now I
wish to know about the test."

Bahoud shrugged again. "It's very simple, really."

Holzer stifled a response. The final test at the Master Camp was legendary. Those who survived it successfuly were themselves the stuff of legend. Bahoud had completed the test in record time—and in a unique way.

"They took us to the middle of Siberia in the winter, dressed us in American military uniforms, and dumped us out of the truck one by one, about twenty miles apart so we couldn't cooperate. They alerted all the area police and military and civilians that U.S spies were on the loose and gave us one week to make our way back to camp in Yessey undetected. It was about two hundred miles on foot through wilderness with patrols looking for you."

Holzer shuddered at the prospect of covering two hundred miles of shelterless terrain in a Siberian winter. On foot it would require a forced march of thirty miles a day through snow without adding the complications of patrols, food, or shelter. The success rate of the "test" at Master Camp was less than one per year. Bahoud was the one in his year.

"Were you given any survival equipment?" Holzer asked.

"If you want to call it that. We all had an electronic transmitter that could be traced by surveillance aircraft. It gave them a fix on our position at any given time, and it had a distress button to use if you wanted to give up."

Holzer knew there was no disgrace to giving up in the "test." He had heard reports that more than forty percent of the "masters" gave up rather than freeze to death. Another forty percent were caught by the patrols—perhaps willingly. The remainder were rescued when their signals became stationary for more than half a day, indicating they were succumbing to the conditions. The Soviets were careful not to lose any of their "masters" if they could avoid it—each of them was far too valuable. The test was designed to see how far a man would go before he would give in, not to kill him.

"You did not need your distress button," said Holzer, prompting him to continue.

"No."

Holzer waited.

"You know what happened," Bahoud said.

"I would like to hear your version."

"There is only one version."

"Then your interpretation of that version. Please."

Bahoud dug another morsel of sand from the cement. "I was the last one in the truck after he had dropped off the other five."

"He?"

"Captain somebody or other. He wasn't connected with the camp, really. He was just a flunky designated to drive us to the drop-off point."

"His name was Malkov."

"Was it?"

"So he dropped off the other five men?"

"Then he drove me to my drop-off site and told me to get out of the truck. He switched on my transmitter and gave it to me and told me to start walking. Frankly, I didn't see the point, so I took his pistol and made him trade his uniform for mine and told him to start walking while I got in the truck with the driver. I remember the driver's name was Slansky, a corporal, not a bad guy. We had a pretty good time."

"You drove off and left Captain Malkov in the middle of Siberia with no survival equipment, no compass, no winter clothing."

"He was going to do the same to me."

"And with no transmitter."

"I gave the transmitter to Slansky when I dropped him off once he got me back to the road to Yessey."

"They found Slansky right where you left him."

"I told him they'd pick him up faster if he stayed in place."

"They got him after half a day. He only had a case of frostbite."

"He was a pretty funny guy. We laughed some."

"Captain Malkov died of exposure."

"Is that right?"

Holzer studied Bahoud for the slightest sign of remorse. They had warned him there would be none.

"According to the report. You returned to Yessey in five hours. That's a record."

"It seemed the simplest way to do it."

"The Soviets didn't agree. Here you are."

"According to them I broke the rules, but that's not true. There were no rules. No one said I couldn't trade places with the captain."

"Apparently it had never occurred to them anyone would."

"I always felt the Russians were a little short on imagination," said Bahoud.

Holzer nodded. "We agree, actually. Did you know that Captain Malkov had a wife and three children?"

"Why would I know that?"

"You never inquired?"

"We didn't have much of a conversation."

"I mean afterwards. After you learned he froze to death. You never wondered about his family?"

Bahoud looked at Holzer curiously, tilting his head to one side.

"He wasn't really part of the camp," Bahoud said finally. "I mean, I didn't know the man, I had no reason to know him. He was just a flunky."

Holzer wrote "flunky" in his notebook. He was not familiar with the word, although he could easily discern the general meaning.

The reports had told him that Bahoud was totally without the sense of social awareness that people call a conscience, but they had not prepared him for the complete indifference of the man. Holzer had known killers, had killed himself, but in every instance some rationale had been offered, some political exigency cited. Holzer knew men who were more than willing to wire up a car bomb and leave it to annihilate any innocent passerby within range—but always for a cause. At least, at the very least, some lip service had been offered. A greater purpose was being served. Some must die that many may be freed, etc. The forms were sometimes hollow, and after too many years of rhetoric and hiding and imprisonment Holzer himself at times wondered if he had not reached the point where he did what he did simply because it was all that was left him to do. But jaded or not, cynical even to the point of insensitivity, Holzer and everyone he worked for at the very least recognized the need to follow the form. Even if they no longer cared about human life for themselves, they recognized that some public show of compassion was essential for the sake of appearance. They knew that others cared even if they did not and accordingly gave a nod to opinion.

Bahoud not only didn't care about the man he had killed, he didn't see why he should pretend that he did. His masters had recognized this indifference for the danger that it was. If he didn't care for anything beyond himself, it would be very difficult to control him. Without ideology there was only money and whatever wealth one party offered another could top.

The Soviets had decided that Bahoud's potential for both violence and betrayal were unbounded. The Master Camp was designed to find the most resourceful, resilient, and toughest assassins and terrorists in the world—but only those who could be controlled.

Still, although useless to them or any of their client states, Bahoud still had a value on a market that was glutted with low-level thugs but bereft of the skilled professional. Economic times in the Soviet Union had become very harsh, and, with signs that the Cold War was thawing and the Eastern bloc crumbling, men like Bahoud became potentially embarrassing. His jailers had offered him for sale and Holzer's people had asked to inspect the merchandise before purchase.

"You've killed before," Holzer said.

"Sure."

"Do you know how many times?"

"You saw the record. I don't know the numbers," Bahoud said. "It was low-level stuff before I was discovered and brought in for training."

"Six times."

"Was it?"

"That we know of. Were there more?"

Bahoud shrugged. "Six, seven. Eight, nine. Somewhere in there, it sounds close enough."

"Do you remember the circumstances?" Holzer glanced at the "circumstances" which he had already copied from the dossier into his notebook. Two men in Northern Ireland in a still poorly understood incident in which Bahoud may have been working for either the IRA or the Protestants. Both men had been stabbed to death. A man and a woman in East Germany during an internal struggle amongst former members and supporters of the Bader-Meinhof gang. The man had been garotted, the woman thrown from a window. In both of those incidents Bahoud seemed to have been working simply as a hired gun, brought in to do his killing and move on.

The last two victims were killed while Bahoud was a member of the Ali al Fatwah Coalition, one of many splinter groups on the murderous fringe of Palestinian terror. The record told in cryptic outline how Bahoud had assassinated two members of the Israeli Mossad, themselves working under deep cover and strict security, while in Greece. The killings had been done at close range, by hand, an extremely rare event in Middle Eastern wet work, where bombs were the weapon of choice and mass attacks with automatic weapons a poor second option. Both Mossad agents had been executed with an icepick to the base of the skull, both in more or less public places, and neither death had been discovered for several hours. It was the daring and finesse of these last killings that had brought Bahoud to the attention of all the major intelligence agencies in the world. The Soviets had gotten to him first, recognizing talent when they saw it. In addition to high intelligence, a skill with languages—and native mastery of English, a distinct bonus—and obvious ability at his work, Bahoud demonstrated a definite, albeit shifting, affinity for terrorist groups. With the proper refinement and training in the right schools, he seemed an absolute natural for work at the highest and most difficult levels.

The Soviets' first doubt came after the psychological tests, which saw Bahoud's potential for violence inching off the scale. His sociopathic tendencies revealed themselves more slowly because he had acquired an ability to cheat on psychological tests. He was quite capable of feigning a sense of morality even though he had none. Holzer wondered where he had learned to disguise himself as normal.

"There's no mention of America in your record," Holzer said after Bahoud had recounted casually his bloody history in Europe. "Before you came to Europe, how many did you kill there?"

Again Bahoud turned his smile on Holzer, and again Holzer was startled by it. It seemed so warm and winning that he almost forgot the circumstances of the interview.

"Are you working for the FBI? Are you wired?" Bahoud laughed.

Holzer smiled grimly. "There will be no prosecution, I assure you. The American authorities and I are—acquainted—but we are not friendly."

"I guessed that somehow."

Holzer had been squatting on the cell floor, a habit he had acquired in Palestinian refugee camps in the last several years. As he stood he reached out a hand to steady himself. His fingers came back from the wall moist and covered with crumbling pumice.

"I think you might prefer an American prison, if it came to that," Holzer said. "I understand they have television."

"They do, among other things," said Bahoud.

"How long were you in one?"

Bahoud paused. "A year. What you call one of my formative years."

"I am not familiar with the phrase, 'formative years.' "

"It means I was young: Seventeen. Too young to do time as an adult."

"A children's home."

Bahoud laughed cruelly. "Not exactly. It was a home for the . . ."

"For the what?"

"You going to get me out of here?"

"Was it a hospital?"

Bahoud studied Holzer as if he had his full attention for the first time.

"A sort of hospital, yeah."

"You were ill?"

"That's what they wanted to find out . . . We had a good time figuring that out."

"It took them a year to decide if you were ill?"

"It took me a year to convince them I wasn't." Bahoud laughed again, and Holzer felt a chill that he could not explain. He was not accustomed to this type of fear, but he was glad his back was against the wall.

"I'm better at it now," Bahoud said, this time smiling with that same, charming smile.

Holzer scribbled *wahnsinnig?* in his notebook with a ballpoint pen. It was the German word for "insane."

"It has been an instructive interview," Holzer said. "I will report to my people. I think we will have you out of here very soon."

"Who are your people? What makes you think I'll work for you?"

"Did I mention working for us?"

"You're not with the International Red Cross; you want something from me. Who are you?"

Holzer hesitated. There seemed no reason not to tell him and he would learn soon enough anyway. "Al Beni Hasan."

"I know the Beni Hasan people. I was with Ali al Fatwah."

Holzer nodded. "There is no more Ali al Fatwah."

"What happened to them?"

"They were removed," said Holzer. "Their politics were incorrect."

"Who removed them?"

"Beni Hasan." This time Holzer expected no response. He was not surprised.

Bahoud nodded as if in agreement with a decision that had been made. "They were too small a group to ever be really effective," he said.

"They are even less effective now."

"Are you a good Moslem, Holzer?"

"You know my name?"

"There aren't all that many Germans working for the Palestinian cause in Palestine itself. We know the ones who are."

"How did you know I was in Palestine?"

"The way you squat. Your pronunciation. Your Arabic is quite good, by the way."

"Thank you. It has required much work."

"And are you a good Moslem?"

"Islam is tolerant of all religions. I am a good anti-Imperialist."

Bahoud rubbed behind his ear. The noise of the food delivery was barely audible from far away.

"Ultimately they don't really trust anyone but a fellow Moslem, you know."

"Ultimately they don't really trust anyone," Holzer corrected him. "Which is the way it should be."

"Absolutely," said Bahoud. "The only one you can finally trust is yourself."

"I'll make my recommendations," said Holzer. "I'll come back to take you out within a week. We have certain payments to make."

The noise of the rattling tin food bowls came closer.

"Can I write a note for you to take with you?" Bahoud asked.

Holzer hesitated, knowing he would naturally screen any message himself.

"Certainly," he said.

Bahoud held the pen against an empty page of Holzer's notebook. "I'm surprised they allowed you in here with a weapon," Bahoud said.

Holzer looked puzzled. "I have no weapon," he said, but Bahoud already was in motion, striking Holzer in the throat with the knuckles of his left hand, then driving the pen into the German's ear.

"How did I know you'd really come back?" Bahoud said as he lowered Holzer to the floor and began to remove his clothes.

Holzer's eyes were still open and his lips moved but only an unintelligible murmur came out. His left arm was twitching, which made it slightly more difficult to peel off his shirt.

When Bahoud had donned Holzer's clothes and dressed the German in his prison rags, he propped him up in the corner with his ear turned toward the wall so the bleeding would not show. Holzer's eyes followed Bahoud as he waited by the door for the food warder to arrive and let him out.

Bahoud glanced at Holzer again, pleased at the open, moving eyes, the murmuring lips, the twitching arm. It looked very lifelike. With luck, Holzer would remain upright in the corner for days.

2

In the first subbasement of a building in Langley, Virginia, is a room with moveable walls that can be transformed within minutes into virtually any configuration and size from a closet to a ballroom to a modern office comprised of a warren of cubicles. The walls are moved by computer and hydraulics and they are real walls, solidly made. A stage designer is employed to decorate with the authenticity of the real McCoy. The stock of furnishings and accessories would be the envy of any regional repertory theater in the country. Four employees of the government serve as stage hands and double as actors in the small dramas played out in this amorphous arena.

In strangled bureaucratic parlance, it is known as VPS, or Variable Proportions Space. To the men who exercise within its walls, however, it is known as the Poe Room, in reference, and perhaps deference, to the room in the Poe story with walls that slowly squeezed in upon the victim.

John Becker was ushered into the Poe Room by a man dressed as a butler. The room this day was a perfect replica of the reception hall in the London embassy of a small and determinedly treacherous third world country. A ''reception'' was underway, complete with buffet table, bar, and ''guests,'' more than twenty of them. Becker took a glass of champagne from a passing tray, noted the location of the ''ambassador,'' the security men steadily scanning the room, the newly appointed ''technical representative'' who was slowly working the crowd, and as many details as he could absorb in the minute before the lights went out.

Reacting like the trained actors they were, the ''guests'' screamed and stumbled blindly about in the sudden darkness. The ''security men'' made their way toward the men they were to protect, moving clumsily amidst the milling gang.

In the VPS control room, several men watched the proceedings on an infrared screen. Everyone in the Poe Room was visible on the screen. Several special characters, the objects of the exercise, wore distinctive marks on their clothes that showed up brightly on the screen. The "ambassador" was marked with an X, the "technical representative" with an O, and Becker with a design that looked very much like a Maltese cross, someone's tongue-in-cheek reference to the Crusades. Within that context, Becker was an unvanquished and rather bloody knight.

A nervous young man named Finney stood at the rear of the group huddled around the screen, craning up on his toes to see the action.

"He moves like a goddamned cat," said one of the observers.

"More like a bat."

"A vampire bat then," said the first, a trace of derision in his tone.

The action was already finished in real time. The technicians rewound the tape and played it again as Finney tried to crowd forward.

"He doesn't deserve that rap," said the second of the agents observing the tape. "He just did what he was supposed to do."

"Uh-huh," said the first observer.

"It's a dangerous business."

"No kidding. It's certainly dangerous for anyone Becker goes after."

"He does the job, doesn't he?"

"And keeps right on doing it. How many has he killed so far? Three? Four?"

"He had to."

"In every case?"

"In the positions he was in, he had no choice."

"After four deaths you got to wonder if he doesn't create the positions himself."

The tape replay ran its course in less than thirty seconds and the crew watched in awed silence.

"Christ," said the first in reluctant admiration. "He is good, isn't he?"

"Run it again. I blinked."

Finney made his way to the front of the room as the tape ran again. Watching the clip was a curious experience. It looked as if one figure were running in normal time and everyone else in slow motion. The figure with the cross moved as soon as the lights went out, starting forward with the same highly trained reaction of a sprinter bolting out of the blocks. While the others adjusted to the darkness, Becker moved. One of the security men stepped forward from his position behind Becker and swung a sap filled with flourescent material at the space where Becker had stood a second earlier. If the sap had hit Becker, he would have been marked instantly as "out of play," but the man's arm swung harmlessly through space and the security man was left off balance by the violence of his own motion.

To Finney's mind, the comparisons to cat and bat were both wrong. Cats stalked and bats flew in erratic patterns, but Becker walked quickly as if he were following a path only he could see. He sliced through the "guests," around the buffet, and behind another security man who was just then starting to move, slightly off the correct line. As the security man reached out protective arms, Becker grabbed the "technical representative" from behind with one arm across the man's throat in what would have been a paralyzing choke hold if the exercise had been for real, lifted him off his feet, and exited through one of the side doors while the security man was still groping for the man he was assigned to protect.

"He can see," said Finney, surprising himself.

The others looked at the younger man and smiled. Each of them had harbored the same suspicion at some time.

"Special light-sensitive contact lenses, maybe," said Finney, grasping for an answer and feeling foolish as the knowing faces grinned at him. "Something."

"Personally, I suspect he's got infrared sensing capability," said the first observer. "Like a pit viper."

"He's just good, Finney," the second agent offered.

"Just?"

"Well, alright, more than just. He likes the dark, he's comfortable in it, I don't know. But it's not a trick; he has no special equipment. He just remembers where everyone is and moves before anyone else does."

"He went *through* people," said Finney.

"At least he didn't kill anybody," said the first observer.

"I've read his records," said Finney. "I think that reputation is a little exaggerated."

"Just like his performance in the Poe Room."

The tape was running yet again, this time with the observers noting the mistakes of the other players in the drama. As far as Finney could tell they all reacted well. Had they been pitted against one another it might have been a draw. But then they all shared one drawback— they couldn't see in the dark.

As Finney was leaving the observation room, the first agent called him back.

"When you talk to him," the agent said, "don't look him straight in the eyes. He's like a wolf; look him straight in the eyes and he'll attack."

"It's bullshit, kid," said the second agent. The first one laughed. "He's actually a very nice guy."

"That's true," said the first agent. "I was just kidding. Becker's just like anybody else—as long as you don't have any open wounds."

"You're talking to a jealous man," said the second. "You'll like Becker, unless he's hungry. Then he'll like you."

Finney exited to a chorus of laughter.

Finney found Becker in the cafeteria where he was talking to a female agent over coffee. Finney knew the woman slightly; they had done time together in Fingerprinting before Finney escaped to a happier job. A joint term in purgatory did not make them the best of friends, but it had established a degree of intimacy that comes from shared tedium.

Finney sat down next to the woman while Becker returned to the cafeteria line. She seemed pleased to see him in as much as her perpetually sardonic attitude ever allowed her to be pleased about anything.

"You're moving in grander circles than when I last saw you, Karen," Finney said.

"Hello, Finney. Somebody said you were here. What are you doing?"

"Messenger service. What are you up to these days?"

"Still Fingerprints and Documents."

"Ah."

"Yeah, ah. I give it another six months, then I'm transferring out."

"Still lusting after Terrorism?"

Karen removed the spoon from her coffee and licked it slowly.

"You and I use the term 'lust' rather differently, Finney. Being a man, you think of it in aggressive terms. You lust for anything you can stick it to. A woman, on the other hand, experiences the end result of lust as a rather intrusive experience.'' She closed her mouth around the spoon, wiggling the handle up and down in Finney's face and leering around the edges. ''So naturally we tend to be more careful.''

She was grinning like a cat, and Finney shifted uncomfortably in his chair.

''You've taken up philosophy since we knew each other,'' said Finney.

''You could call it that. I got divorced.''

''Ah.''

''Exactly. Who are you messengering for?''

''Terrorism.''

''You little shit.''

''Thank you.''

''Are you serious?''

Finney nodded, trying to suppress a self-congratulatory smile.

''You're not that good,'' she said. ''How did you do it?''

Finney shrugged. ''I applied.''

''*I* applied,'' said Karen. She twisted in her chair with annoyance. ''Who did you have to fuck? Or should I ask how many?''

''Many are called, few are chosen.''

''You make me wish I still smoked,'' she said, then sighed. ''Well, congratulations anyway.''

''Thank you.'' Finney nodded toward Becker, who was eyeing the cafeteria options with equal distaste. ''What's he like?''

''Becker?'' She studied Becker's back for a moment. ''I'm getting very mixed signals. I get the feeling that if I made the move he wouldn't say no, but he's not going to make the move himself. I mean, you can tell he likes women—he gives off incredible heat—but something is holding him back, you know what I mean?''

''No.''

''He would be a hard man to get to commit himself. Very reserved despite those eyes.''

''What about his eyes?''

''They sizzle.'' Karen grinned again and swept her blonde hair back from her forehead. ''I'm saying he's very hot and very cold. Nothing but trouble, in other words. Of course, I don't know a woman worthy of the name who doesn't secretly yearn for trouble . . . Hello in there, hello, Finney. You following any of this?''

"I'm following it. You think he's sexy."

"Intensely, but not because he's coming on to me."

"Because he's not coming on to you."

"No, because I don't know what he's going to do, but whatever it is, it will be interesting."

"Why do you women make it all so complicated?"

"Why do you men ever think it's simple?"

Becker had made his selection in the food line and was now making his way toward the cash register.

"Well, to digress from sex for a moment, what I wanted to know was, what is he really like?"

"As what?" she demanded. "As a person? As an agent? As a conversationalist?"

"As an agent."

Karen thought for a moment before answering. "Well, he's lethal, isn't he? How many has he dusted? Seven, eight?"

"I believe the actual number is three," Finney said stiffly.

"Come on. There were three in the Siegurd business alone."

"One, actually."

"I heard three."

"I read the report. The man gets bad press."

"Do you have a case of hero worship going here, Finney?"

"I just like to know who I'm working with."

"You're working with?"

"Well, Terrorism is working with. I've come to fetch him."

Becker approached their table carrying a plastic tray. Finney stood too abruptly, rattling Karen's coffee cup.

"Mr. Becker, I'm Charles Finney with Terrorism. It's an honor to meet you." Finney extended his hand before Becker had put down his tray, then stood awkwardly waiting.

Becker nodded, dropping his eyes, as he shook hands. "Have you met Agent Crist?" he asked, looking at Karen.

"Finney and I go back to our rookie years," she said.

Becker grinned. "As far back as all that?"

"I watched you a few minutes ago in the Poe Room," Finney said. "That was amazing."

Becker kept his eyes on the table as he unloaded his tray. He murmured something under his breath.

"Sir?"

"I've had practice," Becker said more loudly.

"Yes, sir, but so had everyone else in the run. How did you manage to move around so quickly?"

Becker glanced briefly at Finney's face, then back to the table. To his amazement, Finney realized the man was embarrassed by praise. Of all the things he had heard about John Becker, no one had mentioned that he was shy.

"You have to like the dark," Becker said. "Or if you can't get yourself to like it, you have to get over your fear of it."

"I'm not sure how that actually enables you to see in the dark. Just not being afraid of it?"

Becker nodded as if agreeing with something Finney had said, then applied himself to his side order of coleslaw.

Finney looked to Karen for assistance.

She grinned mischievously at Finney. "I tried to explain that already. It's in his eyes." She let the statement sink in. "They generate their own heat."

Becker turned slowly to face her, the corners of his mouth twitching upward as if he were fighting the smile. There was no trace of shyness now as he held Karen with his gaze. Finney watched as the young woman sat upright as if something in his look had braced her. She giggled suddenly with a girlishness Finney had never seen in her, then looked away, abruptly reduced to blushing bashfulness.

Finney wondered if Becker might not have another reputation just as impressive and possibly less inflated than the one he already had for his skills as an agent. He had never seen Karen Crist back down before, much less act like a kitten being stroked on the stomach. In the course of one exchange of glances, Finney was made to feel that his presence was very much out of place.

"Agent Becker?" he said.

This time Becker looked directly at him without a trace of the former temerity. Finney had the sense he was dealing with several men at once and understood what Karen had meant when she said she couldn't tell what he was going to do next but that it would be interesting. She couldn't predict *what* he was going to do next because there was no telling *who* he would be next.

"You've come to get me," said Becker. "Who's sending for me exactly?"

Finney had been warned about the possibility of such a question. "McKinnon is in charge of Terrorism now," he said.

"I've heard," said Becker. "McKinnon is a good man."

"Yes, sir, one of the best."

"Who's his new deputy?"

"Sir?"

"Who do you report to, Finney?"

Finney cleared his throat. There seemed no way to evade such a direct question without making matters worse. "Hatcher," he said, finally.

Again Becker nodded as if in agreement with something. Finney watched as the man took a bite of his sandwich, his eyes fixed on a spot in the air over Finney's shoulder.

Karen understood none of the specifics of the situation but was keenly aware of the sudden plunge the conversation had taken. She eyed both men with interest.

Becker swallowed and took a sip of coffee before speaking. When he spoke, he looked directly at Finney and smiled.

"Tell Hatcher to fuck himself," Becker said. Finney could detect no rancor in his tone. Becker made it sound like good advice. If it hadn't been for Karen's sudden burst of laughter that erupted like a cough, Finney might almost have said Becker's manner was friendly.

"Yes, sir," Finney said. It was his turn to nod. "I see." Finney half rose, uncertain of the protocol in such a situation.

"I suppose I should take that message back now," he said.

"Now would be a good time."

"It was a pleasure meeting you."

"You, too, Finney. And Finney . . . "

"Sir?"

"Don't translate the message for Hatcher. Give it to him verbatim."

3

Taha Hammadi had made a career of calculated caution, of assessing risk and reward, and balancing fear with action. For the most part, his forays against imperialist Zionist targets had been highly successful, providing enemy casualties and loss of property and the attendant— and ardently desired—publicity with only low-to-moderate loss of his own operatives. The reason he could send men into action against vastly superior security forces was that he knew how the security forces would react. They were predictable. Everyone in the conflict was, at some level, predictable. Even he, Taha Hammadi, was predictable. If not to time and place, at least to general intent. Strike me, I strike back. Tap me on the right shoulder and I turn my head to the right. Present me with odds that are too formidable and I back down. I am, after all, a rational man, Hammadi thought. Which was precisely why Bahoud frightened him. Bahoud was not a rational man and did not react as others would, and that made him unusually dangerous. And unusually useful.

"It is a strange place to meet," said Hammadi.

"I like it here," said Bahoud. "Not so crowded." The two men sat in a rowboat fifty yards offshore in lake Como where Hammadi had rowed out with some difficulty to meet Bahoud. Hammadi was no longer young, and sweat dripped into his black moustache and steamed the lenses of his eyeglasses despite the chilly wind that swept across the lake. The transfer from his rowboat into Bahoud's had been very awkward and had left him feeling clumsy and unsettled. Bahoud had hauled him aboard by the back of his jacket as unceremoniously as a fisherman shifting the day's catch. It seemed to amuse Bahoud, who regarded the older man now as if he were to be the source of the afternoon's entertainment. Even as Bahoud pulled them deeper into the lake with strong and measured strokes of the oars, he watched

Hammadi as if the man might tell a joke or burst into song at any moment.

Hammadi caught his breath and struggled to regain his composure. Three bodyguards of the Beni Hassan on shore had watched his undignified boarding of the rowboat. It was not wise to appear the fool to one's underlings, especially men as attuned to the signs of weakness as these.

Hammadi glanced casually toward shore to see if he could find them among the tourists and villagers. They were nowhere to be seen, which pleased Hammadi. He had not really doubted their competence, although sublety was seldom the primary asset of men who carried guns. They were dangerous men, too, but comfortingly predictable. Which was not to say dependable. Hammadi had survived to this age by his ability to detect seismic shifts before they happened. He sometimes thought of himself as a passenger on the iceberg of Palestinian terror that was continually breaking up into increasingly smaller pieces. It was important to sense the cracks before they reached the surface of the ice, and vital to be standing on the largest floe when the split occurred. For the time being, at least, the Beni Hassan was the splinter with the closest association to oil money. That association made the Beni Hassan, although few in numbers, the largest floe around.

"There's one in line outside the bakery," said Bahoud suddenly.

"One of which?"

"Weren't you looking for your men? There's another on the veranda of the hotel, and the third is having a conversation with the fisherman, who's emptying his net. Is the fisherman one of yours, too?"

"No," said Hammadi, trying to hide his annoyance at the ease with which Bahoud had found his men.

"Interesting," said Bahoud. He shipped the oars, and rivulets of water sluiced down the blades and into the boat.

"It took you over a month to contact us," said Hammadi. With a fellow Arab he would have been more circumspect in coming to the point, but Bahoud was an Arab only by genetic chance. He spoke Arabic and knew Arab ways but acted like an American. It was best to treat him as one; it was part of his value. "We had expected to hear from you sooner."

"I didn't need you any sooner," said Bahoud. "Holzer had quite a bit of money on him."

"You are fond of money?"

"Devoted to it."

"Then we can perhaps do business together. We have a great deal of money to offer you for a certain errand. And, of course, we hope you can help to offset the loss of Holzer."

"Something happen to him?"

Hammadi studied Bahoud, who gave every appearance of sincerity.

"Yes. He has certain brain damage."

"Seemed all right when I left him," said Bahoud.

"Yes?"

"Maybe the prison people roughed him up because he helped me get away."

"Perhaps," said Hammadi, hiding his fury at the unnecessary loss of Holzer, a man he had personally liked and one of the best operatives he had for actions in the West. "It is most unfortunate, of course, because we have only a very few western agents, as you know."

"That puts me at something of a premium, I guess," said Bahoud.

"You will be extremely well paid," said Hammadi.

Bahoud smiled broadly, and Hammadi was struck by the unexpected charm of the man.

"If you can accomplish a rather complicated—and difficult—task for us," Hammadi continued.

"I can."

"Do you want to know what the task is before you say you can accomplish it?"

Bahoud shrugged. "I can."

The wake of a passing speedboat caused the rowboat to rock gently. Hammadi glanced at the passengers in the noisy craft. He was horribly vulnerable sitting here in the middle of the lake, but it was the only meeting place Bahoud would agree to, and even that only at the last minute.

Hammadi removed an envelope from his jacket and placed it in Bahoud's hands. Inside was a newspaper photograph and an accompanying article.

"You recognize him, of course," said Hammadi.

"Of course."

"You will see by the article that he is to be in New York in four months' time."

Bahoud glanced at the article that spoke of a planned international convocation of leaders at the United Nations to deal with issues concerning children. Seventy-one presidents, premiers, prime ministers, and other heads of state were to attend. The Year of the Children, proclaimed a headline.

Bahoud snorted derisively. As if the leaders of the world knew or cared about children. As if they could do anything for them even if they wanted to.

"I was a child once," Bahoud said, then laughed.

Hammadi regarded him curiously.

"Just remembering that peculiar pleasure," Bahoud said. "Me and dad. Me and good old dad."

"We know about your father," said Hammadi.

"Think so?"

"He and I come from the same village in the Negev. Mizpe Ramon they call it now. Its pre-Zionist name—its real name—is . . ."

"El Saff," said Bahoud. "I know. Dear old dad used to reminisce about the rocks and the goats and how you had to check your bed for scorpions every night. It sounded like a fun spot to me. Perfect spot for Daddy. Made him the man he was."

Hammadi fought back a desire to strike this insolent young man. "It was a small village, not remarkable. Insignificant to western eyes, I am sure. But it was home. Now the Zionists manufacture electronic components there. The dry climate is very good for the necessary technology." Hammadi spat into the water.

"Technology will never replace a good goat," said Bahoud, laughing.

Hammadi was grateful he did not have a weapon or he would have felt compelled by honor to attack Bahoud. He had no illusions that he would succeed in such an attack. He managed a thin smile instead.

"We would like this man assassinated," he said, nodding his head toward the newspaper article. "Publicly. At this convention at the United Nations."

"Why there?"

"Publicity," said Hammadi. "It will make the greatest impression there. The world will be watching. If one leader is plucked from seventy and slaughtered on the steps of the United Nations, it will make them all uneasy."

"There will be a lot of people happy to see him die," said Bahoud.

Hammadi could not suppress a smile. "Myself among them. How-

ever, more important than his death is the cause of it. It is not enough
that he be killed; he must be seen to be killed by the hand of Zionist
extremists."

"Zionists?" said Bahoud, surprised.

"Who more likely? Who has more motive?"

"Do you have me confused with a Zionist?"

"No," said Hammadi. "But I hope to have the Zionists confuse
you with a Zionist." He glanced again at the shore but again he could
not see his bodyguards. The look on Bahoud's face indicated that he
still saw them, however. "You will penetrate a small group of fanatics
in New York City. They call themselves the Brotherhood of Zion.
Right now they are very small, impotent, a rather silly group of mal-
contents who do little but make speechs and try to disrupt rallies. They
speak of violence but they do nothing. You will transform them into
a powerful action group, a group capable of this type of assassination."

"How do I do that?"

"That is up to you. Inspire them. Charm them. Show them the
rewards of violence. We have a preliminary target for you to help
establish them as a threat. The police must perceive them as a danger
before you strike at the U.N. so that when they take credit, they will
be believed."

"So you not only get rid of him," Bahoud tapped the photo with
his fingernail, "but you get a tremendous anti-Zionist backlash inter-
nationally."

"That is the plan," said Hammadi.

"Very nice. For you. And what do I get?"

Hammadi adjusted his glasses on his nose. "Mr. Bahoud, we have
an oil well pumping just for you."

"I don't drive that much," said Bahoud. "You keep the oil, I'll
take cash."

"Of course. Three million dollars. In installments."

Bahoud was silent. His eyes flickered toward shore, at the various
boats on the water, back to Hammadi.

"The first installment will come when you have successfully arrived in the United States. Five hundred thousand dollars then."

"What's going to keep me from taking half a million and walking
right then?"

"Greed," said Hammadi.

Bahoud laughed, flashing his wonderful smile. "Right you are."

"And the knowledge that we would hunt for you forever."

The smile vanished. "You're on safer ground with greed, Hammadi." It was the first time he had used Hammadi's name. "I don't like threats, and I'm a much better hunter than you are."

"Of course," said Hammadi. "That is why we are hiring you."

"When do I get the other installments?"

"A million when you eliminate your preliminary target, the one that establishes your credibility."

"Is this target a friend of yours, too?"

Hammadi paused. "He was. He chose to retire."

"In America?"

"I'm told it's very nice there," said Hammadi.

"Parts of it," said Bahoud. "The expensive parts."

"You will be able to retire in any part you wish," said Hammadi. "The remaining one and a half million dollars will be yours following the elimination of your final target."

"How do I get the money? That's too much cash to cart around."

Hammadi shrugged. "An electronic transfer to any bank you choose. You can inform us when you decide."

"You have a contact for me in place in New York?"

"Of course." Hammadi removed another envelope from his pocket. "Details are here. Please study them, then return them to me."

"I may want to study them at my leisure."

"That is not entirely acceptable. We must have your decision now."

"Today?"

"Now, I am afraid," said Hammadi. "By the time we return to shore."

Bahoud smiled. "And if my answer is no I get to deal with your three goons?"

"We would not want the project jeopardized by someone who knew of it but was not willing to participate," said Hammadi. "You can understand that."

"Oh, of course," said Bahoud, opening the second envelope. "I either agree or stay in the middle of the lake the rest of my life."

"Or under it," said Hammadi.

Bahoud paused, memorizing the details of contact codes and numbers and the name and address of the first target. His fingers ran over the front of the passport that was included.

"All right," he said after a minute. "Everything seems okay except the money. It's hard to retire on three million dollars these days. I would guess that oil well could pump out at least ten million."

Hammadi had expected some haggling about money. "I might be able to go to five," he said.

"Ten would make me so much happier," said Bahoud.

"It is not my money, you understand. I was authorized no more than five. My principal would have to agree, but I think I could get him to offer six."

"A coup like this can't be valued in dollars," said Bahoud. "And it's not as if you have anyone else qualified to even try. I'm the only man who can do it for you, I'm the only one good enough."

"Naturally we will pay your expenses," said Hammadi.

They settled on eight million as Bahoud rowed toward shore. Fifty yards from shore he shipped oars again. Hammadi's rowboat bobbed gently thirty yards away and parallel to Bahoud's.

After putting the passport in his pocket, Bahoud returned the second envelope to Hammadi.

"I'd be careful about that fisherman your boy is talking to so long," Bahoud said. "Most of the fishermen on this lake have their nets in by mid-morning."

Hammadi turned to look at the fisherman and Bahoud pushed the older man into the water. When Hammadi came to the surface, sputtering and flailing, Bahoud snatched him by the back of his collar and held his head above water.

"Never learned to swim there in goat town, did you? That's the problem with deserts, a definite lack of swimming holes." Hammadi reached for the boat, but Bahoud struck his fingers with the oar, then twisted his collar so the older man was held with his face to the shore, his back to the safety of the rowboat.

"I told you I didn't like being threatened," Bahoud said. "Now who do you think is going to be under the lake?"

Hammadi spit water and coughed. The three bodyguards were in action, two of them running toward a boat, the third swimming directly toward them.

"You have your choices," Bahoud said. "You can tread water until your boys reach you—if you can tread water. You can swim toward your boat—if you could swim. Or you could sink. Sinking is the easiest.''

He released Hammadi's collar and the man's head sunk briefly before bobbing up again. Bahoud made an assessment of the swimmer, who was closing quickly. Assuming Hammadi could keep himself afloat for at least a minute, the bodyguard would be a hero.

"Just kick your legs and move your arms," said Bahoud as he pulled for shore. "And breathe only when you're above water. I'll let you know where to send my money.''

Bahoud was right; the swimmer reached Hammadi first. The two of them floundered about inexpertly for a few moments before the rowboat with the other two bodyguards pulled alongside. By that time Bahoud had reached shore, well away from the fisherman who watched with seeming disinterest.

Crossing through passport control in Montreal should have been simple enough. Canada has no terrorist problem, and what perfunctory border scrutiny of possible suspects they do perform is a pro forma gesture for the benefit of the United States. The passport Hammadi had given him should have been good enough to get into Canada, although Bahoud knew that it would be risky to try to cross into the States with it.

The agent at Immigration just happened to be very young and new on the job. The zealotry of the beginner had not yet been flattened by the endless parade of tourists and returning natives that in six months of time would dull his curiosity and blur the sharpness of his vision. By normal standards of scrutiny, Bahoud should have elicited no interest at all. He did not fit the profile of a terrorist. To all reasonable eyes he was exactly what he pretended to be: a visitor from Poland taking advantage of his country's newly established freedom to travel by visiting relatives in a Polish enclave in Ottawa. The passport was actually authentic, one of several hundred provided to Hammadi and the Beni Hassan by a sympathetic Communist offical just before his party's rule had begun to crumble. Bahoud had supplied the photo and counterfeit stamps himself with the aid of a very competent forger friend from his Red Army days. There was no reason to take a second look at the document—except for curiosity.

The agent—"Meager" was the surname printed on his name

plate—had not yet seen a real Polish passport outside of training class.
He studied the photo, glancing at Bahoud, then slowly turning the
pages of the visa stamps. His scrutiny bore a certain air of demonstrated authority, a display of expertise to impress Bahoud. Meager
had not yet gotten used to his power over people. He could sense their
anxiety, even those with no reason for fear, when he showed the
slightest delay. Merely pausing made people worry, and Meager got
a little charge of excitement from that. There was a small joy in making them sweat.

Unfortunately for Meager, Bahoud's response to the suggestion of
suspicion was not anxiety but action.

"Is there a problem?" Bahoud said, smiling and leaning forward.
The nearest armed security guard was behind him. As he leaned in,
Bahoud knew that his body would shield his actions. The only other
armed guard in the hall was considerably farther away, his head momentarily averted as he spoke to a bewildered tourist seeking direc-
tions. If he chanced to look toward Bahoud and Meager, the guard
would see only a civilian speaking privately to the agent. Many who
passed Immigration were embarrassed about one thing or another that
they didn't want broadcast to neighboring travelers.

Meager looked up at Bahoud, then pulled back slightly as the man's
face bore ever closer. Bahoud's left hand moved toward the passport,
drawing Meager's attention. He was not aware of Bahoud's other hand
until he felt the thumb pressing deeply into his neck just above the
clavicle.

"I think you'll find everything is in order," said Bahoud, smiling.
He removed his passport from Meager's hand, then gripped the
agent's wrist as the man tried to press the alarm button beneath the
counter. Meager's fingers waggled futilely and his eyes swiveled toward Bahoud, then fluttered upwards, giving him the appearance of
swooning as old-time film actresses had fainted and fallen away at the
mention of bad news.

If he had had time, Bahoud would have continued to seal off the
carotid artery until Meager died of oxygen deprivation to the brain,
but seconds were important now. The security guard he could see had
freed himself from the tourist and was now looking in Bahoud's direction and the one behind Bahoud's back could get suspicous at any
time.

Several of the passengers waiting in line had observed Bahoud's episode with Meager, but none knew what they were witnessing. It had all happened too fast and too smoothly to be taken for the act of extreme and near-lethal violence that it was. Bahoud nudged Meager's body back against the chair as it started to slump, then walked briskly to the security guard who was behind him.

"That agent seems to be sick," Bahoud said. It was important to give the guard a false explanation so that it would take him longer to come to the correct assessment. By the time the guard reached Meager, the agent had collapsed onto the floor and Bahoud was in the hallway outside of Immigration, sprinting down the corridor past startled tourists making their way toward Customs.

As others waited for their baggage to appear, Bahoud stepped into a Customs line. He calculated that he had about three minutes before the guards figured out what had happened to Meager, then perhaps another two or three to allow for the inevitable confusion that would ensue. With luck he would be through Customs and into the unrestricted airport by then. Once in the open terminal, he had no doubt he would be able to elude detection. The trick was to make it through Customs and past the set of armed guards who manned the gates to the terminal.

Fifth in line, Bahoud contemplated whether he might have done better to grab a bag, any bag, from the carousel. Arriving after an international flight from Poland to Frankfurt and thence to Canada without so much as a toothbrush was guaranteed to raise suspicion, and questions, and take time to explain. Even if he claimed his luggage was lost, the story would take time to elaborate.

He was fourth in line, then very quickly third. Bahoud thought of taking a bag from the family in front of him that were pushing and carrying nearly a dozen among them when he saw one, then another, of the guards remove his walkie-talkie from his belt. Bahoud slipped out of line and back into the baggage area, blending in immediately among the milling and impatient crowd. As he moved quickly toward the mouth where the luggage carousel emerged from the wall, he kept his eyes on the guards. They were scanning the crowd now.

His timetable had been optimistic and Bahoud reappraised it immediately. Now he had a minute, perhaps two, before the guards realized they did not see the man they were looking for and the alarm was spread throughout the building. Bahoud grabbed a bag that an elderly lady was reaching for and placed it in her hand while in the same motion stepping onto the conveyor belt and through the long rubber strips that screened the baggage area from the interior hallway. He hoped that anyone watching would think he was attempting to free some stuck luggage, but his only real concern was that the guards did not see him at all.

Bahoud dashed along the thin catwalk running parallel to the conveyor belt and burst through another screen of rubber strips to the astonishment of two baggage handlers unloading a tractor load of suitcases.

Bahoud ran a hand through his hair, brushing it from his forehead, and smiled at the men as if they were exactly the people he had been looking for.

"Is this your tractor?" he asked the nearest man. The man stared stupidly back at him.

Bahoud asked the question again in French. This time the man managed to shake his head and point a thumb at his companion. Bahoud turned as if to address the second man and drove an elbow into the windpipe of the first. The second man opened his mouth to protest, then collapsed forward as Bahoud wedged the fingers of his hand into the man's solar plexus.

Killing them was the quickest and safest option, so Bahoud snapped their necks and shoved them onto the catwalk where they would be out of sight for long enough for him to make his escape. He did not know if they were actually dead or merely paralyzed, but for his purposes it didn't matter. Sometimes men were suprisingly resistant to death, and at others they shattered as if made of crystal. He stripped the second man of his uniform jacket and cap and yanked the heavily padded headset from his ears.

Unbuckling the tractor from the luggage trailer, Bahoud swung up onto the vehicle's seat and put on the jacket, cap, and earphones. Inside the terminal the general alarm had been sounded and the doors sealed, but Bahoud was already motoring toward the strip of fence by the far runway that was closest to the highway. By the time the security people finally noticed the luggage tractor nosed up against the cyclone fence and realized that Bahoud had vaulted the barrier and somehow commandeered a passing auto, it was far too late. He was already loose and free on the North American continent. In the haystack of more than half a billion people and ten million square miles, Bahoud had become less a needle than a strand of thread to fit through its eye.

* * *

There were many ways to get fake documents, but the reliability of the copies varied widely and all the methods took time. Genuine passports, on the other hand, could be acquired quickly, although Bahoud knew of only one certain way of doing it.

The waiting room of the Montreal passport office was furnished like a bus depot, with the same disregard for customer comfort. Bahoud sat for three hours on a straightback folding chair, reading a pornographic sex novel, which he had glued into the gutted covers of a text on Zen philosophy. He was no more interested in pornography than the average man, but he had long since learned that a state of semiarousal was the best condition in which to kill hours of waiting. There was no point in trying to read a good book while glancing up every few minutes to study the faces around him. A good book required too much concentration and provided too much pleasure— which could only be diverting. He might become too engrossed because of a reluctance to leave a good narrative and miss the one person who would come by in a day who met his needs. Pornography, on the other hand, required no attention span and no concentration. He could leave it for minutes at a time and return to his place—or pick a page at random—and find essentially the same thing going on with essentially the same characters. And with essentially the same result on Bahoud. And unlike a novel or a book of nonfiction, it was easy to reread a book of pornography immediately. The second time through, when the excitement created by novelty had worn low, it always seemed like a comedy as Bahoud became aware of the repetitive style, the ludicrous dialogue, the simplistic attempts at characterization. Occasionally he wondered who wrote these things, who edited them, who read them.

Just before noon, as the book's heroine struggled futilely to withstand the fourth attempt on her virtue in the course of a day, the man Bahoud had been waiting for arrived. Bahoud closed the book and slipped it into his coat pocket, then rose and stretched. He could tell immediately that the man was the right basic type—a dirty blond with hair receding early as it often did with blonds, features set regularly in a mildly oval face. He looks like me, Bahoud thought, but he doesn't look as good. Many men resembled Bahoud. He had a face of Northern Europe—Germanic, Scandinavian, English—a legacy of his mother's family; but Bahoud thought he had the best face of the type. There was not a day when he didn't look at his reflection in the mirror and feel pleased. He would study himself soberly for a moment, practicing sincerity, sobriety. It was a handsome face to be sure, but also a highly serviceable one because, despite its good looks, it was not distinctive. There were no exaggerated features to stick in the minds of witnesses, no large nose, no vanishing or protruding chin, no scars. His face was a police artist's nightmare, nothing to work with, the kind of generalized blur that could be practically anyone. After studying himself seriously, Bahoud would smile, and admire himself even more as he smiled. He knew the wattage of that smile, understood through happy experiment just what effect it had on women. If anything set his face apart, it was that smile that he could present in a hundred variations from pluckily grinning through tears to ecstatic beaming, and all the gradations in between, and all of them winning. Police artists did not work with smiles, however. In fact, they never even asked about them. Few criminals smiled at their victims, but Bahoud did. Why not? He enjoyed his work, after all.

After appraising the man for face and general build, Bahoud sauntered toward him to get a better estimate of his height. An inch or two differential could be accommodated with lifts or a slump in posture, but if the man was significantly different in size Bahoud would have to let him go and wait for someone else.

He guessed the man was perhaps a half inch shorter than his own 5′ 11″; close to perfect. Best of all, he sported a mustache, a full mustache that drooped over his upper lip and effectively disguised a significant part of his face. Removing his upper lip from view made the man even less individual. Bahoud could grow a similar mustache in three weeks—or buy one today. He didn't like facial hair; it tended to detract from his smile, but for his present needs, it was perfect.

While the man renewed his passport, Bahoud crossed to the coat rack that stood by the door. It was cold outside, but few of the people in the room had bothered to remove their coats, hoping for a short stay. Bahoud had known better and his coat was already hung and prepared. When he put the coat on a hanger on arrival, he had slipped a second hanger from the pipe rack and put it in the inside pocket of the coat.

Now Bahoud put on his coat and walked to the men's room, where he stepped into a stall and bent the wire hanger back and forth until it broke. He did it again close to the hook, feeling the metal heat until it burned his fingers, and then snap. He now had a straight, foot-long length of metal, jaggedly sharp on both ends, which he slid up the inside of his shirt sleeve. He worked one point of the hanger under the ring he wore on the middle finger of his right hand so that the metal was secured just short of his finger tip. The ring was a raised onyx set in a plain steel band. It had no sentimental associations to Bahoud, and no decorative purposes—but it had its uses.

Returning from the men's room, Bahoud sat again, folding his hands in his lap to hide the hanger that ran from his shirt sleeve, across his palm, under his ring, and up to the finger tip. He could feel the other end of the hanger pressing reassuringly against his forearm where it rested against his abdomen.

When the man left the passport office, Bahoud followed him into the blustery April streets of Montreal.

4

Mr. Henley was there today. He always called before he came, so Myra had a chance to dress herself and make a pass at her face in the mirror. It did her good to have a visitor now and then, like someone rattling the bars of her cage to wake her. She was not caged, of course. She could leave if she wished. The door was not barred, there were no chains. She could stir herself for company if she had to. Normally she wore only her bathrobe during the day, not because of slovenry— there was no sluttishness in Myra; she was not given to pink mules or bonbons by the television—but because there was no reason to do otherwise.

She was wearing gray slacks and a white silk blouse, which was open one button too many for strict propriety. She had accentuated her cleavage with a brown liner. She knew, with malicious pleasure, that her mother would be appalled by her wantonness.

She left the door unlatched when Mr. Henley was coming so that he could enter by himself after ringing the bell. It would destroy the effect of her seductive beauty if she had to hobble back to her desk after letting him in. Her other customers sent delivery men, an odd array of disinterested messengers, some of them mildly retarded, men who talked to themselves or talked too much to others. She did not invite them in. Mr. Henley was the only customer who actually entered her apartment.

She sat by her word processor, bathed in the soft light of her reading lamp, back erect, manner proper, blouse opened one button too far. The very picture of the modern lady executive, she imagined, businesslike but sensual. *Cosmopolitan* would be proud.

Her body was turned so that her "bad" arm dangled inconspicuously behind the word processor, the fingers resting just at the level of the desk top. Nature had been kind in that regard, she thought. She could type with that baby's arm; the fingers were as adept and swift as those on her other hand, for all their seeming frailty. In order not to draw attention to that hand, she had trained it to stay motionless at times like this, hidden behind the word processor like a butterfly at rest, not to flutter free until Mr. Henley was gone. Her arm resented the banishment, the fingers itched to move, to wiggle a coy hello, to toy with a pencil and smooth her blouse. Sometimes it took all the effort of her resolution to keep it still, but she was stronger than her willful shrunken limb. She willed it to obey.

"Here it is, as advertised," she said cheerfully, tapping the manuscript that lay on her desk in a neatly stacked pile, edges together. The pages glistened, the ink seemed as black as a squid's. Mr. Henley couldn't keep his eyes off it, she thought. It was so swollen and fresh with promise. He tried, as always, to be polite. Here I sit, she thought, smiling sweetly, breasts accentuated even further as I arch my back just a fraction, demurely alluring on the outside, wanton as a whore within. But Mr. Henley lusts only for his manuscript. He longed to reach out to it, she could tell, to caress it, to make love to it. But decorum prevailed over the writer's ardor. Mr. Henley was always decorous.

"How did it go?" he asked. This was code. Myra knew he was not concerned with how it went; he wanted her to tell him what she thought of it, did she laugh, was she moved, would it be read, admired, praised. She was his first reader every time. He lived alone, had no family, no wife. By the mournful look of him Myra could tell he had no girlfriend. Who, if anyone, read his material after Myra did, she had no idea. He had mentioned an agent once or twice, but whether he actually had the agent or was courting him, Myra was not certain. To be polite, she had asked about the success of previous works now and then. In response, he would always shrug and look away. He was waiting to hear, he would say. Always waiting to hear. Myra could sympathize with that. She was waiting, too.

"It went fine," she said, just a bit ashamed of teasing him. He was such an easy target. He stood uncomfortably, shifting his weight from side to side, as ill at ease as always. She was toying with a button on her blouse as if deciding whether or not to undo it, but she doubted if that added to his discomfort; he had not really seen her, not made full eye contact. He had eyes only for his beloved manuscript. It was a play this time, two acts. Something about a young man's battle with the crushing, dehumanizing effects of the big city. She assumed he was the young man; she assumed the city was New York; she assumed it was all about his life. It seemed to Myra a silly effort, although she had to admit she knew nothing about the theater.

"No problems, then?"

"Not at all," she said.

"Well . . ." At last he could contain himself no longer. He picked up the sheaf of paper, ninety-eight pages of text plus a title page and a page listing the characters. A nice round hundred all together, and he folded the paper as if it were indeed nice and round. Like the curve of a woman's body, her body, Myra thought, to take an example close to hand. Very close to hand. She could see the hairs on the back of his wrist, craning out of the cuff of his shirt sleeve as if stretching for the light. There was hair on the back of his hand, hair on the fingers up to the first knuckle. She longed to touch his hand, to lead it to something warmer, something more receptive to his caress than the pile of lifeless paper.

She looked up and realized that he was really looking at her for the first time. Or at least at her cleavage. He jerked his eyes toward her face, embarrassed, caught. She wanted to reward him for his naughtiness, but she did nothing. Her face revealed nothing. She wanted to tell him he could kiss her breasts if he admired them, but, of course, she did not. Her good hand was still twisting the button on her blouse. If she were to undo the button now, tear it off with a snap of her fingers, how would he react? She didn't know; many responses were possible, but only one of them acceptable, and she didn't take the chance. There must be some way to entice him beyond looking, she thought, there must be ways to let him know she was willing. She was available. She would not slap his face, run away, call for help. He had but to reach out a hand, a finger, he had but to touch her breast, the blouse; Lord, just to breathe upon them. Her nipples were rigid in anticipation; surely they were visible through the cloth, she thought. She had worn no brassiere, she could feel the silk on her skin. There must be ways! But she did not know them. She may be a tease, she thought, but she was neither brazen nor brave. Ultimately she was defeated as much by her lack of imagination as her reserve. She rewarded him the only way she dared.

"I hope you don't mind my saying so, but I liked your play." Her voice was quavering. Could he tell?

"Oh, really?" He looked at her now, no question about it. She had become a source of greater interest than if she had torn her clothes off and writhed on the floor. With a single lie, she had become his fan.

"What . . . What did you like in particular?"

"The young man," she said. "I particularly liked the character of the young man."

"Really?!" He couldn't believe his good fortune, Myra thought. "I worked especially hard on him."

"It shows."

"The young man." He shook his head in wonderment. Of the many right things she could have said, she had apparently hit upon the best. "That's great, that's terrific."

She shifted her weight on the chair to make her breasts bounce. The nipples showed through like a dark, puckered stain. She knew. She had tested the effect in the mirror.

"A straight man is always the hardest to write," he said. He had not noticed her breasts. The script was clutched against his chest now and he tilted it away from his body now and again, like a mother checking her baby's face.

"Is that so?"

"I don't mean straight in the sense of heterosexual. I mean the character with the fewest quirks, the one the action has to revolve around. It's always easier to write someone flamboyant. Like the girl in this."

He looked at her now, waiting for her to say something about the girl in his play. Myra remembered her name was Jan because she had had to type it so many times, but she didn't recall anything about her character. Mr. Henley's eyes were brown and soft and soulful. It would be so easy to hurt him. He'd been a client of hers for at least five years, and to her knowledge he had sold none of his writings. How had he survived? How had he kept those eyes so innocent and kind? But, of course, looks could be deceiving. She should know that better than anyone, Myra thought.

"The girl. Jan," she said, nodding with great comprehension. "I see what you mean. She was easier to write, was she?"

"Oh, yes, much!" And Mr. Henley suddenly broke into speech as if a pipe had been ruptured under the pressure of all those lonely hours of composition. At least she assumed they had been lonely hours. The play he had written suggested he was a terminally lonely man. Terminally. The hero of the play was ineptly suicidal. Was Mr. Henley sheltering ideas of killing himself behind that shy, serious aspect? He seemed so very grateful for her feigned interest. She would gladly give him something better to be grateful for, but he wasn't aware of that possibility. He must think the poor crippled girl can't do it, Myra thought, as if my sexual parts were deformed, too. They weren't.

Mr. Henley was talking in a rush, telling her about the agonies of creation, the theory and the technicalities. He couldn't seem to get the words out fast enough, as if he was afraid this opportunity might vanish at any second. She wondered how long it had been since he really spoke to anyone.

"It's the structure that's so hard in a play," he was saying. "The dialogue isn't hard. I've got a sort of gift for dialogue. I don't mean a big gift. I don't mean like Mamet or anything, but I don't labor over it; but the structure, putting the whole thing together into the proper shape, even knowing what the proper shape *is,* that's what's so difficult!"

He paced as he talked, clutching the script with one hand, gesturing with the other. He reminded Myra of Howard, all that frustrated energy, never able to be completely still, even in his sleep. Howard usually took the same route Mr. Henley used now, desk to sofa, sofa to door, door to desk, as if there were a rut worn into the floor. It was so uncomfortable to watch these men test the perimeters of their cage this way; as if their skin were burning with claustrophobia. She wanted to tell them that the only way out of the cage is to accept it, but Howard had never listened and she wouldn't presume to advise Mr. Henley. In his case it may be just excitement, she thought.

Her concern must have shown on her face, and Mr. Henley had misinterpreted it as annoyance, for he had abruptly stopped talking.

"Well . . . I guess that isn't of much interest to anyone but me," he said apologetically.

"I think it's interesting," she said brightly, but too late. The moment had passed. Like any lonely person, Mr. Henley was quick to retreat into his solitude. The appearance of needing someone is worse than the loneliness, Myra thought. Are we lonely because no one wants to listen to us? Or do we assume we are not worth hearing and shut ourselves off? Whatever the answer, the result was reinforcement. The lonely got lonelier because they were lonely and didn't want others to know it. I could tell him that I understand this, that I suffer from the same symptoms, if for different reasons, but it would only offend him to hear it, Myra thought. He would not appreciate being lumped with his crippled typist as another social misfit.

"Thanks again," he said, walking backwards toward the door.

"Do you want to look it over?"

"I'm sure you did your usual great job," he said. He paused for a moment, as if wanting to say more, but afraid he'd said too much already.

"It was nice talking to you," Myra said.

"Oh! It was nice talking to *you* . . . well . . . "

She smiled and arched her back one last time, an exercise in futility. Her baby hand yearned to twitch, but she willed it to stay quiet just a moment longer.

"I'll see you next time I have something," he said, then fumbled for the doorknob. Suddenly he can't get away quickly enough, she thought. With a final nod he was gone, moving so rapidly he nearly collided with the door before it was fully open. Myra sat at her desk for a moment, fighting the sense of disappointment that was surging up from her stomach. It was not as if she liked Mr. Henley all that much. She barely knew him. He was attractive enough, in a neutral way, although he would sink into a crowd of middle-class Americans in their early thirties like a snowball in a snowbank. His only real appeal, she had to remind herself, was not his big soft eyes or his obvious need, but simply his propinquity. He was there, so she wanted him. Now he was gone and she had all but forgotten him already, she told herself. She would have yearned for the television repair man or the pizza delivery boy just as ardently as she yearned for Mr. Henley, and would have forgotten them as quickly. Out of sight, out of mind.

She sometimes flattered herself that she was a spider in her web, awaiting a choice morsel. Like the spider she was not selective. One fly would do as well as another; she did not pine for one with brown eyes and the stain of a typewriter ribbon on his fingers—unless that one happened to get caught in her web. Then, of course, she saw it as the best meal of all.

But she knew she flattered herself by the comparison. A spider is efficient and lethal. She does catch her prey, enmeshes them in her web, bites and paralyzes them, then sucks them dry. Myra outlined her breasts and unbuttoned her blouse before a callow and unsuccessful young man who had no interest in her except as a reflection of himself. If she was a spider, he was a tree, something on which she could hang the web of her foolishness, but totally indifferent, oblivious.

In a surge of self-disgust, Myra buttoned her blouse to the neck, then lurched toward the door to lock it. The crutches were as much a nuisance as a help for short trips and she seldom used them when she was alone at home. They were for public consumption because they gave her a more gracious air, a gliding motion much more aesthetic than her cripple's hobble, she thought. She could get around as fast as anyone else with her hobble—she'd had a lifetime to refine it— but she feared that she looked like something less than human, a beetle or a crab. A cockroach scurrying from the light, perhaps. She was grateful that she didn't have to watch herself.

She was halfway to the door when there was a tap and it swung open. Mr. Henley was there, talking, apologetic, and Myra was frozen in the middle of the room, bent as if arrested in mid-fall.

"I'm awfully sorry, I forgot to pay you," he said, half the speech out of his mouth before he even entered, the checkbook in his hand. Then the awareness of what he was seeing struck him and he gaped. Myra imagined a force to his astonishment and horror so palpable that it seemed to hit her like a shock wave. Astounded, she realized she was really falling. She clawed at the air with her baby arm. It had something to do at last, and it flapped grotesquely in his face. And then she was on the floor.

The next moments were so embarrassing that she scarcely registered them. She knew that he helped her up and returned her to her chair. He talked incessantly, babbling on with embarrassment and apology while he wrote the check. Her face was on fire with shame; she could not look at him, could not speak to him. She was certain she could feel his revulsion pulsing toward her in waves. He had placed her in the wrong position in the chair; nothing was hidden, the baby arm hung short of her waist, the leg jutted out to the side as if trying to pull her away. She folded both arms across her chest, the normal one hiding its little sibling, but it didn't matter anymore, she thought. He wasn't looking at her. Nothing could make him look directly at her now, she thought. She felt like Medusa discovered in her boudoir, her serpentine coiffure writhing in full freedom.

Finally, mercifully, he was gone. She didn't bother with the door this time but sat at her desk, letting her tears quench the fire on her cheeks.

5

Edgar Allen McKinnon suffered from a pinched sciatic nerve that nagged with the insistence of a toothache. The pain radiated down from his left buttock through the length of his leg and into the foot where he had begun to loose sensation in his little toe. It was a pain for which there was no relief other than bed rest—a luxury he would not grant himself—and it made McKinnon very angry most of the time. When he was not angry he felt like weeping from frustration, but his subordinates never saw either aspect of his reaction. What they saw was what McKinnon allowed them to see, and after a career spent studying and thwarting covert enemy actions, McKinnon allowed no one to see much of anything. His doctor knew something of his pain; his physical therapist knew more. But no one knew about his inner rage.

What Finney saw was what all of McKinnon's subordinates saw, an almost eerie self-control that manifested itself in a voice lowered always to a near whisper and a manner that suggested the kindliness of a saint. Finney was inexperienced enough to believe what he saw.

"What were his exact words, Mr. Finney?" McKinnon leaned forward suddenly in an attempt to ease the pain which Finney interpreted as interest. He glanced nervously at Hatcher, McKinnon's deputy, who sat in a chair next to his boss's desk. Hatcher had already heard Becker's message and his face was contorted now into the unreceptive aspect of a fist.

"His exact words, sir?"

"Please, Mr. Finney." McKinnon called everyone "Mister," which was regarded not as courtesy but as an oddity within the Bureau, where "Agent" was the normal term of formal address.

"I'm not sure I can recall his precise words, sir," Finney lied.

"At my age I could understand a memory failure, Mr. Finney. At your age, it's bothersome. What exactly did Mr. Becker say?" McKinnon smiled with such patient forbearance that Finney could never have guessed it was to hide a sudden spasm of pain that tore down the director's leg like an electric shock.

"He said that Special Agent Hatcher—I mean Deputy Director Hatcher—"

Hatcher dilated his nostrils at the distinction as if it gave off an odor.

Christ, I didn't say it, Finney thought. I'm just the messenger. Hatcher had already turned on Finney when the young agent delivered the message the first time. He looked as if he was about to take another large chunk of his ass.

McKinnon waited, eyebrows raised in anticipation.

". . . He said he could fuck himself," said Finney. "Sorry, sir."

McKinnon wrote on a notepad as if taking down the message.

"Sorry, Mr. Finney? For the language, or the message?"

"Uh . . . the language, sir."

Hatcher expelled his breath noisily.

"And the message, too, of course," Finney added hastily.

"I've heard the language before," McKinnon said, "but thank you for your concern for my sensibilities. Sit down, Mr. Finney."

McKinnon turned slightly to face Hatcher, the better to watch his discomfiture. It was his relish for Hatcher's embarrassment that had made him extract the verbatim account from Finney in the first place. Keeping Finney in the room increased the embarrassment and would prevent Hatcher from whining too vociferously. It was Hatcher's whining that McKinnon disliked most about the man, but there were other unpleasant qualities to choose from.

"Your personal experience with Becker was not entirely a happy one, Mr. Hatcher?"

"I believe he was working under some misunderstanding," Hatcher said stiffly.

"Apparently. The question then is, is this misunderstanding going to prevent his working for us."

"He can be told to," said Hatcher.

McKinnon arched his back slowly, stretching the muscles. It was the only posture that afforded him any relief. When the sciatica was at its worst, he longed to hang upside down to alleviate the pressure on his spinal disc. The mental picture of himself roosting head down like a bat while conducting interviews made him smile.

"Actually, that gets a little complicated," he said. "Becker is currently with the Bureau of Alcohol, Tobacco and Firearms. We're not really in a position to give him orders."

"He can transfer," Hatcher said. "He's been with three different departments in the past two years. He's a troubleshooter."

"But he has accepted those transfers," said McKinnon. "I'm not entirely certain he would accept a transfer to the Bureau again."

"Why not?"

McKinnon turned to Finney. "Did he indicate why not, Mr. Finney?"

"No, sir, not really."

"Just a general distaste for Mr. Hatcher?"

"Something like that, sir."

McKinnon nodded. He, too, had a general distaste for Hatcher, but the man had been promoted by McKinnon's superiors, to whom Hatcher's blend of flattery, bootlicking, and overall sycophancy apparently held a greater appeal than it did for McKinnon. Unable to advance any specific complaint against the man himself—other than a vague but genuine dislike for him—McKinnon had held his tongue and accepted the appointment. He did not believe in running his shop on the basis of personal affinities, and there was nothing in Hatcher's record to disqualify him. To the contrary, it was quite a good record. He covered his ass well, McKinnon had to admit. On the other hand, Becker, whom McKinnon genuinely liked and admired, had a dossier as checkered as a Tartan kilt. He was the kind of man everyone wanted to work with—except perhaps Hatcher—and the kind that no superior would ever promote beyond his current status as an operative. Becker had no desire to be in charge of other men; it was Hatcher's only ambition.

"Do you return this distaste, Mr. Hatcher?"

"How do you mean?"

"Do you dislike him?"

"I don't dislike anyone, sir. I do my job, whatever my job may be, to the best of my ability. I don't see where personalities need to enter into it at all."

In other words, you lack all personal integrity, McKinnon thought. Becker, on the other hand, was crawling with it. Which was why Hatcher was deputy director and Becker was not. A department full of Beckers would be chaos. A department full of Hatchers would lack spark and brilliance. The choice, almost inevitably, was for mediocrity, McKinnon realized, and the thought made his back hurt even more.

"Actually, sir, I don't see where it needs to be a problem at all," Hatcher was saying. "There are other agents besides Becker."

"Do you know any who are as good at this kind of thing?"

"I'm sure there are some," said Hatcher.

"I'd appreciate their names, Mr. Hatcher," McKinnon said. He held his pen poised over the notepad.

Hatcher tried to smile his way out of it. He had not anticipated such a lack of support. A simple assertion of Becker's qualified abilities should have been enough for his superior. Was McKinnon actually pitting the value of a single agent against that of his own deputy? What was it about Becker that brought forth this kind of attitude from others?

"I actually haven't seen his record over the past few years," said Hatcher.

Finney shifted in his chair. He had personally reviewed Becker's record with Hatcher himself.

"It makes for interesting reading," said McKinnon. To Finney's horror the director turned to him. "Isn't that right, Mr. Finney?"

Don't involve me, Finney wanted to scream. If he admitted he was familiar with Becker's record, it was certainly implying that Hatcher knew it, too—or should have. If he denied knowing Becker's record, it made him look negligent and incompetent. There was no way to do anything but lose. McKinnon was evidently waiting for an answer. For the first time Finney wondered if the saintliness were just a facade after all.

When in doubt whether to kiss the ass of the deputy director or the director himself, choose the director. Finney was certain he had been taught that lesson in his first week of training.

"Very interesting reading, sir," Finney said. Then, trying to give Hatcher some kind of out, he added, "Although we went after him so quickly that I didn't have time to study it as carefully as I would have liked."

McKinnon inclined his head slightly, as if acknowledging Finney's efforts at statesmanship.

"I suggest you brief Mr. Hatcher, then," McKinnon said. "Bring him up to date on Becker's career." He turned to face Hatcher, whose face again had taken on its resemblance to a fist. Blush red color showed itself along his hairline, while the area around his mouth seemed to be drained of color. "You'll want to be familiar with it so you can make conversation when you talk to him, Mr. Hatcher."

"When I talk to him, sir?"

"I want you to fetch him for us," said McKinnon.

Hatcher straightened in his chair. My ass is dead, Finney thought. Somehow or other, I'll have to pay for this indignity.

"Personally, sir?"

"It's the personal touch that means so much," said McKinnon. He lowered his face to his notepad to conceal his grin.

Two days before his meeting with McKinnon, Hatcher had driven with his wife into a wooded section of Virginia, just far enough away from Quantico that there were deer running through the trees, not FBI trainees. As he and his wife sat over their picnic in the numbing silence that had become their pattern over the years, a doe had peeked its nose into their small clearing and paused tensely for at least a minute. Hatcher's wife had squeezed his hand in excitement, urging him to share the thrill of the moment. It was the first time she had voluntarily touched him in weeks, he realized, as he sat very still, trying to mimic her exhilaration. It annoyed him that an animal could cause her to gasp when he could not—not that he tried much anymore. Their mating had become nearly seasonal, like the deer's. They coupled once in spring, once in summer, and so forth, and during the long interim Hatcher just tried not to think about it.

The doe slowly stepped into the clearing, followed by two fawns, newly born, not much larger than a collie dog, their legs stick-thin and frail. As indifferent to their presence as if Hatcher and his wife were statues chiseled from native stone, the deer began to browse. Hatcher glanced at his wife and saw tears welling up in her eyes and her lips tremble as if she were whispering so softly Hatcher could not hear her two feet away. She was staring at the deer as if they were a saintly apparition, come expressly to confirm her faith in beauty and innocence. Despite the tears, Hatcher's wife was smiling beatifically. He didn't think he had ever seen her quite so happy. It was all he could do to keep from strangling her.

The deer worked patiently across the clearing, pausing frequently to lift their heads and listen. Once the mother turned to the fawn next to her and licked its face. The second fawn took this as a cue to nurse and butted its head fretfully against its mother's nipples. His wife squeezed his hand the harder to add emphasis to the scene, and from the corner of his eye he could see her turn her face toward him. She was biting her lip to keep from wailing about the sheer maternal serenity of the moment—and she wanted Hatcher to know it. There, she seemed to be saying. If only you would treat me with such sweetness. Turn to me with spontaneous affection to kiss my face. Love me with the gentleness of a deer.

Hatcher worked to smile for her, feeling the effort in every muscle in his face. Hypocrisy was a tool he could wield with great facility at work but found difficult to handle at home.

A larger deer appeared where the other three had emerged from the woods, a buck with large and heavy antlers crowning his head. Hatcher's wife sucked in her breath in awe.

Hatcher lifted his arm and pointed it like a rifle at the buck. All the deer bolted immediately, tails flashing white as they vanished back into the trees. Hatcher had squeezed off three imaginary shots before the buck was completely gone and felt a certain sense of triumph that sustained him against his wife's silent fury on the long ride home.

Hatcher remembered the moment now as he stepped into the basement gymnasium and saw Becker standing on the balance beam. He wanted to lift the silent rifle of his arm and blow the man away, if only to prove he could do it, but with Becker it would be a very foolish gesture. Even though his back was toward Hatcher, Hatcher was not entirely certain that Becker would not somehow detect the motion and the animosity behind it. And, given that it was Becker, there was a real, albeit remote, chance that he would assume the motion was truly threatening and wheel around and blow Hatcher's head off. Neither alternative seemed a very good way to begin an interview designed to win the man over to Hatcher's side.

While Hatcher stood quietly in the doorway, Becker lifted one foot off the balance beam and rested it against the inside of the opposing knee, then stood without wavering, his arms crossed over his chest. He looks like a stork or crane, Hatcher thought. Or a picture of a Masai warrior on the savannah, tending his cows. But the Masai always had a spear in one hand for support.

Hatcher moved into the gym until he was facing Becker.

"In a minute," Becker said. He had his eyes closed.

Some Zen thing, Hatcher thought dismissively. Balancing on one foot with your eyes closed. He reminded Hatcher of scenes from various American karate movies.

Becker put both feet on the beam and walked forward with his eyes still closed, his arms still folded on his chest. His feet were pointed to the side like a dancer's. He stopped two inches short of falling off and walked backwards, eyes still shut.

For a happy moment Hatcher thought Becker would step off the back of the beam, but again he stopped just short of the end and stood stock-still. Becker let his arms fall to his sides, took a deep breath, and suddenly dipped his head and rolled forward into a somersault on the four-inch-wide beam. He rose up to his feet, arms out like wings, and leaped straight up, yanking his legs into a pike position before landing on his toes. Without pausing Becker bent his legs and propelled himself into a backwards somersault, rolling over with his head on one side of the beam. As he used the momentum to come to his feet, he wobbled to one side, waved his arms futilely, then fell off the beam, landing lightly on his feet.

"I always have trouble with that part," Becker said. His eyes were still closed. Without opening them he leaped up and to the side, scissoring his legs, and was suddenly standing on the beam again.

Finally he opened his eyes.

"Very nice," said Hatcher, smiling wanly.

"Put your feet together," Becker said. If he was surprised to see Hatcher he gave no indication.

Hatcher put his feet together, still forcing the smile.

"Now close your eyes," Becker said.

Just standing on the solid floor Hatcher found himself swaying within seconds of closing his eyes. He snapped them open and spread his feet apart once more.

"I see," said Hatcher. "Very impressive."

"Just a trick," said Becker. "And an awful lot of practice."

"Do you practice it for some purpose?"

Becker stripped off his gray T-shirt and used it to wipe the sweat from his face. "I hope not," he said.

Becker walked toward the locker room, leaving Hatcher to follow or not.

"Have you ever studied the Innuit?" Becker asked as he removed his sweatclothes in the locker room.

"The ...?"

"The Innuit Indians. Eskimos."

"No, I haven't studied the Eskimos. Why should I?"

"For your philosophical enlightenment. Before the white man introduced them to rifles and snowmobiles, they used to live on a near-starvation diet during good times and bad. Even when times were plentiful and there were lots of seal and whales and they could have gorged themselves for several years at a time, the elders wouldn't let the people overeat because they knew that inevitably hard times would come again and if they were used to the good life they might not be able to adjust to the bad."

The locker smelled of wintergreen, which conjured up memories of sprained ankles and torn muscles for Hatcher. He had not been in a gym or locker room when he wasn't required to for years.

"Sounds like a pretty joyless way to live," said Hatcher.

"It was a way to survive," said Becker. "I'm in favor of survival."

Becker kicked off his shorts and stood, naked, reaching into his locker for a towel. Hatcher was always uncomfortable in the presence of naked men and he studiously kept his eyes on Becker's face.

"How do you feel about survival, Hatcher?"

"I think you might have misunderstood how things happened last time," Hatcher said.

"Well, yes, I might have," said Becker. "I was sort of preoccupied with dealing with two men trying to kill me while my backup was lost in traffic somewhere."

"I was delayed no more than a minute ... "

"How long do you think it takes to die?"

You would know more than I do about that, Hatcher thought. You've caused enough deaths to qualify as an expert. He wished Becker would at least wrap the towel around his waist. There was no way to maintain one's dignity while talking to a naked man, particularly when one's eyes kept wanting to glance down. Hatcher kept his gaze focused squarely between Becker's eyes.

"My driver screwed up," Hatcher said.

"It's always somebody else's fault with you, Hatcher. There's always someone you can blame and dump on in your report, but the screw-ups just keep happening, don't they?"

"Not actually," said Hatcher. "If anyone else thought that way I wouldn't be deputy director, would I?"

"The only people who think that way are all the men who ever served under you," said Becker, walking toward the shower.

Hatcher stood at the entrance to the shower, his face averted.

"We could work out some accommodation," Hatcher said. "I understand that personalities conflict sometimes."

"It's not your personality I object to," Becker said. "It's you."

Hatcher laughed humorlessly. "Well, these things can be worked out," he said.

Hearing no response, he turned to see Becker with his head directly under the stream of water, his eyes closed. Taking careful aim with both hands, Hatcher pointed his finger and with immense gratification blasted Becker four times.

When Becker returned to his locker, Hatcher was sitting on the bench, playing with the crease in his trousers.

"We have unsubstantiated reports that a terrorist has entered the country from Europe in the past week," Hatcher said.

Becker turned his back to Hatcher as he toweled himself dry.

"What kind of reports?"

"An Israeli asset trailing the movements of the Beni Hassan reported a rather peculiar meeting between an unidentified man and Taha Hammadi." Hatcher pinched the trouser crease and ran his fingers the length of his thigh. He ignored the fact that Becker was presenting him with his backside. Under the circumstances he chose to interpret it as discretion rather than insult.

"The unidentified man met with Hammadi in the middle of lake Como and then dumped the old man into the water."

Becker laughed. "He did us all a favor."

"He wasn't trying to drown him. We don't think. He was just buying time to get away. Hammadi's bodyguards pulled him out, but he kept them from going after the other man." Hatcher paused while pinching the crease in the other leg.

"Strange, don't you think?" he said finally.

"Did the Israeli asset go after him?" Becker asked.

"He was apparently working as a fisherman. There wasn't anything he could do without blowing his cover."

Becker pulled on his pants and sat to put on his socks and shoes. He knew that Hatcher was feeding him small bits at a time, like luring a pigeon near enough to capture by dropping crumbs of bread progressively closer to the trap.

"Interesting," said Becker. "But so what?"

"Two days later there was an incident at Montreal passport control involving an incoming passenger from a flight from Poland. The passenger killed two baggage handlers and nearly killed the Immigration agent before commandeering a baggage truck and vaulting over the runway perimeter fence."

"How nearly killed?" Becker asked.

"Carotid ligation. Possible brain damage. The Immigration agent doesn't remember the incident or the man, but that's normal after that sort of trauma. There were witnesses, but it's the usual botch-up. Some think he's tall, some short, some think he's fair, some dark . . . "

"They agree it's a man?"

"A young man. Youngish. Late twenties, early thirties. And apparently a real pro. The whole incident was very quick, but no one remembers his doing anything the least bit hurried."

Becker hated to ask because he hated to give Hatcher the satisfaction, but he could not deny to himself that he was intrigued.

"Any reason to think it's the same man?"

"Not really. But the Beni Hassan have used a number of Polish passports in the past. This guy came on a Polish flight." Hatcher shrugged. "McKinnon found it an 'interesting concurrence.' The guy was a pro. He bolted at passport control, which means he wasn't just smuggling something; he was the contraband himself."

Becker buttoned his shirt and tucked the tails into his pants.

"Sounds like a Mountie problem to me."

"If that's as far as it goes," said Hatcher.

Becker knew it wasn't as far as it went, but he did not want to ask Hatcher any more questions. The man's smugness was growing with each inquiry.

Becker started for the door. "Always nice seeing you, Hatcher."

"The next day, in Montreal, a man named Robert Carmichael was found murdered and dumped into a refuge bin at a construction site. If they hadn't happened to finish the job that day, they wouldn't have found the body for at least a week. If at all.''

"Canada's getting to be dangerous," said Becker, pausing in the doorway. "It's time we all headed for Australia. Be sure to give McKinnon my best."

"You'll like this part," Hatcher said, still sitting on the bench. "Carmichael was killed by a foreign object rammed into his ear. They found a wire coat hanger in the dumpster but don't have the lab check on the blood yet."

Becker leaned against the door jamb and studied his shoes for a moment.

"Why do you think I'd like that particular part, Hatcher?"

"Just a figure of speech," said Hatcher.

Becker raised his gaze to Hatcher's face. After a moment Hatcher squirmed uncomfortably. Becker was capable of scaring him just by looking at him.

"I didn't mean anything by it," Hatcher said. "No need to take offense."

"I don't enjoy hearing about how people die," said Becker.

"Of course not. I didn't mean that."

"I don't like knowing about details. It doesn't give me some perverse thrill, as you seem to be implying."

"I meant nothing of the sort. Truly."

"What's more, I don't like you, Hatcher."

"I know. But we're professionals."

"Sometimes people die in the course of this work," Becker said. "Nobody is happy about that. Nobody enjoys it."

Bingo, thought Hatcher. Got him right where he lives.

"I didn't mean to imply that," said Hatcher. "Although . . . "

Becker took a deep breath as if bracing himself for the next stupidity to come. As Hatcher paused, Becker tilted his head to one side, like a bird studying a worm. Or the next crumb, Becker thought to himself. He already knew he was going to step into the trap, but he didn't want Hatcher to think it had been a certainty from the start.

"Although . . . a man who takes the time to prepare a weapon like eight inches of wire hanger—you'd think he might enjoy it," Hatcher said.

"I assume you have a description of the dead man at least," Becker said.

"It matches the identification of the man who tossed Hammadi in the lake. He killed somebody who looked like him and took his wallet, credit cards, driver's license ..."

"And passport," Becker said, finishing Hatcher's thought.

"Correct. And about one hour after the coroner estimates Robert Carmichael was being put in the dumpster, someone named Robert Carmichael rented a car and drove to the border crossing."

"In New York."

"Nope. Windsor. And into Michigan."

"Detroit."

Hatcher nodded.

"He took the diagonal through Canada. A lot faster that way than going through the States and around the Great Lakes."

"And Detroit has the largest Arab community in the country," Hatcher said.

"Is it established he's an Arab?"

"No, but working for them. One day after 'Robert Carmichael' crossed into Detroit, the National Security Agency picked up an electronic transfer of funds from Libya to the Allied Arab Bank of Michigan. Two million dollars."

"Not that unusual," Becker said.

"No, but the account was brand-new."

"Established under the name of Robert Carmichael," said Becker.

"Three hours before the transfer. We tried to make a small wire transfer account to the same account yesterday just to see if it was coded."

"It was already closed," said Becker.

"How did you know?"

"That's what I would have done," said Becker. "He knew the name was traceable eventually. Take the money, get out of Dodge. Establish a safer identity when you have the time." Becker paused for a moment, his eyes fixed on the wall behind Hatcher.

"What else?" he asked finally.

"Why do you think there's anything else?"

Becker smiled slowly and returned his eyes to Hatcher. "Because what you've given me isn't quite enough to get me and you would hate to have to go back to McKinnon without me. What do you have left to bait me with, Hatcher? The man's gone, right? No more "Robert Carmichael," no more bank account. The rented car was returned or disappeared. You haven't got any record of the credit cards being used since he arrived in Detroit—but then with two million in his pocket, he wouldn't need credit cards. He's gone, right? Disappeared somewhere into America with a ton of money, which he's going to have to earn some way or other."

"All correct," said Hatcher.

"So what more do you have to dangle in front of me?"

"Nothing about this guy . . . There is one other thing that might interest you, though. Probably not related. Just an 'interesting concurrence' that McKinnon thought I should pass on to you."

Becker waited, giving Hatcher his moment.

"Willie Holzer is dead."

Hatcher noted with gratification that Becker was genuinely surprised—and more. There appeared to be almost a note of sorrow in Becker's voice, though given the history of the two men that seemed hardly likely or appropriate.

"The son of a bitch," said Becker.

"Way overdue," said Hatcher.

Becker sat on the bench, dropping the gym bag between his feet. "Willie Holzer."

"I don't pretend to grieve over him," said Hatcher.

Becker swiveled his head toward Hatcher. "I don't pretend to grieve over him, either."

"You can't seriously be sorry he's dead."

"I mourn my enemies, Hatcher. They're often more important to my life than my friends. Willie was a murderous bastard, but he was sincere about it. He believed in what he did . . . so, finish it up."

"What do you mean?"

"What was the interesting concurrence?"

"Willie died because somebody pushed a ballpoint pen into his ear."

Becker nodded slowly as if he had known it all along in some way.

"Ask the Mounties to dust the Montreal passport office for prints," he said.

"Why?"

"That's where I'd go if I wanted to find someone who fit my description and to be sure he had a passport on him. He probably had to sit around there for a while unless he got lucky. If we get lucky we can get a print.''

"There will be thousands of prints in a place like that.''

"That's what computers are for, Hatcher.'' Becker stood and walked to the door again. This time he did not turn back, but Hatcher knew there was nothing left to say. The pigeon was in the trap.

6

Late afternoon was the dangerous time for Myra. Her work was done and her imagination was free to conjure what it would. The apartment seemed as resoundingly empty as a cave, and she could sense her anxieties building drop by drop like stalagmites in every corner. In time their steady accretions would cause them to fill the room, clogging off the light and air and space and she would be imprisoned upon her mother's carpet, beneath her mother's framed prints of English fox hunters and baying hounds, imprisoned, and ultimately impaled as the stony point of her anxieties grew toward her body and finally through it. Would her body grow around it like a wounded tree around a nail, she wondered, or would it kill her in torment and fear?

She turned to her telescope, but today it had little joy to offer. Her brother, Howard, thought she used it for astronomical observations, and so she had, from time to time, but the lights in the city are far too bright for any meaningful sightings and, at any rate, she had but a small quadrant of the sky visible from her window.

The telescope was for people, targets far more luminous for Myra than stars, and she watched them with unabashed interest. The miracle of optical lenses could take her north as far as Fiftieth Street before an apartment building intervened. To the south her vision extended through an architectural rift in the skyline for nearly a mile down Second Avenue. A stop light at Twenty-ninth and Second allowed her to watch motorists scratch themselves, adjust their clothes, pick their noses while imagining themselves invisible within their cars. To the east she could see the United Nations complex and beyond it the East River. Diplomats and tourists, ships and seaplanes, and past it all, in the farthest stretch available to her, Myra could penetrate far into Queens.

Today the telescope held no interest for her. She was drawn, as she knew she would be, toward her brother's room.

Howard's room held for Myra the familiar thrill of a bad habit long practiced in private. It emanated sex and sin and secrecy, guilt and self-indulgence, the essence of her brother. In a way, the room was more truly Howard than the person himself, for there were no restraints in the room, no token courtesies, no public repressions, no masks or images other than his true self. By violating his wishes and penetrating his sanctuary, Myra felt closer to Howard than any other time.

The lock had presented no barrier for years. When she opened the door, she was greeted first by the odor, a mixture of male sweat and old underwear, of sex and frustration. He masturbated in here, she knew, furiously and constantly, spilling himself into one of a series of old socks which he eventually removed, sneaking them out of the apartment in the pocket of his raincoat, destined for the nearest trash basket; and the room itself had the sense of an engorged penis, Myra thought, hot and quivering and ready to explode.

It looked like the cell of a sex-crazed monk. The furnishings were monastically spare, the same bed, the same book shelf, the same straightback chair and desk he had had since early teens. Somewhere on the surface of that desk, buried now beneath the clutter of his obsessions, were his initials and Myra's, carved in a heart with an arrow piercing through. Two drops of blood completed the design, gouged out of the pine, the wood still unvarnished twenty years later. She had carved that sign of love for her brother when he was fourteen and she was twelve, did it from an irrepressible need to let him know how much she cared for him. Even then he was virtually the only male in her universe, at least the only one who treated her with enough respect to mistreat her. He yelled at her, punched her, bullied her, acted as if she were his sister, another competitive human being, and not a creature to be pitied or coddled. Myra would have burned their initials into their flesh if she could have. His reaction on discovering the maiming of his new desk was exactly what she had expected—he howled and beat her, rolling her under his body on the floor and pummeling her with his fists until their horrified mother pulled him off. She cried, of course, but the blows never really hurt. The real pain came from her mother's insistence that Myra was not to be treated with the same big brother brutality as any other naughty girl.

He had added a reading lamp that clipped onto the head of the bed frame, but otherwise Howard had changed nothing in the room. A yarmulke and prayer shawl hung on a hook behind the door. On the desk was a photograph taken when he graduated from high school. He glared at the camera, furious with the photographer who must have been their mother. His hair was slicked back, a sure sign of her intervention, and his lips were curled into the sneer he wore most of his teenaged years. Despite his attitude, Myra thought he looked quite handsome, young and strong and full of promise. He looked the way she remembered their father. One arm was draped over Myra's shoulder and her body was turned into his, as if with affection, and it was with affection, but also to hide her arm and leg. She, at least, was smiling, pleasing her mother, being a good girl, a photographic imitation of the perfect fifteen-year-old daughter, pretty, happy, radiantly nubile. The camera lies so readily; it has no attention span, Myra thought ruefully. Anyone could feign perfection for the length of a shutter click.

There was no picture of their mother on the desk, but in the bottom drawer, wrinkled and pushed to the back behind reams of paper for Howard's typewriter, was an old snapshot of both parents. There was a long slash through their mother, which had been taped together again imperfectly so that her two halves didn't match properly. It was probably as good a description of her as any other, thought Myra.

Howard had been paid yesterday, so Myra expected new material today. She looked first on the top of the pile by his bed, but she knew it could be anywhere in the mound. Howard shuffled through the books and magazines as if they were cards, seeking old favorites or simple words and images he hadn't seen recently. Several pin-ups from old copies of *Playboy* were stuck to the wall by yellowing tape. He had used pushpins to reinforce the tape, and the girls dangled at odd angles amid a papered background of classic cars. The pictures were very old indeed; there was no pubic hair displayed, only the airbrushed skin as glossy as the paper on which it was reproduced. Myra's personal favorite, a brunette with a sweet, understanding smile, adorned the wall directly under the banner for Howard's "party." Her brother's two passions, sex and politics, pinned to his wall, each as self-delusionary and masturbatory as the other, she thought.

His tastes had become more jaded lately, or at least more specific—

or perhaps the magazines had changed their style. Howard was Myra's only source of knowledge there. In any event, he had started buying picture books. There was no nonsense about text here, just photo after photo of naked bodies engaged in a variety of display and activity. It was raw stuff, nothing left to suggestion, but perhaps that was the trend to Howard's obsession, she realized. His imagination was flagging and he needed all the details provided for him.

Myra found what she thought was a new book. The cost of these things was appalling; she objected to the money wasted. But the paper was good quality, the pictures would last. This one, like most of the others, showed a couple mating. He sported a sandy mustache and needed a haircut, and there was a mole on his left shoulder. The book was not designed to make the man the subject of interest, but Myra couldn't help studying him. Why did he do this? Was it fun, could it conceivably be fun there in front of the lights and the photographer, being sucked and handled by a woman he felt nothing for? Judging by the results, part of him liked the treatment. He put her on her back on the bed. She was ready for him, her face a parody of desire. Myra knew it to be a silly, vain exercise, and yet she compared herself to the woman in the pictures; she imagined this man mounting herself, splitting her. She heard him whispering her name in her ear, nothing more, just her name, Myra, Myra, Myra. She could feel herself taking him in. God, how she wanted him! I am bursting like a cow with a swollen udder, bellowing for release, she thought. She was tired of herself, her own fingers, her own hand. Myra wanted the warmth of another human. She could simulate *sex* with an object, but she couldn't feel another's breath on her face, she couldn't imagine a tongue in her mouth, on her body, moving to its own, unexpected rhythms. She knew herself too well; there were no surprises left.

She dropped the book, disgusted with herself, and looked for other amusements. On the desk, surrounded by a bayonet, an Israeli helmet, a throwing star, stood Howard's typewriter. Behind it, unused in years, was a spring with wooden handles, a mail-order device for strengthening the hand. For several months Howard had been never without it, pumping ceaselessly in a vain attempt to transform himself into a tower of strength. It didn't work and he tired of it, or else decided to concentrate on a more pleasurable way of exercising his hand. There was the beginning of a new manifesto in the typewriter, another of his mad ramblings. She would have to retype it cleanly on the word processor for him when it was finished, Myra realized, so she didn't bother to read it now.

His writings no longer troubled her as they once did when she thought they actually meant something. In the beginning she feared for him; it all seemed so intense, so deranged, so full of paranoid malice. There was no arguing with him; he had his facts marshalled, his polemics set and polished. He would not debate the subject. He would orate, and as he did he would get angrier and angrier as if Myra and Myra alone stood in the way of his changing the world. It became so much easier to avoid the topic.

When he founded the "party" and began bringing the other members home, she once more became concerned. They were such a scruffy bunch, so dull and spiteful, Myra couldn't imagine where he found them, or how they found him. Was this how her Howard appeared to others? Mean-spirited and nasty, poor white trash on a mission? When he spoke in the park, did people glance at him and dismiss him as crazy, in need of a haircut and a sedative? Myra hated to think that, but that was how the other members looked and they, too, might have sisters who cared for them and saw them differently.

Myra's concern had vanished again the more she listened to their meetings. They were a pathetic group, really, for all their talk of violence. They had the hatred but no more method than little boys playing a game of war. They were disorganized, inept, adrift. Children posing as Zionist avengers. It was an ugly sight, but not one to fear.

7

The skinheads had arrived. Howard watched them massing across the street, an array of malice in leather jackets, dangling ear rings, clenched fists bedecked with large rings and bronze knuckle dusters. They carried only one sign, but that was no surprise. The skinheads were not long on literacy; they specialized in direct action.

Howard inched closer to Borodin, his angry Russian enforcer. Huge and stupid, Borodin's flat-planed face bespoke strength and violence. Unless the skinheads were even dumber than they acted, Borodin would be the last man they would pick on for a direct test of strength. He was what passed for Howard's palace guard, a peasant to the core, mutely loyal and indifferent to subtlety.

"They're here," said Hart, clutching Howard's arm.

"I see them," said Howard. He knew that Hart was watching him to see how he performed as leader. Hart was jealous, not to be trusted. The first sign of weakness from Howard would bring Hart forward, snapping at him like a hyena.

"What do you want to do?" Hart asked.

"You go stay by Wiener," Howard said. "He's new, he might panic."

"What's the plan?" Hart insisted.

"I'll let you know when you need to know," said Howard. "Don't worry about it, that's my job. You just take care of Wiener."

Wiener stood on the end of their picket line, holding a sign proclaiming the need for Jewish might. He was a skinny young man, scarcely more than a kid, and his eyes darted nervously from the skinheads across the street to his own pathetically thin echelon of fellow supporters.

This was the third time in as many weeks that the thuggish neo-Nazis had shown up in counter demonstration. As he watched Hart move back down the line, Howard wondered if his jealous rival wasn't passing the Brotherhood's plans on to their enemies, just to put Howard's leadership to the test. How else to explain their appearance at today's demonstration by the Brotherhood of Zion outside the Japanese embassy? Howard himself had decided upon the demonstration only yesterday when he read of the Japanese premier's latest thoughtless insult to the Jews and Israel, likening them to aggressors. It was the kind of insensitive act that Howard could not let pass without action, but hardly the sort of thing the skinheads would have picked up on.

The first two encounters with the neo-Nazis had slipped by without bloodshed. Howard had managed to maneuver his men away the first time before the thugs had arrived in force and there had been little more than a few shoves. The second time had threatened to be uglier, but the police had arrived before it erupted and chased the skinheads away to the jeers and taunts of the Brotherhood.

Howard hoped he could forestall things long enough this time for the police to intervene again. He wondered if they even knew. Howard and his men had only been on the scene a few minutes themselves, and the Japanese in the consulate might not even have reported the disturbance. If he could have done it surreptitiously, Howard would have phoned them himself, but as an outspoken advocate of Jewish strength and violence in the cause of Zionism, he could hardly afford to be seen hiding behind the police for protection.

"What do you want me to do?" Solin asked, sidling next to Howard. Of all the members, Solin was the most violence prone, the most dangerous.

"Just hang on," said Howard.

Solin spat contemptuously. "That's what you always say."

"And that's what I mean," said Howard. He could hear his voice rising. He hated having his authority questioned almost as much as he hated being in charge. "Just hang tough until I give you orders."

"What if they start something?"

"They probably won't," Howard said, wishing he could believe it. "Let them yell, it's a free country."

He glanced down the line to Hart, who stood next to Wiener. The newcomer looked as if he were going to cry. Hart looked back at Howard, catching his glance. His lip seemed to curl.

"Pick a man," said a voice close to Howard. He turned, startled, to see a stranger standing beside him. The man was blond with ordinary features.

"What?"

"Pick a man. Each of you pick a man, and when it breaks, go straight at him. Don't hang back, don't wait for him to come to you, don't be defensive. Go straight to your man and hit him hard."

Solin looked at the stranger and nodded. He liked the sound of the advice.

"Who are you?" Howard demanded.

"A fellow Jew," said the man. He flashed a smile and Howard felt better immediately. "My name is Meyer Kane. I wish we had something like the Brotherhood of Zion in Detroit."

"What do you mean, pick one?" Solin asked. "I want them all."

"Don't be greedy," said Kane. "Take one that's close so you can get to him right away. Surprise is important." Kane turned to Howard as if seeking confirmation. "Right?"

"Well, yes. That's right," said Howard.

Kane turned his attention to Borodin. "In your case, you should pick that little guy with the gold tooth."

Borodin pointed to a huge skinhead with a spider's web tattooed on his bare scalp. "I ought to take him."

Kane looked at Howard and grinned conspiratorially as if only the two of them understood what was going on. "Why, because you're both big? Take the little guy and smash him fast. This is a street fight, not a joust between knights of honor. The idea is to hit them first and hard and spread some terror in the ranks. Right?"

Again he turned to Howard for confirmation, as if Howard knew anything at all about street fights. Howard nodded, not trusting his voice. He didn't know where this stranger was leading, but it felt so good to have someone around who know what he was doing.

"Do you think you ought to spread the word to the rest of the men?" Kane asked. "So there's no confusion about who's going after who. Those two on the end . . . what's their name?"

"Hart and Weiner?"

"Yeah. They look a little rocky. Maybe they should go after one guy together. You think?"

"That's what I would have thought," said Howard.

"You want to tell them? I would, but they don't know me."

Howard nodded. He felt the reins of command slipping away—and the burden. "Right," said Howard.

As Howard moved down the line, Kane removed his belt and wrapped it around the knuckles of his right hand.

"I'll take the big one," he said to Borodin. "He'll be expecting you, so I'll have the element of surprise." Borodin nodded.

"And I'll get the little guy with the gold tooth."

Kane flashed his full smile at Borodin. "We're going to make a great team," he said.

"Kick some ass," said Borodin, grinning in response.

Children, thought Kane, alias Bahoud. Children playing at adult games. They don't have a clue, neither side of this skirmish. Not the skinheads, not the Brotherhood of Zion. Nothing of significance is accomplished by cracking a few heads in the street. Most people are glad to see both camps fighting each other; it kept their attention away from the good people.

Howard had returned to Kane's side.

Kane put his hand on Howard's shoulder. Half a block away he watched the television news van pull to the side and emit the cameramen and the reporter. Kane had called in the news story about to happen less than half an hour ago. The response was impressively quick, probably better than the police.

"Stick close to me," Kane said.

"Now?" asked Howard. He held back.

"Let them see you leading," said Kane. He slipped his hand behind Howard's back and pulled him off the curb so that the two of them stepped into the no-man's-land of the street together. Kane glanced to his left and saw the cameramen responding immediately to the first sign of action by shouldering their cameras. Kane turned slightly to his right so that his back was to the camera.

"Do you think we should ... " Howard was protesting as they approached the skinheads, still hoping for a way out.

"No other way," said Kane. "You got to do them before they do you."

Kane looked in the face of the largest skinhead, who was now only a step away. The big man was snarling.

"Kike!" he yelled.

Kane smiled at him. His body was completely relaxed, his manner as casual as if he were just stopping by to say hello to an old friend.

"We were wondering ... ," Kane said as he hit the big man squarely on the bridge of his nose with the belt buckle. He knew immediately he had broken the man's nose. As the big man's hands flew to his face, Kane stepped hard into the side of the man's knee, then grabbed him behind the neck and threw him face first into the street.

"Kick him," Kane said to Howard.

Howard stood staring at the big man moaning at his feet. The attack had been so fast that no one on either side had yet reacted at all. Howard had felt as if he were watching a movie; he had never seen anything so swift and brutal in real life.

"Kick him. Now."

Howard blinked, looked up at Kane who was asking him to do the impossible, and saw the television cameras running toward him.

"Now!"

Howard watched his foot move as if it were someone else's. Someone else's shoe that hit the big man's ribs and then, more amazing, drew back and did it again as the big man jerked and groaned and tried to roll away.

Across the street the Brotherhood surged suddenly forward at the same time as the skinheads came to themselves and started toward Kane and Howard. For a moment Howard knew he was finished as the furious neo-Nazis surrounded him, but Kane thrust forth an arm and one skinhead fell and he kicked out once and another dropped, and then Kane yanked Howard through the opening as if he had created a door with a magic wand. Howard caught a glimpse of Solin smashing one of the smaller thugs in the mouth, and then Kane was pulling him harder and they ran and ran until Howard could scarcely breathe and the violence was several blocks behind them.

Howard leaned against a building and gasped as Kane stood in front of him, scarcely winded, looking back to see if they were pursued.

"Leaders shouldn't get arrested," said Kane. For the first time, Howard noticed the sound of sirens. "You have to stay free in order to plan the next move," said Kane.

Howard nodded, still gasping. He had no desire to go to jail; he had heard all too often about what could happen to a novice there.

"What we need now is a safe place to go," said Kane.

"I have an apartment," said Howard.

Kane smiled and Howard felt warmed by it. "You and I are going to make a great team," said Kane. "Let's go to your apartment."

"I have a sister," Howard said.

They had arrived at Howard's building on East Forty-fourth Street. Kane stood with his head back, looking up at the thirty-five stories like a gawking tourist.

"Nice neighborhood," said Kane. "You must be rich."

"Not really. My parents bought the apartment a long time ago and left it to us."

"Nothing wrong with being rich," Kane said. He scanned the surrounding buildings with their awnings and uniformed doormen. "Don't apologize for it."

"I'm not. I'm really not rich. I mean, I have enough to live on, I guess. If I ever tried. I work, you know. I don't know if I'd have enough without my salary."

"What do you do?"

"I'm a chemist with a drug company." Howard mentioned one of the industry's famous names.

"Oh, yeah? What kind of drugs?"

"They make them all, but I work on . . . cough syrup."

"Nothing wrong with that."

"I could do better, I could do a lot better. I should be running the department by now—but my boss is an anti-Semite."

"The bastards are everywhere," Kane said heatedly.

"They are," Howard agreed. He nodded at the doorman, who inclined his head minimally as Howard and Kane passed into the lobby. "That prick of a doorman, for instance. He treats me like shit even though I pay his salary."

"That can be fixed," said Kane, turning on his heel. Howard caught him by the arm before Kane reached the doorman.

"No, no, that's okay," said Howard.

"We can get you some respect real fast," said Kane. He pushed back through the glass doors with Howard holding back, stammering.

"No, no, no . . ."

The doorman had a florid, beefy face and a nose that showed the signs of too much alcohol. He looked at Kane and Howard with a bemused indifference.

"Your name?" Kane said.

The doorman paused a telling second before answering. "Terence O'Brien. And whom do I have the honor of addressing?"

Howard waited for the sudden explosion of violence, but Kane merely smiled and extended his hand.

"So you're O'Brien," he said. "Howard has told me about you. You're the friendly one."

"I try, sir," said O'Brien. He found himself instantly taken by the man's charm. O'Brien knew blarney when he heard it, but it was a welcome change from the casual arrogance of most of the residents.

"Pleasure to meet you, O'Brien. My name is Kane. I will be staying with Howard for a while, so we'll be seeing a good deal of each other."

"Right you are," said O'Brien.

Kane placed a bill in O'Brien's hand. O'Brien smoothly folded it with two fingers and slipped it into his pocket without a glance.

"If there's anything I can be doing for you to make your stay a more pleasant one, just let me know, sir."

"You were right, Howard," Kane said. "He is a good man."

"The best we have," said Howard, picking up his cue.

"There is one thing, O'Brien. My ex-wife. You got one of those?"

"Don't tell me," said O'Brien.

"You know the story, then. There's the question of some back alimony. The bitch would like to attach my left leg, you know what I mean? There's a chance she's got private detectives after me. Maybe worse, who knows. Do I have the money? Would I give it to her if I did? You see what I'm saying?"

"I follow you, sir."

"So, if anyone comes asking about me, you've never seen me. Or am I wrong?"

"You're not wrong, Mr. Kane. I've never seen nor heard of you."

"But let me know who's asking questions. Fair enough?"

O'Brien smiled.

"Fair is fair, sir."

"And we'll have another conversation again in the future," said Kane, winking. "Tell your relief man . . . ?"

"Sanchez."

"Tell Sanchez I'll be having a word with him later, too."

"He'll be glad to hear it, sir. And a pleasure to meet you, Mr. Kane. Mr. Goldsmith."

This time when they entered the building the door was held wide for them.

"Did you think I was going to hit him or something?" Kane asked as they entered the elevator.

"I—I wasn't sure," said Howard.

"You must think I'm a pretty violent guy. You can't go through life punching everyone who deserves it. You'll end up in jail. And you and I have more important things to do than that, don't we?"

Howard chuckled halfheartedly. He had no clear idea of what Kane had in mind. In fact, now that the panic and adrenaline of the confrontation with the skinheads had abated, Howard realized he knew nothing about his newly found friend at all. That he was a friend had been demonstrated without question. That Kane himself needed a friend was also clear in the quick and almost desperate way he had latched onto Howard. Needing a friend was a state with which Howard was very familiar. He had felt as if he needed a friend all his life since his mother died. Myra was a friend, of course. More than a friend, certainly, but hardly a protector. She required so much protection herself she could hardly be expected to offer Howard any in return. But this man, whom he knew not at all, liked him, he clearly liked Howard. That much was evident in the smile he bestowed, a signal of friendship that could not be feigned, Howard was certain.

True, Howard was a little afraid of Kane, but he was used to that. He had been a little afraid of his mother, too.

As the elevator doors opened at the thirty-fourth floor, Howard paused, half in and half out of the elevator.

"I have a sister," he said.

"You told me," said Kane.

"I mean, I have her with me. She lives with me."

Kane stared at him blankly. There had been no mention of a sister in the apartment in Taha Hammadi's dossier on Howard. Either the Beni Hassan agents in New York had done sloppy work or the sister was a new development.

"She doesn't go out much," Howard said. "I mean she doesn't really go out at all. Not really." The blank look left his new friend's face and was replaced with polite curiosity.

"Oh?"

"She's a shut-in," Howard said. He never knew exactly how to define Myra, but it was a problem that seldom came up anymore since he almost never referred to her.

"A shut-in?"

"Sort of a cripple." The word sounded strange to Howard. He never thought of Myra in those terms except in the presence of others. To him, she was simply his sister, sometimes loveable, sometimes horrible, but a fixture, no more in need of explanation than the building itself. "Sort of. She owns the apartment, too. My mother left it to both of us."

"And you take care of her?" asked Kane.

"She's pretty self-sufficient except with . . . "

"Except with what?"

Howard laughed with surprise at the notion. "Except with people," he said. "She's kind of shy. Oh, Christ, I should have called her and told her I was bringing you home."

"Well, we're here now."

Howard could already imagine Myra's reaction to the sudden presence of a stranger, the embarrassment that bordered on hysteria, those beautiful eyes wide in horror. It would make her sick, literally sick. And later, she will kill me for sure, Howard thought. How could he have forgotten to call her, at least. What was he thinking, bringing this man to stay with him? He tried to think back to the chain of logic that had developed into the present predicament, but all he could remember was the rush of events, the strength of Kane's will propelling them both to safety. They needed to get off the streets, Howard knew that much. There had been some story about Kane's having no place of his own, some brief discussion of the obvious solution, Howard's apartment. And now they were here.

Kane stood outside 34B, Howard's apartment.

"I can wait outside while you tell her," Kane said. "You know, if I'm a problem or anything. The police may not have a good description of us yet, I'll probably be all right."

"No, no," said Howard. He took his new friend by the arm as he unlocked the door. "You're welcome here. Come meet Myra."

Howard told Myra in her room that they were going to have company in the apartment. He had expected a scene of outrage and thus barreled into his argument with a full head of steam, not noticing until he was well launched that he was meeting no resistance.

"It will only be for a while," he said. "He doesn't have a place, he just arrived, I don't think he's got any money. He could stay in Momma's room."

Myra studied him curiously but without outrage, as if she did not fully understand him yet, Howard thought.

"He—uh—helped me out today," Howard said lamely. "He was a lot of help, really. I think he can be really useful in the Brotherhood . . . ''

Howard trailed off, surprised at how weak it all sounded now. There had seemed such urgency at the time. And how could he possibly explain the incident of violence with the skinheads to Myra when he was still trying to digest it all himself? Mention of the Brotherhood was usually enough to incite her contempt all by itself: a city street brawl was not likely to impress her favorably.

She continued to study him curiously.

"I know how you feel," Howard said. "But he's very friendly and he—uh—he likes me a lot." Howard dipped his head in embarrassment. Someone's affection for him was not a topic that usually came up. "I think he's got a slight case of hero worship. I mean, because of the Brotherhood and everything, and they don't have one in Detroit, and he can—I really think he can be useful, Myra. He can do some things none of the others can and . . . ''

"Okay."

"What?"

"Let's see him, then."

"You want to meet him?"

"I ought to if he's going to live here, don't you think? Give me a minute to put myself back together, and I'll come out and meet him. We'll decide if he stays after that. If he's a moron like Smolin, no way."

"No, he's not stupid . . . ''

"I don't like Hart, either."

"He's not like that. He's not like any of them. He's a normal guy."

"Then he's not like any of the 'Brotherhood,' that's for sure."

"You don't really know any of them, to be fair."

Myra had watched the meetings of the Brotherhood through the crack of her door. Afterwards she would dissect the membership with scathing comments that Howard found difficult to bear and equally difficult to refute. The members were not yet the elite corps that Howard aspired to—but they were a beginning.

"Go tell him to part the hair in front of his eyes and get his knuckles off the floor," said Myra. "He's about to meet a lady."

She dismissed Howard with shooing motions. He returned to the living room wondering as he often did just where Myra got some of the mannerisms she displayed. How could she go from weeping disconsolately one second and the next be some sort of movie version of a siren in her boudoir. "Put herself together?" He had never heard her say anything like that in his life. She had always had an active imagination.

Kane was standing at the window, next to Myra's telescope, looking out at the city.

"Great view," Kane said. "What's that big space down there?"

"United Nations Plaza," said Howard.

"No kidding. The U.N.? I didn't know that was here."

"Yes."

"I thought it was in Washington or something."

"No, right there on the river."

"You must spend a lot of time just looking, I'll bet."

"Not really. You get used to it. I've had that view all my life."

"Did you ever see what's his name, the president?"

"He doesn't really go there very often. He's mostly in Washington." Howard paused, looking for a delicate way to phrase things. "I'm sorry, but I've forgotten your name."

"Meyer Kane."

"Howard Goldsmith." Howard extended his hand and they shook, awkwardly. This is not going to work, Howard thought. I don't know the man, why would I want him living here with me, not to mention Myra. I was just swept along, the whole thing was like a tidal wave. From the moment he materialized at my shoulder it was as if some irresistible force lifted me and carried me to this minute. Now that I'm in my home, there is no threat, no Nazis screaming at me, no huge thug to be kicked, no one to run from. I will tell him I'll help him find a place to live, ask him to join the Brotherhood, but live with Myra and me? No way.

Then Myra stood in the doorway of her room, leaning against the jamb. She wore a floor-length silk dressing gown embossed with dragons that Howard remembered from his mother. He hadn't seen it in years and had never known Myra to wear it before. The gown covered her bad leg, and the long, full sleeves masked the withered arm. Myra's hair was loose and brushed out and it flowed to her shoulders.

She's beautiful, Howard thought with a shock. My little sister is a beautiful woman.

"Hello," Myra said in a voice huskier and sultrier than any Howard had heard before. "You must be Howard's friend."

Kane turned from the window and studied Myra for a moment before speaking. The corners of his mouth moved upward in just a hint of a smile.

"I'm Meyer Kane," he said.

"Meyer, I'm Myra. Do you think that will be confusing?"

"I'm sure we'll manage to keep each other sorted out."

She gave Kane an openly appraising look. "You look capable of sorting things out."

"Howard told me about you, of course. But he didn't tell me how lovely you were."

"Howard doesn't know," said Myra. "He's just a brother."

There was a look on Myra's face that Howard had never seen before—again except in the movies—and it took him a moment to put a name to it. Seductive, he realized with surprise. Not only beautiful but seductive. It was a day for the unexpected.

Myra's arms were crossed over her chest. She lifted them slightly as she shifted against the door jamb and her cleavage became more evident. Howard resisted an urge to tell her to close her robe. She and Kane were having a conversation of banalities that seemed to fascinate both of them. There was an undercurrent to their talk that Howard sensed but felt excluded from. Everything either said seemed to amuse the other in a very restrained way. Howard saw no humor in any of it.

"Have you shown Mr. Kane where he'll be staying, Howard?" Myra asked without taking her eyes off Kane.

"Not yet."

"I think mother's old room would do," she said.

Howard could not suppress a snort of laughter. What was this, a mansion with dozens of choices? It was mother's room or the sofa. She was acting very strangely, and Howard didn't like it at all.

"I'm not sure . . ." There was something in Kane's look that made Howard stop. He had been going to say he wasn't sure that he wanted

Kane to stay, but the intensity of Kane's look somehow made refusal an impossibility.

"None of us can be sure, Howard. Life is filled with uncertainty."

Now she was teasing him. This, at least, was more familiar ground; he had to cope with this attitude often enough, although not coming on top of such a grand manner.

"I was going to say I'm not sure Meyer wants to stay here."

Myra looked at Kane and arched an eyebrow. Just one eyebrow, Howard noted. Where did she get this stuff all of sudden?

"Mr. Kane? Do you want to stay here?"

"It will be a pleasure," said Kane.

"I certainly hope so," said Myra.

For the first time Kane gave free rein to a full smile. Myra blushed and dropped her eyes.

At that moment Howard knew he had made a terrible mistake, although he was not sure what kind.

8

"People touch things," explained Special Agent Karen Crist. To her surprise she had been sent to Montreal to "advise" in the effort to find identifiable fingerprints in the passport office. As an American advisor on Canadian territory, her mission was partly diplomatic, partly as a reminder to the Canadians to do a thorough job because Washington took the matter seriously, and partly—and by far the smallest part—to offer technical assistance. The Canadians needed no real assistance—fingerprinting was a craft, not an art, and it attracted few geniuses—but they did need some reminding of the significance of the job. A passport office, any government office, is a vast space to fingerprint.

Karen was performing the role of diplomat now as she carefully explained her specialty to the manager of the passport office. It had been necessary to open the office overnight to a legion of officers in and out of uniform, and the manager resented the intrusion as well as the fact that he had to stay up late for it.

"People are like monkeys, really," she said. "Over a period of time they touch everything within reach, and most of it they're not even aware of."

"Uh-huh," said the manager without much interest. He was watching a man blow powder from a plastic bulb onto the surface of a desk.

"As part of our training they have us watch a film of people who are put in a room and don't know they're being filmed. It's a 'Candid Camera' type of thing, but there's no gimmick and no surprise. We just want to study how many places they touch over the course of an hour. Do you know what they touch the most?"

The manager looked at Karen. He did not like being included in the conversation.

"What people touch the most? I don't know. They're sitting down, is that it?"

"They're just alone in a room for an hour. They're free to do whatever they choose, but there are magazines to read, a television, chairs, a sofa, so on. It's like a living room."

"What they touch the most? The television controls, I guess."

"Their faces," said Karen. "Most people are in constant contact with their faces, almost as if we wanted to make sure we're still there. We rub our eyes, stroke our chins, scratch our heads, pick our teeth, pick our noses, rub our noses, squeeze our noses, tug at our ears, squeeze our lips, run our fingers through our hair—and pick up a lot of oil to make better fingerprints then, by the way, although rubbing our noses is good for that, too."

The manager had been about to pull on his earlobe. He let his hand drop to his side, then into his pocket.

"Our hands are going non-stop. After our faces we touch our bodies the most. A person who thinks he's unobserved acts as if he has a bad case of fleas. In an hour's time he will scratch every place conceivable, on the outside of his clothes, under his clothes, some people even take their shoes off and have a go at their feet. None of this leaves any useable fingerprints, of course."

The manager suddenly had a very hard time knowing what to do with his hands. He tried to hold them still, and the harder he tried the more they twitched with the need to move. All of his body seemed to itch at once.

"But in addition to grooming ourselves like so many apes, we touch everything else, too. Not just pencils, pens, magazines, glasses, ashtrays, telephones, armrests, countertops, door handles, all the things you might have some reason to touch. We touch lamps. If the light is off, we reach up and touch the bulbs. We reach under chairs, we trace the patterns in wallpaper, we straighten picture frames, we remove fly specks from mirrors, we drum our fingers on anything available while we read. In fact, while we're reading our fingers go practically berserk and explore things and places our conscious mind doesn't even know to be there. One woman removed all the brass nails in the upholstery of an armchair and put them back again while reading an article on how to please your lover. Afterwards she didn't remember anything about it. Another guy wandered around the room and picked up and overturned every chair, which means he left prints on the legs of the chairs. He looked under the chairs, swung them up and down a little, then put them back. When they asked him why later, he said he didn't know, just to get the feel of them. They got one perfect fingerprint of this guy from a metal caster on the bottom of one of the legs.''

The manager crossed his arms over his chest, tucking his fingers into his armpits.

''You know the old joke about how an Italian can't have a conversation if you tie his hands behind his back? Well, the truth is, none of us can explore the world without our hands. We fondle everything top, bottom, and sideways, feeling every facet, checking all the angles—and leaving prints, or partial prints, a good percentage of the time. If you ever see anyone who doesn't use his hands, you might be looking at someone with severe mental problems.''

The manager let his hands fall to his side again then rubbed them together.

''So what you're saying, this guy you're after probably left some prints,'' said the manager.

''Unless he was wearing gloves or soaked his hands in soapy water every twenty minutes to keep the natural oil from the sebaceous glands off his skin.''

''Would that work?''

''It would keep him from leaving fingerprints, yes. It might make it a little tough to function in the world, of course. But I don't imagine that's the case with the guy we're after. The problem here is not finding prints; it's identifying the ones we find. There will be thousands in this room and even more in the restroom.''

Karen surveyed the progress. A film of white powder was moving inexorably across the room like a steady drift of snow. I'll have to remind them to do the floors in front of the chairs, she thought. If the vinyl had only been swept and not mopped since the suspect's visit, traces could remain there. People touched floors when they tied their shoes, when they dropped things, when they saw things. Some pressed their entire palms to the floor instead of touching their toes, even in public places like this. There would have been a lot of waiting and muscles required stretching.

''But if I was soaking in a hot tub and my fingers got all wrinkled up the way they do, and I took a knife and killed my wife, no one would know?'' the manager asked.

Karen looked at the man for a moment. ''I think you'd find divorce would be simpler.''

The manager shook his head. ''This is Quebec, mademoiselle. We are Catholic.'' He shrugged his shoulders. ''It is not a simple matter.''

Karen decided not to smile and encourage the man, although he was grinning at his cleverness. She did not find it funny.

The only good thing about this peculiar assignment, she reflected, was that when she did the necessary computer work, she would get to report to Becker. That might be interesting. Working under him, as it were. It was Becker who had asked her to make the trip to Montreal. There were others who could have done it—although no one any better, she thought—but he chose her. Maybe just because he knew her personally, of course. Or maybe because he knew her and liked her, she thought. Maybe he wanted to get to know her better, too. You have a habit of belittling yourself, she thought. You also have a habit of overrating yourself to compensate for the belittling. The truth about you lies somewhere in the middle. She wondered what truth Becker perceived about her—if indeed he thought about her at all.

She allowed herself to think about Becker's hands and where they might wander on her. Karen wondered if men thought about sex as much as women did. And if so, why they were always in such a rush to get it over with.

Briefings at the Federal Bureau do not often take the form usually presented on television or film with a slide show in a darkened room and lots of agents watching freeze-frame photos of dangerous spies and demented drug dealers. It happens that way occasionally, but far more often it unfolds as a simple conversation between the parties involved, the briefer distilling into common English all of the important data.

That was the way in which Karen Crist gave her report on the fingerprinting of the Montreal passport office, but since it happened in the office of Director Edgar Allen McKinnon, head of Terrorism, it was anything but a simple conversation.

McKinnon leaned forward onto his desk as if to catch every word, his face serene, his manner as saintly as ever.

"We will distribute your report of course, Ms. Crist," he said in his near-whisper, "but in the interest of speed, I thought you might tell us directly. If that's all right with you."

"Of course, sir," said Karen. "I'll be happy to."

"That's very nice," he said, abruptly leaning back and swiveling to the side so that he faced Becker, whose chair was drawn up beside the desk. McKinnon turned his eyes to Karen. She was seated on a paisley sofa with Hatcher perched stiffly beside her. It seemed to Karen that Hatcher and Becker were in reversed positions, but she was not in any condition right now to infer the political ramifications of the seating chart. She was far too nervous.

McKinnon arched an eyebrow at her, which she interpreted as her signal to begin.

"If we're after speed, I'll skip the technicalities, sir. The cleaning service was last in the passport office on Wednesday night. Robert Carmichael renewed his passport—and was killed—on Thursday. The Canadians ran their check on the room on Monday night, which means, assuming the cleaners were fairly efficient, that we got five days of latent prints, including those from Thursday, plus all of those in the out-of-the-way places that the cleaners never get, which may go back for months."

"I understand," said McKinnon.

"All told we got about nine thousand distinct prints or partials, about half of them from the employees and the cleaning crew. The rest of them were of unknown origin."

"Nine *thousand?* In five days' time?"

"People touch a lot of things," Karen said.

"So it would seem. Sorry to interrupt."

Hatcher shifted his weight on the sofa. His discomfort was apparent, but Karen did not understand what caused it. She knew what was causing her own. McKinnon and Becker were watching her as if they were a pair of hawks and she was their next meal, hopping her way stupidly across the meadow. She surreptitiously rubbed her moist palm on her skirt. Was her skirt too tight? She wished she had worn slacks so she could cross her legs without giving the wrong signal. This was not the time to appear to be a woman in a room of men; this was the moment to be a special agent and nothing else.

"We ran all of the remaining prints through our computer and the Canadians did the same."

"They were cooperative?"

"The Canadians? Yes, sir, very."

McKinnon nodded slowly as if making a mental note about the cooperation of his northern neighbors.

"You prepared all those prints and ran them in just three days?" It was Becker who spoke this time. "You must have been working awfully hard."

Thank God someone noticed, Karen thought. "We drew extra help from some of the other departments. And we did work late," Karen said deprecatingly. *Good girl. Say "we," not "I." Seem selfless, part of the team. Don't mention that you haven't slept in three days. They can probably tell that by looking at you, anyway, but let them come to the conclusion that you've made heroic efforts on their own.*

"We eliminated all the females, which was about sixty percent."

"Oh, really?" This time it was Hatcher.

"More women travel abroad than men, although businessmen travel more frequently."

"I didn't know that."

"Widows," said Karen.

"Women are more adventurous generally," Becker said. Karen looked at him with surprise. It was a startling comment, particularly coming from him.

"They read more, they participate more in the arts, they travel more," he continued.

"Well, if you say so," said Hatcher, unconvinced.

"They're interesting people. You should get to know some," said Becker.

McKinnon smiled beatifically, turning his gaze first to Becker, then to Hatcher, who seemed on the verge of commenting again.

"I'm sure we could all improve our understanding," said McKinnon. "First, however, let's let Ms. Crist continue to enlighten us on the point at hand."

"Agent Becker said to prepare a primary list of suspects from those who had any criminal activity in their background. . ."

"How do we know he's a criminal?" Hatcher demanded. "You could be overlooking him right at the beginning."

"We don't know he's a criminal, we don't know he was at the passport office, we don't actually know that he exists. We're working in the dark, and when you do that you go on certain assumptions. The first assumption is that just because the lights went out doesn't mean the world disappeared. It's still there, you just can't see it. If we're looking for a man who killed Robert Carmichael with a coat hanger, he is not your average citizen who decided to get a passport the easy way—Did you dust the coat rack for prints, Crist?''

"Yes, sir."

"Good. I'm just G-7 like yourself, by the way. You don't need to call me 'sir.' '' He smiled at her as he said it.

"If I'm going to find this guy, Hatcher, I'm going to have to do a lot of guessing. If I guess wrong, I'll back up and try again, provided I'm not already too late to get him. Meanwhile, I'll have to be lucky. One of the guesses I'm making is that a man who is worth two million dollars to someone in Damascus didn't just arrive on the scene without having some skirmish with the law earlier in life. I may be wrong. He may have been a model citizen up till now. He may not be an American or a Canadian, but again I'm guessing that he is or has spent a lot of time in one of our countries or he wouldn't try to pass with a Canadian passport. If I'm right and we use Carmichael's general description with three or four inches for height and ten years give or take for age, we can filter out a lot of unlikely candidates. If I'm wrong, we still don't know who he is, which is where we started. Okay?''

Hatcher shrugged. "Fine by me. It's your case."

Karen could feel the resentment rising from Hatcher like heat.

"Agent Crist?" Becker said.

Karen resumed her report. *I'm walking in a minefield,* she thought. *I could get blown off my feet and never know what hit me or what I did to set off the explosion. Keep your eyes straight ahead, girl, and don't try any fancy footwork.*

"We used the filter Agent Becker suggested, sir," she said, addressing herself to McKinnon. "Screening for age and general physical characteristics, we cut the list down to fifteen names, all of whom have police records in the United States, and one of whom has been arrested in Canada as well."

"Which brings us to this?" McKinnon tapped the report on his desk.

"Those are the fifteen names, sir." As the three men all looked at their copies of the report, Karen took the opportunity to tug at her skirt. Almost done, she thought. Whatever made me think reporting to Becker would be exciting? This was as much fun as standing very still under a hornet's nest that someone else was poking at with a stick. Maybe if she didn't budge at all, she wouldn't get stung. Maybe. The hostility between Becker and Hatcher was strong enough to form a force field of its own, and McKinnon looked very much like the mad scientist who knew how to control it. Karen wondered why all the men thought of McKinnon as so saintly. She could see something behind his eyes, but it certainly wasn't warmth. Men were lousy judges of character, she thought. They were too impressed by position and facade. Women, who were masters of facade, knew all too well how much it could hide.

"Well, Ms. Crist. That seems to be that."

"Good job," said Becker.

Karen got to her feet and the men pointedly did not. Such courtesy was now considered sexist. Don't sway those hips, she said to herself as she walked toward the door. She could feel all of them looking at her until she was through the door and out. In the hallway she took her first deep breath in ages.

At least Becker had said "good job." McKinnon had done nothing but dismiss her. She had wanted to knock McKinnon's socks off, of course. He was the one she wanted to work for, Terrorism was where she wanted to be. But she had very different reasons for wanting to impress Becker. She would have to take his "good job" and be satisified with that. Professionally, that is. But then there were relationships other than professional ones.

The three men studied their copies of Karen's report in silence. The names of the suspects were listed alphabetically. Becker ran his finger slowly down the list, then back up again. He held his finger on the first name on the list and waited for the others to look up.

McKinnon lifted his head first, then waited for Hatcher.

"I assume you see it," McKinnon said, looking at Becker.

Becker nodded.

"See what?" Hatcher asked.

"I'll take it myself," said Becker. To Hatcher he said, "Get someone to check out numbers two through fifteen. I want to know their past histories, where they've been for the past six weeks, where they've gone since Montreal, where they are now."

"What about number one?"

"I'll check him out myself," said Becker.

Hatcher nodded agreement and looked again at the top name on the list. Finally he could not prevent himself from asking.

"Why that particular one?"

"See the age at which those fingerprints went on file?"

"Yes? So?"

"He was too young," said Becker.

"Too young for what?"

"For his fingerprints to be kept on file. Somebody made a special effort. I wonder why."

Becker visited the Detroit police headquarters, where a rather bewildered clerk offered little help.

"It was before my time," the clerk said. "I don't know why it would have been done that way. I mean, the procedure is, if a perpetrator is a juvenile at the time of commission of a crime, his prints are supposed to be removed when he becomes an adult."

"I understand that," said Becker slowly. The clerk seemed intimidated by Becker's FBI badge, and Becker tried to take him through the procedure carefully. "Perhaps he wasn't a minor by the time he was released from custody."

The clerk studied the card in front of him. Biographical data covered the top; the bottom of the card was covered with fingerprints in black ink. It was the original of the copy stored in the computer's memory and unearthed by the FBI master computer.

"Well, he was, actually. Of age, I mean, when he was released. Actually that's why he was released; they had to let him go by statute when he became an adult."

"Could that be why the prints were kept on record?"

"Shouldn't be. The law's pretty clear. Juvenile stuff is not supposed to be kept in the main files—I'm not saying it's a good law, but it's the Michigan state ordinance and we follow it."

"I understand," said Becker.

"I'm just talking prints, you understand," the clerk said. "It's not like the record is supposed to be erased entirely. That depends on the nature of the offense. The severity of the offense, you see."

"I do see," Becker agreed. "You don't want to keep a teenage shoplifting charge hanging over a person forever."

"Well, that's the reasoning," said the clerk. "But if the guy burns down the house with his family in it—you'd want to keep a note on that, even if the kid was only fourteen at the time. You see?''

"I do."

"But this guy you're looking for, he didn't burn down the house, did he? In fact he wasn't actually convicted of anything."

"Really?'' Becker asked politely. He was perfectly capable of reading the charge sheet himself but thought it politic to let the clerk explain it. "So why was he in jail?''

"Well, technically, he wasn't. He was arrested on a charge of assault, but you see this here? This note of 'psy ev'? That means psychiatric evaluation. They took him off to a shrink right away. Judging by this he never came to trial at all. They just kept him for psychiatric evaluation for ten months until he turned eighteen years old and they had to let him go."

"They kept him for evaluation for ten months? Why would they do that?''

"Short answer?'' The clerk shrugged. "He was a nutcase. Probably somebody thought he was dangerous but wouldn't be convicted of anything to make him do real time. He was a minor, remember. This way they could keep him off the streets for ten months, anyway."

"Or cure him?'' Becker asked with seeming innocence.

The clerk laughed. "Oh, sure. Or cure him. That's probably it." The clerk stopped abruptly when he realized that Becker wasn't laughing with him.

"Were you serious?'' he asked.

"You don't think people with mental illness can get cured?''

"People with mental illness? Yeah, sure, I guess, what do I know about people with mental illness? You mean claustrophobia, fear of flying, that sort of thing? Sure, maybe they get better, why not? But kids who put their parents in the incinerator? Get cured? In the D Center? Nooooo, I don't think so."

"What's the D Center?''

"The Detroit Center for Juvenile Analysis. It's where they sent your boy. Whoever saved his prints for posterity probably came from there, too."

"You've got a special psychiatric facility for juvenile offenders? A ward of their own?''

"A ward?'' The clerk looked at Becker as if he were hopelessly naive. "Agent Becker, this is *Detroit*. We got a whole building for it. In this town the bad guys start young. Got to get a head start. They got their careers to think of, you know."

Becker had never liked to listen to cops laughing. It was far too cynical a sound and carried little humor.

Like many of the public buildings built during Detroit's long reign of glory and prosperity, the D Center looked good from the outside, a robust creation of steel and stone that blended elements of the classic and the modern. Externally the building looked like the city that had built it, strong and wealthy with pretensions to taste. Internally it reflected the city that now used it, drab and decaying, and all but given up in the fight to even maintain itself. Improvement seemed out of the question.

Becker sat in the office of Dr. Harold S. Posner, a man whose face seemed to be in the same process of decay as the building around him. He had worked in the facility as a young man fresh out of college, been transfered to other institutions throughout the Michigan system of penal correction, and sent back finally to the place where he had started, but now as the chief administrator. To Becker he seemed beyond tired, he appeared bone weary. Not old so much as abused and worn out.

"I remember him," Posner said. "We had him nine, ten months, then had to let him go."

"Had to?"

"He turned eighteen."

"Does that mean you would have kept him longer if it had been up to you?" Becker asked.

"This was what, seventeen years ago? It was my first year out of school. Nothing was up to me."

Becker was shocked. Posner could not have been older than his forties if he got out of school seventeen years ago. Becker had guessed him to be in his early sixties, just hanging on until retirement.

"I couldn't even prescribe medicine without someone reviewing what I did. Not even dosages. So what I'm saying, my opinion didn't count for *bubkes*. They were going to let him out soon, eighteen or not."

"They?"

"There's a board. This is a government operation, there's always a board."

"They saw no reason to keep him, then?"

"They thought he was perfectly sane. Well, perfectly is not a term with strict application in this business. They thought he had had a psychotic break—which, frankly, many of them sympathized with given the conditions of abuse he lived under—and that he was now stabilized." Posner fingered the edges of the file that had been placed on his desk by his secretary. Becker noted that he had not opened the file and seemed to have no need to refresh himself on the case. "He fooled them."

"How?" Becker asked.

Posner paused, studied Becker for a moment. "Are you familiar with psychiatric terminology, officer?"

"A bit."

"A bit isn't quite enough, so let me skip the technical terms. They change too often, anyway. He wasn't drooling, his eyes didn't roll in their sockets. He looked perfectly normal, quite charming when he smiled, actually. He was bright, very bright. He knew right from wrong. He knew what society expected him to do and not to do. There was only one difference between him and you or me. As I said, he knew right from wrong—he just didn't give a shit. Now understand this, he wasn't a lunatic of any kind, he wasn't a sadist—don't imagine that kid you knew in eighth grade who liked to pull the wings off grasshoppers—he wasn't abnormal in any way that you could spot. I mean that literally—that *you* could spot—unless you have unusually acute powers of perception. No offense, but the members of the board didn't spot it, either, and they were all trained physicians and therapists."

"But you spotted it," Becker said, encouraging him to continue.

"I was on the ward, I was fresh out of training and eager to go. He was my first real patient, all my own. Plus I had a hint to work with."

Becker waited.

"He had tried to kill his father. That's why they brought him in. That's sort of a clue, don't you think? You'd have to be pretty stupid to ignore it. That's not fair. Sympathetic, maybe, not stupid. He was covered with welts, thin lines, almost as sharp as if someone had taken a blade to him. His father had beaten the hell out of him with a coat hanger—apparently over a period of years. The neighbors knew about it, the family knew about it, nobody intervened—well, it's an old story, isn't it? The kid is abused, he becomes an abuser. Someday, when he gets old enough, daddy is going to give him one lick too many and junior will finally realize that he's bigger than daddy now, and stronger, and younger—and just as filled with violence. Most kids just belt the old man and leave home, of course. Some of them use a weapon, usually a gun—and in many cases that's a psychotic break— I'm not saying this cynically, it happens, it's understandable, and with treatment nothing like it will ever happen again.''

''But you didn't think it was just a break this time.''

''Most did, I didn't. It seemed a justifiable analysis on their part— and from a distance it was. But I was with this kid, remember. I sat knee to knee with him, I looked in his face, I asked him questions and gave him tests—I studied him.''

''How did he do on the tests?''

Posner put a finger in the air, as if to say *ah-ha!* ''The first ones were revealing. He showed—I said I wasn't going to get technical, let's just say he looked sick. Disturbed. Dangerous. Just on the first tests. Then he seemed to catch on to what was required. I told you he was very bright. When he took the later tests he looked normal, real normal, abnormally normal if you see what I mean. Squeaky clean. Those are the tests the board saw.''

''Why didn't you show the board the first tests?''

''Couldn't find them. They disappeared. Not only the tests but my notes on our whole first week of interviews. Everything vanished as if he hadn't even been here. A mystery, no?''

''As you said, he was a smart boy.''

''Smart is one thing. A potential for violence is another. A complete lack of social conscience is another. Put them all together and we're not talking about a troubled youth. We're talking about a man who has become a concealed weapon. The current term is sociopath. It sounds a little sterile to my taste. Do you remember Ted Bundy?''

''Of course.''

''Killed how many women? Everybody thought he was a nice guy, a hell of a guy. A charmer, in fact. They call him a sociopath. Legally sane, knew what he was doing, knew it was wrong. He didn't hear voices, the devil didn't make him do it. He did it because it provided him with what he wanted—in his case a sexual need—and the fact that what he wanted was contrary to the wishes of the women didn't mean anything to him. He just didn't give a shit. I'm not saying my patient has any significant sexual component to his character. He was a functioning heterosexual as far as I could tell, so he doesn't have that aspect in common with Bundy. What he does share is the total indifference to the means he uses to achieve his ends, whatever they may be. If he wants something and you're in the way—look out.''

"And you were convinced enough of this diagnosis to keep his fingerprints on file?"

"How did you know that?"

Becker shrugged. "Somebody cared enough to circumvent the statute. You sound like you cared."

"I was young, you have to remember. I just couldn't see this kid walking into society and disappearing, especially since I had witnessed the way in which he had learned to fool people. And he did learn. Hell, if I had given him the final interview instead of the first one, I would have let him go, too. Anyway, I figured someday the cops would need to find him. I had a friend on the force who had a friend in Records—you know how it's done. It was no skin off their nose. If anyone ever raised a fuss they could call it a clerical error and let it go at that."

Becker nodded agreement. He did indeed know how it was done and there were no police departments in the country that he had ever heard of that would punish a clerk for keeping an offender's prints too long. The laws concerning juveniles and their treatment were not made by the police.

"And I was right, wasn't I?" Posner demanded. "Everyone thought I was being overzealous because I was young, because he was my first patient, because I wanted to make him—and thus myself—more important than the facts justified, blah-blah, bullshit. But I was right after all. He has done something or you wouldn't be here. What's he guilty of?"

"Right now the only thing we know for sure he did was go to a passport office in Montreal."

Posner was visibly deflated. "Whatever that means. Whatever you suspect him of, he's capable of. Believe me."

Becker remained silent.

"You don't believe me, do you?"

"Can you look in there and give me any specifics of his 'assault?' " Becker asked.

Posner tapped the folder. "I don't need to look. I've forgotten hundreds of cases by now, but not my first."

Posner opened the file for the first time and withdrew a photograph and handed it to Becker.

"I'll have a copy made and return it," said Becker.

"I remember what he looks like," said Posner. "Nice-looking boy, isn't he?"

Becker nodded. "Wouldn't pick him out of a crowd, but he's nice-looking."

"You're trying to pick him out of crowd now, though, aren't you? What do you want to know?"

"How did he 'assault' his father?"

"He took the coat hanger away and used it on him."

"He whipped his father?"

Posner smiled, a trace of triumph mixed with the weariness. "You really don't get it, do you? Do you think I'd be spending all this energy over a kid who whipped his father? Especially a father who richly deserved it? He didn't whip him with the coat hanger. He tried to kill him with it. He stuck the point in his old man's ear."

Becker sat bolt upright in his chair.

"What?" Posner asked. "Did that get your attention?"

"It did, Dr. Posner. And I can see why it got yours seventeen years ago. He didn't kill his father, though?"

"It's a tricky way to do it. He was young, you understand."

"Do you have an old address in there for the boy's father? I'd like to talk to him."

"It's still his current address. In fact, it's in a sister institution. I used to see the old man when I worked there. You won't be able to talk to him, though."

"Why not?"

"He can't talk, he can't think, he can't feed himself. A relatively small but vital section of his brain was damaged by his son, who, by the way, never thought to inquire about his father until my fifth session with him. And even then I brought up the subject first. The first time he didn't seem the least bit interested. But then that was still his first week and he was learning. The next time I brought it up, in a week or two, he did a pretty good job of feigning remorse. He might even have squeezed out a tear or two.''

"But you didn't believe him.''

"Not for a second. Do you know how hard it is to pierce the skull with a coat hanger? Do you know the strength it requires? Or the diligence? It would take work . . . I didn't believe him for a second. Would you?''

Becker smiled grimly. "Dr. Posner, I'm not a great believer in accidental killings or killings of passion. I have to think that most of the time people who kill other people do it because on some level they wanted to, or at least realized that death was a very possible end result. And since they wanted to, that kind of eliminates any real remorse, as far as I'm concerned. If you wanted to kill somebody for the length of time it took to get your gun or pull out the knife, then you knew what you were doing. If a man backs the car over the family cat in the driveway, that might be an accidental killing. Might be. Remorse after the fact is just so much eyewash.''

"You sound as if you've given the matter some thought.''

"I've done more than that. I've killed some people.''

"Intentionally? . . . Sorry, that's what you're saying, isn't it? Of course it was intentional, but in your line of work, justified . . . Right?''

"I thought so.''

"And you feel no remorse.''

"No remorse . . . Guilt. Lots of guilt.''

"That's understandable. Still, if they were justified killings . . . I mean justified in your own mind.''

"Absolutely justified in my own mind. And legally. They were all self-defense, they all occurred during the attempted arrest of a resisting felon, etc., etc., etc.''

Posner nodded sympathetically. Without thinking he had fallen into his professional mode.

"The point is—I killed them.''

"Could you have done otherwise?''

"Not and live to tell about it.''

"So?''

"The point is . . . never mind.''

"What is the point? Tell me, I don't . . . You just said that on some level people who kill people want to do it. But your circumstances were different, weren't they?'' Becker did not answer. "I see . . . Have you talked to anybody about this?''

"I'm not really trying to get a free session, although it probably looks that way.''

"No, no. I could recommend some decent people in private practice . . . I mean, if this thing troubles you.''

Becker smiled wanly, then sighed, for the moment sounding as weary as Posner looked.

"It troubles me. It doesn't plague me. One more thing about Roger Bahoud. Was he an Arab?''

"An Arab? Oh, I see what you mean. The name is Arabic. His father came from Palestine, but Roger was just a kid from a slum in Detroit. I never saw any ethnic identity of any kind. He didn't identify with groups, or his family, or his crowd, or anything but himself. A sociopath is far too selfish to think of himself in terms of others. Unless it suits his purposes.''

Becker rose to leave. "Thank you, doctor. You've been most helpful.''

"I did the right thing keeping those prints in the file, didn't I?'' It was an assertion, not a question.

"I think you did.''

"About the other thing . . . I could give you some names, or the Bureau must have people you could talk to.''

"If you make your living at the carnival by diving into the tank from one hundred feet up, you shouldn't complain to the carnival owner about the thrill you get jumping off of high places. They would like to think I'm normal.''

"Nobody's normal, Agent Becker.''

Becker grinned. "You're telling me?''

When Becker closed the door on his way out, Posner looked down at the file on his desk with the name "Bahoud, Roger'' printed across the top. Seventeen years ago. Roger would be thirty-five years old now and very practiced in his ways, whatever they had become. Cunning and skilled, no doubt. Becker was cunning and skilled, too, Posner could see that easily enough. In some ways he reminded Posner of Bahoud. They were about the same age. Their looks were not dissimilar. And Becker, judging by the facts he had recited, was very dangerous, too. The difference was, Becker had a conscience. Posner

wondered, if it came to it, whether guilt would slow Becker down
enough to make the difference. He hoped not. Becker was disturbed
by the things he did and the way he felt. Bahoud was not disturbed,
and it was that lack in him that took him from the ordinary realm of
severe character disorder to the level of monster. For a second Posner
felt a twinge of guilt himself. That was not the way to think of any
human being; but then Posner shrugged. If I haven't earned the right
to that opinion, who has, he thought. To hell with the smotheringly
tolerant psychological view of mankind. It was Posner's experience
that there were an awful lot of sick people in the world—and a few
monsters.

Becker found Namer Bahoud in the institution's sunroom. There
was a solitary window with southern exposure but little else about the
room that could be considered sunny. The walls were a shade of pea
green that gave the entire facility the look of a place long forgotten
and given over to mold and lichens. The occupants, too, had been
long forgotten. They were the pacific ones, the placid patients who
required only the occasional feeding and cleaning and changing of
diapers. They caused the warders no trouble and thus were "rewarded" by being wheeled daily to the sunroom, where they sat and
slumped in their various attitudes of vegetation. They were out of the
way for the day so the staff could devote their ministrations to those
inmates whose dementia required attention or restraint.

A television played without the sound. Becker assumed it was for
the benefit of visitors since none of the patients could lift his head
high enough to look at the screen. Not that there were any visitors
beside himself. Maybe it was just a sign of the culture, he thought. A
television had become the inalienable right of everyone, even those
who could neither see nor hear it.

"He can't talk, you know," said the male nurse who led Becker to
the senior Bahoud.

"I know," said Becker.

"He can't hear, either." The nurse was tall and lean and wore a
gold chain visible under his tunic. Becker noted the basketball sneakers, unlaced, beneath the white uniform pants. The nurse looked as if
he were ready to break into a fashionable dash to escape the institution. Becker could not blame him.

"He can't do anything. He's a veg."

"I know," said Becker. "That's been explained to me."

"Can't do a thing . . . Can't even die, poor bastard."

"Do you think he wants to?"

The nurse looked once around the room where half a dozen patients, each nearly indistinguishable from Bahoud, sat folded over in their chairs.

"Wouldn't you?"

"Don't go by me," said Becker. "I might feel like doing a lot of things you wouldn't."

"I doubt it," said the nurse, grinning.

"Don't," said Becker. "You'd be wrong."

After a pause, the nurse said, "Well, there he is. Mr. Namer Bahoud. You've seen him and that's about all you're going to see. He doesn't move or anything. What you see is what you get."

"Thanks. I'll just sit with him a while if that's all right."

"It's all right with me. I guess it's all right with him, too . . . But you won't get through to him, you know. In case you're planning a conversation or a miracle cure or anything. There's practically nothing still working in his head. I mean, sometimes people come in here, they've seen movies and stuff, they think they'll say the right thing, tap the subconscious, something like that, and get a response the doctors couldn't get. Forget it. They've done brain scans on these people. There's no activity."

"I understand," said Becker. "I'm not hoping to talk to him. I just want to sit with him for a while."

"Sure."

"Okay?"

"Hey, have a good time." The nurse started to leave, then stopped. "Are you a relation?"

"No," said Becker.

"Friend of the family?"

"No."

The nurse nodded as if everything suddenly had been clarified.

"I ask because he hasn't had a visitor since I've been working here."

"Uh-huh."

"That's seven years, six months, three weeks, two days."

Becker looked at Namer Bahoud. The man's eyes were open and gazing vacantly at the floor.

The nurse could not let it go. "So you're just going to sit with him? You're not related, you don't know him, you're just going to sit there?"

Becker slowly turned to look at the nurse.

"Go away," he said.

For a second the nurse considered defying Becker, but a closer look made him reconsider quickly. He left without a further word.

Becker studied Bahoud for a moment. His face seemed to be still that of a man in his forties, as if the absence of mental activity had brought with it a cessation of the aging process. Namer would be close to sixty years old now, Becker knew, but except for the hair, which had turned white, he probably looked much the same as on the day on which he had given his son one whipping too many.

Feeling he had to say something, Becker touched the old man's hand. The skin was very cool to the touch.

"I've come about Roger," Becker said. "Your son, Roger."

The old man did not blink, did not stir. Becker saw no quickening of intelligence behind the eyes. He had not expected to. He was not sure exactly what he had expected to happen when he came but it was nothing rational, certainly. None of the miracles of which the nurse made fun. It was not that he had hoped to jar the man back into life— Becker believed the results of the electroencephalograph—but rather that he hoped to have the old man jar something in him.

Like gravity, he thought to himself. All mass had it. I tug on you a little, you tug on me a little. It happened when two people encountered each other. However slight and fleeting the contact, each mass gave a little, took a little. The difficulty was to measure the size of the response. And it was just there, with that nearly imperceptible twinge of reaction, of psychic interchange, that Becker's genius lay. He could read it where others did not notice it at all.

The effects lay in the tone of voice, the catch of breath, the flicker of the eyes, the muscle that moved for no reason, the way the hands were clasped. Becker did not precisely study these reactions in others; they were too swift and small to be consciously noted or calibrated. He simply let them happen, trusting that they would be there, captured like light on film, revealing far more than the photographer ever saw.

But then that was with another human being. Bahoud senior scarcely qualified as that. If he gave off any psychic gravity, Becker did not feel its pull.

After a few moments he began to feel foolish sitting with the im-
mobile old man and would have left then except for a reluctance to
give the nurse the satisfaction of having been right.

His conversation with Posner continued to play in his mind. The
man had tried hard to help, not only with the investigation; he had
tried to help Becker as well. He had offered to give Becker names of
specialists, people who could presumably help Becker with his own
mental problems, whatever Posner perceived those problems to be.
People always wanted to help him, Becker thought. They were so
eager to pry open Becker's can of worms. But once the can was open
they wouldn't have to deal with Becker's worms; Becker would. They
wouldn't have to get the worms back into the can. Becker would.

Better by far to keep them canned, Becker thought. Don't mess
with them, don't think about them, pretend you don't see them lurking
in the corner of your mind. Lurking? He wasn't sure he had the right
image, but he was positive he didn't want to pursue the line of thought
any further.

He returned his concentration to the old man. Namer Bahoud was
as still as sleep, his body responding only to the steady motion of his
breathing. Nothing here to see, Becker thought. Nothing to learn. An
exercise in futility. Perhaps the whole trip to Detroit had been a waste
of time. He could have accomplished much the same results by telephone, so what had been the point in talking to Posner in person?
What had drawn him?

And if I want to keep the can of worms closed, why am I so eager
to hint at it? He had not needed to have that little dialogue with Posner
about killing; it had not been relevant to the case . . . Or had he needed
to mention it? Did he have a compulsion to bring his own problems into view? What was he looking for, a free session from the
psychologist? Show it and then take it away, that's the behavior of
a tease, Becker thought. Was that what it was all about, some psychological flirtation? Or did he do it to make himself seem more interesting? You think Bahoud has problems, doc? Take a look at
mine. But then don't show him. Great, John. Outstanding work.
You should have taken him up on his offer of help. You need it,
you really need it. But I won't get it, Becker told himself. I won't
get help in self-examination, because I'm afraid of what I'll see. I'll
flash it at other people, hoping they can give me an off-the-cuff di-

agnosis, a quick fix. But I'll be damned if I'll look at that can of worms myself.

Becker smiled in self-deprecation. I want a miracle cure, too, he thought. And I've come to a great place for it.

Becker started to leave when suddenly Bahoud coughed, his body rocking back in the chair. The eyes blinked rapidly and the man coughed once more. For a moment there was animation in the face, a sort of puzzled wonderment at all the activity before the features fell once more into their stuporous repose.

It was only an autonomic reflex, Becker knew. The muscles of the diaphragm reacting to the intrusion of foreign matter into the lungs, but that second of life had triggered Becker's imagination. He had seen, for a fleeting moment, the man who had been Namer Bahoud.

Becker squinted his eyes and the old man seemed to dance and swim in his vision, and in his mind Becker could picture him seventeen years ago, the coat hanger in his hand.

Namer Bahoud in his kitchen, dressed in work pants and a T-shirt, the dark hair curling up from the opening at the neck, forcing its way through the cloth. In an anger which seemed to spring from nothing and flashed into a fury with nothing more to fuel it than the presence of his son. Becker could see the boy, too, backing away, knowing he would be hurt again. Again and again and again in an endless chain that stretched back to the beginning of time and forward to infinity.

Namer Bahoud raised the hanger. He was a strong man, as strong as Becker's father, as tall as Becker's father, his face curled into the same snarl of disdain. He beat his son with a passion bordering on contempt. Not hatred, but a sort of withering scorn for one so young, so small, so innocent and helpless.

But the younger Bahoud was no longer so helpless. No longer small, long since past innocence. We grow, Becker thought. Despite the blows, despite the scorn, we grow. Maybe not straight, but we grow.

Becker saw his father lashing down with the coat hanger, then saw young Roger Bahoud catching the man's arm. Perhaps for the first time. His father's face, astonished at the resistance, then furious, struggling against a grip he had heretofore dismissed with ease. Becker saw Roger Bahoud rise, no longer cringing against the blows, saw him lash out with his fist, felt the harsh shock of bone hitting flesh.

Then, the world turned upside down. The father on the floor, baffled, the son over him, panting, his own fury unleashed at last.

Bahoud senior sat still as stone in his chair, but Becker no longer saw the real man, he saw the man on the kitchen linoleum with its pattern of gray and black octagons, as familiar as mealtime, as sullen and lowering as mealtime.

The man on the floor swore but his jaw was hurt, his lips already swelling, and the words came out incomprehensibly. He rose to one elbow and Becker saw Roger Bahoud kick him and the older man fell back. When he spoke again there was anger in his voice, but no contempt.

Becker saw Roger Bahoud with the coat hanger in his hands, saw him bend the metal hook until it was straight as a blade. Becker saw him fall on his father, saw him use his weight to pin the older man on his back, his knees to fix his father's arms against the linoleum. His left hand clamped on Bahoud's throat, his right hand moved the wire stilleto to the man's ear. The father's eyes widened in disbelief, then horror as he felt the first touch of cold metal on his ear lobe, inexperienced, searching, but determined.

You taught him, old man, Becker thought. Doesn't every teacher want his pupil to surpass him? Consider it success.

Becker heard the grunt of effort as Roger Bahoud thrust with the wire. He saw the old man's eyes freeze abruptly into place.

For the first time Becker saw Roger Bahoud's face, saw the expression of effort, the tightening of the lips, the icy concentration in the eyes. The angles of the face were still softened by youth, the skin smooth and wrinkle free, the beard still more fuzz than stubble.

The young man realized what he had done as his father ceased to struggle beneath him. A look of grim satisfaction settled on his face, then slowly changed as he turned his head slightly and looked right at Becker. Like a man who has just had his first taste of a dish that will become his favorite food, Roger Bahoud smiled the slow grin of recognition.

Becker hurried from the hospital and into his car and drove until he was certain he was out of sight from the nurse. Then he pulled to the curb and tried to settle his breathing. The face of young Bahoud that had turned and grinned at him, pleased with his first kill, had been Becker's own.

The can of worms he did not want to open, the can of worms he had imagined as lurking in the corner of his mind—they weren't worms, Becker thought. They were serpents, and they weren't lurking. They were writhing.

9

They were changed. Something had happened to them, Myra didn't know what, except that it had to do with Meyer Kane's arrival and the brawl. Whatever it was, they were charged with an electricity, a vitality, an—the word seemed incongruous to her—*intelligence* that they had never shown before.

They were in the living room now, this weekly gathering of clowns, the revolutionary incompetents of the "Brotherhood," Myra's six stooges, as she thought of them. Seven now, with the addition of Kane, but it was hard to think of him as anybody's stooge. They sat on her mother's good furniture with its dainty floral patterns like baboons upon a stool. Warthogs at an English tea, she thought. All those delicately—and expensively—brocaded roses crushed under the insensitive and boorish butts of Howard's group of dancing bears. Her mother would have died to see it. No, she wouldn't die, she would act, Myra corrected herself. She would throw them out, back into the street where they belong. And so should Myra. Then she should grab Howard by the ear and send him to his room. And I would, too, if I didn't have to leave my room to do it, thought Myra.

Tonight she might even get away with passing among them instead of peering through the crack in her door. They were so excited she didn't think they would notice her. After all, they were watching the most fascinating thing of all—themselves.

They were replaying the tape of the newscast for the seventh or eighth time. Each time they saw something new, some further proof of their virility and cleverness.

"Right there is where I hit the guy in the balls," said Hart. "The camera turned away just at the last second and missed it, but I got him square in the nuts, didn't I, Wiener?"

Wiener grinned and nodded but didn't say yes, which meant Hart was lying. Howard despised Hart and Myra could see why; he had that lean and hungry Cassius look about him and it was obvious he wanted to be the leader, although he had no qualifications at all, save ambition.

Howard, who was nobody's definition of a leader, at least had intelligence, Myra thought. For the most part. She had to qualify it, because organizing the Brotherhood was the dumbest thing she'd ever seen him do—except stay in it.

"Freeze that. Right there. Freeze it!" Solin wanted to watch himself hit someone. In some ways he was the oddest of the bunch, a red-necked cracker Jew from Georgia. A hillbilly with all the backwoods mentality and a wad of chewing tobacco in his cheek right now. He spat into a Styrofoam cup. Her mother would have killed him outright. What made him think he was a Jew, Myra couldn't imagine. Maybe someone had told him the hill people were the lost tribes of Israel and he took it from there. Howard welcomed him in, of course. There was no litmus test to join the Brotherhood. With six members—seven now with Kane—Howard could not afford to be choosey.

Even Bobby Lewis was excited. His acned face glowed brighter than usual tonight; he was no more immune to violence than the rest of them. Myra had had hopes for Bobby Lewis, once. He had seemed the most nearly normal. Howard said he was married and had a baby girl. He was soft-spoken, almost sweet, and when he talked he made a kind of sense—assuming anyone made sense in the context of the Brotherhood. Myra had a sort of yen for Bobby at first, acne and all. He had the look of gentleness about him—but not tonight. He was cheering and jeering at the tape as raucously as the rest of them.

They act as if it's football, Myra thought. But it was not football. They were watching themselves hit other people and reveling in it. Actually, the only real blow that seemed to land with any effect was thrown by Kane, with his back to the camera, the blow that dropped the giant skinhead. And then Howard, inconceivably her Howard, her inwardly furious and frustrated but always cowardly brother, kicked the man. Kicked him and kicked him. Full faced, on camera. That was what they were all responding to. It was Howard's act—or Kane's and Howard's joint thrashing of the giant—that gave the rest of them the courage to surge forward and allowed them to see their own ineffective swats and kicks as powerful blows.

Myra had become an expert on the tape, more so than they, because she had watched it as often as they had but her ego was not involved. Not that the truth of it mattered, of course. What counted was their perception, and in their own eyes they had been transformed instantaneously from a motley group that heretofore had tried to picket and whine their way to power into an action group. *They think they are a sort of Jewish S W A T team,* Myra realized. *The Mogen Davids destroying the Goliaths of neo-Naziism.*

Kane turned off the tape to loud moans. They could have watched themselves all night.

"Howard wants to get on with the strategy planning. Don't you, Howard?"

"That's right," said Howard, a little too late to be convincing. He was just as fond of looking at himself as the rest of them. Could it be that Kane didn't love the tape as much because his face was the only one not showing?

Hart whispered something in Solin's ear as Howard rose and began one of his windy speeches.

"Screw that," said Solin. "We want to watch the tape."

"Well . . ." sputtered Howard.

Borodin was chewing gum. A bubble came from his mouth like a pink bladder.

"Turn the tape on. We're tired of hearing you blow, anyway," said Solin, Hart nodding encouragement at his side.

Myra could see the color draining from Howard's face. Was this the insurrection he had always feared? He had been tolerated as the leader of the Brotherhood of Zion only because he was the originator—and because none of the others had had the wit or strength to snatch the leadership from him. Hart had conspired darkly, but this was the first time he had enlisted a confederate.

"I—uh—I thought we should talk about what to do next, but of course we can do that later, if that's what we all want."

"Sit down, Howard," said Solin. He crossed to the television to put the tape back in the vcr.

"Take your seat," said Kane. He spoke as calmly as if he were a teacher in a classroom, but there was no mistaking the menace in his voice. Solin turned as if spat upon, his red neck burning.

"Who you talking to?"

"Sit down and listen to your leadership," said Kane. "Sit when you're told to."

Wiener laughed nervously. Bobby Lewis was watching with his mouth open.

Myra thought Solin looked like he was going to explode in a gush of venom and tobacco juice. His face was aflame. He stepped in front of Kane, who remained seated. Solin's legs straddled Kane's, then clamped Kane's knees together. He pushed his pelvis toward Kane's face.

"Now see the trouble your mouth got you into, sucker?" Solin said. He was smiling in a filthy, anticipatory way, as if he expected something nasty to happen.

"Now men . . ." said Howard, his words deflated by the tension in the air.

"Your mouth got you into it, it looks like your mouth is going to have to get you out of it." Solin thrust his crotch against Kane's face. "What say now, sucker? Want to use that fat mouth for what it's good for?"

Kane brought his forearm up between Solin's legs so hard it actually lifted him off the ground. Solin stumbled backwards, bending over, his hands clutching at his groin. He gasped horribly and his face had turned deathly pale. Kane had still not gotten out of the chair. Solin turned slowly around the room, as if looking for comfort or support. The expression on his face was not only one of pain but injustice, as if Kane had cheated and Solin expected someone to spring to his defense. Everyone else was too shocked to do anything. Hart, his puppet master, was as transfixed as the rest.

"Now sit down," said Kane calmly. "We've wasted enough time on you already."

Solin's breath came back to him at last. He had fallen to his knees. "I'm not finished with you, you son of a bitch," said Solin.

"I think we can dispense with him," Kane said, looking to Howard. "He's too stupid to learn, too mean to train. Do you agree?"

Howard didn't seem to understand. Like Solin, he looked around the room as if for an answer.

Kane stood and kicked Solin in the chest. Solin fell on his back, his mouth working silently. Kane grabbed his feet and dragged him to the door, then slid him into the hallway.

"You're done," said Kane, closing the door.

The others were dumbfounded, except for Borodin, who had finally been jolted into action. He stood, towering over Kane. Myra cringed inwardly for the smaller man. Although the violence had stunned her, she felt a grudging admiration for the way Kane had handled Solin. Borodin, however, was clearly too much for him, she thought.

"We never said we wanted to get rid of him," said Borodin.

"Your leader said," said Kane. He seemed unperturbed by Borodin's mass. "Howard said."

"*We* never said," said Borodin.

"This organization is not a democracy," said Kane. "Our leader gives an order. We obey it. Is that clear?"

"I don't know you," said Borodin. Myra thought he looked at least a foot taller than Kane.

"You just met me," said Kane.

"I don't know you," Borodin insisted stupidly.

"You sit down now," said Kane in the same tone of voice he had used with Solin.

Howard said, "I think . . .," but it was clear what he thought didn't matter. Myra winced at her brother's ineffectiveness. Borodin had balled his fists and assumed a crouch. He would not be as easy to deal with as Solin, Myra thought. Kane would be crushed—Myra was not sure how she felt about that.

"Take your seat," said Kane, and suddenly something was in his hand. He held it easily at his side, but away from his body so Borodin could see it. It was an icepick.

"Sit," he said. He didn't seem angry or threatening, Myra thought. Only his actions frightened.

Borodin sat without a word.

"It's true, you don't know me, any of you," said Kane, "except for our leader's introduction. So I'm going to show you something about myself."

He put his left hand on the pile of typing paper on Myra's desk.

"Like all of you, I am here to serve our leader. Together, with his guidance, we will achieve our goals. His goals are our goals. His desires are our desires. His needs are our needs. Our leader knows that we have many, many enemies. Our people have always been besieged by enemies and those today are no less dangerous than those of the past. Today, however, we know how to deal with them, today we can speak to them in the only language they understand. We can move these enemies not through reason—but through fear. As they would do with us, if they could. They fear what they do not understand

and cannot control. The Brotherhood will become the tool of that fear. It will require courage and dedication from all of us. I want to show you that I have that courage and dedication.''

They were listening raptly. Myra had never seen them like this, they looked almost intelligent. Were they responding to his message, she wondered, or to the man who had just crippled Solin and cowed Borodin? And the leader he referred to with such respect. Could he possibly be talking about her brother?

Kane spread his thumb and first finger far apart atop the typing paper, then held the icepick above his hand. Fearing what he was going to do, Myra tried to look away but found her gaze riveted on him. He put the point of the pick on the web of skin between thumb and finger and pressed down. The others gasped and Myra cried out, but no one heard her. The icepick was through his hand, sticking into the paper. He did not move or scream.

''We must be prepared to suffer,'' he said. Blood was seeping into the paper.

''We must do what must be done, for our leader and our cause,'' he said. His body was on the edge of spasms. His face was twisted into a snarl, but he faced them, looking at them, not the metal sticking from his flesh. He stayed like that, eyes glaring at them, body shaking, forcing them to look at him and not his hand. Myra could not look but could not look away.

Finally he removed the icepick, withdrawing it as calmly as he inserted it, the expression on his face unchanged. He continued talking, but Myra didn't understand what he was saying for several moments.

The others watched him, rapt, but Myra was sure that they, too, were mesmerized by his actions and not his words. He lifted his wounded hand, palm toward them, like a man protesting innocence, and blood ran over his wrist and into the shirt sleeve.

''For our leader and our cause,'' he said, and Myra realized he had been repeating this phrase. ''For our cause and for our leader.''

He moved to Howard, who had watched his performance with the same gaping awe as the others.

''Our leader,'' Kane said and gestured for Howard to stand.

''For our cause and for our leader,'' Kane said. He held his awful hand aloft over Howard's head, an act of horrible benediction.

''For our leader,'' he repeated, this time with an edge of command.

Hart was the first to respond. "For our leader," Hart said. The others caught on and joined him uncertainly at the end of the phrase.

"For our leader," said Kane. The bloody hand was still over Howard's head. Kane's eyes had shrunk inward from the pain, giving him a crazed look. He was a self-styled John the Baptist, stumbling out of the wilderness, half-mad with the ecstasy of his mission to proclaim the Christ, Myra thought.

"For our cause," he said, continuing the litany of this grotesque baptism.

"For our cause," they repeated, in unison this time.

"For our leader," said Kane, biting off the words.

"For our leader!" said the others, eager now to win his approval.

Myra thought Howard looked like a man awaking from a dream in which he has received everything his heart desired, but now, in full consciousness, cannot recall what it was he won.

Howard recovered himself enough to adopt the proper mask. He looked strong and resolute and seemed to think the cheering was really for him.

For the first time Myra was truly frightened for Howard and his clowns. At last they had a leader. And it certainly wasn't Howard.

Kane turned from them and took a step toward Myra's door. He took a napkin from the table and wrapped it around his hand, then stepped even closer to Myra's door, his back to the others. His eyes met hers and he winked at her.

Myra was dumbfounded. Had he known she was watching? Was it all a game of some kind? For whose benefit? Hers? Howard's? Theirs? Or just Kane's own?

Kane had turned to face the others. He sat next to Howard.

"I think you wanted to talk about targets," he said to Howard, who nodded agreement. The others leaned closely to listen.

10

Edgar Allen McKinnon leaned forward over his desk and for once his smile reflected human warmth and not an attempt to conceal the pain in his back. He liked Becker and enjoyed talking with him. McKinnon thought that the two of them had much in common; he saw something of his earlier self in the younger agent. A certain quality of steel that a few agents possessed and the rest could only feign. Becker didn't need to posture, he was the genuine article. Men like Hatcher, perfectly useful men, dedicated, hardworking men, could spend their careers following procedures and routines and they would do credible work. The business was like that; it would yield to perseverance and attention to detail. But in the larger sense, they would never understand it. They would never show a genuine feel for it. Becker had the feel for it. It was the difference, McKinnon reflected, between a man who fished with a net and the angler who used a line and a lure he'd made himself. Both would catch fish, but only one of them understood the quarry.

Becker had specifically requested a private meeting without Hatcher, so McKinnon assumed that Hatcher would be the topic of conversation. But from the opening greeting McKinnon understood that something far more important than bureaucratic haggling was troubling Becker.

"I want off the case," Becker said after the brief pleasantries.

McKinnon straightened in his chair. This meeting had suddenly come to look as if it were not going to be so pleasant after all.

"Go ahead, tell me," said McKinnon.

Becker shook his head. "I don't think I want to go into it. It's a personal matter."

"What is it, John? Hatcher?"

"I can live with Hatcher if I have to."

"So?"

"I'm here on temporary assignment. Volunteer assignment. I can leave without cause if I want to."

"Tell that to civil service. I'm sure you're right about it. Now tell me what the problem is."

Becker paused, considering whether to answer.

"You've killed men," Becker said finally.

"Yes," said McKinnon. Normally he would add the disclaimer that it had been in self-defense, but with Becker it seemed a silly formality.

"Several," Becker said.

"Four," said McKinnon.

Becker paused again. McKinnon waited, his eyes on Becker, who was studying the floor as if he expected an answer to his unspoken question to rise from the carpet.

"How did it make you feel?"

McKinnon had been asked the question many times before. It was usually the third or fourth query at cocktail parties and lectures. He had a pat answer, well rehearsed, filled with horror and loathing and self-serving remarks about duty and the greater good. It was an answer that satisfied most questioners because it matched their expectation. McKinnon knew it would not serve for Becker.

He shaped his answer carefully before answering.

"Different each time," McKinnon said.

Becker nodded in understanding.

"How about the fourth time?" Becker asked. "How did you feel then?"

"Like it was time for a new line of work," McKinnon said.

"That's too easy," Becker said.

"All right. I felt as if I was getting too good at it. Too efficient. I felt as if it didn't trouble me as much as it should."

"Anything else?"

McKinnon studied Becker for a moment. At first he had thought he knew what Becker was getting at, what he needed to hear. Now he was no longer certain.

"I felt like I'd become a magnet of some kind and this wet work was seeking me out," McKinnon said.

"As if it was seeking you out?" Becker asked.

McKinnon nodded.

Becker paused.

"Not as if you were seeking it?" Becker asked.

"No," McKinnon said, surprised. "I never felt that."

Becker was visibly disappointed.

"Is that what you feel, John?" McKinnon asked. "That you're seeking it out?...John, I've read your file, I know it well. You didn't seek anything out. You were assigned to a case. Other people put you on the case, just as I put you on this one. You couldn't know ahead of time how they would turn out."

"Unless I caused them to turn out that way."

"They were self-defense. Every one of them. You didn't line anybody up against a wall and shoot him, you protected yourself. The only way you 'caused' anything to happen was by not allowing the other guy to kill you."

"There are subtler ways."

"That's ridiculous. I know you, John. You wouldn't do anything like that. Why would you?"

Becker shrugged. "Why. Try an easier question."

"Have you been listening to the gossip?"

McKinnon immediately realized he had made a mistake.

"Gossip?" Becker asked. "Is that what they say about me? That I caused those killings?"

"It's just malice. A lot of people are jealous of your success. What do you care what they say behind your back?"

"There's a lot of truth to folk wisdom," Becker said. He was smiling, but McKinnon did not think he was amused. "Maybe they've latched onto something."

"John, ease up. You get too involved in your cases. I know that's why you're so good at it, but it's just a job, not a calling."

"It started that way. Just a job. I wasn't at all sure I would even like it."

"It's an acquired taste," said McKinnon.

"Yes," Becker said slowly, drawing out the word. "A taste. That's what you might call it. A taste. And I've acquired it. A taste. I like that, it sounds very refined."

"Stay on the case, John. I need you. You've got your teeth into it already, I can see that."

"It's not my teeth I'm worried about."

McKinnon sighed. "What are you worried about? Exactly. I want to be helpful if I can, but if it's just a general malaise you're feeling,

I don't know that I'm the right man to talk to. I don't know the questions to ask or the advice to give.''

"You haven't asked the big question,'' said Becker.

"What is it?''

"The same one I asked you. How did you feel after the fourth killing?''

"All right, I'm asking. How did you feel after the fourth killing, John?''

Becker shook his head. "I was just joking.''

"How did you feel? It's fair enough, you asked me. How did you feel?''

Becker turned away from McKinnon, his face tense.

"John?. . . How did you feel?. . . How terrible can it be? It's not as if you liked it, after all . . . John?. . . You didn't like it, did you?''

Becker turned back to McKinnon and looked him squarely in the face. Despite his experience, McKinnon felt both fear and pity in a measure he had seldom experienced.

The moment was too intense and neither could sustain it. McKinnon looked away, feeling he had stared into the torment in Becker's soul. It was not a sight he had wanted to see.

"We have people you can see, if you want to talk,'' McKinnon said. "Some of them are pretty good.''

"Shrinks.''

"Counselors. They're there to help. There's a man named Gold, I've heard very good things about him.''

"I'm a little leery of shrinks.''

"Why's that?''

"I haven't seen very many good results, have you?''

"That's not really my area, John. Some people swear by them.''

"The only people I know who swear by them are the people who can't get off the couch after five years. They need the shrink's approval to tie their shoelaces.''

"Our people aren't like that. They're there to help you deal with specific problems and get you back to work. Gold is particularly good at it, I hear.''

"I'll think about it.''

"It wouldn't hurt to at least meet him. See what you think of him.''

"Maybe.''

"You need to talk to someone, John."

"I'll find someone."

"Not just anyone."

Becker laughed. "No, not just anyone. I have to find someone who knows what the hell I'm talking about. Not many would."

Becker stood, ending the interview on his own.

"I want you to stay," McKinnon said. "You can work this other thing out."

Becker paused with his hand on the door.

"I think you can catch this son of a bitch," McKinnon said.

"I think so, too," said Becker. "That's what scares me most."

"Will you do it?"

"Maybe when I catch him, I can have that talk with him about my problem. The thing is, he's one of the few who would understand."

"You'll stay on the case?... He's a bad son of a bitch, John, who-ever he is. You can catch him."

Becker paused a moment longer in the doorway. "I'm not worried about catching him. I'm worried about catching what he's got."

"I don't know what a comment like that means. He's a bastard, a stone cold killer. He killed two men at the Montreal airport, nearly killed another, killed a third when he stole his passport, and he prob-ably hasn't even started his real job yet ... "

"And why do you want me for this case? Particularly. You've got an army of agents."

"And I'll use them, too," said McKinnon. "Or you will. They're good enough but they need direction. You have a special talent."

"And what is that special talent?" Becker demanded.

"You have a feel for it, you have a special feel for the work."

"A feel," Becker said flatly.

"Call it what you will. You seem to be able to almost anticipate what a certain type of man will do. I don't know why, John. I don't know how. Maybe you do. All I know is that it's a very, very rare gift. You seem to be able to get into their minds."

Becker smiled humorlessly. "What if I can't get out again?"

McKinnon chose to ignore the question and its implications.

"You're on the side of the angels in this, John. We need you. You can do some good, an awful lot of good, get this guy off the streets."

"I'll think about it," said Becker.

"Did something happen in Detroit?"

Becker looked at his hand where it rested on the doorjamb. He studied the tracery of his veins for a moment.

"I submitted my report."

"Very dry, very proper. What happened?"

"I visited with Roger Bahoud's father," Becker said slowly.

"Yes?"

"The man used to beat Bahoud. One day Bahoud stuck a coat hanger in the old man's ear and left him for a vegetable."

"And you saw the old man?"

"I was with him for close to an hour."

"And what did he say?"

"Oh, he can't talk," said Becker. "We had a nice conversation. It was kind of a sentimental journey. Just like old times."

After a pause, McKinnon said, "Stay on the case, John. Talk to Gold if you want. I'll set up an appointment. Or don't talk to him, that's up to you. But stay on the case."

"I'll let you know."

"Stay on it, John."

Becker left and McKinnon drew his notepad toward him. He wrote the word "Becker," paused, then wrote "Gold." After a moment he crossed out "Gold," and stared for a time at the word "Becker."

McKinnon stretched and realized with some amazement that for the last several minutes he had been entirely unaware of his pain. He tore the note with Becker's name on it from the pad, crumpled it, and dropped it in the wastebasket.

When all was said and done, McKinnon had to admit to himself that he was a lousy shrink and a lousy father confessor. He might even be a lousy friend. But he was very good at getting what he wanted.

It was night and the lights in Kane's and Howard's rooms were finally off. There was an ambient glow that came from the city below and never left on the darkest of nights, but otherwise the apartment was dark, and Myra could come out at last. She felt like a werewolf, slipping out of her cave to answer the moon, transformed into a misshapened sport of cruel nature. In the movies the werewolves were always reluctant monsters, struggling against their bizarre metamorphoses when they could. Good people at heart who longed for the silver bullet when they knew it was the only thing that could release them from their terrible bondage to the moon. Vampires seemed to love their calling, and no one missed them when they were gone, but werewolves had Myra's sympathy.

Kane had not seen her since that first meeting two days ago. She had taken her meals like this, late and on the sly. If she could manage to just be there, she thought, limbs composed and hidden, like an actress discovered as the curtain rises, she would spend some time with him. She thought he was intelligent; he would respond to her smiles, her jokes. He would like her—as long as she did not move. But she would need a curtain to fall before she could make her exit. If she could be queen for an hour or two, horny Queen Elizabeth (the "virgin" version, not the proper matron of our time) with painted face and orange wig in place, she would grant him an audience, flirt with him in her royal way, taunt him, tease him a bit with the unattainable glories that lay behind her ermine robe, and then dismiss him so that she might leave the throne and hobble unseen to her bedchamber.

Since she could indulge these fantasies only in her mind, she stayed within her room. She had seen him, of course. She had watched his every move through her door, but he had not so much as glanced in her direction since that startling wink yesterday. She was no longer sure that she had seen it right. She may have imagined it, she thought, disturbed as she was by his actions with the icepick. He had certainly given no further sign that he was aware of being observed. But he was aware of her; she had heard him ask Howard if she ever came out of her room. Once, when they ate their TV dinners together, he had inquired of Howard if they should ask her to join them.

Howard had looked horrified, then muttered something about how Myra liked her privacy. Poor Howard. He loved her, she knew, but didn't want to share her with the world.

Myra prepared her meal of pasta and salad—why was she staying slim? For whom did she watch her figure?—and ate it leaning on the counter, the macaroni almost too hot for her mouth. It was dark and the men were asleep, but she was not sure that Kane would not come out again. She hadn't seen him long enough to trust his habits. With an apple in hand for desert she limped back to her room, reminding herself of the Disney witch offering Snow White the poisoned fruit.

Witches were always hunchbacked, of course, and she was not. Her back was smooth and erect, and in the mirror she could see the traces of her spine as straight as a zipper, but when she walked she had to bend over to accommodate her bad leg, so she felt like a hunchback.

No sooner was she in her room than she heard a door open and Kane was in the living room. He wore only a towel around his waist. As he moved to the window to look out on the city, Myra could see him clearly. My God, he is beautiful, she thought. His chest was thick and strong and covered with hair that ran from the declivity in his throat down across the broad mat of his pectorals and continued in a thinner line until it vanished under the towel. His legs were covered with hair also and the muscles in his calves were bunched all the time as if he were standing on his toes. Myra thought he looked so strong, so male, so much better than the men in Howard's magazines with their inflated torsos. Kane looked *real* and only feet away from her. He looked like a bear. A beautiful, beautiful bear.

She tried to control her breathing so he couldn't hear her, but to her own ears it sounded as if she were gasping. Kane leaned forward to look through the telescope and the towel fell to the floor.

My God. He was huge. And beautiful. Lord, how beautiful. Was that a normal state? Lord, what a thing to carry with you, and what a shame to hide it under clothes. It was the first she had seen in the flesh.

Kane played with the telescope, scanning the city, but she was scarcely aware of what he was doing; she could only will him to stay there forever, as nude and unashamed as Adam.

Too soon he tired of the telescope and stretched himself, leaning back into the brace of his hands in the small of his back and arching, thrusting his pelvis forward in Myra's direction. Oh, Christ. He retrieved the towel with a flick of his foot but did not put it on as he turned his back to her and walked to his room. His buttocks clenched and released with each step.

Was there not some way she could have kept him there? Could she have offered to show him the sights through the telescope? Should she have suggested a cup of hot milk for the sleepless? Or should she simply have torn off her nightgown and fallen to the floor before him?

At last she flopped down onto her bed. She was so excited she would not sleep. She would masturbate, she knew, but still she would not sleep. He is here, in my apartment, she thought feverishly, a strong, savage man who frightens and excites me. Only feet away, only a few seconds away. Out the door and across the living room and into his bed. She could even crawl the distance in less than a minute. She could—but she wouldn't.

Would he come again tomorrow night to look upon the city? She prayed he had insomnia; she would certainly have a case of her own.

11

Becker ate while Hatcher talked, running down the list of suspects whose fingerprints had been found in the passport office. Becker had requested the meeting in the cafeteria for three reasons: He did not want to be in Hatcher's office because he was automatically in a subordinate position there; he wanted something to look at other than Hatcher or Hatcher's letters of commendation that littered the walls of his office; and, finally, he chose to meet in the cafeteria because he knew it annoyed Hatcher.

"I'm listening," Becker said. His eyes followed the newcomers entering the cafeteria.

"I wasn't sure," said Hatcher.

"I listen with my ears, not my eyes."

"Well, that much about you is conventional, at least," Hatcher sniffed.

"You were telling me that one of the fifteen suspects is dead," said Becker. He bit into his sandwich, glanced at Hatcher, then across the room again.

Hatcher referred to his list. "One is dead, cardiac arrest. He died at home the day after he renewed his passport. One is under arrest and incarcerated in a Montreal jail. He was involved in a barroom brawl and pulled a knife on someone."

"That's not our boy," said Becker.

"How do you know?"

"The man we're looking for is not that stupid. No one would pay him two million dollars if he was. What else?"

"Six are currently abroad, one in England, one in Australia, the rest in various places in Europe. We have checked on all six and they are all traveling on their own passports. Not Robert Carmichael's."

"That leaves seven."

Hatcher shifted in his seat. "That's how my math comes out, too."

"Look, Hatcher, it's great that we have so much in common. We both listen with our ears and we can subtract eight from fifteen. But let's not dwell on our similarities. It doesn't exactly constitute common ground."

"I'll be happy to keep it to business, for my part."

"Good. What about the other seven?"

"We have located and interviewed three of them. One is a former arsonist, one an officer in the Canadian Army who was court-martialed for striking an enlisted man, and one killed his wife twenty years ago and has been out for five."

"Scratch all three."

"Why? They all are capable of violence. Why scratch them off the list?"

"Because you found them. Our boy isn't going to kill someone for a passport, then stand still to be questioned. There are too many ways he could be found out. Whoever he is, he isn't tame. He's going to be one of the missing. Tell me about them."

"There are four whose whereabouts are unknown. Lester Gannon, a fugitive for the past six years, wanted for aggravated assault, assault with a deadly weapon, assault with intent to kill. He has a prior arrest list long as your arm and has been underground for six years . . . I like him."

"Go on." A woman in her forties passed Becker's table and Becker watched her legs approvingly.

"Rickard Finkbeiner, native of Germany, resident of Canada since 1984. No known political activity. No criminal record. His prints were on file from when he registered as a legal alien. Whereabouts unknown for two years."

"Where in Germany?"

"Bonn. Born in Leipzig . . . Leipzig is East Germany."

"You like him, too, Hatcher?"

"Born in East Germany. Crossed the border into West Germany when he was twenty-three—certainly old enough to have been indoctrinated and trained. Sits quietly for two years, comes to Canada, keeps on sitting for another five years, establishes himself as harmless, trustworthy. Then vanishes completely? Yes, I like him, too."

"Keep going."

"Moishe Pinter. Israeli citizen in U.S. on a student visa. A post-

doctoral candidate in mechanical engineering at Rochester Institute of
Technology. No record of having been in the passport office—but, of
course, his prints were there. Hasn't been seen for over a week.''

"He could have gone in there with a friend."

"Thirty-three years old. That's pretty long in the tooth to be a post-
doc in engineering."

"He's a slow learner."

"Hasn't been seen since Carmichael's murder."

"Probably shacked up with a girl, getting his ashes hauled."

"For a week?"

Becker laughed. "You wouldn't understand that sort of thing,
Hatcher, but yes, a week. But you like this guy, too, don't you?"

"He's Israeli; that already triples his chances of being a foreign
agent. This country is crawling with Mossad people, and we have
more Israeli agents working on American soil than any other nation-
ality. Particularly in technological fields. The chances of his being an
agent are pretty good, just on the face of it. And a terrorist to boot?
Why not? The Israelis certainly do more than their fair share of bump-
ing people off. Usually with some discretion, I grant you, but the
victims are just as dead. You don't have to hijack a 747 to be a
terrorist. Why don't you like him?"

"The money came from Libya."

"The Israelis are capable of pulling that off."

"They're capable, but they usually don't. Most of the time they
use a Swiss bank. Or London. Or New York. Amsterdam. Tripoli? I
haven't heard of that."

"There's always a first time," said Hatcher. "For that matter, turn
it around. Maybe they used Tripoli because it's Arab money, just the
way it would seem. If I were an Arab terrorist and could pass for an
Israeli—what would be better? Can you think of more effective cover
than that?"

"Yeah, I can. Total invisibility."

"Great. How do you get that?"

"You drop out of sight seventeen years ago and you don't reappear.
That's what Roger Bahoud did."

"So did a lot of others. Disappearing is no great trick. All you have
to do is die. How do you know Bahoud isn't really underground somewhere?"

Becker sighed. "Did you forget where we started from? Bahoud's prints were in Montreal, that's how I know he's not dead. How many killers have you heard of who murder by introducing a foreign object into the ear?"

Hatcher watched Becker's eyes and turned to see what he was looking at. Karen Crist had just entered the cafeteria. She noticed the men looking at her and nodded.

"I've heard of it," said Hatcher. "It's not common, but I've heard of it."

"You're right, it's not common," said Becker. He glanced at Hatcher, then returned his gaze to Karen, who had entered the food line. "It's extremely uncommon. That's what Bahoud did to his father as a juvenile. That's how Carmichael was killed . . . "

"His father?"

"He got an early start. A precocious kid. That's how Willi Holzer died."

"What's Willi Holzer got to do with this?"

"I don't know. I just know it's a very rare method of killing. I know Bahoud used it."

"Once. Seventeen years ago."

"And now two victims die that way within a month of each other."

"Two out of several hundred thousand who were killed in the world in the last few months. Not much of a connection," said Hatcher.

"No, but a nifty coincidence. If we're looking for a terrorist, old friend Willi is a good place to start. He was connected with the Beni Hassan last we knew, right?"

"He was seen with them."

"Seen how? Having tea? Paying a social call? He was connected with them. Beni Hassan are bankrolled out of Libya, the money sent to the Detroit bank was from Libya. Willi and Carmichael died the same way as Bahoud's father. Plus Bahoud got a ringing endorsement from the shrink who treated him. I mean, he was talking about a kid primed and loaded and just waiting to go off."

"Seventeen years is a long time to wait if you're that ready."

"We don't know that he waited. Only that we never caught him."

"So, you like Roger Bahoud."

"I don't like him, I love him. I like the others, too, but they don't have quite the same sex appeal as Bahoud."

Karen passed their table carrying a tray and nodded again.

"Stick around," Becker said to her.

She passed them without comment.

"So, we have our favorites," said Hatcher. "Among the suspects, I mean. What would you like to do next? All four are possible, all four are whereabouts unknown. We don't know the potential target, we don't know the time frame. What do we do?"

"What's your idea?"

Hatcher knew that Becker asked only to embarrass him. He did not, in fact, have any clear idea what to do. I am not an idea man, he thought to himself in justification. I am a manager. Besides, McKinnon had made it perfectly clear that this was to be Becker's case. Any ideas had to flow from Becker.

"Follow the money," Becker said after pausing long enough to make Hatcher's discomfort clear to both of them. "He'll put it somewhere. He took it as a bank check, that's treated the same as cash. The banks should report any deposit of cash larger than $10,000."

"Should. They don't always."

"Granted. Let's hope they do what they're supposed to. He may just plunk down the whole two million somewhere, but my guess is he'd split it into four or five different accounts to draw less attention to himself."

"What if he doesn't put it in a bank? What if he stuffs it in his mattress?"

"Then we don't catch him that way. He might put it in a safe deposit box, of course, but only if he thinks he's being watched and can't use it or even touch it. I don't think he knows we're onto him; it was just chance that the Israeli agent saw him drop Taha Hammadi into the lake. For all he knows Carmichael's body was compacted and dumped into a landfill and never found. If he thinks he's not being watched he would want the money where he could get at it from a distance. A wire transfer means a bank account. Pull some strings, put on some heat with the banking authorities, maybe we can even trace that bank check. Concentrate on the cities over a million in population; that should limit the search a bit."

"Why?"

"Because historically that's where terrorist activity takes place. You hit the nerve centers, not the periphery. You don't try to scare the folks in Keokuk, Iowa. You want to terrify the people in New York, Washington, L.A. They're the ones who control the media. They're the ones who can influence government.''

"I'll put Finney on the money.''

"Good. And keep me posted on any activity involving any known terrorist groups, any international figures no matter where they're from, any unusual criminal activity, anything unusual reported at an airport, an embassy or consulate, the office of any international company—all the routine reports. I want to see them immediately.''

"You'll have it.''

"Also, assemble a calendar of events for the major cities for the next six months. Sometimes they like to time their little surprises with anniversaries. If there's a centennial in Seattle, I want to know about it. For that matter, get me a list of any major event of any kind, sports, entertainment, political convention, whatever. Anything that's apt to draw a crowd of more than ten thousand, say. I want to know who, what, when, and where.''

"You can't possibly check all of those out. Rock concerts alone . . . ''

"I didn't say I was going to check them out, I just want to know about them. Talk to the agencies that book the tours for this kind of thing.''

"There must be thousands.''

"Probably. Don't worry, I don't plan on attending. I just want to know. I want to hear what's happening and maybe something will strike a responsive chord.''

"You mean you're . . . ?''

"Guessing. Sure. Hatcher. How do you think I do it, a Ouija board? I look at the same possibilities they do and hope that the same thing stands out to me that caught their attention.''

"That means you have to think like they do.''

Becker studied Hatcher until the other man began to squirm.

"That's right,'' Becker said at last. "I think like they do.''

Becker glanced at Karen and caught her looking at him. He lifted a finger to indicate he would be with her shortly.

"And get in touch with Interpol. Find out if there have been any killings within terrorist groups or other political groups in the past fifteen years or so that involved Bahoud's little trick of going through the ear.''

"For the past fifteen years?"

"A man with tastes like that hasn't been inactive. He just hasn't fallen within our territory till now, but you can bet he's been working somewhere. One thing, he likes his work."

"How do you know that?"

"Because it's hands-on, it's close, you can't get any closer unless you hug them to death. A man who doesn't like his work kills people by dropping bombs, setting fires, anything remote, but this guy— Bahoud whether you want to admit it or not—this guy gets as close as he can. He might kiss them on the neck before he slips in the wire."

"Nice image, Becker."

"You think there isn't something sensual about killing that way? You can feel it going in, feel it meeting obstruction, you push hard, harder, feel the object snake its way in, penetrate, feel the softness of the brain. You hear it, hear the flesh tear, hear your victim breathe and cry out and gasp and moan. If you do it from the front, you can watch, you can see every nuance on the face, the surprise, the horror, the pain, maybe a very quick plea for mercy in the eyes. You can feel the warmth of the victim's breath in your face, you can smell his dinner. And all the time you're pressed against him, you have to be tight against his body to kill that way, you can feel him struggle, writhing against you, then the stop, the complete stop—or maybe he twitches, maybe he continues to writhe long after it's done . . . I'd say a man would develop a taste for that sort of thing."

Hatcher stared at Becker. "You've got a very vivid imagination," he said finally.

"Have a talk with Interpol. Beni Hassan didn't hire a virgin for this job. Bahoud's been killing for a long time, and he must be very good at it or he wouldn't have been given that kind of money."

Becker left Hatcher and carried his plate to the table where Karen Crist sat. Hatcher muttered "sick" under his breath.

"Can I join you?"

Karen had been nursing a bowl of soup to last until he got there, but now she feigned surprise.

"Please."

"I'm sorry about the meeting at McKinnon's the other day. You sort of got caught in the crossfire. Sorry."

"I didn't mind. It was instructive."

"It's a quick way to learn, like sticking your finger in the wall outlet."

"There did seem to be a bit of electricity in the room," Karen agreed. "You and Hatcher have a little history, I guess."

"A little blood under the bridge, yes." Becker wet his finger and picked up a crumb from his plate. "Is he watching us now?"

Karen looked casually in Hatcher's direction.

"Like a hawk," she said.

"I'd tell you to give him the finger, but I understand you'd like to work for him."

"Well, not him, precisely. I'd give my left nut to work in Terrorism, though."

"Considering the circumstances, not much of a sacrifice," Becker grinned.

"You're right, a meaningless statement. Let me rephrase it. I'd give Finney's left nut to work in Terrorism."

"Does he know you think that highly of him?"

"Finney? We're just friends, as the saying goes."

"What's the fascination with Terrorism?"

"That's where the real nasties are. If I'm going to spend a career chasing bad guys, I'd rather go after the ones who blow people up than the ones who commit wire fraud or embezzlement."

"You like them nasty, do you?"

Karen laughed. "Why do I think that's a trick question. Have we changed topics all of a sudden?"

Becker looked at her evenly, giving nothing away, missing nothing. Most men looked her in the eye only fleetingly, Karen thought. Their eyes shifted all over the place when they spoke, returning to her only occasionally, and briefly. Becker behaved that way when speaking to other men, she had observed him. But speaking to women he reversed the process, looking mostly at them and away only sporadically. He's awfully comfortable with women, she realized. And he certainly lets you know he has your attention. His gaze alone established an intimacy beyond what most men ever achieved. His words were considerably more ambiguous.

"Would you like to change topics?" he said at last.

"I don't know which topic we're on, or which several. I have no problem with double entendre, either—as long as I know that's what we're doing. Normally I would know."

"Why not now?"

"I find you very hard to read," she said. "And I would hate to misread you."

"Maybe it's because you don't know me well enough."

"Maybe. I suspect very few do know you well enough."

"There have been some."

"Are there any now?"

Becker tilted his head slightly as if pondering whether, or how, to answer.

"Are there any who know me well enough to know what I'm talking about?" He paused. "Not right at the moment. How about you?"

"Divorced," said Karen.

Becker laughed. "He didn't read you right?"

"Or read me too well." She shrugged. "I was just too young to be married. I still had too many wild oats to sow. You know what I mean?"

"I've heard of the condition. Not usually in women, though."

"It's a new age," said Karen.

"I've read about it. I was never sure if it was just theory or if people were actually behaving differently."

"You haven't tried any research on your own?"

"I don't go out much," Becker said. "I'm not very good company." He looked away for the first time. Shy, thought Karen. Or very clever.

"Oh, I bet you are," she said. "In your old-fashioned, traditionalist way."

"No," he said darkly. "I'm really not." His mood had changed so abruptly and so completely it was as if a cloud had passed over his face.

Karen paused before speaking. Somehow the moment for innuendo had vanished.

"Oh," she said. "And for a moment there I thought you were going to ask me out."

Becker looked at her again and his mood seemed to lighten.

"Even though I'm not good company?"

"I'm glad you didn't," she said. "Because since I reported to you on the Montreal case, you're at least technically my superior. And there are very strict Bureau rules about sexual harassment by a superior case officer."

Becker grinned at her. "Good thing I didn't," he said. "My record is checkered enough as it is."

"On the other hand, there's no prohibition against a junior asking her superior out." She held her breath. A rejection seemed as likely as acceptance. She really did not know how to read him, she admitted. But on the other hand, what an interesting language to learn. Becker was far and away the most intriguing agent she had met, with the most impressive record and the most tantalizingly ambivalent attitude. He would be not only a feather in her cap, but the cap as well. If he accepted.

"I warn you, you won't have a good time," he said finally.

Karen breathed in relief.

"Oh, you don't know. Maybe I will. We all define a 'good time' differently. I like them nasty, remember?"

Becker studied her carefully for a moment, slowly shaking his head.

"Remember, you asked for it," he said at last.

Kane allowed himself a few minutes to rest before the meeting. Stretching out on Mrs. Goldsmith's bed he reviewed the day with satisfaction. The bedspread was knobbled with a thousand twists of cloth, the kind of chenille spread he had not seen anywhere in thirty years. He enjoyed idly playing with the material as he lay there. The knobs made him think of a woman's nipple. It had been entirely too long since he had felt that particular pleasure. For a time he had thought he might have to sleep with Howard to solidify his hold over him. He was prepared to do so if necessary, but Howard had proven most compliant without sex. If he had a sex drive, it was totally inverted, Kane assumed. Or sublimated into this obsession with the Brotherhood. Whatever the case, it didn't need to concern Kane and in the meantime it allowed him the freedom to contemplate Howard's sister. He had seen her only once, lounging in the doorway of her bedroom the day he arrived. If she was crippled as Howard said, Kane certainly hadn't noticed. She looked damned good to him. Very pretty in an innocent sort of way. And sexy. Or, at least, her notion of what sexy was like. People who had sex on their mind didn't need to play it that hard, but she could learn. Kane would be more than happy to teach her. It had been entirely too long. And if she was inclined to stay in her room, so much the better. He had no intention of sporting her around in public.

His mind drifted away from Myra and returned to the day just past. He had spent much of it dealing with his money, an activity that always pleased him. Starting with Chase Manhattan for the deposit of the original bank check, he had broken the two million dollars into four equal pieces and put the remaining three into smaller banks. At each bank he received temporary check forms and was assured he would get permanent ones within a week. To each bank he gave a different address and name. The addresses were postal boxes at different mail delivery sites throughout Manhattan, which were accessible day and night. Once he had the permanent checks he would break the money into smaller portions and deposit it in various mutual fund money markets by mail. To each of the mutual funds he would give still other addresses. When the money was spread widely enough he would close the bank accounts and the original postal boxes, thus eliminating any trace of himself. Within ten days' time the money would be invisible but, just to make sure, he would wait the required thirty days, then close all of the money market funds and move the cash into still other mutual funds.

The work was not yet done, of course. Each account required a separate social security number, which meant he would have to do a little leg work to acquire some legitimate ones, but he had time for that. Meanwhile, it had been simplicity itself to slip into Howard's room and find his social security number on his bank book. Kane had supplied the four New York banks with Howard's number. It would do until they got around to checking it—if they ever did—for by that time the money would be as clean as a four-time scrubbing could make it, and Kane's association with Howard would be long since dead. As would Howard.

He was vulnerable for about a week, until the new checks came, but it couldn't be helped. Laundering money took a little time in America; that was just the way things were. The regulations that had been put into effect to catch drug dealers with their massive deposits had made it difficult for anyone dealing in cash. Money was simply not as fungible as it should be, and cash, large sums of cash, caught people's attention. Chase and the other banks were required to report his cash deposits, and he assumed that in another month or so some clerk somewhere would make note of them and, most likely, ignore them. He was not a drug dealer, after all. He was engaged in no known criminal activity—that is Robert Carmichael was not. Nor, at this point, was Howard Goldsmith. There was a risk that eventually someone would pick up the trail, but Kane had had no choice. If he had spread the Detroit deposit via conventional banking means, it would have left a path a mile wide straight from the Detroit deposit for any investigator to follow. He could not have taken the money in cash in the first place and just kept it on him or tucked it away someplace. Not in New York City, where he was liable to attack by any crack addict on any corner, or where his room could be burglarized at any time. Plus cash had the disadvantage of any other belonging; its hiding place had to be visited. If Kane had to move quickly he did not want to have to return first to his cache site; he wanted to be able to leave instantly. With the money safely in money market funds, he could get at it at any time, from anywhere in the world. All he needed was a telephone.

The few days' vulnerability was worth the risk. Do it right the first time and you don't have to worry about it later. No one was after him, anyway, he was fairly certain of that. In Canada, yes. But Robert Carmichael's body was under several tons of garbage by now and the loss of his passport was unknown to anyone but Bahoud. The Chase Manhattan account was under the name of Carmichael by necessity because that was the name on the original bank account in Detroit and was thus the name on the bank check, but the likelihood of anyone tracing it seemed extremely remote. They would have had to be onto me immediately, Kane thought, and no security service in the world was that efficient. The only way any agents would make a connection would be if someone tipped them off ahead of time. Hammadi and the Beni Hassan were hardly likely to do any tipping to the FBI. They were not exactly bosom buddies with the G-men. Yes, he reflected, it was safe enough. Now he had to prepare for his second installment from Hammadi. With accounts into which he could deposit the new money, Kane would not have to concern himself with any of this nonsense the second time around. Of course, first he had to meet the terms required for the second installment.

"A preliminary target," Hammadi had called it. After his banking, Kane had done the initial work on the target. It had been as easy as looking in the phone book and making a few calls. What was there about America that made everyone so careless? Did they really think the ocean presented an insurmountable barrier to revenge? Or did they believe the propaganda that said the FBI was too effective to allow for successful penetration? That reputation was undoubtedly spread by the FBI itself, Kane was sure. They couldn't be that good, not in a country this vast. Just look at their record against drug dealers. Laughably inefficient. True, they had caught a few Colombian assassins before they did their jobs, but Kane was no Colombian with a machine gun tucked into his belt.

Perhaps Sulamein bin Assad was simply foolish enough to think all was forgiven because of his age. If so, his memory had failed him along with his sense of security. You did not walk away from your allegiance where groups like the IRA, the PLO, Al Fatah, or the Beni Hassan were concerned. Or, you did not walk away and live to tell about it. Age was no excuse, nor health, nor decrepitude, nor a lifetime of devoted service. Sulamein bin Assad may have been counting on all four, but he was wrong. Nor would hiding in a mosque provide sanctuary. Did the old man believe he was living in the Middle Ages? Modern politics were not about to be stayed by religious considerations, no matter how much the Moslem groups might cloak themselves in the mantle of Islam.

The buzzer rang and Kane heard Howard moving toward the intercom. It would be the first of the Brotherhood. Probably Hart, Kane surmised. Hart could not wait to get to meetings now. His resistance to Howard had been transformed to assiduous allegiance. The others were much the same, eager now for what was to come. Excitement was intoxicating, as Kane knew full well. Violence and danger were as addictive as any drug in their own way, and Kane was now their chief supplier. Through Howard, of course. Howard must be the middleman, he must be the one the others thought of as their source. You could become very attached to your local pusher. Like Pavlovian dogs, Kane wanted the members of the Brotherhood to worship the man who pushed their buttons—and it must be perceived to be Howard. Kane had been blatantly in control in the beginning—and that had been necessary—but now he must take a backseat and run Howard by remote control, counting on their sessions alone together to keep Howard moving in the right direction. The man was smart enough, certainly, all he needed was sound counsel and constant bracing.

Kane heard the buzzer ring several more times and waited. Let Howard greet them. He would join them himself later, just like any other member. Howard would be in charge.

12

The psychiatric counselors kept on staff by the Bureau share one floor of the secondary office building next to the main headquarters in Langley. The building was taken over as temporary space as the Bureau continued its thirty-year expansion under the legendary aegis of J. Edger Hoover in the late 1950s. The temporary space had soon become permanent, and the counselors themselves were installed as a nod to the prevailing notions of mental health in the late 1960s. Hoover would have preferred that any agent who found himself in psychic turmoil sat down for a good chat with his local clergyman, but Hoover was gone by then and his successors had come to understand that the rigors of hunting and occasionally shooting other men produced problems that were beyond the scope of the average minister or priest. The collection of counselors brought at least the perception of a scientific approach to the abiding mystery of the spirit.

Gold's office was a small one in the middle of the building, which meant a view of the airshaft. Becker assumed he was a younger man without any of the perquisites of seniority. The outer office did not even have a window and there were only three chairs. Either Gold was not very busy or he was efficient and didn't keep people waiting around.

An agent, whom Becker knew slightly, emerged from the inner office, gave Becker a furtive glance, then left quickly. Guiltily, Becker thought. As if he'd been caught indulging an impulse weak and dishonorable. Not a very fashionable or understanding point of view, Becker realized, but he recognized it as his own nonetheless.

Gold stood in the door leading to the inner office. Becker disliked him immediately. The psychologist wore a slightly bewildered look, as if wondering what transgression had landed him amongst the tangled and decidedly resistant psyches of the FBI. He was broad in the hips and appeared to be spreading like a pear, a decidedly womanish shape, and his feet splayed to the side when he walked. The ducklike waddle was a feature he shared with Hatcher, which didn't help him in Becker's eyes.

"Becker?" he asked, extending a hand. "I'm Gold. I'm very pleased to meet you. You've got quite a reputation."

"Have I? As what?"

"As a very special agent. A man with great talents."

"What kind of talents do I have a reputation for?"

"Have I hit a sore spot already?" Gold inquired. "The session hasn't even started. It was intended as a compliment."

Gold stepped to one side and beckoned Becker into his office, but Becker stood his ground.

"Let's establish credentials first," said Becker. "Just so we don't waste anybody's time."

"I've got some diplomas on the wall behind my desk," Gold said. "Very impressive. I was a dedicated student."

"Congratulations."

"Thank you. Or were you wondering, If he's working for the government, how good could he be?"

"I was wondering how good you could be. Period."

"Come on in and find out. It only takes an hour."

"I won't need that much time," said Becker. "Just a few questions."

"Shoot . . . Sorry, wrong place for that. Go ahead, ask."

"Did you ever kill anybody?" Becker asked.

"No."

"Did you ever want to?"

"Physically, do you mean? No, not really."

"Did you ever even hurt anyone?" Becker asked. "Physically."

"Do I have to say 'yes' to pass this test? I haven't lived that kind of life. Violence hasn't played a big part. I'm a wuss, maybe even a sissy. There were a few kids who liked to kick my ass when I was in grade school—more than a few, actually. A lot of kids liked to kick my ass when I was in grade school. I cried easy. That made me kind of popular, in my way. At least it assured I always had fellow students around me, lined up to take a poke at the blubbering baby."

Gold stared at Becker. There was no trace of either pride or self-pity in his voice.

"Does that help?" Gold asked.

Becker smiled. "Not really, but nice try."

"But I have listened to an awful lot of stories from men who have killed people and felt dreadful about it, and I've heard from a lot more who were so scared they soiled themselves."

"Haven't mentioned my category yet," Becker said, forcing a grin.

"Give me a chance," Gold said. "Maybe we'll find you're not so unique as you think."

"Hell, I'm not unique," Becker said. "I see people like me all the time. People like me are my specialty. The only thing unusual about me, Mr. Gold, is that I'm on this side of the fence."

Becker started toward the outer door.

"Give it a try," said Gold. "All you've got to lose is your pain."

Becker chuckled. "Mr. Gold, my pain is the only sign I've still got a conscience." He turned to leave.

"Perhaps another time," Gold said. Becker was already in the hallway.

"Perhaps," said Becker. "But not likely."

When Becker was out of sight, Gold said, "I'd say it was an absolute certainty."

Back in his inner office, Gold debated whether to take a nap during the free hour Becker had just handed him. Instead, he picked up his telephone and asked to speak to McKinnon.

"I've been doing some research," Howard said. "And I've found us a target. Someone who can serve as a signal to the rest of our enemies that we mean business."

The others murmured excitedly at the suggestion of action.

"His name is Sulamein bin Assad," Howard said, rolling the foreign sounds contemptuously on his tongue. "He used to be on the council of the PLO."

The noise of the others grew even louder at the mention of the enemy. Like dogs being trained to kill, thought Kane. Wave a rabbit in front of their face, taunt them with it. He sat on the edge of the group beside Wiener, leaning forward as eagerly as the others—but no more. Muttering excitedly in concert with them—but no more.

Howard quelled them with a look and Kane smiled inwardly. He's getting good at it, Kane thought. He's beginning to believe the power is really coming from him.

"He retired from the council about five years ago and came here to live."

"Here?" Hart asked incredulously. "In America?"

Howard smiled patiently as if dealing with an enthusiastic child. "In Brooklyn," he said.

The others exploded in a roar of indignation. Brooklyn, a borough with mythic connections to the heart of the American Jew second only to Israel itself. The PLO in Brooklyn? Unspeakable degradation.

Howard raised his hands and they quieted with difficulty. "There's a big Syrian and Arab community there, as you may or may not know. He's living there now. In a mosque."

"How do you know?" asked Wiener. Kane glanced at Wiener curiously. He had not expected the question to come from him. Hart, perhaps, who was the smartest still, despite his obeisance. Or Bobby Lewis who maintained a certain gloss of normality about him. But not Wiener who seemed so shy and insecure.

"I have sources," Howard said.

Hart was the first to nod with understanding. The leader had sources. Of course. As it should be.

"It's best that you not know them," Howard continued. "It's important not to compromise them."

Hart nodded again and this time the others joined him. They did not need to know *how* he knew, of course. It was sufficient that he did know.

"Now what we are going to do"—Howard said, pausing for effect—"What we are going to do is pay a visit to Sulamein bin Assad. All of us. A social call." Howard laughed and the others joined in. Kane chuckled with them.

"We're going to show him how welcome he is in America."

"I'll show him how welcome he is," said Borodin, smashing his fist into his open hand.

"*We'll* show him," Howard corrected him. "We'll show them all. And we'll show them the way *I've* got it worked out."

"Sure," said Borodin. "I didn't mean . . ."

"When I say and where I say and how I say."

"I didn't mean . . ."

"Understood?"

Borodin nodded meekly as the others stared at him.

"Good," said Howard.

Like a duck to water, Kane thought with satisfaction. *He's got all the makings of a petty tyrant except the power of enforcement, and that I can supply.*

Howard leaned forward to the others conspiratorially.

"We're going to do it now, tonight, and we're going to do it good, and we're going to make it known that we did it so that everyone understands that the Brotherhood of Zion is here and a power to be reckoned with. We're going to make Mr. Sulamein bin Assad regret his years with the PLO."

We'll do better than that, Kane thought, although none of you know it yet. You must learn to walk before you can run, but don't worry, boys, I'll have you up and sprinting before the night is over.

13

Karen was grateful that afterwards Becker did not pull away. He continued to hold her and gently kissed her face and her eyes for minutes afterwards. Only gradually did he slacken his grip on her as if he had discovered during the act that she was too precious to let go. When they parted at last it was so slowly that it seemed almost a continuation of being together.

His patience seemed without end. First, when they had arrived at her apartment and she was fairly jumping out of her skin with nerves and anxiety, he had held her, just held her close to him, for the longest time until she gradually began to relax. When he finally kissed her it was with a tenderness that shocked her. She had never liked kissing Larry, her husband, and as a result their sex had never started with gentleness and built to excitement—it had simply commenced. Becker's lips explored hers with the tentative touch of shyness, a caution that matched her own. Gradually the kisses warmed and only then, when she had already given over to him, did his hands begin to explore her body.

His hands were also a revelation to her. They seemed to genuinely like her, all of her. With warmth in his palm and fingers, he explored her everywhere, caressing her arms, the soft hollows of her neck, the planes of her face. He moved his fingers through her hair with a sensuousness that made her gasp. Why had no one ever caressed her scalp like that before?

She found herself trembling again, but this time not with nerves. She realized with the joy of revelation that she was actually being made love to and every inch of her was being cherished and appreciated.

When he finally touched the top of her breasts she felt as if they wanted to leap up to meet his hand. When he put his lips to her breasts she sensed the thrill throughout her whole body.

Karen had not thought it was possible for her to be fulfilled her first time with a man. She had never before relaxed enough nor trusted enough to allow herself release. But with Becker it came upon her in a succession of huge waves that roiled and rocked her. She cried out shamelessly and clung to him until finally the waves receded to ripples.

But when she was done, he was not, and he took her there again when she had thought it was not possible to return. Arching her back, baring her teeth, panting like a Lamaze student in transition, she peaked when he did, matching his convulsions with her own.

And afterwards he took her down so gently, kissing away her tears and staying with her until she was finally ready to release him.

Not only had Becker surprised her—shocked and stunned her, really—but she had amazed herself. After her divorce she had tried very hard to change her attitude toward men and sex. Men could have sex without emotional involvement, why couldn't she? What did orgasm have to do with anything but nerve endings? Masturbation was just physical stimulation, nothing more, why not the same for sex with a man? Take your pleasure and move on, she told herself. Be as cold and independent as those bastards. It would be so much easier. No more anxieties, no more endless efforts to please, no more tears. Be as inhuman, unfeeling, and uninvolved as they were. It seemed like such a good idea. The only problem, she now realized, was that she couldn't do it.

But damned if she'd let Becker know it.

They lay together for a long time, she with her head on his chest, he with one hand idly stroking her arm.

"And you said you were no fun," she said at last.

"That's when I thought you would probably want to go dancing."

"Do people still go dancing?"

"I don't."

"I think I can live without that," she said. "Although I must say you do have a pretty good sense of rhythm. And . . ."

"What?"

"Never mind."

"Tell me."

"Bad idea. Really. Forget it."

"Okay," said Becker.

Karen held it in for three more breaths.

"Are you always so much in control of yourself?" she asked, immediately regretting it. "I shouldn't have asked that."

"It's all right."

"That's not criticism! Believe me! It was, you were, astounding—but how do you do it?"

"Slowly," said Becker.

She laughed. "Yes, I know. Bless you."

She moved her body slightly and her breasts brushed against his chest. Her nipples were hard again. Don't be greedy, she said to herself.

"Can I ask you another question?"

"Sure," he said. His hand stopped stroking her arm.

"Are you sure you don't mind talking about this? I mean, I shouldn't be telling you this, but this was a unique experience for me. I don't mean there have been all that many besides my husband, but there have been some . . . "

She rolled her head away, grabbed a pillow, and pressed it over her mouth.

Becker gently pulled the pillow away.

"What?"

"I've got to stop talking."

"Okay," said Becker. He was propped on one elbow, looking down at her. A dim glow from the street lights filtered through the window and she could see him grinning down at her.

"You know I can't help myself. You should help me but you're taking advantage of me by letting me babble on."

"You want me to hold the pillow?"

She put a finger to his chest and ran it slowly through the hair. There was a sheen of moisture on his skin. So he did sweat after all, she thought with satisfaction.

"I've been with quite a few men in my time. I don't mean tons, but quite a few, all right?"

"All right."

"I'm no whore."

"Would I be here if I thought that?"

"Look, none of those guys—and some of them were pretty sophisticated—but not a one of them . . . Everything you did was right. Everything. You seemed to know what I wanted even before I knew. How do you do that?''

She put the pillow on her face again, then immediately removed it.

''You don't have to answer. I even embarrass myself . . . But how do you, really?''

''It's simple enough.''

''No one else seems to know it.''

''I do the same thing I do when I'm trying to catch somebody.''

''I don't understand.''

''When I make love to you, I do my best to become you. So when I do this''—He pressed her nipple with his thumb and Karen felt a jolt throughout her body—''I know you want me to do it. And when I do this . . . ''

He took her breast in his mouth. Very quickly Karen stopped waiting for the rest of the sentence. To her disappointment he lifted his head.

'' . . . I know you want me to keep doing it.''

''You have that right,'' she said. ''In fact, if you'd care to continue . . . ''

''But there are things you don't want me to do,'' Becker said, and his tone had become more serious. ''There are things that make you uncomfortable, no matter how aroused you are.''

Karen sat up in the bed and moved against the headboard. ''Yes, there are.''

''But someone did these things to you some time, didn't they? Someone did things to you that you didn't want them to do.''

''I don't want to go into this,'' she said.

''It wasn't your husband. You're much too strong to let anybody mistreat you as an adult.''

''I don't want to talk about it,'' she said.

''All right,'' Becker said. ''I'm just showing you how I do it.''

''How you do which? Hunt somebody or make love?''

Becker paused. ''The process is similar,'' he said. ''The result is different.''

Karen crossed her arms. ''So while you're making love to me you're analyzing my sexual background? Very nice.''

''I'm not analyzing. It's not an intellectual process. I'm feeling. I'm feeling what you're feeling. And when I do certain things, or start to do certain things, I feel your resistance. Your fear. We don't get most of our fears as adults; we bring them from childhood. So I assume someone did something to you as a child."

"Did you bring any fears from *your* childhood?"

Becker laughed. "Oh, yes."

"What?"

"You tell me," Becker said.

"I don't know."

"Oh," he said. She could hear the disappointment in his voice. "Okay."

"How would I know?" she demanded. "I don't really know you."

"Never mind. I thought maybe you could. It doesn't matter."

"Why did you think I could? Because I'm an agent? Does that mean I can figure out my bed partners by having sex with them?"

"Not just because you're an agent, no. Hatcher couldn't, to take an outstanding example. I thought maybe you were different."

"Why?"

"Because you want to be," Becker said.

"I want to be different?"

"Very much. Hatcher doesn't want to be. He wants to be ordinary. Powerful, but ordinary."

"And you don't want to be ordinary?" she asked.

Becker shrugged. "I don't think I have any choice in the matter. Perhaps you do. Maybe I've misjudged you."

Karen slid back under the covers and stared for a time at the ceiling.

"You haven't misjudged me," she said at last. "And you're afraid of the dark."

Becker was silent for a long time. Karen began to suspect he had gone to sleep, or had not heard her.

"How did you know?" he said finally.

"You told me, the first time I met you. You had just done something in the Poe Room that Finney was talking about. He asked you how you could move so well in the blackout and you said you had to get over your fear of it."

"People don't usually believe me when I say that," Becker said.

"I did. I knew you meant it and I also knew you didn't want me to believe you meant it."

"Good for you," he said. Karen was not certain how to read him.

"Are you afraid now?"

"No," Becker said. "There's street light coming in the window, I can see your face. It's only total darkness that bothers me."

"Total darkness is hard to find."

Becker laughed mirthlessly. "You have to go looking for it."

"What did he do to you in the darkness?" she asked.

Again Becker was silent.

"Which time?" he asked finally.

"The worst time," she said.

Becker exhaled slowly. "I'm not ready to go into that."

"Okay."

Becker lifted himself onto his elbow and looked down at her.

"How did you know it was a man who was in the dark?" he asked.

"You don't have any trouble relating to women," she said.

Becker grinned, then fell back to the bed.

They lay together in silence. At length she touched his arm. He jerked instinctively, then relaxed under her touch.

"It wasn't your fault," she said. "You know that, don't you?"

"I know that."

"Nothing he did to you was your fault. You were just a little boy."

"I know."

"It took me a long time to realize it myself," she said.

Becker reached for her and they clung together. When they began at last to caress each other and to glide from comfort to passion, Karen allowed herself to feel Becker's sensations as well as her own.

It was, she realized, the second time she had been made love to, and the first time she had made love herself.

With blessed timing, his beeper did not sound until they had finished.

She ran her hands across the muscles of his back as he spoke on the bedside phone to Finney.

"Sorry to bother you at this hour," Finney said. Becker glanced at the glowing face of the clock. It was midnight. They had been in bed for three hours. "But you said you wanted to be notified right away if anything unusual showed up."

"Go ahead, Finney."

"Give Finney my best," Karen whispered, then giggled. "Never mind, I don't have any of my best left to give."

Becker shifted the phone to his other ear and pushed the pillow over her face.

"I put the screws to the Treasury and they obliged by reminding the major banks of their responsibility to report cash deposits over $10,000. We also reminded them of their rather shabby record, recently, and of the laundering indictments in Miami and New York."

Becker let the young man tell him things he already knew. It was his only moment in the sun and small enough recompense for a great deal of hard—and boring—work.

"Director McKinnon put in a word or two, also," said Finney.

"I bet he did," said Becker.

"Everyone pays attention to Director McKinnon. I mean *everyone*."

"As they should," said Becker.

"Yes, sir, that's true. So we got the major banks to report within twenty-four hours for at least a week. They grumbled a lot, but they've been complying. Normally they aren't obliged to report those deposits for thirty days, but Director McKinnon talked about national security and all that. We assumed he would make the deposit at a major bank because that amount of money would cause too much of a stir at a smaller one . . . "

It had been Becker's assumption in the first place, but he saw no point in reminding Finney. Becker could tell by the pause in Finney's voice that the young agent had finally come to the point.

"I've put all the reports through the computer every night and done the analysis you suggested, and I just now came up with something you might be interested in." Finney cleared his throat in a vocal equivalent of a drum roll. "This morning Chase Manhattan in New York City received a cash deposit of a quarter of a million dollars from a Robert Carmichael."

Becker expelled a long, low breath.

"Agent Becker?"

"I'm here, Finney."

"We don't know that it's the same Robert Carmichael, of course," said Finney. "It's probably a fairly common name, after all."

"Probably," said Becker. "But as someone once said, there's no

such thing as a coincidence. Good work, Finney. Go to bed. I'll call
you in the morning.''

"Yes, sir. Thank you, sir.''

Becker hung up the phone and rose from the bed.

"I can't stay,'' he said.

"It's already been too good to be true,'' said Karen. "Why press
it?'' She hoped her disappointment didn't sound in her voice.

"Get some sleep, you're going to need it. We're going to be very
busy in New York.''

"We?''

"I'm going to call McKinnon and tell him I need you.''

She spoke very softly. "Do you?''

He stood at the foot of the bed, looking down at her as he buttoned
his shirt.

"Don't worry. You'll pull your own weight.''

Karen smiled. It was the first time all night that he'd been wrong.
That wasn't what she had been worried about at all.

The Sunni Moslem mosque on Dykeman Street in Brooklyn was in
a converted church that had once served a congregation of Evangelical
Lutherans of the Missouri Synod. The spire had been truncated and
the more overt signs of Christian symbolism had been chiseled from
the exterior stonework, but the architecture was still unquestionably
American Protestant. A building fund had been established with the
ultimate goal of topping the building with a dome in the tradition of
Arabia, but the congregation was not wealthy and the fund grew
slowly.

But Moslem or Christian, it was clearly not a synagogue, Howard
noticed with some relief. Tonight's action was not about religion, of
course, but violating a house of worship gave him some uneasiness
anyway.

"They do it to us all the time,'' said Hart, sounding as if he was
trying to convince himself.

The Brotherhood stood on the street opposite the mosque. The hour
was late and Brooklyn, unlike Manhattan, not only slept at night but
in spots it practically rolled up the sidewalks. The streets were all but
empty, the lights within the mosque were out.

"They do far worse to us,'' said Howard.

"If we were the PLO, we'd have a bomb," said Bobby Lewis.
The others were quick to agree.

"They knock over graves in our cemeteries," said Wiener.

"They fucking *kill* us," growled Borodin. "What's the matter with
you guys? He's PLO. I don't care if he's hiding out in the middle of
Mecca. We got him, don't we? Let's get the bastard."

"Borodin's right," said Howard. "They made the rules a long time
ago, nothing sacred. We have nothing to reproach ourselves for."

Kane sensed that Howard was working up to a speech. He much
preferred talk to action and Kane touched Howard on the arm as a
reminder of his real mission.

"Right," said Howard. He may have misgivings about the action,
but with Kane at his side, he had no fear of the action itself. Kane
would take care of it, he knew that. He looked at each member of the
group in turn, locking eyes, trying to buoy them with his own feeling
of confidence. "Let's go," he said, and they swept across the street
like a wave of trouble.

Kane slipped the lock on a side entrance and Wiener stood nervous
guard outside the door as the others went into the mosque. After re-
assuring himself that they had not been seen, Wiener took a can of
scarlet spray paint from his pocket and went to work on the side of
the building. Even the hiss of the pressurized paint sounded loud to
him and he worked with a shaking hand, looking about constantly to
see if he was being watched. He was no graffiti artist and his lettering
lacked the fanciful craft of the boys from the ghetto, but the words
were clear enough. "Never Again," they screamed. "PLO Must
Pay!" And finally, as a signature, the initials "B.Z." in letters four
feet high.

Kane led them into the basement with no attempt at silence. When
they pushed open his door, Sulamein bin Assad was already awake,
swinging his legs toward the floor. He was an old man, more than
eighty, and in poor health, but fifty years of paranoia had kept his
instincts for survival sharp. Kane had allowed Borodin to storm
through the door first to absorb any shock that was waiting for them,
and now he was forced to step around his hulking comrade as Assad
reached under his pillow. Kane clamped the man's arm and secured
the pistol with ease, holding it in the air for the others to see.

They froze, dumbfounded by the sight of the firearm and equally
surprised by the seeming frailty of Assad. He was very old and wast-

ing away. His arms jutted from his sleeveless T-shirt as thin as sticks and mottled with liver spots. This was not how they had pictured the enemy. Someone with the grizzled face of Arafat was what they had expected; a hook-nosed Arab with fiery eyes and checkered kaffiyeh on his head. They had not sought their grandfather, ancient and embarrassing to behold in his semi-nakedness.

But Assad did not view himself as a relic, nor had he lived this long without a powerful will to live. He threw his free arm around Kane's neck and tried to choke him, still struggling with his other hand for the gun. Kane dug backwards with an elbow into the old man's ribs and as Assad gasped and loosened his grip, Kane pivoted and drove the elbow into his face.

"Help me," Kane said.

The others hung back. Kane grabbed the stunned Assad from behind, locking his fingers behind the old man's neck, and lifted him from the bed. Blood spilled from Assad's mouth as he moaned in pain.

"Help me with him," Kane repeated.

Howard looked nervously from Kane to Assad. The old man seemed so helpless, Kane so much in control. But Assad had gone for a gun, he would have shot them. He was PLO.

Kane's eyes caught Howard's and fixed him, demanding action. They had discussed this scene privately in the apartment. Kane had explained the need for Howard's dynamic leadership in just such situations. It was only his unwavering leadership that could bind them together and allow them to do the things they must do for the Brotherhood to succeed. Howard knew that, he agreed with it. Kane could only assist him in these things, Howard must play the leading role. There was no question about this. A leader had to lead, or he would be quickly supplanted by someone else who would. And none of the others were worthy, Howard had not needed Kane to convince him of that.

Howard stood directly in front of Assad as Kane held him upright. Up close, the old man did not look so harmless. His eyes burned with hatred.

"You don't know us," said Howard. "But we are your worst nightmare."

"Scum," the old man said.

"We are Zion's revenge. Tell the world, old man, that it is no longer safe for your kind. We are the Brotherhood of Zion, we are the avengers. We will find you wherever you hide and we will root you out and we will expose you to the world. We will punish you. You may never strike with impunity again.''

And then the hard part. Wincing even before he landed the blow, Howard struck the old man across the face.

"PLO," Howard said, as a curse.

He stood back and gestured to Borodin. For a second Borodin did not understand what was expected, then he stepped up eagerly.

"PLO," Borodin said.

The old man tried to spit as Borodin lifted his fist, but his lip was swollen from Kane's elbow and saliva and blood dribbled down his chin just as Borodin smashed his fist into Assad's face.

Kane felt the old man go and knew he was finished after Borodin's blow, but he kept him upright in his grip, clutching his hair to keep his head from sagging onto his chest. One by one the others stepped up to take their turn, each spitting out the word "PLO" as they struck the old man.

As the others proceeded to ransack the office, Kane dropped the old man back on the bed.

"Let them know who we are," Howard said, nodding agreement as Hart sprayed "B.Z." on the wall. For good measure Howard scrawled "Never Again," and "B.Z." on a sheet of paper torn from a book and put the note on the old man's chest.

Bobby Lewis was kneeling by the bed, searching for Assad's pulse. Howard looked at Lewis quizzically. He didn't want anyone dead. Roughed up was one thing, but a killing was too much. PLO or not. Sworn enemy of his people or not. He and Kane had discussed the matter at length. They had agreed that violence had its purpose, but murder was out of the question.

"He's all right," said Bobby. "His pulse is strong, he's breathing okay."

Howard sighed with relief. The old man's face looked like hell, but it was a very small price to pay for a lifetime of plotting against Israel. The trick was to keep reminding oneself of that justification and not simply respond to the sight of a frail old man who had been badly battered.

Kane was at Howard's side. He pressed Assad's gun into Howard's hand. Startled, Howard nearly dropped the weapon before putting it into his pocket. It was right that he should take it, of course. He would decide what to do with it later, but he could hardly leave it behind for the old terrorist to shoot them in the back.

And he was still capable. One of his eyes opened and glared at them with hatred. The other eyelid had been hit by a ring and had swollen already to the size of a golf ball.

The old man swore at them in Arabic and tried again to spit.

"Is it time to go?" Kane asked.

"Yes," said Howard. He forced himself to look directly in Assad's face again as he leaned over the bed. "The Brotherhood of Zion," he said, raising his voice because the old man looked so battered. "Tell them we are the avengers. Tell them who did this to you."

Wiener grinned broadly as the others came out of the mosque, making no attempt to hide his relief.

"Did you do it? Can we go?"

"We split up now in case the police get onto us," said Howard. "Each of us will get home separately. They'll be looking for a group, they won't bother us singly." Howard glanced at Kane, who nodded imperceptibly. It was the plan they had agreed on.

"We're going to be all over the newspapers and television tomorrow," Howard continued. "But just lie low and don't start bragging to people that you're the ones who did this. We want them to fear and respect the Brotherhood, but we don't want them to know who we are. You all know this, right? Take off now, I'll be in touch."

They dispersed into the quiet Brooklyn night. Kane squeezed Howard's shoulder once, giving his silent approval and support for a job well done, then turned and walked swiftly away from him.

Kane walked half a block, glanced behind him, and saw Howard making his way toward the subway station. Kane stepped out of sight into a doorway until Howard was gone, then he sprinted back to the mosque. He did not fear the police. Assad's status in the country was too shaky for him to risk involvement with the police, which also meant no publicity. Sulamein bin Assad had not survived to his age by broadcasting his presence to the world. Alive, he would bring them no publicity. A defaced mosque might get them thirty seconds on television, but that was not at all what Kane had in mind.

Assad had managed to get to his feet by the time Kane reentered the room. He was still punching a number into the telephone with a shaky hand when Kane kicked his knee and knocked him to the floor. Kane hung up the phone and paused to look down at the old man. The fire had gone from his eyes and had been replaced for the first time with fear. He had withstood the group assault with contempt, but the sudden presence of one man alone meant something very different. This one was no bumbler or speech maker. Assad recognized his own kind.

"Who are you?" Assad asked, but he did not really expect the man to waste time talking to him. He was right.

Howard had been in bed for only three minutes before he heard Kane let himself into the apartment. He lay on his bed, listening as Kane went about the business of preparing for sleep. The shower ran for a long time. The toilet flushed. Howard knew that he himself would not sleep for hours, if at all. He had no desire to close his eyes and see Assad's distorted face. But he did not want to be with anyone else, either. If Myra had been awake, he would have talked to her. He might not have told her what he had done. No, he definitely would not have told her, because although, on balance, he was very proud of his actions, he knew she would not sympathize. But he would have talked to her, anyway. She calmed him, she comforted him with her presence. She loved him, he knew it and he felt it, and there were times when he was certain she was the only one who ever would for the rest of his life. Until Kane came alone. He thought maybe Kane loved him, too, in a way. Not in the same way, of course. It was as much hero worship as love, perhaps. There was an indisputable element of that in Kane's affection, but more, too, Howard thought. He is really fond of me; he values me for myself. Still, Howard would have talked to Myra tonight, not Kane.

He heard doors close and then the sound of footsteps in the living room. He wondered what Kane was doing out there in the middle of the night.

Kane wrapped the towel loosely around his waist so that it would fall if he nudged it. The living room was peaceful and very quiet. At the height of thirty-four floors, little of the street noise penetrated, at least not at this hour of the night when honking and sirens were greatly reduced. Howard made no sound in his room and Kane knew he would be lying on his bed, staring at the ceiling or the paraphernalia of the

Brotherhood. Adrenaline took a long time to subside completely. Kane himself was still high from it and he was as tolerant of it as any long-time abuser; he could just imagine the jolt Howard had received tonight. If he slept by morning he would be lucky.

But it was not Howard Kane was concerned with. He moved across the room toward Myra's door, then passed in front of it as if going to the bookshelf. It was open just a crack. He pressed himself against the wall just next to her door, out of her sight but close enough to hear her. After a moment he heard her move slightly, trying to see him from another angle, and then he smelled her. She used a light perfume, or perhaps just a powder. It had the familiar odor of talc with a hint of some flowery fragrance added. And who was she wearing this for? Kane smiled to himself. Not for brother Howard, that's for sure.

She was still up and waiting for him. Good girl. She had gotten used to their little meetings quickly.

Kane took a book from the shelf and returned to Myra's view. As he had the night before, he paused at the telescope and looked into the eyepiece. The angle was as he had left it, and the United Nations plaza sprang clear to his eye. With just a touch of the control the focus was as sharp as a rifle sight.

There was nothing new for him to see now. He would need bodies, traffic, the constant flow of humanity in and out of the U.N. before he could make further plans and adjustments. That would come by day, and tonight he could feel Myra's eyes on him as he posed by the telescope. He eased his elbow back while pretending to adjust the controls and nudged the towel, which obligingly fell to the floor. He could sense her intake of breath.

Kane glanced at the book in the glow of the window, riffled a few pages, and changed his mind. He walked toward the bookshelf again, toward Myra's door. He passed within inches of the door and his naked flesh responded to the heat coming from her room.

Almost, Myra, he thought. You could reach out and touch it, couldn't you? Almost. But not tonight. Howard is awake tonight and I'm not sure you want it enough quite yet. But soon, little girl, soon.

The silence from the living room lasted too long for Howard's curiosity. He rolled from bed and eased the door of his room open a crack. His first thought was gratitude that Myra was asleep and did not see Kane standing stark naked in the glow of the street moon with an erection so stiff it looked painful.

His second thought was something very different and new to him. It troubled him and excited him and disgusted him. But he could not look away and as his breath became shallower and shallower he grew almost dizzy with excitement.

14

On the shuttle flight from Washington to New York City, Becker telephoned McKinnon, who, as usual, was in his office before his assistants.

"I've decided to stay on the case," Becker said.

"Excellent."

"But I'll need some help."

"Hatcher will give you whatever you need . . ."

"No," said Becker. "I mean help with the problem we discussed before."

"Ah, yes. Gold told me you had stopped by."

"Not Gold. I think I can work this out with the assistance of a fellow agent."

McKinnon paused. "You found someone who understands?"

"I think so. I think she can help. I think I can help her at the same time."

"I see," said McKinnon warily. He waited for Becker to continue, but he was not in any doubt as to his decision. He would give Becker what he wanted, however unorthodox it may sound. Becker was on the case because he could accomplish what an army of Hatchers could not, and bending rules, particularly in Terrorism, was more the rule than the exception.

"I want you to assign Agent Karen Crist to this case and send her to New York," Becker said.

"It's done," said McKinnon.

"Thank you."

"You do understand it might raise a few eyebrows," McKinnon said.

"She is an agent."

"I'm not arguing, John. You're the best judge of the situation and what you need. I'm merely reminding you of realities."

"I've thought about it," said Becker. "I know it has its risks."

"I'm thinking of Agent Crist, as well," said McKinnon.

"Yes." Becker paused. "Ask her if she'll volunteer."

"And if she won't?"

"Would you stay in Fingerprinting and Documents if you had a way out? She's eager to work for you."

"Eagerness and frustration make for incautious decisions. I will do whatever you want, John, but I think it's my duty to ask if you're sure you're doing what is best for this young woman."

"I'm not certain of anything."

"Well, that's candid. I'm not asking for iron-clad certainty. I just want to be sure you've thought it through."

"I have. I think it will be good for her as well."

"Then she's on her way," said McKinnon.

"One other favor," Becker said.

"Of course."

"Let me tell Hatcher."

"It's going to put his nose seriously out of joint," McKinnon said.

"That's why I want to do it," Becker said.

McKinnon replaced the telephone and arched back into his chair. It had been an interesting call with which to start the day, even though it had ended on a disappointing note. McKinnon had no idea how the young woman would be of any help to Becker beyond the obvious, salacious assumption, but McKinnon didn't care if Becker resorted to magic crystals or communing with dolphins. The disappointment had come when Becker requested to tell Hatcher. McKinnon had rather looked forward to doing that himself.

Becker was greeted at LaGuardia by two New York City policemen and an FBI agent holding a sign bearing Becker's name.

"Good news," said the FBI man after identifying himself to Becker. "We've got a murder."

"Oh, that is good news," Becker said wryly. The irony was wasted on the other agent.

"The perp killed an old man in Brooklyn. We thought you'd like to go there right away."

"What better way to start the day."

One of the cops chuckled and the agent looked around, puzzled, afraid he'd missed something.

"You're going to like this part," the agent continued. "The victim was killed by a sharp instrument introduced into his ear canal."

"Polite, isn't he?" Becker asked.

The cop laughed loudly this time, and the agent turned to look at him as if he were demented.

"What?"

"Introducing the instrument, that's polite," Becker explained.

"Oh, yes," said the agent.

"It's a pun."

"Yes, I do see that."

"Not very funny, though," said Becker.

"Perhaps not," said the agent.

"You're not related to Hatcher by any chance?"

"No, but Deputy Director Hatcher is in town. He said he'd meet with you after you'd been to the crime scene. He thought you'd be pleased to hear the news."

"Delighted," said Becker.

The agents followed the policemen, who spirited Becker through the crowds and into a waiting patrol car.

"Deputy Director Hatcher said you had requested to be advised of any assaults that used this M.O. I'd say this was a very good start," the agent said.

"This is a strange profession," Becker said.

"Pardon me?"

"I don't think even undertakers get this happy about a murder."

"No one is really *happy*, of course."

"Ah, well, what is happiness?" Becker asked.

"I don't follow."

"Philosophy," said Becker.

The agent regarded Becker oddly.

"Who was the victim?" Becker asked.

The agent cleared his throat and hesitated. "That's a matter of some embarrassment," he said at last.

Becker was driven to the mosque in Brooklyn, where he briefly studied the crime scene. The body had already been efficiently removed and hustled to the autopsy, but the basic story was easy enough to read from the chalk outline on the floor. The old man had put up quite a struggle, Becker thought. Still, the killer had gone to the trouble to hug his victim close, to immobilize him, to do it the way he loved to do it. It was more dangerous for the killer that way, but the agent had been clear enough. A sharp instrument introduced into the ear canal. With a victim who was fighting back, the killer was exposing himself to harm to get that close.

"It must be one hell of a sensation," Becker said aloud, to no one in particular.

The cops then drove Becker to see Hatcher. The agent who had met Becker at the airport watched him go. He shrugged, unimpressed. He had heard of Becker's record but had seen nothing special about the man unless you counted irreverence special. The agent thought it a detriment, himself. He did not envy Hatcher his task in dealing with Becker.

Nor did Hatcher.

"Did we know Assad was in the country?" Becker asked without preamble.

Hatcher had learned not to expect the normal courtesies from Becker.

"We knew," he said uncomfortably. "He came into the country about eighteen months ago, just walked in, visa in hand, quite legally. Somebody blinked, didn't see him."

"Was he on the State Department list of persona non grata?"

"Of course. Somebody at Immigration just screwed up."

"Somebody screwed up when they gave him a visa in the first place," said Becker. They sat in the New York FBI headquarters at Federal Plaza in an office that had been hurriedly cleared for them.

"He got it in our embassy in Greece. He said he was coming for medical treatment—which was true. Apparently he's dying—was dying. Something about the blood, I don't know. It wasn't hard believing his story. Some clerk, somebody, just didn't check him out thoroughly enough."

"So we let a member of the PLO executive council come to live in Brooklyn."

"Ex-member of the executive council," Hatcher said.

"If there is such a thing as an ex-member."

"He had been inactive for three or four years because of his health," said Hatcher.

"He was active enough for someone to want him dead," Becker pointed out. "When did we learn he was here?"

"A year ago, little more. After he'd been here for several months. Getting him out looked too embarrassing. He had come in legally, he was old, he was sick, he was living in a mosque and giving classes in religion . . ."

"And we would have had to go to court to extradite him and look like inhumane incompetents in the process, right?"

"Something like that," Hatcher agreed.

"Do we have the full autopsy yet?"

Hatcher tapped a manila folder.

"And?"

"He was beaten, a broken rib, hairline fracture of the jaw, contusions, et cetera." Hatcher paused, reluctant to give Becker the plum. Becker flipped open the folder. "But the cause of death was a sharp object introduced into the brain. Apparently it was one of those spikes on a base you use for putting bills on. They found one in the room. The people at the mosque say it wasn't theirs. The assailant must have picked one up from a deli counter somewhere. We're checking on it."

"Bahoud," said Becker.

"Maybe."

"Roger Bahoud."

Hatcher shrugged. "It might be coincidence. What's this graffiti? What's B.Z.?"

"I don't know. But it's Bahoud."

"If we assume it was, then we've missed him, haven't we? He's probably in South America by now, spending his millions on the beach."

"The money's still in the banks, I checked . . . I'm not sure this is what he's here for."

"Why not?"

"Was Assad worth two million dollars? He was a dying old man. Why not just let him die and save yourself some money?"

"Revenge. Sending a message, something like that."

"Possibly. What's the message, who's sending it to whom?"

"Who wants the PLO dead? The Israelis, of course."

"This is not the Mossad's style," said Becker. "They'd love to take a PLO exec alive. Show trials are more their style."

"Oh, come on, Becker. There are bodies all over the world the Mossad have left strewn around like so many bread crumbs. Those guys take an eye for an eye every chance they get."

"But not this publicly. And not in this country. They might blow up an office in Tunis, they might make a raid in Algeria . . ."

"Or Greece, or England. I could cite you at least four murders off the top of my head . . ."

"All right," Becker conceded.

"You just don't like the obvious. How are they going to kidnap somebody from the U.S. without pissing off their primary—hell, their only ally. Snatch a Nazi or two from Bolivia or Argentina, fine, but they're not going to flaunt our laws that publicly. Privately, sure they do, constantly. But we're talking about international headlines for months if they kidnap someone from our jurisdiction. We're talking about the president making noises about shutting off the five billion annual aid budget. Maybe even losing the vote of a congressman or two."

"Probably not."

"No, probably not. But still, there would be so much flak . . ."

"So you think they hired a killer to come in, spray graffiti, desecrate a mosque, recruit a gang of vandals. Why not just do the guy and make him disappear? Why all the fuss?"

"Sending a message, as I said. It's clear enough, isn't it? 'PLO Must Pay,' 'Never Again.' That's the message. The graffiti part? To avoid exactly the kind of incident we've been talking about. Blame it on good old 'B.Z.,' whatever that is. That way we don't blame the Mossad. Or at least the press doesn't blame the Mossad, which is the point, after all."

"I don't like it," said Becker.

"Why not?"

"Would the Mossad hire a sociopath like Bahoud when they have plenty of politically motivated and dependable assassins willing to do it for patriotism alone? Why waste the money? It's not as if it were a tough assignment. Anyone could have walked in and done Assad at any time. Two million dollars buys a lot of expertise. More than two million, of course. Probably at least four million."

"Why?"

"Would you pay a hired killer everything in advance? You wouldn't even pay a baby-sitter in advance. He's getting another payment when his job is done, you can be sure."

"His job is done," said Hatcher.

"I don't think so," said Becker. "But it will be soon."

"What makes you think that?"

"He's too careless. Bahoud is a terrorist, not a criminal. He's leaving too many clues behind, and that's because he knows it doesn't matter. He doesn't care if we get onto him eventually, which means he's not going to be around by the time we do. Clues don't do you any good if the man has hit and vanished. Whatever he's going to do, he'll do soon."

Becker rose and scraped back his chair, ending the working session.

"By the way, Hatcher. You'd better get another desk in here. I've asked McKinnon to send some help."

"You asked—you asked McKinnon for help? I'm your help, for, God's sake!"

"No need to take it personally. This will assist me in getting the job done."

"You're supposed to go through me! Any requests go through me! You can't just go to McKinnon whenever you feel like it."

"McKinnon didn't seem to mind," said Becker.

"You're doing this to get me, aren't you?" Hatcher demanded. "You've never liked me for some reason, I don't know why. I've bent over backwards to be decent to you, but you've always held something against me. It's my rapid advancement, isn't it? You hate it because I've gotten ahead so fast."

"Try deep breaths," Becker said. "You're changing colors."

"You think McKinnon will read your ploy as suggesting my incompetence, don't you? Well, you're wrong. He's too smart for that."

"He is smart," Becker said, smiling. "That's why he's sending Agent Crist."

"Who the hell is Agent Crist? I've never heard of him."

"From Fingerprinting."

"Fingerprinting? Why are you bringing someone from—I don't know any Agent Crist—that girl?"

"Woman."

"Jesus Christ!"

"Keep breathing," Becker said.

Hatcher did indeed keep breathing. After four deep breaths and several seconds' pause, he asked, "Why—just off hand—why do you need a fingerprinting expert?"

"That's not her area of expertise I'm after," said Becker. "And that is not a set-up line for you."

"May I inquire what line of expertise you are after from Agent Crist?"

"If we were hunting an embezzler, Hatcher, or a forger, or organized crime, you would be competent enough."

"Thank you."

"But we're hunting a killer, a man who does it for a living, or for fun, or both. That's a different category of mind. Or soul, if you like. He thinks—and feels—on a wavelength entirely different than yours, Hatcher."

"Thank God."

"Yes, indeed, be grateful. You have certain skills, and they're fine for ordinary work. For this kind of person, you need other skills. A deeper understanding."

"I thought that's what you brought to the case," Hatcher said.

"It is. I think Agent Crist might have it to, although she may not realize it yet."

"And you're going to help her find out?"

"Something like that."

"Sweet," said Hatcher. "I always like to see an experienced man reaching down to help the younger ones. Is there anything she can help you with in return?"

"Yes, as a matter of fact, I think there is. McKinnon thinks so, too."

"McKinnon has more interests than I realized."

Becker stood directly in front of Hatcher's face, his expression tight and threatening.

"If you smirk, Hatcher, at any time—when she gets here, now, later, any time—if you smirk even once, I will feed it to you. Do you understand me?"

Hatcher took a step backwards and smiled very carefully. "Shall we get on with things?" he said. He made every effort that the smile did not become a smirk.

15

Howard woke her with a tapping at her door. She was surprised to find herself asleep; she felt as if she had lain awake all night long, unable even to close her eyes. Myra knew that she had stayed up for a least an hour after Kane went to his room, glued to the door, hoping for his return. He didn't come back, of course. Once he had his book, there was no reason to, but she could not stop herself from hoping. And then when she finally fell upon her bed she still had lain there for what seemed forever, running the scene over and over and over in her mind. Kane's naked body, lean and hard with muscle, moving so lightly, so gracefully yet with such power.

Howard entered her room and sat on her bed. He was dressed for work, but his face was puffy and his eyes bleary. He could not have slept enough himself, Myra thought. She had heard him come home just minutes before Kane. They had been out with the ''Brotherhood,'' she knew, doing whatever goonish thing they did late at night. Baying at the moon, probably, she thought.

Before Kane had arrived in their lives, Myra always had breakfast together with Howard. It was one of her favorite times—and his too, she thought. He was always calmer in the morning before the day had stirred up his paranoia, before new events brought forth new demons. He was more tractable in the morning, and they would often have conversations that were almost fun. It was as close as he ever got to being silly. By evening when he returned from work he would be as dark and threatening as thunder, brooding over slights from his boss, his co-workers, the world as manifested in the events of the newspaper.

Since Kane, however, Myra had stayed in her room until they both were gone for the day. She had not realized how she missed their breakfasts together until she found Howard sitting on her bed.

"Listen, Myra, we have to do something."

"About what?"

"Kane."

"What about Kane," she asked cautiously.

"I . . . I think we ought to ask him to go."

"Why?" She was startled but struggled to keep it out of her voice. She knew she must be careful not to let Howard know of her fascination with Kane. She was certain he would not understand.

She changed her tone of voice. "I thought you were getting along fine."

"We're getting along okay."

"He's helpful in the Brotherhood, isn't he? You told me he was."

"Yeah, he's helpful. He's more than helpful."

"Then why do you want him to leave?"

"For your sake," said Howard.

Oh, my poor benighted brother, she thought. If we're doing it for my sake, let's strip Kane naked and lock him in the living room. I'll leave a trail of crumbs leading to my bedroom.

"I don't mind him," she said calmly.

"It's not fair to you," he said.

"I don't mind."

"You're living in your room like a hermit."

"I don't mind the inconvenience as long as he's helpful to you."

"I can't allow you to make that sacrifice," he said.

Now this was very strange, Myra thought. Neither of them was given to self-sacrifice for the other, but now they sounded like some strange version of O'Henry's "The Gift of the Magi."

"I don't think it's healthy for you," Howard continued, and there was something in his choice of terms that made her realize he was troubled in a way he couldn't talk about.

"Of course it's healthy," she said. "Don't be silly. The air in here is the same as it is in there. I still get my exercise vaulting around the apartment when Kane leaves during the day. What's unhealthy about it?"

"I don't mean it that way."

"How do you mean it?"

Howard couldn't look at her. He studied the far wall, displaying an unusual interest in the items on her vanity table. To her surprise he

touched her bare arm. Howard was not a toucher, and only with reluctance did he allow her to give him an embrace. Sometimes when
he had his headaches he would have Myra massage his temples and
the thick, corded muscles of his neck and shoulders but even that only
briefly before he shrugged her off.

"I don't think he's good for you, okay? I mean, why are we arguing? He's my friend, I brought him in here. It was a mistake, so
I've decided he's got to go."

She carefully said nothing. There was an agenda there which she
did not know. It was never wise to attack Howard head-on in any
event. He was easily enough led by indirection, but confrontation was
a mistake. He was too insecure to be bucked; he would fight irration-
ally if she presented him with a simple no.

"He's not . . . There's something . . . I don't know," he said, struggling. Myra could tell he knew but didn't want to say. "I think there's
something—perverted about him."

"Perverted?"

"You wouldn't understand," he insisted. "I just don't think it's a
good influence for you to have him around."

"Howard, I'm a grown woman. What threat could his influence be
to me?"

"You're grown, but you don't know anything about life. Just trust
me."

He was so uneasy that Myra thought he must be talking about sex.
He was blushing; he still refused to look at her. Could he know about
her voyeurism? How would he know?

"I'm afraid something might happen," he said.

Myra was afraid that something might not, but she dared not say
anything now. She would have to find a subtler way.

"I think we have to tell him to go," he said, and Myra realized he
meant *she* would have to tell him to go. "The problem is, I can't do
it because of the Brotherhood. I'm his commander, you see, and I
can't just suddenly tell him I don't want him living here anymore.
That would antagonize him and, Myra, we can't afford to lose him
now. Maybe in a little while, but not now. We're really starting to do
things now, things are really coming together. Pretty soon, sooner than
you think, we're going to be known, I mean *known,* and we'll be able
to get all the members we want. Then maybe we can let him go, but
not yet."

Myra knew her role and determined to play it while looking for a way to change it.

"Do you want me to tell him to leave?"

"He can't very well argue with you, can he? I mean, this is your apartment, too."

"What excuse should I give?"

"Tell him it makes you uneasy to have him around. Don't hurt his feelings or anything, don't get him mad, just tell him you want the place to yourself again. For God's sake, he'll understand. I'll tell him I tried to talk you out of it but you insisted."

"All right," she said, smiling inwardly at the notion of Kane's making her uneasy. Uneasy hardly did justice to the way he made her feel.

Howard was so relieved he kissed her, another fairly rare occurrence and performed awkwardly, self-consciously. And then Howard was gone and Myra was left to ponder what to do.

Mr. Henley had called and asked to come over with a rush order. The afternoon sun was streaming through the windows and the apartment was getting hot. Myra had unbuttoned her blouse to the navel but not to seduce Mr. Henley this time, and she would be sure to button it to the collar when he came. She had dressed very simply this time in slacks and blouse. No siren, she.

There was a sound at the door. It could not be Henley, he had not been announced by the doorman. Kane walked in. He had never been home this early. It was the first time she had seen him face to face since the day he arrived.

"You left the door unlocked," he said. "That's dangerous."

"A client is coming," she said.

"There are dangerous people in this city," he said. She expected him to go to his room, but he took a chair from the dining room table and straddled it backward, facing her.

"Yes, I read about them," Myra said.

She tried to return to her work. She felt her face was flush with embarrassment, or was it excitement? The first few lines she typed were filled with errors and she backed up and did them all again, grateful that he could not see what she was doing from where he was sitting.

"It's nice to see you," he said.

"Yes. We've been managing to miss each other," she said, glancing at him to show the bare minimum of politeness before continuing her work.

"I thought you might be avoiding me," he said. There was a trace of irony in his voice. He was taunting her, she thought.

"Why would I do that?"

"I don't know. I thought maybe you didn't like me."

"I don't really know you at all," she said, her eyes on the terminal. "I can't have an opinion one way or another."

"Really? I feel as if I'm being watched all the time."

She looked at him. How did he mean it? Did he know about her at night? Did that mean he was doing it *for* her? Did it mean—what did it mean?

"What do you mean?"

She looked back at her work, afraid to see his face when he answered, but he did not answer. She heard only the sound of her fingers on the keys. The silence stretched. Finally she looked at him again.

He had been waiting for her. His look was one of knowing irony that suddenly blossomed into the warmest smile she had ever seen. More than warm, it radiated something from him, something that seemed to pierce her and touch her deep inside. She tried not to shiver.

Myra found herself smiling back. His eyes were smiling too, his whole being seemed to exude—what? Something more than charm. Something more than warmth. He had locked his eyes onto hers and for the moment she couldn't look away.

"I had hoped we'd get to know each other better," he said.

"Why?" she blurted out.

"Because the first time I met you I sensed something that I wanted to get to know."

"What did you sense?"

Again he smiled. It was not just the beauty of the smile, it was the disarming sincerity of it. And something else.

"Someone lonely, someone with much to give—and no one to give it to. Maybe I'm wrong, or maybe I'm projecting. I feel that way myself, so maybe I'm just putting my feelings onto you."

Myra didn't know what to say. He could not have described her more succinctly. How could she reply?

His eyes moved down for a second, then back to her face, and she realized that she had not buttoned her blouse.

The intercom blared. She could not get to her feet and limp to it in front of Kane.

"Would you get that, please?" she asked. "It's Mr. Henley. Just tell them to send him up."

Kane crossed to the door and Myra frantically buttoned her blouse, but he turned back before she had finished and caught her.

"Why don't you send him away?" he asked.

"Send him away?"

"I'd like to . . . talk some more." ·

But he meant more than talk, didn't he? Did he? Myra's imagination had made a fool of her so many times. And if he did mean more than talk? She was suddenly terrified. She had sat in front of him with her blouse open to her navel; naturally he thought she was offering herself. And she had been, in her heart at least. But now her bluff was called. What if he wanted to take her, she thought. What if he wanted to send Henley away so that he could spend the afternoon loving her? Or just as bad, what if he didn't? What if he only talked? The one prospect was suddenly too scary, the other too frustrating.

"I'm afraid I have to see him," she said. "He won't be long. We can talk afterwards, if you like."

But she could see that the ardor had already left his eyes. He told the doorman to send Henley up.

A glaze of politeness covered his face now.

"He's a lucky man to have you so devoted to him," he said. "Howard didn't tell me you had such good friends."

"Oh, no, no. He's not a friend." She knew she was too quick to say that. "He's just a writer, not a very good one, I don't think. He supports himself working for the government or something."

A flicker of interest in Kane's eyes. He was moving toward his room but now he stopped.

"He works for the government?"

"I think so. He writes in his spare time. I think that's all he does in his spare time."

"Which government? New York City?"

"The federal government, I think. I'm not sure. I could ask."

Kane seemed to freeze for just a fraction, as if his mind were caught in a strobe light and she could see one thought in transition.

"If it comes up. I always wondered where writers get their inspiration."

"You could stay and talk to him, if you like."

"I don't want to intrude."

"He'd probably be flattered," she said. It would probably be the first time anyone had ever shown any interest in Mr. Henley at all, Myra thought, the poor man. If one excluded her misguided attempts to seduce him, that is.

"No," said Kane. "He probably looks forward to his visits with you."

"This isn't a regular visit," she said. "It's a last-minute urgent thing."

Again the barest flicker of hesitation from Kane. But then it was gone and nothing showed on his face but the sheen of courtesy.

"I'll leave you to it," he said and stepped into his room.

Myra did not hear the door click shut, although it appeared to be closed. Her imagination was running away with her again. She had just gone through a whole flush of fantasy, she told herself. Kane was being polite to his hostess, earning his keep with a few kind words of flattery, that's all. All the rest was her projection, not his, she thought.

Then Henley was in the room, wearing his usual dour expression of self-concern.

She inquired about his play.

"These are all rewrites," he said, brandishing a sheaf of papers. She could see the deletions and handwritten changes from where she sat.

"The producer wants a clean script by tomorrow. He's an idiot, an idiot. He's ruining my play. And do you know why? Because it's too expensive! He knew that when he read it! He knew that when he agreed to do it! All of a sudden I have to take out a character so we can pay one less actor. I have to take out the character of Annie. Do you remember her? She's my favorite!"

"Mine too," she lied. She didn't remember any of the characters.

"It's a small part, sure, but it's important. I had to give all her lines to the doctor. It makes no sense, but it's cheaper . . . What do you think?"

Myra had no idea what he meant.

"Should I have done it? Do you think I'm selling out?"

"No."

"It's not like I had any choice. God, the theater is so depressing. It's all about money, you know."

"I know," she said sympathetically.

He sighed, blowing the air up through his mustache.

"Do you think you can do it?" He riffled the pages in front of her face. "It seems like a lot, but it's really not. You've got it all on a disc anyway, don't you? It shouldn't take you too long."

"By tomorrow?" She studied the sheets for a moment. "I can do it."

Henley was greatly relieved and relaxed for the first time.

"Thank God."

He sat in the chair Kane had occupied. Now he wanted to talk. What was going on here today, Myra wondered.

"So how are you?" he asked as if he had just noticed her sitting there. "Everything okay?"

"Fine. How are your friends at work reacting to your success?" she asked.

"At work?"

"Don't you work for the government?"

"I didn't know I told you about my work," he said.

"You mentioned it once," she said.

He nodded slowly, trying to remember.

"I don't usually talk about it," he said, more to himself than to Myra.

"Ooooh, very hush-hush," she teased.

"Not really," he said. "Just very boring." He glanced around the room.

"Your voice sounded very different on the intercom today," he said in a non sequitur as abrupt as her own.

"What do you mean?"

"When I was in the lobby and the doorman rang you? You sounded like a man when you said to send me up."

Myra lowered her voice. "Oh, really?" she growled. "I have to stop those hormone shots."

He smiled, but he was not amused. He scanned the room once again.

"I thought you had company," he said.

"I have a brother," Myra said and was amazed at herself. Why was she lying? She didn't know, but suddenly she realized she didn't want Henley to know about Kane living there any more than she wanted Kane to know about the strained social relationship she had, or nearly had, with Henley.

Myra looked toward Kane's room and the door that may or may not have been closed. If he was listening—and why should he be?—what would he make of her response? She didn't know what to make of it herself.

"I didn't know that," said Henley, and he seemed relieved. Again, her imagination was running amuck.

"There's no reason you should know," she said, "unless you're studying me."

"That's right," said Mr. Henley. "I work for the FBI. I need to know all about your subversive activities."

He smiled wanly. Even he was not amused by his joke.

They chatted for another minute, but the mood was strained. To tell the truth, she thought, she did not know how to relate to Mr. Henley except as the temptress and that, God knew, was hardly appropriate anymore. They were no longer quite in a strictly business relationship, but Myra couldn't keep showing her cleavage and batting her eyes at the man anymore, either. They had never had a friendly relationship. She didn't really know how to make it work.

Mr. Henley left, leaving Myra to decipher his rewrites. She began to work at once, trying to ignore Kane's door. Was he naked in his room? Was he striding back and forth, hugely erect, fantasizing about her? Did he lurk there, waiting for a sign from Myra, a word, the crook of a finger, before he burst forth and lifted her into his arms and laid her on the dining room table and ravished her there on her mother's polished oak?

Howard was right, he must go. He is not good for me, she thought. He forced her to confront the truth about herself. She was all desire and no will. She was spineless. My character is more deformed than my body, she thought.

Kane startled her when he suddenly emerged from his room. He glanced at her, smiled mildly, then disappeared into the kitchen. She heard a drawer open. He rummaged about, but the sounds were too muffled to be silverware clanking against each other. He was in the tool drawer with the screwdrivers and string, she thought. Maybe he was looking for rope with which to tie her to the bed.

Then he was out of the kitchen but there was nothing in his hands. He walked to the door, ignoring her, but then stopped and stared at her for a moment. The intensity of his look confused her and she returned to her work. He came to her, stood in front of her, forcing her by his presence to look up at him.

"You missed a button," he said and touched her blouse. Slowly, lingeringly, his fingers fastened a button on her chest.

Astoundingly, Myra let him do it. She did not move, she could not move. It was all she could do to breathe. His fingers were burning a hole in her chest, and she was nearly dizzy with the rush of blood. Her eyes fixed on his belt. She could not watch his fingers, she could not look in his face. It took forever in a moment and when he was finished he walked out the door. Myra was left alone to pant aloud with excitement and near panic.

He touched me, she thought. And then aloud, "He touched me."

16

In a police department uniformly understaffed, the New York City division with the worst workload was the Terrorism Squad. The potential for terrorist activity in the city was immense. Packed with virtually every ethnic group under the sun, possessing the nation's most important newspaper, the news headquarters of two television networks, consulates of every nation represented in Washington, and the United Nations itself, the city had all the elements necessary for a terrorism explosion of major proportions. And yet, oddly, there was very little activity. The fact that no major terrorism incident had ever taken place in the Big Apple had two significant effects on the Terrorism Squad. One, it had allowed the department to cut the squad's operating budget to cover little more than the payroll of the five full-time employees. Two, it had served to increase the anxiety level of those same five men. They saw the past history of non-activity not as an answer for the future but as the quiet before the storm. In their view, the longer the peace, the more violent the war to come.

In 1989 Captain Ed Genesse led the squad. By nature quiet and pleasant when dealing with his own men, he took on a more combative nature when talking to outside law enforcement agencies, most notably the FBI. It was an attitude with which Becker was familiar. Law enforcement was as much a matter of turf as it was crime prevention. Pride was involved, and budgets, and pecking orders.

At the moment, however, Genesse was being cooperative. It was easy to do because Becker had admitted to ignorance. Genesse was also ignorant of the issue at hand, but as this was his turf, he did not have to admit it so blatantly.

"I've got PLO, I've got Druse, I've got the JDL, I've got Croatian separatists, I've got Chinese tongs, I've got skinheads and neo-Nazis

and white separatists,'' Genesse said. "I've got—or I had—Sulamein
bin Assad. We knew he was here before the feds did.''

Hatcher smiled sourly. "Immigration let him in,'' said Hatcher.

"Right.'' Genesse waved vaguely in the direction of a bank of filing
cabinets that looked close to collapse from overloading. "I've got
anti-Castro Cubans, I've got Puerto Rican separatists, I've got a former Weatherman working on Wall Street, I've got IRA, and I've got
a British agent who is here unofficially to keep tabs on the IRA. I've
got communists of about a dozen different stripes and at least that
many anti-communist groups . . . '' Genesse paused for breath, inhal-
ing dramatically.

Hatcher moved into the pause. "The Bureau has all of those and a
good many more, as I'm sure you realize,'' he said dryly.

Genesse was not finished. "*Plus* I've got all the gangs in the city.
They gave me the gangs because they figured I didn't have enough
to do. And now, of course, I've got this *farblondjet* Year of the Children meeting at the U.N. Seventy-six world leaders. Seventy-six!
Whose idea was this? Washington's? Great, it doesn't happen in
Washington. It happens here. Any one of these groups can decide to
go after the leader of his choice. It's like a smorgasbord. Why don't
we sell tickets? All you can blow up for a buck.''

"You're doing an amazing job,'' said Becker. "I don't know how
you've managed to keep a lid on it all until now.''

Genesse was not averse to flattery when he was convinced it was
deserved. "Only by working my ass off.''

"What you don't have is somebody to get all this information into
the computer for you,'' Becker said, nodding toward the files.
"Hatcher, do you think we could spare a specialist just to help out
with the computerizing of all this valuable information?''

Hatcher, a past master at greasing his superiors, balked at doing it
with inferiors. He saw no point in rising through the ranks if one had
to still be patient and accommodating with the underlings. He could
not recall any of his bosses who had ever been solicitous of him.

"Perhaps,'' he said.

"Would you like somebody for a few weeks?'' Becker asked. "He
wouldn't interfere with procedure, of course.''

"Christ,'' said Genesse. "Would I like some help? Would I like
some budget slack? Would I like a promotion?''

"Hatcher will see what he can do for you," said Becker.

"God will reward you," said Genesse. "I certainly can't."

"You might tell us about 'B.Z.' " Hatcher said.

"Didn't I tell you? I thought I told you. I don't know who the hell they are. We talked to the B'nai Brith and some of the other Jewish groups. They never heard of them. They deplore their actions, they say such activity has no legitimate place in the Jewish community, blah, blah, blah. I mean, we're assuming this is a Jewish group that dusted Assad. The 'Never Again,' 'PLO Must Pay,' defacing the mosque. We talked to the Jewish Defense League. That kind of rhetoric is in their line of work, at least. They never heard of 'B.Z.' We hear nothing on the street. Whoever it is, they're new, which means they're small. Apparently they're nasty. They mean business."

"They've killed a man," Hatcher reminded him.

"I am aware," said Genesse. "That already puts them way ahead of most everybody else. All of those groups have killed people somewhere in the world, but not many of them operate that way in the city. Believe me, I want to know more about them as much as you do." Genesse paused.

Hatcher started to speak, but Becker cut him off with a glance.

"Now they may have transmuted, of course," said Genesse.

"How do you mean?"

"Started out one way, then switched into a different area. That happens sometimes. A lot of the student groups in the Sixties started peacefully, then grew more radical and violent as they went along."

Hatcher sniffed. "What you're saying, then, is you don't have anything at all on this B.Z."

"What I'm saying," said Genesse, "is that I got about as much on this B.Z. as you feds have got. But I ain't coming to you for help."

Becker laughed.

"I don't find that remark particularly funny," said Hatcher.

"No, I didn't think you would," said Becker. He turned to Genesse. "Captain, I won't lie to you. We don't know a damned thing. You can see that, and we're on your playing ground. You know the city in ways we couldn't ever hope to learn. We're in a real squeeze here; we don't have much time and frankly we're getting desperate. There's a man loose in the city we need very badly. I'm pretty sure he's connected to Assad's death, which means he's connected to B.Z. If there is such a thing. If it isn't just a smokescreen he created. If B.Z. is real, you'll hear about it eventually, probably sooner than later, right?''

"I'll hear about it,'' Genesse agreed.

"We need to know right away. Right away. We're at your mercy.''

Genesse shrugged. "No problem.''

"I'm counting on you,'' Becker said. "I know I couldn't be in better hands.''

Becker and Hatcher left Genesse with a promise to have the computer operator there the next day.

"I didn't picture you as the type to grovel,'' Hatcher said as they exited the police station.

"We need his cooperation,'' Becker said. "We don't need to remind him how grand we are.''

"He would cooperate anyway. That's his duty.''

"He would cooperate *eventually*. That's his duty. And eventually isn't soon enough for us. Bahoud isn't going to give us many openings, and they aren't going to last long. We have to act immediately or it will be too late.''

"You're worried,'' Hatcher said with some satisfaction. "I didn't know you had it in you.''

"Yeah, I'm worried. We don't know anything, we haven't got anything, Bahoud has all the cards, all the advantages. We don't have squat.''

"Sure we do,'' said Hatcher.

"What have we got?''

"We've got you,'' Hatcher said dryly.

"Funny.''

"Now who's lost his sense of humor?''

"This son of a bitch has now killed four people in a week. That kind of taxes your sense of humor, especially when you don't think you can stop him.''

"You've got a lot of respect for this Bahoud.''

"Respect isn't quite the word,'' said Becker. "He's very good, he kills easily, and he's got time on his side. But respect isn't the right word.''

"What is?''

"I don't know,'' said Becker. "I'm not a psychologist.''

"You feel something psychological about him, is that what you're saying?"

Becker shook his head with impatience. "You wouldn't begin to understand and I don't have the time to explain. Be sure to get a computer man to Captain Genesse right away."

"We can use Crist for the job," said Hatcher.

"No, we can't use Crist for the job. I've got other work for her to do."

"Uh-huh," said Hatcher.

Becker turned slowly to face Hatcher, but Hatcher had already pivoted and walked toward his waiting car.

17

Henley lived in a brownstone in a fourth floor walk-up apartment on West Eighty-sixth Street, less than half a block away from Riverside and the Hudson River. His apartment was technically considered a studio, but the designation was laughable to Henley when used to describe a twelve-by-eight-foot box with the bathroom in the hall to be shared with the other "studio" dwellers on his floor. To Henley the room had all the charm of a crypt, and not much more space. It was, however, all he could afford, and it had the one spectacular benefit of access to Riverside Park and the river. He would have died without the river, Henley thought.

Returning from his visit to Myra Goldsmith, Henley walked the stairs to his apartment with the notion of resuming his day's work, but once inside the door the oppressiveness of the room overwhelmed him. Turning on his heel, he went back down the stairs, past a man in the lobby seeking a name on the mail boxes, and out into the street. When he reached the river he stood for a moment with his face to the sun, his eyes closed. The sound of the river lapping against the rocks of the bank reassured him. They would have sounded the same anywhere in the world. He could be beside the Thames, the Ganges, an Alaskan stream, and the sound of water on rock would be the same. The scent of moisture would be the same, the coolness of the air blowing from the water would be the same. For the brief moment he was not in Manhattan and that, and that alone, was his relief from being in a city he had learned to despise with all the loathing of the healthy man for disease.

The sun was moving toward the artificial horizon of the buildings on the Jersey shore and Henley estimated that he had about three quarters of an hour left before dark. Walking was his exercise, his period for meditation, his entertainment. He walked to relieve stress, he walked to spur his imagination, he walked to observe humanity, and he walked to alleviate his crushing loneliness. He did not, however, walk at night. His state of mind had reached the point that he never felt safe while afoot anywhere in the city after dark. He avoided the world after sundown with the same superstitious terror of a medieval peasant shying from the forest. And virtually every morning the newspapers reaffirmed him in his wisdom as they printed stories of still more people being mugged everywhere, uptown and down, east side and west, in "good" sections and bad.

Henley started walking north. He would go as far as 100th Street while the light was still at its best and be back in the eighties when it started to fade. That way he could always sprint for home if need arose. Henley believed that flight, ostentatious flight, was the only defense against muggers. More than once he had broken into a run down the middle of the roadway when suspicious characters got too close. A mugger would not chase you down, he thought, because it would bring too much attention to himself. If he were more of an athlete, he would put on jogger's clothes and trot everywhere he went. The secret to survival, he was convinced, lay in keeping a sphere of unbreachable space around him. Twenty yards was a comfortable radius and if anyone came closer than that from behind when he was on the streets after dark, Henley would assess the threat, size up the potential mugger, and either change his course or break into a run. He did not particularly mind looking like an idiot running in the motorway amid the traffic. He would rather take his chances with the cars than the muggers.

Not everyone was a potential threat, of course. His paranoia had not reached that level. Like border police, he had a profile in his mind. Most people did not fit that profile, but in a city of millions, many, many did.

At a particular outcropping of rocks, Henley stepped over the railing and squatted atop the boulders. He had seen a family of water rats scurrying about in this area and he knew their nest was someplace close. He did not find the rats threatening because they were living outdoors. He assumed they found their sustenance from the river somehow, not from garbage cans or people's kitchens. Henley had convinced himself they were a different species of rodent than the one that filled the city dwellers' nightmares. Apart from the birds and a few squirrels, they were the only wild things living in the city and he felt a certain kinship with them. They, too, were living in a hole in stone amid dangerous neighbors.

If he stayed as he was for a moment or two, the rats would get used to him and go about their business openly. He looked warily around to see if his borders were secure. To the north a woman pushed a baby carriage and behind her the park was littered with people strolling on the grass or playing basketball. None were on the walk along the river's edge, however. To the south Henley saw a man standing on the walk, watching the ships go by. It took Henley a moment to remember where he had seen him before. He was the man Henley had passed in the lobby of his brownstone. Waiting, no doubt, for someone to return. The man did not fit Henley's profile, and Henley put him out of his mind.

Before long the rats appeared, scurrying through their errands, slipping in and out of the crevices of the rocks and occasionally pausing to turn a curious eye on Henley. He was far enough away not to present any imminent danger, but if he moved so much as one step closer they would dive for cover. He did not blame them; they had their safety zones and he respected that.

When he looked again Henley saw the man from the lobby coming toward him. Henley watched closely as the man passed on the other side of the railing and kept going north. He did not look at Henley, but Henley kept track of him until he was out of the danger zone. Even though he did not fit the profile, he had some characteristics of it. He was young enough to be dangerous. He looked fit. (Henley did not regard fat men as a threat.) He wore sneakers.

Henley stood and stretched and the rats fled for safety. Henley smiled. Not everyone is your enemy, he thought to the rats, and to himself. He was, after all, very much aware of the paranoia that had seized him since coming to the city. Being aware of the situation did not make him feel safer, of course, but it did make him feel sane. He was still capable of laughing at himself and his caution, which meant it was still within reasonable bounds.

He walked north for several more blocks, letting his mind run freely through the rewrites he had done, the ones he felt he ought still to do, the raving success that his play would be, and all the earthly rewards that would follow. Thought of the rewrites led him to thoughts of Myra Goldsmith. He had almost connected with her, he felt, and was still mystified by what had happened.

Thinking of Myra, he turned and started back toward home. A horn blared angrily and Henley looked toward the street, which at this point was elevated above the river walk. The sidewalk abutting the street also had a wrought-iron railing and leaning against it, looking out to the river once again, was the man from the lobby. He did not look at Henley, but Henley had the distinct feeling that he was being watched.

Not watched, stalked. The man had been in his lobby, perhaps that's where he picked Henley out as a victim. A man alone walking by the river close to dusk. Henley had worn his tweed jacket, his "writer's jacket," to Myra's. He must look prosperous, an easy victim. And now he was being followed until he dropped his guard.

The man stepped away from the railing and toward the street at his back. Because of the elevation, he was quickly out of Henley's sight. But which way had he gone? Back to Henley's building? He was closer, he could get there before Henley could, and if Henley entered the lobby and found the man waiting there, what could he do? Take out his key, turn his back to the man, enter the building? They warned you never to do that, didn't they? He was suddenly uncertain what behavior one was supposed to adopt in the face of danger. If he left the lobby and went into the street, what then? It would be dark, it was nearly dark now. He had waited too long.

There was another possibility, of course, and Henley was aware of it. His imagination could be scaring the hell out of him for no good reason. The man had come to visit someone else in the building, found them not at home, and had gone out to the river to kill some time while waiting. He had done essentially what Henley was doing, following basically the same route, and why not? It was a sensible, pleasant thing to do.

Henley started walking quickly toward home, abandoning the walk along the river's edge and slicing diagonally across the park. Riverside Park was nothing like Central Park. Many city blocks long, it was never more than a hundred yards wide, and Henley traversed it in seconds. He climbed the hill, pulled himself over the railing, and was on the sidewalk next to Riverside Drive, several hundred yards ahead of where he had last seen the man from the lobby.

He oriented himself quickly, perceived no danger, but his senses had been alerted and he walked now with a growing unease. He looked behind him; an old man was in the distance, two women closer at hand. No threat. The pedestrians across the street moved to the north and to the south, Henley saw only women coming toward him. There were only three blocks to go before he reached home. He decided to approach his apartment from the opposite side of the street. From there he could look directly into his lobby and assure himself it was empty before he entered it. There was no place to hide in the lobby and if the man was there, Henley would keep going and come back later. He would go to a movie if necessary. He was certainly not such a valuable victim that a mugger would wait all night long for him to return.

And now he was only one block from home. He had been monitoring pedestrians to the side and front continually and he turned to look behind him again. Abruptly, startlingly close, a man stepped from between parked cars and onto the sidewalk. Henley reacted without thinking and broke into a sprint. The man had circled back and was going to take him from behind, probably jumping him just as he entered the lobby. Henley dashed into the street amid a blare of horns and zigged through the traffic like one of his rats in the rocks. He reached the far sidewalk and saw pedestrians on the other side looking at him with curiosity. Let them look. He was not embarrassed about survival. At first he did not see the man among them but he was still running and the shadows were heavy now. He was there, Henley was certain, and probably stunned by the quickness of Henley's reactions.

Henley continued to run all the way to his building. Breathing heavily, he looked back as he vaulted up the stoop. The man was nowhere to be seen, the lobby was empty. He would be safely within his room long before the man could even reach the steps. He did not fumble with his keys but worked them quickly and calmly. He took the stairs on the run, reaching the hallway of the fourth floor with a final spring of energy before leaning over the railing to look back down the stairwell. No one was on the stairs, no one was entering the building. He had won.

As he inserted the key into his apartment lock, the first feeling of foolishness came upon him. He was jumping at shadows. He had not even waited long enough to get a good look at the man who had materialized from between the parked cars. For all he really knew he was running from nothing at all.

But I'm safe, he thought. Maybe a fool, but safe.

He entered his apartment and switched on the overhead light, which clicked and blazed for a fraction of a second before flashing out.

Momentarily blinded by the lightbulb that had gone off like a flash-bulb, Henley cursed and crossed the room toward the floorlamp beside his chair.

When he snapped on the lamp he saw the man from the lobby sitting in the chair, smiling. He held an icepick in his hand, but it was his smile that frightened Henley the most.

"You're breathing awfully hard," Bahoud said. "Have you been running from something?"

After cleaning the icepick on the bedsheet, Bahoud ransacked the apartment, looking for evidence that Henley was working for the government. He had suspected that Henley was not a threat when he entered his apartment. Federal agents were not particularly well paid, but they could afford to live better than this. There was no evidence whatever that Henley was with the FBI or CIA or the police or even the local school board. Still, he could not afford to take the risk. He had heard him tell Myra he was in the FBI, he had heard him express an interest in Kane's voice on the intercom, he had asked probing questions. The chances that he was onto Bahoud/Kane had been remote in the first place, but there was no advantage to taking unnecessary chances.

He needed two more days. Henley's death, even unnecessary as it was, was a very small price to pay to assure him security for those two days. Especially since it was a price Bahoud did not have to pay personally. From all he could tell from the available evidence, Henley died without lovers, without family close enough to warrant a picture, without much of a life at all. The only one who lost by his death was Henley himself, and even he wasn't complaining. He had made no protest at all when Bahoud struck, he hadn't even cried out. It had been as if Henley had expected it to happen. Accepted it. Not like Sulamein bin Assad who had struggled to the end. Bahoud found it curious how differently various people reacted to the prospect of death. Not at all predictable, which was why it was best to do it quickly.

Bahoud put Henley's body in the closet and covered him with an overcoat and a jacket. Anyone who discovered the body would have to find it by looking, not by a chance glance through the window. He doubted that the body would be found within two days, and it would certainly take several days after that before the police made inquiries to anyone as remotely connected to the deceased as his typist. By then, Bahoud would be long gone. And so would Howard and so would Myra. The trick now was to keep the brother and sister favorably disposed toward Kane for the next two days. He had sensed a growing remoteness on the part of Howard, as if the man's fear of Kane was outdistancing his gratitude. Myra was well in hand already, and would be even more so after tonight. Howard he could start working on in the morning. There were ways to bind others to oneself. All you needed was to be prepared to do them. And for eight million dollars, Bahoud reminded himself, he was more than ready to do absolutely anything.

He had two million already in hand. The second installment of another two million was due when the death of Assad was verified, which Bahoud expected would be done on the evening news. The final payment of four million would be due when he completed the assignment. As he surveyed the mess in which he had left Henley's apartment, Bahoud did some calculations concerning his fortune. Eight million at four percent in tax-free bonds was $320,000 a year. Net. He could live on that. He could do better than that, of course, but it was not a bad base figure.

The apartment looked as if someone had tossed it looking for valuables. There had been no valuables beyond a used television and a manual typewriter, but how was a burgler to know that ahead of time? What a disgusting place, Bahoud thought. How could anyone allow himself to live in such a hole? I've been in bigger dungeons that this, he thought to himself with a laugh as he stepped into the hallway and made sure the door was locked behind him.

18

Howard went straight to the television, waving Myra away impatiently. He sat too close, as always, and had the sound louder than necessary, as if he were half deaf and half blind. She had seen him watch television this way since he was a child, nearly squeezing himself into the set.

The news was on and Howard did not turn to her until he was certain the current story did not interest him.

"Did you tell him to leave?" he asked as the newscaster spoke of an airline tragedy. Even then he turned only partway to Myra.

He acts as if he's being sucked into the machine, she thought.

"Not really," she said. She had forgotten she was supposed to get rid of Kane. Since their encounter earlier in the day she had thought of little else but Kane, but certainly not about getting rid of him.

"Why not? Jesus, Myra. I asked you to do something . . . "

The newscast changed topics and Howard swiveled back to watch. He turned to her only when he was sure the story did not concern him. The anchorman spoke of the upcoming meeting at the United Nations to highlight the Year of the Children. In an unprecedented gathering, the heads of state of seventy-six countries were to convene in New York. There had never been anything quite like it, the newscaster assured his viewers. Howard paid no attention.

"Do it tonight," Howard said.

"I don't want to do it," Myra said. She knew she had to proceed with caution. If Howard suspected she wanted to keep Kane in the apartment, he might freak out. Not in front of Kane, of course, because he was afraid of Kane, but in front of her. Myra had seen a lifetime of Howard's tantrums; she had been raised to live in silence in order not to provoke them. Even now she dreaded the prospect of facing one.

"It should come from you," Howard said.

"I don't see why. He's your friend."

"Why do you always question everything I say?"

"I don't. But this is an ugly job and I don't see why I have to do it for you. It's your responsibility . . . if you really think it's necessary to ask him to leave at all."

"It's necessary."

"Okay."

"You have to remember, Myra, I know a lot more about the way the world works than you do."

Poor Howard, she thought. If only that were true. He operated in the world with such a veil of naïveté and paranoia. It was odd how much the two qualities were linked. One needed a massive dose of innocence to believe that the rest of the world *cared* enough to be working against him.

The television screen suddenly filled with a picture of the mosque, then the graffiti sprayed by Wiener's shaky hand upon the wall. Myra saw the slogans, the initials B.Z. The camera was then inside the mosque in Assad's monastic room to show the disruption of furniture, the initials repeated on the wall, the blood stains on the bedclothes, and, finally, the pool of blood upon the floor.

Howard gasped. "Did he say dead?!"

The newscaster had just told of the killing of Sulamein bin Assad at the hands of unknown assailants. The victim was described as a professor of theology and a specialist on Middle Eastern affairs. Howard was talking so loudly she could not make out the rest of the story.

"He wasn't dead, Myra!"

"How do you know?"

"He was fine, he was fine."

"Howard, how do you know about this?"

"Did they mention the PLO? Did they say he was PLO?"

Howard searched the channels frantically, looking for a repeat of the story. He found it at last and this time they listened to the story in its entirety.

The mayor decried the crime, claimed to be scandalized over the desecration of the mosque, joined the Islamic community in its sorrow, announced that the city would not tolerate such incidents. The police had witnesses, who had seen several men in the vicinity of the mosque at the time of the killing. They did not know the significance of the initials "B.Z." They said a note had been found but did not reveal the contents. They were working on a number of leads and expected arrests soon.

There was no mention of Assad's lifetime association with the PLO. They spoke of his age, his ill health, his reputation for piety. They said no autopsy had yet been performed but the presumptive cause of death was a beating by persons unknown.

Howard paced furiously, neither speaking nor responding to Myra's questions. When the phone rang, he jumped for it, then froze with his hand on the receiver. He let it ring a second time before he picked it up, trying to compose in his mind what he would say to Kane.

"Hello?"

"I got you by the balls, hon," said a male voice.

"Who is this?" Howard asked.

"I got you by the balls and I'm going to start squeezing. You have got balls, ain't you, Howard?"

Howard recognized the Southern drawl, the mean spirit behind it. "Solin?" he said.

Solin saw the story first on a television screen over a bar where he was drinking in the company of noisy Irishmen. Solin didn't like the Irish—he didn't like any of the goyim as a matter of principle—but they were raucous, good-humored, and feisty and reminded him of home in Georgia. His distaste for goyim was newly arrived at, a result of being in New York where Jewish consciousness was high. Back home he had thought of himself as Southern first, then Jewish. Being Southern, of course, had been a point of great pride. In the North, it was regarded by many as a sure sign of slow-wittedness and deep bias. When they heard his accent, half the Yankees acted as if he were a slave-owning plantation colonel, the other half as if he were a red-necked sheriff unleashing his dogs on a freedom march. Being Jewish, on the other hand, was an asset. They laughed at the way he said the prayers with his slow-tongued country pronunciation, but they grudgingly accepted him. Not as one of them, exactly—he was still too Southern, too crude, too much the cracker—but at least as a relative. A red-necked Jew from the hill country of Georgia, as strange a discovery as the sudden appearance of the pitch-black Jews of Ethiopia. Jews, well, yes, maybe, possibly, *technically,* but certainly not us, not of our kind. However, technical membership was an advance for Solin. He was not a Yankee of any stripe, technical nor hypothetical, and never would be.

He had come upon Howard and the Brotherhood like a drowning man upon a raft. There had been no membership test, no qualifications necessary. He had told Howard that he was a Jew and wanted to kick some ass, and Howard, in his desperation to recruit, had embraced him. Or had come as close to an embrace as that bloodless city boy could, Solin thought. Solin didn't know for sure that Howard was a pansy, and he certainly preferred to think he wasn't, so he let it go at that, but that boy was *weird*. All that talk, all that endless chatter about history and theory and vigilance and vengeance. Solin liked the revenge part. He could relate to that. A whole lot of people in this city could use a quick kick upside the head and Solin would be only too happy to oblige.

The other guys in group were all right, in a soft, Northern sort of way. Except for Borodin. There was nothing soft about Borodin except his brain. They all talked too much, of course. And thought too much, which was worse, which was why they were paralyzed all the time. But they were all right. They accepted him as part of them. They were a kind of semblance of home, the only semblance he had up North. They weren't much of a family, but they would have to do. His real family hadn't been all that much, either.

It was Howard who had taught him a harsher concept of the goyim and instructed him in the dark forces of society that were all around. Solin needed no tutoring in paranoia. He had always known most of the world was against him, but Howard had put a sharper face on the enemy. In the tiny town where he had grown up, Solin could not afford to hate all non-Jews. There would have been no one left to associate with. *All* the good old boys were goyim, and Solin was never fool enough to hate himself right out of drinking buddies. In New York, however, percentages made hating much easier. There was a vast matrix of Jews in which he could nestle while comfortably despising everyone else.

Still, he preferred to drink with the Irish.

Solin could only watch the picture on the television screen when the news story about the mosque came on. The din of voices was much too loud to allow him to hear the sound of the newscast and some idiot had started to sing close to his ear. He saw the letters

"B.Z." on the side of the mosque and stood up off his stool, moving closer to the screen.

Had the Brotherhood done this? Of course. What else could the initials B.Z. stand for? Spray painted on a mosque? It had to be them. Damn! They were finally doing stuff, kicking some ass at long last. And without him.

His initial pride turned to anger. They had let him go as if he meant nothing to them. Not one of them had tried to help when that Kane sucker-punched him. None of them came out to the hallway to see if he was all right. No one called him the next day to ask him to come back. He had been with them in the brawl with the skinheads—and had that ever been fun—and he had shared their jubilation as they watched themselves on tape, again and again. And then they had allowed a newcomer to kick him in the balls and unceremoniously dump him out of the apartment.

The anger settled and deepened into a thick bitterness that seemed to coat his mouth and throat. Police were looking for the perpetrators who had defaced the mosque, he could tell that much by watching the interview with the cop on television. A number to call with information flashed on the screen and Solin walked through the crowd to the telephone.

The phone was answered on the third ring and a voice announced that all officers were busy at the moment and the next available officer would be with him as soon as possible. Solin hung up. He had a better idea, anyway.

Solin punched another number into the phone and this time Howard answered.

"I got you by the balls, hon," Solin said.

"Who is this?"

"I got you by the balls and I'm going to start squeezing. You have got balls, ain't you, Howard?"

"Solin?"

"Howard?" he mocked. "Is that you, Howard?"

"What do you want?"

"The law's looking for you, ain't it, Howard? The law's looking for you—and I know where you are. How about that?"

"What do you mean? What are you going to do?"

"I already done it, Howard. I called the cops three minutes ago."

There was a pause and Solin could hear the sound of the television set in Howard's apartment in the background.

"What did you say to the police?" Howard asked finally. His voice was very calm. Precise.

"I told them who B.Z. is. I told them where to find your ass."

Again a silence.

"Who you talking to, Howard? You talking to that asshole Kane? Tell him I'm going to give the cops his name first."

"I'm not talking to anyone," Howard said.

"Tell Kane he's going to get what's coming to him."

"I thought you said you'd already spoken to the police."

"I had a preliminary conversation," said Solin, grinning to himself. He could work poor old Howard like a yo-yo. He could yank him around as much as he wanted to. Why blow it all at once when he could string it out and make Howard suffer, make them all suffer, as long as he wanted?

"Where are you?" Howard asked.

"Having a drink with my buddies." Solin held the phone in the air so Howard could hear the noise in the background. "Hoisting a few with my friends."

"I think we should talk about this," said Howard. "There's no need to do anything rash."

"You got that much right," said Solin. "I ain't going to do nothing rash. I'm going to do it real slow. I'm going to slip it to you and your asshole pals inch by inch and I'm going to love every bit of it."

"Let's meet. We can talk . . ."

"Good night, Howard. The next sound you hear may be the police knocking on your door. Sleep tight."

Solin hung up and returned to the bar with a glow of satisfaction. Let them dread it. Let them fear Solin and his retribution. He'd get his own back, one way or the other. He might call the police or he might not, depending how he felt. Right this minute, he felt damned good.

Solin returned to the bar, ordered another beer, and asked the bartender to change the channel on the television. As he drank the beer the news story about B.Z. and the mosque came on the new channel.

"Hey," he said loudly. "I know them peckerwoods." The bartender and several customers looked first at Solin, then at the television screen.

"They're assholes, every one of them," he drawled, enjoying the sudden celebrity.

Solin was home in time to catch the late news on his own television without the distraction of the people in the bar. He planned to watch it with the satisfaction of knowing that Howard and the others would be doing the same thing, viewing their handiwork again, but this time worrying. About him. None of them had called to see how he was. None of them. Not even Borodin. Well, screw them all. Let them suffer, wondering when Solin would drop the other shoe. Let them wait for his surprise.

But when the news came on, it was Solin who was surprised. Without the sound in the bar, he had only understood the Brotherhood's action to be the defacing of a mosque. Now he heard for the first time that a man had been killed. Not just killed but beaten to death, or at least Solin inferred that was the cause of death. The police were vague about that, but the reporter made it clear that the old man had definitely been beaten.

To death? Solin could not picture it. Not that bunch of featherweights. Borodin was dumb enough, but the others wouldn't allow him. Hart? Wiener? Lewis? Howard? The idea was laughable. There wasn't enough violence in the four of them to pop a beer can. They lost their guts when they lost me, Solin thought . . . except for the newcomer. Kane. It had to be Kane's doing.

Solin wrote down the number on the screen as his telephone rang.

He recognized Howard's voice, thin and frightened.

"I've been calling you all night," said Howard.

"Well, well, good old Howard. You probably called to see how I'm doing, I imagine. You're probably wondering about my health, ain't you, Howard?"

"Naturally I'm concerned. How are you?"

"I'm mean, that's how I am. I'm a mean-assed redneck, didn't you know that, Yankee?"

"You seem very angry . . . "

"Did you call to ask me back into the Brotherhood, Howard? That's probably why you called, ain't it? You missed me?"

"We do miss you, actually."

"And you want me to join the Brotherhood again? I don't know,

Howard, that's mighty kind of you, but it may be that I resigned just in time. You killed a man.''

"It was a mistake.''

"That's a dangerous mistake, Howard. The cops aren't very understanding about that kind of mistake. What happened, couldn't you control Kane?''

Howard was silent. Solin could imagine him sweating in his apartment, caught by the balls and not having any idea what to do about it. He laughed into the phone.

"Hey, Howard, you called me, remember? You got something to say, or not?''

"We'd . . . you didn't call the police, did you?'' Howard's voice sounded next to tears.

"Call about what, Howard? What would I call about?''

"We'd like you to come back,'' Howard said.

"Oh, is that right?''

"Yes, we would. All of us. Very much.''

"All of you?''

"Yes.''

"Does that mean *you* want me back, Howard?''

"Yes, certainly, yes, I do.''

"And does that mean *Kane* wants me back?''

"Yes, I'm certain he does.''

"You're certain? You don't know?''

"He's not here, I haven't spoken to him, but I'm certain he would want you to return. We miss you, we . . . ''

"Okay.''

"Okay? You mean you will?''

"Sure thing, Howard. You didn't think I'd be the kind of guy to bear a grudge, did you? I'll be happy to come back. But there's just one thing, just one little thing. Kind of a ceremony. There ought to be a kind of ceremony to welcome me back, don't you think?''

"Certainly.''

"Just a little token like.''

"Absolutely. We'll have a party . . . ''

"Oh, no, hon, nothing all that grand. I just want you to kiss my ass.''

Solin could barely keep from laughing into the shocked pause.

"I am deeply sorry,'' Howard began.

"I'm sure you are, but I don't want an apology, honey. I want you

to kiss my ass. You and Kane. Both of you. On your knees. To kiss
my ass. And I'd like you to come over here and do it, Howard. I
don't think I should have to come to your place, do you? I want it
over here and I want it tonight. Otherwise, I might get lonely. And if
I get lonely, I'll probably pick up the phone and call people. You
know how it is. Sometimes you'll talk to just about anybody to hear
a friendly voice, you know? I might even call the police. I understand
they have a hot line open all the time just for people who want to
talk to them.''

"Kane isn't here."

"Find him, Howard. Then the two of you get over here and kiss
my ass.''

Solin hung up and laughed until he rocked back on his sofa with
his feet in the air.

Kane and Howard stepped from the cab in front of Solin's building
on Twelfth Street and paused for a moment looking up.

"The third floor," Howard said. "Three C. On the corner of the
building." Howard could see the light still glowing in the window. It
was a little past midnight.

Howard started toward the building but Kane held back, still looking upward. Howard glanced up again. There were no shadows against
the window, no sign of movement. Still Kane held back, looking.

"Do you see something?" Howard asked.

"I see what I need," said Kane, and he started forward, but not
toward the entrance to the building.

The telephone lines climbed down the side of the building from the
roof and slipped into the basement via an alleyway barely wide
enough for a man to squeeze into. Kane slid into the alley sideways
and grasped the lines where they entered the building. The phone
wires ran in with the cable television lines. It was possible to distinguish the two, but easier not to bother.

"What are you doing?" Howard asked, his voice dropping instinctively to a whisper.

"He hasn't made the call yet, right? Let's make sure he doesn't."

"I thought . . . I thought we were going to do what he asked."

"If we have to, Howard." Kane pulled a pair of rubber-handled
wirecutters from his rear pocket. One by one he snipped the wires
going into the building, carefully avoiding the power line.

"However, it is my hope we won't have to." Kane slid out of the passageway and back onto the sidewalk. "Don't you agree?"

"I was hoping we could just talk sense into him," Howard said. ". . . Is that everyone's telephone you cut?"

"Not to worry, Howard. It's the middle of the night. The phone company will be here in the morning." He patted Howard's cheek, grinning. "We have to break a few eggs to make this omelette. Not many. Somebody may have to do without cable TV tonight, but it's for a worthy cause, right?"

"Right."

Solin was coy as he spoke on the intercom.

"Did you come to kiss my ass, Howard?"

Kane nodded and Howard answered, "Yes."

"You came at a good time," Solin said moments later as he opened his door a crack. Kane and Howard stood in the empty hallway. "My cable just went out and I need some entertainment."

Kane grinned over Howard's shoulder.

"We'll give you some entertainment."

"I'll bet you're looking forward to it, ain't you, Kane?"

"Yum-yum," said Kane. "Can't wait."

"How about you, Howard? You eager to get at it?"

"Could we not do this in the hallway, please?" Howard asked. "It's embarrassing enough as it is."

"No, it ain't," said Solin. "It ain't nearly embarrassing enough. I just realized that a few minutes ago."

Kane could see only Solin's right eye and the right side of his head. The chain on the door crossed him at chest level. If the chain was the only impediment, this would be easy.

"I mean, if you come in here and kiss my ass, who's going to know? Just me. That's not good enough. I've decided I want you to do it in front of everybody. At a full meeting of the Brotherhood."

"You just lost, cracker," said Kane.

"Think so, smart-ass? Howard's willing, ain't you, Howard?"

"You tried for too much, Solin," said Kane. "Now you're not going to get anything."

"Tell you what, Howard," Solin said. "I can see by your face that you don't like the idea, so I'll make you a better offer. I'll let you off the hook. You don't have to kiss my ass now or any other time. All I want now is for that peckerwood with you to get down on his knees in front of the membership and open his pussy mouth and suck my dick.''

"Sounds fair," said Kane, smiling. "Sounds like a good deal. Why don't I come in now and get in some practice?''

Kane stepped around Howard and stabbed his arm through the door. The icepick hit Solin in the cheek and he staggered back, howling. With his right hand Kane applied the wirecutters to the chain, at the same time leaning his shoulder into the door.

Kane felt the chain yielding to the cutters as the blade bit more and more deeply. The link had almost snapped by the time Solin recovered himself and hurled his full weight against the door. Solin was wiry, strong, and desperate and for a moment he bore Kane backwards.

Kane thrust the wirecutters into the gap to keep the door from closing all the way.

"Howard!" he commanded, and Howard put his weight against the door, too.

"I got a gun, motherfucker!" Solin cried.

"He does have one, I think," Howard said, his eyes wide as he looked at Kane.

"Then go get it, asshole," Kane said to Solin. He had slipped the icepick in his pocket and was pushing against the door with all his weight.

The resistance gave way abruptly and the door snapped open against the chain again. Kane could hear Solin rummaging frantically in the kitchen as he put the wirecutters to the chain again. Solin was on his way back as the first half of the chain link snapped.

Kane stepped away from the door as Solin slashed the open space between door and jamb with a butcher knife. With a startled cry, Howard leaped back.

"So much for the gun theory," said Kane.

Solin was wailing wildly on the other side of the door. "Try it now, motherfucker! Come on, motherfucker, come on in now! Try it now!''

"Another time, perhaps," Kane said. He grabbed Howard by the arm and pulled him away.

"He'll report us for sure, now!" Howard said as they reached the sidewalk.

"How?"

"He'll call the police!"

"His phone doesn't work."

"Not now, maybe! It will tomorrow."

"Tomorrow," Kane observed, "is another day. He hasn't made it through this one, yet."

"What are you talking about?"

"Go on home now, Howard," Kane said. They had reached Fourteenth Street and Kane waved at a cab.

"You're not going to try to get in there?" Howard was horrified.

"Of course not. He's armed and a man could get hurt."

"What are you going to do?"

"Just talk to him. Wait until he's calmed down, then talk to him, reasonably. In a way he'll understand."

"He's not going to listen. He sounded crazy."

"Then I'll wait. He'll listen to reason in time. Everyone does, eventually."

Kane put Howard in a cab and walked a block until he found a wino sitting in a doorway.

Kane put a dollar in the man's hand, then took his wine bottle as the man was muttering thanks. When the man protested, Kane pushed his head against the concrete of the building until he stopped arguing. One block further on he found the remnants of a cardboard box in a trash can. Carrying the wine bottle and the box, he returned to Twelfth Street and positioned himself across the street so he could see Solin's window and the door to his building.

It was easy to imagine Solin sitting just inside his door, holding the butcher knife, not daring to go to sleep. Kane had not felt bone on his thrust with the icepick and he assumed he had merely pierced Solin's cheek flesh. Not much of a wound; it had probably stopped bleeding by now. Still, it would be enough to serve as a reminder to Solin. Enough to keep him scared as well as angry. Kane preferred a scared target. Fear made men stupid. Cautious, of course, but seldom of the right thing.

Kane settled into a doorway, sitting on the cardboard, watching Solin's window. He wished he had some pornography to pass the time, but then one couldn't ask for everything. Besides, he realized, he had some real life erotica to reflect on. He began to think about Myra and smiled.

Hatcher got the news from Captain Genesse just before dawn. He thought at first of calling Becker but then decided to tell him in person. Hatcher did not want to dissipate his sense of victory by leaking any portion of it over the telephone. He wanted to see Becker's face when he told him—and he wanted Becker to see his.

It was policework, Hatcher thought triumphantly as he approached Becker's hotel room. Good old-fashioned policework. No mumbo-jumbo. No unorthodox theories, no half-cocked approaches. It was good old-fashioned policework of the type that Hatcher had been taught and practiced.

Hatcher rang, waited, then rang again. He had resorted to banging on the door when Becker finally appeared.

Becker opened the door only partway, leaning around it as if he were inadequately dressed. Hatcher thought he had a guilty look, although he could have been merely sleepy.

"We've got a lead on 'B.Z.,' " Hatcher said, watching Becker's face for reaction.

"Good for us. Did you ever think of calling first?"

"I figured you were about to get up, anyway," said Hatcher. "Why, did I disturb anything?"

"Thanks to my incredible powers of concentration, no, you didn't manage to."

Hatcher thought he heard the muffled sound of a giggle in the background. Becker appeared to be suppressing a grin.

"I didn't realize you had company," said Hatcher. He leaned to one side, trying to peer around Becker. There was some movement deeper in the room, the sound of clothing rustling. Someone was dressing.

"I didn't realize it was any of your business or I would have told you," Becker said.

"I'll wait out here," Hatcher said.

"Try the lobby. You'll be more comfortable."

"Captain Genesse is picking us up in ten minutes," Hatcher said, glancing at his watch.

"Agent Crist will join us," Becker said, closing the door. "I'll notify her."

Hatcher stood for a moment in the hallway, glaring in impotent anger at the door. He weighed his options carefully, then lifted an imaginary machine gun and drilled a hole through the door. Feeling a little better, he went to the lobby to wait.

Karen was fully dressed and applying makeup by the time Becker returned to the bedroom.

"Do you think he knows I was in here?" she asked.

Becker watched her rub coverup over blemishes he had never seen. Her fingers fairly flew and the entire proceeding required a fraction of the time he took to shave. When she was done he saw no trace of makeup, no hint of the artistry applied. The practiced wizardry of the working woman. He detected no change in her appearance, but then he had not seen the need for any changes in the first place. He liked her face the way it came.

"He may suspect it," Becker said.

"It's against every regulation," Karen said. "He could hang me." She sounded matter-of-fact, not worried.

"He wants to solve the case," Becker said. "He's not quite stupid enough to do anything to jeopardize that. Not quite."

"He's not stupid at all," said Karen. "There are a lot of things wrong with Hatcher, but he's not stupid."

Becker shrugged.

"Do you think it's wise to take me along now?"

"Yes, I think it's wise," said Becker.

"May I ask, strictly objectively, why? I mean, I'm dying to go, don't get me wrong, but isn't it going to antagonize him unnecessarily, cramming me down his throat like this?"

"McKinnon said you were on the case."

"Yes, but only because of what you said to McKinnon."

"What did I say to McKinnon?"

"I don't know," she admitted.

"You want to learn, don't you?"

"Yes," she said. "Very much."

"You won't learn manning a desk."

"Is that why you brought me? To teach me?"

Becker did not answer.

"Or was it because you like sleeping with me?"

"I like sleeping with you, but that's not why I brought you."

"I didn't think so. You would always find someone to sleep with. Why did you bring me?"

Becker tied his shoes then stood.

"Time to go," he said.

"Why, John? Why did you bring me with you?"

Becker turned to her and took her face in his hands. She brushed his hands away.

"Why?... What did you tell McKinnon about me?"

"I told him I thought you had something special," Becker said.

"What?"

Becker leaned over to kiss her. Karen put her hands on his chest and pushed him away.

"What do I have that's special? A lot of women can kiss. Is it my breasts that are so special? My ass? What?"

"They're all special, but that has nothing to do with it."

"Then stop acting as if they did. Tell me what you said to Mc-Kinnon about me that made him jerk me out of Fingerprinting and rush me here ahead of at least a dozen other agents."

Becker walked to the doorway and waited. Karen watched him from the bedroom, her face angry and determined.

"My sex has been used against me often enough. I don't mind if it works in my favor for a change, but if that's all it is, I want to know it."

Becker opened the door.

"I told McKinnon you were a lot like me," he said. "But that you didn't know it yet."

Becker left the room, closing the door behind him.

Karen sat for a moment longer on the bed. "Christ," she said aloud. A lot like Becker? The thought scared the hell out of her and she wished he hadn't told her.

Like any experienced policeman, Captain Genesse knew the value of serendipity, although he would call it luck. It was, in reality, a combination of effort, preparedness, maintaining the right contacts in proper working order, and good fortune. Over the years he had learned that the good fortune usually happened if everything else was in place. Getting the tip on Solin was a perfectly ordinary example.

"A guy named Kerrigan runs a bar," Genesse explained to Becker. Hatcher and Karen were in the car, too, but Genesse had found it easier to talk to Becker and let Hatcher listen in if he wanted to. He liked Becker, he liked his direct and no-nonsense approach to things, his ability to pierce right to the heart of the matter. He wasn't sure where the young woman fit into the scheme of things, but she certainly looked good and he didn't mind having an audience to play to.

"An Irish bar on the East Side," Genesse continued. "A guy owns a bar, he wants to maintain good relationships with the police."

"Sensible," said Becker.

"Not only for diplomatic purposes, but some of his regulars are on the force. He does favors, they do favors back. Mostly he just keeps his ears open."

"What did he hear?" Hatcher asked.

Genesse had his own timetable for telling the tale and he did not appreciate being hurried by Hatcher. He ignored him.

"So he hears something that might be of interest, he passes it on to a detective acquaintance of mine who is a regular at Kerrigan's. Now this detective acquaintance I don't happen to like very much— and I can tell you this because I don't give you the man's name— but I don't ever let the detective know this. On the contrary. I cultivate this guy. I cultivate *every* detective. This way instead of a staff of five working for Terrorism, I got a part-time staff of—I don't know—a hundred, two hundred."

"That's a lot of cultivating," said Becker. "You ever get tired of it?"

"From the minute I get up in the morning," Genesse admitted. "But what are you going to do? I need the extra help, I couldn't begin to cover the job otherwise."

"Your lips must be fixed in a permanent pucker," Becker said.

Hatcher sat upright, certain that Becker had offended the man.

Genesse looked at Becker, saw the little grin, and laughed.

"I do kiss a lot of ass," Genesse said. He heard the woman stifle a laugh.

"Obviously to good effect. What did Kerrigan tell this detective acquaintance of yours?"

The time was right and Genesse was now happy to come to the point. He had been talking so much because of the woman, but enough was enough.

"A guy was in there drinking last night, a semi-regular, you know, a familiar face but you don't really know him? He was very interested in the newscast about our 'B.Z.' friends and the mosque and Sulamein bin Assad. He made Kerrigan change the channels so he could watch it twice. Then he started talking about how he knew those guys."

"B.Z.?"

"Yeah, B.Z. He was going on about how they were a bunch of assholes."

"Probably a pretty good bet."

"So Kerrigan asks around, does anybody know this guy. Somebody knows somebody who comes up with a name. After closing up he calls his detective buddy who calls me when he gets off his shift. And here we are. Sorry about the hour."

Genesse pulled his car to the curb beside a hydrant. He pointed to a building across the street.

"His name is Solin. Isaac Solin. Calls himself Ike."

The three men and the woman stepped out of the car and approached the building. Thirty yards away a drunk lay sleeping under some cardboard, his empty wine bottle where it had fallen on the sidewalk, inches away from his open fingers.

The street was still in heavy shadows, the sun only slightly above the horizon.

Solin awoke with the first light, startled to find that he had fallen asleep in his chair. Another chair was jammed under the door handle to secure it from attack. The butcher's knife was still in Solin's hand, cradled on his lap. It took him a moment to remember the events of the preceding night, but if the specifics were missing for a time, the fear was there from the moment he awoke.

He had made a plan the night before as he sat in frightened vigil at the door and he recalled it now. There was a public phone on the corner of Twelfth Street. He didn't know if it was working, but he prayed that it was. First he would call 911 and report a murder. That should bring cops right away. He wasn't certain that Kane was crazy enough to attack him on the street, but he might be, he just

might be. After he had called the cops, he would call the 800 number and report the Brotherhood. Once that was done, there was no
reason for Kane to endanger him anymore. The harm would have
been done. After that, with the police swarming in the area—maybe
even giving him protection, who knows?—Kane could try whatever
he wanted. Nobody would be nuts enough to try to attack Solin
then.

And then, when he had dealt with Kane and the Brotherhood, he
would go to the emergency room of the nearest hospital and have a
doctor look at his cheek. It throbbed even now, an insistent reminder
of Kane's threat.

Solin put the butcher knife inside his belt in the small of his back,
then untucked his shirt to conceal it. If Kane was still around, let him
think Solin was unarmed. Let him try that bullshit with the icepick
again, let the bastard try.

He checked his pockets to make sure he had a coin for the phone,
then peered carefully into the hallway before setting forth. He pulled
his door shut, heard the lock click into place, then touched the handle
of the butcher knife for reassurance.

Halfway down the stairs he heard voices outside on the stoop, then
the buzzer in his room rang behind him. Someone was ringing to be
let in. He couldn't imagine Kane would think Solin was stupid enough
to release the outer door for him, but then he had misjudged Kane
twice already. Solin paused on the stairs, his heart pounding. He was
so close to the freedom of the streets. Behind him, the sanctuary of
his room was no longer safe. If Kane had returned, he must have
brought some means of getting into Solin's room. Solin's only safety
now was to have Kane arrested. Removed. Solin had to make the
phone call.

He peered cautiously around the bend in the staircase until he could
see the feet of the people on the stoop. There was a woman with them.
Kane wouldn't come for him with a woman.

He could hear the buzzer sound again in his room, and then in the
apartment next to his. They weren't after him, Solin understood with
relief. Whoever they were, they wanted into the building and were
ringing all the bells until someone let them in, but that didn't mean
they wanted him personally. Solin took a step down the stairway, then
another until he could see their faces.

Three men and a woman. The woman was a looker, the men were in suits. A couple of them looked like cops, but they certainly were not from the Brotherhood.

Solin opened the front door and squeezed past the people on the stoop. They brushed past him and through the open door. One of the men, the one who looked like an athlete, lingered in the doorway as the others hurried up the stairs. The man studied Solin, who could see him from the corner of his eye.

The street was empty. Solin glanced at his watch. It was not even six o'clock yet, the sun was barely up. A garbage truck was just turning the corner on one end of the block, a derelict was sleeping it off under a piece of cardboard several doors away in the other direction. Otherwise, the city could have belonged to him alone.

"Ike?" the man on the stoop asked tentatively.

Solin began to walk, not looking back toward the man. Why had he spoken his name? Solin didn't know the man, he was sure of that. Nor did the man know Solin, not with any certainty. Had Kane sent these people to get him? He could think of no other explanation for such an urgent visit at this hour of the morning, with a woman or not. Whoever they were, whatever they wanted, it wasn't good for Solin, he knew that much. They sure as hell didn't come to tell him he'd won the lottery.

He glanced back and saw the athletic-looking man vanish into the building after the others. Foxed them, he thought triumphantly. I'm too damned smart for them, too smart for Kane, too smart for anybody.

Solin set out briskly, not running but moving fast, his eyes scanning the cars to make sure Kane wasn't crouched down in the backseat of one of them. His path took him past the derelict and he could smell the stench of spilled alcohol rising from the pavement. The bum seemed to have poured as much of it on the sidewalk as he did on himself. Solin glanced at the shape of the man under the cardboard as he passed, noticing the shoes. They were running shoes, good ones, expensive. Well, those people could always find the money for the things they valued, couldn't they? Typical.

Two steps past the derelict Solin felt the hand at his back and then the forearm at his throat choking him. Kane pulled the butcher's knife from under Solin's shirt and held it in front of Solin's eyes.

"Kneel," Kane said.

Solin fought for breath. Kane kicked him on the back of his legs and Solin fell to his knees.

"There's something I want to show you," Kane whispered in his ear. "Are you listening, Solin?" He released the pressure on Solin's throat just enough for Solin to gasp assent.

"I'm not going to hurt you, but there's something I want you to see. I think it might change your attitude toward me," Kane said.

"I . . ."

Kane tightened his grip again, choking off Solin's voice.

"You can tell me what you think afterwards," Kane whispered. He lowered the knife from in front of Solin's face. "You see? I'm not going to hurt you, I just want you to see something. It's important. Just under that car there. Do you see? Turn your head to the side, you can see better that way."

Solin felt the pressure ease a bit on his throat. At least he could breathe.

"Turn your head to the side," Kane insisted.

The pressure of Kane's forearm eased still further and Solin turned his head to one side, trying to look under the car. He could no longer see the knife. Kane's right arm had vanished from sight.

"See?" Kane asked. "Do you see it?"

Solin tilted his head even further, trying hard to find what Kane wanted him to see. There was nothing under the car but an oil spot.

He felt something metallic touch his ear, then a blinding light exploded in his head just before he died.

"See?" Kane asked.

Kane pulled Solin's body into the doorway and covered his head with the cardboard. He nudged the wine bottle to within a few inches of Solin's outstretched fingers.

Kane admired his handiwork for a moment. Solin looked like any of a thousand other homeless lying in a doorway. There may have been a time when someone would disturb him or report him, but not now, not in New York. Solin would lie where he was until the body began to smell or the dogs got to him.

After wiping his fingerprints off with the edge of his shirt, Kane tossed the butcher's knife in the nearest trashbasket. The icepick he placed in his own belt.

It was still early, Myra would probably be asleep. Well, the time had come to wake her. Kane had spent much of the night thinking about her, whiling away the uncomfortable hours with fantasies. Now it was time for reality.

He walked to the end of the block and hailed a cab.

After no one responded to their repeated knocks on Solin's door, Becker turned to Genesse.

"I think you should check the address. You left that in the car, didn't you, Captain?"

Genesse grinned. "I'll go get it," he said.

Becker looked at Hatcher and waited.

"What about her?" Hatcher asked.

"It's a learning experience," Becker said.

Hatcher started to speak, then changed his mind and turned to follow Genesse down the stairs.

"What's going on?" Karen asked. She could hear their footsteps stop and knew that Hatcher and Genesse were waiting on the stairs below, just out of sight.

"See no evil," Becker said. "Look at that door there." He directed her to the door behind them.

"What about it?"

"Keep your eyes on it. I thought I saw some movement."

Karen did as she was ordered, keeping her back to Becker. She could hear his manipulations of Solin's lock behind her.

"Huh," he said after a few seconds. "Why do you suppose he'd leave his door open?"

As Karen turned to see, Becker was already stepping into Solin's apartment. The door was wide open.

It took no time at all to find that the apartment was empty. It was Karen who discovered the chain.

Becker studied the linked metal, the one link half broken, its open end sheared.

"God damn it!" he exclaimed as he ran for the stairs.

Becker swept past Genesse and Hatcher, taking the steps three at a time as he vaulted down. He hit the street in time to see a man stepping into a cab a block away. The man looked back at Becker momentarily before the door closed and the cab moved off.

Becker ran toward the end of the block, yelling back to Genesse and Hatcher, who had just come out of the building to turn the car around. He beat them to the corner by several seconds, but he knew he was already too late. He could see several cabs in the far distance, but he knew that none of them was the one he wanted. Bahoud would have turned out of sight at the first opportunity. One more cab in a city awash in yellow taxis.

Hatcher leaped from Genesse's car and joined Becker.

"What? What is it? What?"

"We just missed the son of a bitch," Becker said, looking back toward Solin's building. Karen had come out on the run but had stopped.

"Missed who? Solin?"

"Both of them, I'm afraid," Becker said. He watched Karen, who had gone to her knees beside the derelict covered with cardboard.

"We walked right by the bastard."

"Who? Solin?"

"Yes, God damn it. Solin. And Bahoud."

"Bahoud?" Hatcher asked, but Becker was already trotting back toward Karen and the crumpled body on the sidewalk.

As Kane stepped into the cab he looked back toward Solin's building, where a man burst into the street and started running toward him. Kane closed the cab door and spoke to the driver.

"Take the first right," he said. He watched through the back window as they turned and the street behind them vanished. No sign of the running man. Kane was safe. But he was also alerted. There was nothing at Solin's apartment to lead to Kane, he knew that comfortably enough, but still it had been very close. And if they were that close, it was the connection with Henley he had to fear. How had the bastards gotten onto him so fast?

Kane gave the cabbie an address two blocks away from Howard's apartment. He would walk the rest of the way just on the odd chance that they could somehow trace the cab. He didn't think it was likely, but now was the time for caution. He wished he had Henley to do over. He wished he could have disposed of the body. It was a big loose end, but still, given any kind of luck at all no one would come across the corpse for several days. And Kane didn't need several days. He now needed only one.

Kane leaned back against the seat and allowed himself a deep breath. It had been quite an engrossing evening after all. He had killed Henley around sundown, Solin at sunup. And to top it all off he was going now to have some sport with Myra. The night's work had made him horny.

19

Myra lay awake. The pounding of her heart was too loud to allow her to sleep. Through the door she heard the sounds of Kane moving about in the living room. She felt as if she could hear them through a wall of concrete, though they were as slight as the flutter of a bird's wing. The spot on her chest where his fingers had touched her flesh still burned as if it were going to singe a hole all the way through her body.

He was at the telescope; she could hear him adjusting his stance solidly before it. She could hear the telescope move silently on its bearings, hear him blink his eye as he peered through the glass. She felt as if she could hear the towel fall to the floor, hear it as it parted the air, hear it as it collided, crumpled, folded. She could hear the sights of the city as they streamed through the telescope. When he turned to look at her door, the pivot of his neck was like the crashing of the sea upon the shore.

There was no need to see any of it, only danger in the view. She forced herself to lie perfectly still upon her bed. If she went to the door, if she peeked through the crack, she knew she could not control herself. She would open the door, she would shrug off her nightgown and stand before him as wanton as a whore. She must not look; just to listen was hard enough. She had the will to stay on her bed, but she could do nothing to control her mind. It was filled with him, engorged and bursting with the look of him, his scent, the touch of those hard muscles, the velvet softness of the hair on his chest. She could almost imagine his lips on her, almost, but that much finally eluded her. She had never felt a kiss; she could not completely imagine it, there was no sensory memory on which to draw. She had an analog for the rest. She could do, had done, the rest of it to herself, but her lips had tasted only the flesh of her own hand and arm, her brother's cheek. Almost more than anything else Myra longed for him to kiss her. Almost more. She simply longed for all of it, any of it, and yet she could not take it. Her cowardice was even greater than her lust, she thought, and she disgusted herself.

And then all the desire and all the fear and all the self-loathing turned to anger. Myra was furious with him for having brought all of this out in her. He must go. Howard was right, Kane must leave, and now. In the morning she would tell him herself, she resolved.

She heard him moving toward her door. He sought a book from the shelf on the other side of her bedroom wall. He would take it and go to his room as he always did, she thought, and the hardest part of this torture would be over. The worst part, the long, bitter recrimination, the agony of frustration contemplated in endless leisure, still lay ahead, but she was used to that. That would be easier to handle than holding herself still upon her bed.

The door moved! He was opening the door to her room, he was in the room! He stood at the foot of her bed, looking down at her, the light from the window slanting across him like a spotlight. He was completely naked and erect as a post. He said something but now that he was there, Myra could suddenly hear nothing. She was deafened by the roar of blood within her ears.

Now her sense of smell ran riot. She detected the odor of soap and shampoo and beneath that his own smell—Oh, God, he was moving, he came to the head of the bed, he stood beside her. He was inches from her face; she tried to look up at him but her eyes wouldn't rise. There he was, within her reach. He was as large as all those men in Howard's magazines, but he was life-size, huge. Surely he would hurt her, he would split her, he would kill her, she thought.

He spoke again, but she still couldn't make out what he said. So close, so close, so many years of longing, so many dreams, so much time and energy and hope poured into fantasies—she reached out her good hand and touched him. The heat was astounding.

He knelt upon the bed, spreading her legs and his motion pulled him away from her. She reached for him and he pushed her back, then his hands were yanking at her nightgown and it was off, she didn't know how. His touch was rough and hot, and oh, my God, oh my God, his mouth was on her breast. Oh, she had not known. *Oh. More. Oh, God. More.*

The fear was gone. She didn't care what he did, he could hurt her, kill her—and she thought she might do the same to him. She tore at him, she bit his shoulder, her good hand clawed at his back, and the baby arm clung to him for dear life. Her good leg swung over his thighs and pulled him even closer to her. He could not get away, he must never get away, he must never leave.

He lifted his face from her breast, grinned at her, his teeth as white as bone in the moonlight.

"Kiss me," Myra said. "Please kiss me."

He kissed her while his hands continued to probe and caress. His breath was sweet, she was surprised, it tasted of toothpaste. His lips were hard and so active. They raced across her, pressing, nipping, moving. Myra wanted him to linger, she wanted to experience the feeling, but it was too fast, too urgent. His tongue was in her mouth, probing, searching. She responded in kind. This was not the kind of kiss she had longed for, not the kind that ended movies and broke women's hearts, but she had seen this one on the screen, too. She did what he did, hoping she was doing it right. It all seemed so frantic. Her body was frantic but her lips wanted to be beguiled. He is having sex with my body, she thought, and I want to make love with my lips. But she did what he did and found an excitement there, too.

She reached for him again. She could feel him against her leg but she wanted to hold him. This part of him was such a mystery; she didn't know how long she would have, she must learn everything so quickly. She had him and she heard him sigh. Her hearing had returned. He breathed heavily, almost angrily, as he parted her legs roughly and positioned himself between them. She was still holding him and he prodded ineffectually at her. Doesn't he know how, she wondered. Can't he find his way? This sudden ineptitude surprised her. She guided him in.

I probably did it wrong, Myra thought. I probably didn't do what I should have, what I could have, what he wanted. He must be disappointed, and so, she confessed to herself, was she. A bit. Not in him. He was a wonderful lover, she was sure of it, but in the experience itself. It was exciting, terribly exciting. She had almost blacked out from all the sheer stimulation of it. Her nerve endings were shrieking from the overload. But . . .

She had expected too much, it was her fault, she thought; no experience could live up to such expectation. But. It was so fast, so

frantic. It all seemed to take place almost without her, or just in front
of her as she struggled to catch up to it. It was all just beyond her
reach. *He* was there, he must have thought he was with her, but she
never quite caught up, he leapt from stage to stage without her.

But she had done it! She would not die a virgin! And next time
she would be better, she would keep pace with him. If there was a
next time; she hoped there would be a next time. That couldn't be all
there was to it. Myra wanted to know the rest, she wanted to know
the magic that inspired the songs and poems and moved the world.

He slept now. When he awoke would he give her another chance?
She thought he would, but it would be full day when he awoke. Her
arm and leg would not be cloaked in darkness then. He had not really
touched either of them this morning, although he must have felt her
arm upon his back. If he was revolted, he did not show it. But daylight
was different. She did not know how he would act. Please, God, let
him be kind, she thought.

Her touch awakened him, as she had feared it would. As she had
hoped it would. He smacked his lips twice, then turned in her arms
and buried his face in her neck. His breath was stale, but the rest of
him was fresh and eager.

Myra wanted to talk to him but he was between her legs already
and this time he slipped in without her guidance. Look, Ma, I'm doing
it again, Myra cried in her mind. Little Myra had a lover. Crippled
Myra was not afraid. Was not afraid. Was not afraid to live.

Howard was in the door. How could she not have heard him? Kane
was in her and Howard was in the room. He looked as if he had been
shot. He looked as if Myra had done the shooting. He stood there
with his mouth open, horrified, too astounded to speak. If Kane was
aware of him, he didn't seem to care, he kept on pumping.

Myra closed her eyes, she didn't know what else to do. At least it
removed Howard's blighted image from her vision.

Oh, grow up, she wanted to tell him. It's only Myra fucking the
house guest. Or the house guest fucking her. She seemed to have little
to do with it, but it did feel good. It felt so good. Much better than
last night, though localized. Last night was an overload, this was specific. She opened her eyes and Howard was gone. Thank God. She
was not quite wanton enough to abandon herself to lust while he was
looking on, and it did feel so good. Abandonment was called for.

But then it was over. Kane was growling, snarling in her ear, sounding savage, vicious. Desperate. His whole body was rigid, he lifted his head, she saw his face, his teeth bared. He glanced down at her, glaring in anger. And then he released his breath. Myra had not realized he was holding it until he let it go explosively, then succumbed to a succession of panting sighs. He fell on her again, then rolled off. Not yet! She didn't want to release him yet, and she gasped at the withdrawal. She tried to hold him a little longer, moaning her disappointment, but he shrugged her off and was out of the bed, standing, stretching, his back to her.

The sun was now coming directly in the window and it made the hair on his arms and legs shine like a halo. Myra heard the outer door close. Howard had left. She would have to spend much of the day thinking about Howard, she realized. How to explain to him, how to deal with his reaction. But not yet. Thank goodness, not yet. She had a few minutes left to bask in the memory of Kane. Her body was still warm from his. Hairs from his chest and stomach were on her skin.

"How's he going to take this?" Kane asked. It was the first time he had spoken to Myra since his unheeded muttering when he first came to her and even now his back was to her.

"I don't know," she said. "He was in the room, he saw us."

"I know," said Kane. "I heard him coming."

He moved to the door.

"Will you come again tonight?" she asked.

He turned and looked at her for the first time. She was suddenly embarrassed and pulled the sheet over her lower body. There was nothing she could do about the baby arm.

"Sure," said Kane.

Myra wanted something sweeter, some recognition of communion. She wanted to ask if she was all right, did she disappoint, did she fail him. She wanted him to touch her softly, not for sex, just to touch her. It seemed she wanted so many things. It was simpler before when all she wanted was the impossible, all she craved was the experience. Now that she had had that, she seemed to want so much more.

20

The agent who had met Becker at the airport with the news of Assad's murder sought him out again.

"Great news," the agent said.

Becker looked at him quizzically, waiting.

"Deputy Director Hatcher wants to see you immediately."

"Even you can't think of that as *great* news," Becker said.

"No, that's not the news," the agent said. "There's been another murder!"

"Who this time?"

"A man named Henley, lives on the West Side."

"Any known connection with Bahoud?"

"None at all—except the way he died. Deputy Director Hatcher thought you'd be really excited. Two in one day."

"I'm wetting myself," said Hatcher.

The agent tilted his head to one side.

"The deputy director thought you'd like to ride to the scene with him."

"One treat right after another," said Becker sourly.

"I know," said the agent with enthusiasm. "It's a great day."

"I don't deserve it," said Becker.

As he slid into the backseat of the car to join Hatcher, Becker said, "Any further theories about Assad?"

"Other than the Mossad? I think it covers the ground pretty well."

"I've got another theory. The only thing wrong with it, is you may have been right."

Hatcher was startled by the admission.

"About what?"

"You once said that being an Arab terrorist who could pass himself off as an Israeli would be one hell of a disguise, or something to that effect. I didn't pay any attention at the time, but you may have been onto something. What better cover for an act of Arab terrorism than a militant Jewish organization? The act is done for Arab reasons and the Jews get blamed.''

"How do you get the Jews to do it?''

"I'm not sure,'' said Becker. "You bend them some way. A couple million dollars might help.''

"You think B.Z. is a Jewish group?''

"It doesn't have to be, but if it *appears* to be it serves the same purpose. Let's say you were an enemy of Assad who wanted him dead but no repercussions. You kill him, smear some paint on the mosque, and who gets blamed? Automatically? Who are the public enemies of Islam, of the Arabs? Who are the high-profile suspects? It seems to me it works pretty much the same whether it was a Jewish group that did it or just someone making it look that way.''

"It sounds rather elaborate.''

"If they just wanted to kill Assad, it is. But I told you, I think they, he, has another target. Assad was just a test run. Or paying off an old debt. Or maybe establishing credibility.''

"Credibility?''

"For 'B.Z.,' '' Becker said. "Before Assad was killed, no one had heard of them. Now we've heard of them, now we know them as a slayer of a former PLO leader, a defiler of mosques, someone who uses Jewish slogans and therefore is probably Jewish. Whatever they do next is going to be seen in that context. Let's take the reverse analogy. If you are an established Nazi and you make statements about pure blood, we know immediately what you're talking about. We don't think you mean viruses. The point is, whether B.Z. is a Jewish group or not, they are now set up for us with a history, a point of view, a lethal past. Whatever happens next is going to be seen in that context.''

"And what happens next? Assuming you're right that the Assad killing is not what it was all about.''

"If I knew what happens next, Hatcher, I'd quit this job and make a fortune reading palms.''

"I thought that's what you were good at. Thinking the way the bad boys think.''

"No,'' said Becker. "What I'm good at is feeling the way the bad boys feel.'' They fell into an uncomfortable silence. Becker knew he had said too much and Hatcher had heard more than he wanted to hear.

After a time Becker spoke again. "Have Finney get a list of the heads of state attending the U.N. session on children."

Hatcher was relieved that the topic was once more business.

"Are you kidding? That session is crawling with security people. Every man there has his own security guards, plus the Secret Service, plus the FBI, plus every spare New York City cop. Nobody's going to get within two blocks of the U.N. plaza tomorrow. You'd have to be insane to pick a target there. And you don't think our boy is insane, do you?"

"Oh, no, he's very sane. He's just not very nice. And he's working for the Beni Hassan, remember? They're terrorists, Hatcher. Not criminals. They're not trying to avoid detection, they *want* publicity. The more the better. What better place to get the terrified attention of every nation in the world? A gathering of seventy-six heads of state, and one of them is killed. Or many of them. Through the biggest security net this country could provide. You can't get much more publicity than that."

"If the Beni Hassan killed someone at a U.N. conference on children, the rest of the world would be so outraged Beni Hassan wouldn't have an ally left."

"Maybe. If Beni Hassan got blamed for it. But if B.Z. got blamed for it . . ."

"A known Jewish group."

"With one killing already to its credit."

Hatcher whistled one note. "That's not a stupid idea, is it?"

"Of course they'd have to pick a target that B.Z. would want to kill. It wouldn't serve any purpose if they bumped off the prime minister of Western Samoa, for instance."

"So who would B.Z. want dead?"

"What were the slogans they painted on the mosque?"

Hatcher stared out the window for a moment. The car had pulled to the curb as the two men continued to talk.

"PLO Must Pay. Never Again. B.Z."

"There's your target," said Becker.

"PLO?"

"Let's find out if Arafat is attending the session."

"The PLO isn't a member of the U.N."

"They've got observer status. This is the Year of the Children, Hatcher. Everyone there comes off looking like a saint in his concern for the children of the world. Arafat is too smart a politician to miss out on an opportunity like that."

"You think the Beni Hassan want Arafat dead?"

"They have for several years. Arafat has more enemies within the Palestinians than without. He's the one immovable obstacle that's keeping all the other groups from gaining power."

"So the Beni Hassan pays to have Arafat assassinated by what appears to be a radical Jewish group. Thus producing a major backlash against Israel."

"And getting rid of Arafat, and enlisting sympathy for their cause, and making the United States look culpable for allowing it to happen, and on and on. It's not two birds with one stone, it's a whole covey."

"So," Hatcher said slowly. "So, if true, what do we do next?"

Becker shrugged. "Find Bahoud. The U.N. session is tomorrow. I'd guess that's how long we have. Find Bahoud. See who he's killed now, and why."

Becker walked past the police cordon and into the building on West Eighty-sixth Street. Karen Crist was waiting on the stoop.

"The body was found by Mr. LeFraque over there." The homicide detective, whose name was Riordan, inclined his head toward a balding man, who was talking to another detective in the corner of the little room. He pronounced the name Le-*frak*. "He came to pick up the deceased, they had an appointment. Finally he got the super to let him in. Says he knew the deceased wouldn't miss the appointment unless he was seriously ill."

Becker looked at Henley's body still crumpled in the closet. A trickle of blood had dried along a wavering line from his ear to his open collar.

He heard the intake of breath behind him as Karen Crist looked at the body. He gave her a moment before turning to look at her. She had composed her features by then, but her coloring gave her away.

"Two in one day is a hard way to begin," Becker said.

Karen nodded, but refused the out he offered. She knelt for a closer look.

"I'll want to know what you think," he said.

She nodded again, swallowing hard.

"And what you feel. Especially that," he continued.

She looked away from Henley's body for the first time, questioning Becker. "How I feel?"

"Not just what you feel. I want to know what he felt."

Becker drifted across the room toward LeFraque. Karen forced herself to look again at Henley's crumpled body, the pathetic rivulet of dried blood from his ear. What he felt? What did Becker mean? How the dead man felt? What did Becker want from her? For a moment she thought she might be sick, but the impulse was weaker than it had been when she knelt beside Solin's body on the sidewalk. She had fought it back that time, she could certainly do it this time. Amazing, she thought, how quickly one could adjust. To anything. Even to death. It was a very disquieting thought.

"He was going to have rewrites for me," LeFraque explained to Becker. "I'm a producer. A theatrical producer. Henley was a playwright. I was producing his play. That's why I came by. Normally a playwright would come to my office, but Henley was weird about traveling around the city. He would do it, but he was more comfortable if I picked him up."

"Rewrites?" Hatcher asked.

"For the play. His play. Our play. We had a meeting scheduled today with the director. There were some changes that he had to make in order for us to attract a star—I can't tell you how important that is these days. No one will go to the theater without a star's name on the marquee. It doesn't matter if they can act as long as they've been on television. Something you can promote, you know?"

"I don't go to the theater," Hatcher said.

"No. Neither does anybody else," said LeFraque.

"They don't live very well, do they?" Becker said.

"Who?"

"Playwrights."

LeFraque looked around the tiny apartment as if noticing it for the first time. "Not the good ones," he said.

"Did you find the rewrites?"

"No. The script isn't here. He must have taken it to a typist."

"He wouldn't type it himself?"

"If he had a word processor, maybe." LeFraque pointed to an aging portable typewriter on the desk. "He couldn't afford one."

"But he could afford a typist?"

"I gave him an advance. Option money," LeFraque said, as if he regretted it.

When Hatcher and Riordan had left the apartment, leaving only a forensic man to dust and measure and scrape, Becker caught Karen's elbow and kept her from departing, too.

"Now, tell me about it," Becker said. She looked at him blankly. "Tell me what happened, how you see it."

Karen took a deep breath. She felt as if she were back in school and being quizzed on a subject she barely understood.

"Well, the perpetrator was probably known to the victim. There's no indication of forced entry, which means the victim let the perpetrator in the door. Except for the method of killing, which suggests Bahoud, I would have thought it was a robbery, the place has been turned upside down . . ."

"If it was someone who knew him, why would he rob him? Look at this place, the guy didn't own anything, he didn't have any money. The television isn't stolen, the cassette player is still here."

"He was looking for something specific, something incriminating . . ."

Becker touched her arm again.

"You're giving me what Hatcher could give. Let's start over. Walk me through it."

Karen walked toward the bed. "Blood stain on the sheets, but smeared. I'd guess he cleaned the weapon here." She crossed to the closet. "No signs of violence on the victim apart from the ear. That's strange because . . ."

Becker was looking at her, shaking his head impatiently.

"What do you want?" she asked. "I don't know what you want."

"You're not trying. You're not using what you have," said Becker.

"I don't know what you want from me," she said, anger showing in her voice.

Becker pulled her to the hallway, closed the apartment door in her face.

"You're the killer," he said. "You're Bahoud. What do you feel?"

"Feel? What do you mean . . ."

"Come on, Karen," he said impatiently. "You're outside his door, you've got a weapon, you've come to kill. What do you feel?"

Karen stared at him.

"Your throat is tight with excitement," Becker said. "You try to control it but your chest is heaving. You can hear your breath. It sounds like a wind storm, the roar of blood in your ears is deafening. You can't believe the man on the other side of this door can't hear it. You want him to come to the door, God, you want him to come, you want him so bad now, it's like sex. You're ready to burst but your partner keeps pushing you away, you can't stand much more of it. And then a miracle. The guy did not hear the roar of your blood or the storm of your breath, he just comes to the door and opens it and you're in!"

Becker pushed open the door and propelled Karen in before him. She pulled away from his grip.

"Now what?" Becker said.

Karen shook her head.

Becker sat in the upholstered chair, jerked Karen so her back was to him and pulled her down. He put an arm across her chest, pulled her back into his body. His finger touched her ear, his lips were against her hair.

The forensic man working the closet looked up at Becker and Karen, then returned to his work.

"Now you've got him where you want him," Becker said. "Your victim is stunned, shocked, you can feel his indecision. He can't believe what is happening to him, he still doesn't know what you're going to do. You lean into him, feeling his body warm and strong against yours, beginning to struggle now. That's good, that's good. You want a bit of struggle, not too much, not enough to make the job hard, but enough to give you pleasure. And it does give you pleasure. You're more excited than ever, the roaring in your ears is almost too much to take. You're shaking now, your whole body is quivering with the excitement. You love it. There's nothing like it, no sex, no power in the world like it. You try to postpone it a little longer, just a little longer, but then you can't wait another second. You touch the ear with the icepick. You thrust, feel his body react against yours, cling to him in that second, savor it, make it last, that final convulsive twitch . . . "

Becker released Karen and she bounded away from him. She was glad the forensic man was in the room; she fought back an impulse to cry out.

Becker stood over her, lifted her to her feet. His face was flushed.

"And then you take the body to the closet, push it into the corner, cover it with a jacket. What do you feel now?"

"I don't know," Karen said, her throat constricted.

"Nothing," said Becker. "You feel nothing at all."

He turned his back to her and walked to the window.

It took Karen the better part of a minute to get control of her emotions. She could not recall when she had ever felt so frightened.

"I'm going now," she said at last.

Becker did not turn to look at her. "I'll see you at the hotel later." He sounded very strange to her, clotted and restricted as if something were spilling out of him and getting in the way of his voice.

"Yes," she said. "I'll see you later."

She hurried from the room and into the street. She gulped in breaths as if she'd never get enough air.

Karen Crist awoke and realized she was alone in the bed. It took her a second to remember where she was and she had already reached for her weapon before it came back to her. The bed where Becker had lain beside her was warm. His movement when he got up must have awakened her.

The night had been exceptional in its intensity. Becker had come at her with such a passion it had seemed almost like an attack. The strangeness of his behavior at the murder scene in the afternoon was still with Karen, and her participation was tinged with a fear that she tried to deny to herself. There was something more than lust operating with Becker, too. He had taken her as desperately as a drowning man bursting to the surface, gasping for air. Afterwards he had been as tender and solicitous as ever, but the act itself had had the urgency of rape—except that Karen was so willing. The experience added to her growing sense of disquiet. There was a concentration of emotion in Becker, a turbulent vehemence barely contained beneath the taciturn surface that she did not think she could either match or understand. He reminded her of a tame wolf, normally docile and pacific, but with the potential within for a ferocity and strength that no domesticated species could equal. No matter how "tame," the wild animal would eventually return to the wild. Becker was out of her control, beyond her capacity to soothe or serve, harness or lead.

She found him sitting in the living room of their hotel suite. The table lamp beside him was on.

"What's wrong?" she asked.

"I woke up," he said.

"You didn't have to get out of bed."

"I didn't want to disturb you."

"You wouldn't disturb me just being awake."

"I needed the light on," he said.

"Was it that dark?"

"Yes."

She stood beside him, one hand on his shoulder.

"Are you afraid of what might happen to you in the dark? I mean, that your father will do those things to you again?"

"Did I say it was my father?"

"I just assumed."

"No," Becker said after a pause. "I'm not afraid that anyone will hurt me. I'm past that."

"What is it, then?" Karen knelt beside his chair and looked at his face. She was not at all sure she wanted to hear his answer, but she knew she should ask. They were approaching a borderline and he could step over it or not, he could reveal himself and she would have to take him in, she would have to open her heart to him, or he could chose not to; he could leave matters where they were with her on one side of the border and himself on the other. She hoped he would not step across the line. Romance and excitement and wonderful sex would be transformed into something deeper and far more dangerous and Karen did not welcome the change. But she had to ask, she had to offer help.

"It's what I do in the dark," he said. "That's what I'm afraid of."

"What do you mean?"

"It's what . . . At first it's fear. Just fear. I don't mean *just* fear because it's terrible. It's immobilizing, it's paralyzing . . ."

"Not you."

"Of course me. But I'm used to it, I've felt it many times and I know I can get past it. It's the way I get past it that really scares me."

And here it was, the line drawn in the air. She could go back to bed, she could leave it alone, let it hang there, and things could stay as they were. Or slowly wither and die, as excitement always did. At least it was territory she knew and understood and could ultimately deal with. Who knew what demons lay in Becker's uncharted country? But even as she hesitated she knew she would ask.

She had to. It was one of the things that made her different from a man, she thought.

"How do you get past it?"

Becker was quiet for a very long time. Karen could hear the light bulb beside her ear humming as if it were under stress.

Don't answer, she thought. Just don't answer.

"I become him," Becker said. "Worse, I become worse than he ever was. I do what he only wanted to do."

He had spoken the words into the empty space in front of him, but now Becker turned to face her. His eyes pleaded for forgiveness, absolution.

Karen rose and pulled his head against her body. He clung to her, his body begging for comfort.

"You're not a bad man, John," she said, knowing it was so inadequate.

"Not always," he said.

"The men you . . ."

"Killed," he said.

"They were all bad men. They had all murdered. You had no choice, they left you no choice."

"Did they leave me no choice? Or did *I* leave me no choice?"

"It wasn't your fault. You did what you had to do," she said, but she was no longer sure it was true.

"I'm afraid that . . ."

"You've never hurt anyone except in self-defense. You've never harmed an innocent person, you couldn't, I know you couldn't."

"No, I haven't . . . because so far I've come back."

"Come back from where?"

"From being him. What if next time I don't come back?"

He wanted help so desperately, she thought, but she didn't have any to offer. She didn't know what to do, what to say.

"Thinking bad things doesn't make you bad," she said. "We all think bad thoughts, horrible, evil thoughts. But we don't act on them. That's what makes the difference. A person is what he does, not what he thinks. Behavior counts."

"You don't understand, do you?" he asked, and she realized that it was what he really wanted; not to be absolved or forgiven, but simply understood.

"No," she admitted. "I don't understand."

"I thought you might," he said. "On some level."

She shook her head. "I'm not who you thought I was, John. I'm not even who I thought I was. You were wrong about me, I don't have what you have, I don't share your gift . . . "

"It's no gift."

"I don't share your pain. My fear is my fear, not yours, it's done different things to me."

"I'm sorry," he said.

"Oh, no."

"I tried to make you what I needed. It was unfair."

"You do need someone, John. But it's not me. I wish it could be, but it's not."

He clung to her in silence for a while. When he loosed his grip at last Karen pulled off the T-shirt she had worn to bed.

He looked up at her, past her breasts, and grinned slowly.

She stroked his head, then pulled him against her once more so that his lips touched her naked flesh. He pressed his lips to her navel and reached for her breasts. She moaned and leaned into him.

It was a cheat, she knew, but it was the only comfort she could give him.

Bahoud rode the elevator from the thirty-fourth floor to the basement, stopping at five floors on the way down, stops for which Bahoud had pushed the buttons himself. This was a residential building and elevator use during the mid-afternoon, although random, was never heavy. Five stops was much slower than it would normally be. It was his worst-case scenario and even then the descent was very rapid. He could expect to get from Myra's apartment to the basement in less than two minutes. Once in the basement, he walked toward the storage rooms.

He passed the new power plant of the building, which hummed day and night, he passed the incinerator, no longer in use, and paused outside the storage rooms where residents stashed property too large to keep in their apartments.

The door was locked with a ludicrously simple device designed to keep out vagrants looking for a place to sleep. It was useless against a professional and Bahoud had it open in less than ten seconds.

The room was close to bursting with the rejects of people cramped for space. There were old bicycles, children's carriages and trikes, outgrown but too encased in memories to be disposed of, several sets of free weights for exercising, one of them still in the original packaging, lamps, chairs, a dining room set, mattresses resting on end, furniture of all styles and ages. There were enough steamer trunks to start a small shop and, behind two of them, covered by a set of ancient drapes, Bahoud found his rifle.

It was a Remington 700, the U.S. Army's sniper's rifle, complete with a collapsible tripod. The telescopic sight was a Leupold M8-36X with a duplex reticule. The weapon had been given to him by a nervous Lebanese in Brooklyn, who handled the rifle case as if it contained nitroglycerine. Bahoud had purchased the scope separately from a store in Manhattan. It was a miracle of modern-day optics, the dull matte finish belying the spectacular precision of the lenses it contained.

Bahoud had tested the combination of lens and rifle once, in the gathering dusk of the Jersey swamps. Despite the bad light he had seen his target, a Cranshaw melon half the size of a man's head, as clearly as if it were across a room. In fact it had been four hundred yards away. The first shot had exploded the melon, the second had ripped through a fragment of melon still spinning in the air. He had not bothered with a third. It had taken him thirty seconds to set up the tripod and take his aim. Without rushing he had repacked the dismantled gun and collapsed tripod in the case in a minute and a half. On the day of the assassination, of course, he would not need to bother with packing the rifle. He would leave it there along with Howard's corpse. The assassin who had taken his own life for the great good of the cause.

Bahoud merely looked at the rifle to be sure it was undisturbed. Next to the rifle case was a crumpled brown grocery bad and inside the grocery bag was a flashlight and a plastic shopping bag. From the shopping bag Bahoud withdrew the uniform of a plumber, complete to the name "Gene" sewn in looping cursive in red thread above the breast pocket.

The uniform, a dull brown coverall, had never been worn. Bahoud slipped it over his street clothes. It was too large in the sleeves and legs and he rolled them all up. Pushing aside cartons, Bahoud made a place on the floor large enough to lie down. Keeping his head up, he rolled back and forth across the little space, dirtying the uniform. Brushing himself off with a few perfunctory pats, Bahoud returned the cartons to their original positions and slipped the rifle case behind the steamer trunks once more.

Wearing the uniform and carrying the flashlight Bahoud slipped out of the storage room, relocked the door, and stuffed the shopping bag inside the front of the overalls. He ran the zipper of the uniform up and down several times to be sure it wouldn't jam when he needed it.

Like most high rises erected in Manhattan in the vast post-WW II construction boom, the building on Forty-third Street was constructed according to post-1948 codes. As the new structures went up, back to back and side to side without intervening space, they were built with common subbasements that allowed access to all. Like landlocked countries, all the high rises required a corridor to the outside. (A corridor that did not detract from the fashionable frontage.) The interconnected subbasement system allowed a common entrance for the conduits and deliveries of an earlier time. Gas fittings, plumbing, sewage pipes, electrical cables, steam pipes, telephone lines all snaked in from their arteries under the streets and all required space for their servicemen to get at them in time of need. From a single main entrance, this cadre of servicemen could reach several buildings at once. The subbasements spread like warrens beneath the ground, sometimes covering an entire square block.

Seldom used today and tightly shut at all entrances, the underground grid is dark and claustrophobic. It was built for the convenience of the high-rise occupants, not for the convenience of the service people who must maneuver past pipes and cables and frequently squeeze through crawl spaces to get where they are going. Lighting is poor and infrequent and as Bahoud made his way under the Goldsmith building, he made it even worse. As he went, he unscrewed the few bulbs casting a feeble light in the gloom. He did not expect to be followed when he came to this exit after the shooting, but it was better to be prepared, and he was certain that whoever came after him would not be carrying a flashlight. It was a small precaution, but the kind that sometimes made a difference.

Bahoud's light shone upon the doorway, an opening in the cinder block wall, that led under the adjoining building. It was here that he would deal with anyone following him. One step behind the wall would put him out of sight, assuming the pursuer had any light to see

with, and he would have to come through the narrow door; there was
no other way. Bahoud would wait on the other side and the business
would be quickly done.

He trained his light around him. Pipes and cables danced in the
beam like so many serpents. Astounding how much support was
needed to run a building. Now and then he heard a rat scampering
away as he approached, but he did not see any.

Bahoud reached the steel door, opened it, and emerged into the
basement of a building fronting on Third Avenue. In thirty seconds
he was on the street, his face in sunlight.

Bahoud glanced at his watch. Under five minutes, he noted with
satisfaction. Even allowing for delays it was still less than five minutes
from the apartment on the thirty-fourth floor to the street on Third
Avenue. One city block away from where the shot had taken place,
unseen, or if seen, unnoticed. The most efficient police force in the
world could not throw up a cordon in five minutes, and even if they
did, it would not extend this far beyond the suspected source of the
shot. If he did not fall and break his leg, he would be free and away
in five minutes. If he did break his leg, it might take him another five
minutes to drag himself to Third Avenue. Still with more than enough
time to spare. The great beauty of working in a place like Manhattan
was the almost immediate invisibilty. He could disappear like just
another ant in an anthill.

Bahoud walked downtown to the first coffee shop. He ordered coffee at the counter, then went into the restroom where he slipped out
of his uniform. Folding the uniform neatly, he slipped it into the shopping bag with the flashlight, then returned to the counter, paid for his
coffee, and walked back to Myra's building.

It was a very congenial walk. Bahoud was pleased with himself,
with his work, with the ease with which everything was falling into
place. The seduction of the woman had been easy, even fun. Some
sacrifices in the line of duty were a lot easier to make than others. He
had not found her body as distasteful as he had feared. The withered
arm had surprised him with the smoothness of the flesh, the strength
it possessed while pulling on his back. He had expected it to feel
dead, or skeletal, but it was clearly alive. The leg had not been much
of a factor, although she had used the good one for all it was worth.
He smiled at the memory. He had been terrific, of course. She had
been needy, then greedy and surprisingly adept at it. She wasn't prac-

ticed at it, exactly, but it was obvious to Bahoud that she had some experience. Maybe the brother, what with the two of them living together like a couple of hermits in a cave the way they did. Why not? That sort of thing happened all the time. He wasn't sure what Howard was capable of in that area—he certainly wasn't capable of much in any other area. Bahoud was grateful he didn't have to prop the guy up anymore. Once Bahoud stepped away, Howard would collapse like an empty sack, and the "Brotherhood of Zion" along with him, but by then it wouldn't matter. They both would have served their purposes. The Palestinians would have a martyr; Hammadi, or whoever was behind him, would have a clear shot at leadership; the Arabs would have more fuel to consume in their anti-Zionist furnaces; and the United States would have a major international embarrassment. Hammadi's sponsor was getting his money's worth out of this. And, of course, so was Bahoud.

As he approached his building, Bahoud wondered if he had time enough to take another whack at Myra before the brother came home. Last time had been very basic; this time he had a few tricks he might teach her. She seemed a very willing pupil. He thought at one time he heard her say she loved him. But then she was making lots of sounds, he couldn't be sure. One thing he was positive about, however, was that she wasn't going to try to evict him now. He had the time he needed from her.

O'Brien was waiting for him.

"Ah, Mr. Kane," he said. "The very man."

"Hello, O'Brien. How are you?"

"Fine, sir, and thanking you for asking, Mr. Kane. You recall that little business you spoke to me about? Concerning the ex-wife?"

Kane was immediately alert.

"What about it?"

"Well, sir, you said there might be some private detectives asking about you, if you recall, sir?"

"Someone was asking about me?"

"Well, in a manner of speaking. Two of them, there were. They claimed to be with the Secret Service, very impressive-looking badges and so forth. They were checking all the apartment buildings in the area, asking if there had been any strangers around, anyone suspicious, any new tenants within the last three months, that sort of thing."

"What did you tell them?"

"Well, sir, they said they was Secret Service, but how was I to know? They said they were concerned about the big to-do at the U.N., but then they would say that, wouldn't they? I mean, if they were private detectives, they wouldn't come right out and tell me, now would they?"

"Probably not," said Kane

"Indeed not, that's exactly what I thought. I said to myself, O'Brien, where does your loyalty lie, man? With some greeding, grasping, vindictive bitch?—you'll pardon my saying so, but that's how you've described the lady yourself. I have no personal knowledge of her."

"Quite right."

"Or does your loyalty lie with an upstanding, honest man who would like to keep a bit of his earnings for himself? Yourself being the man, Mr. Kane, of course. A man who has been most courteous and generous with me in the past—and will no doubt continue to be in the future."

"You're right about that," said Kane, pulling his wallet from his pocket.

"I knew I would be, sir. So naturally I did not mention you. If they were detectives, then shame upon them for lying to me. And if they were truly Secret Service men, then it would hardly be a honest man like yourself they're looking for."

Kane pressed two fifties from his wallet into O'Brien's hand.

"You are a friend, O'Brien. I hope I can be as good a friend to you."

"I'm sure you will be, Mr. Kane."

"And let me know if anyone else comes around, will you?"

"Well, now, there's the thing, sir. It's been a very busy morning here. There's a gentleman upstairs with Miss Myra right now."

"Who is it?"

"Name of Becker, sir, and this one had a badge, too. He wasn't asking about you, mind. He just wanted to see Miss Myra, but I thought it was the kind of thing you would be interested in."

"It is, indeed."

"So I thought."

"Did he say what he wanted to see her about?"

"No, sir, he did not. He just announced he was FBI and wanted to talk to her. You know how they are, sir. Very closed-mouth."

"Are you sure he said FBI?"

"Oh, yes, sir, Mr. Kane."

Kane paused, trying to keep his face calm. They could not possibly be onto him yet. It wasn't possible, there was no way to trace him.

"What did he look like?"

"Oh, about your size, sir. Brown hair, I think it was. About your age, too, I would say."

Kane nodded. "That could be her brother."

"Her brother?"

"My ex-wife's brother."

"This one had the look of cop about him, Mr. Kane. I didn't need to see the badge to believe he was FBI. It's them eyes, you know. They all have those eyes, like a dog when he hears something and his ears go up? Cops have got the same look to them, all the time. Like they're suspicious of everything."

Kane nodded again. "That's him. He is a cop, actually. But in Philly, not here, and he's sure as hell not FBI. Another one lied to you, O'Brien."

O'Brien waggled his head over the perfidy of mankind.

"I want to get a look at this guy, but if it is her brother I can't afford to let him see me. How can we do this?"

"You could wait across the street there, Mr. Kane. I could give you the high sign when the gentleman came out."

"There's no very good place across the street, do you think? Won't he see me when he comes out?"

"You could be right, sir." O'Brien rubbed his fleshy chin. "You know the pharmacy on the corner there, sir? If you could wait in there by the window, I could step out into the street when the gentleman in question comes down—like I was hailing a cab, you know. You can see me when I'm in the street and I can give you the high sign from there."

"Very good, O'Brien."

"There was once a very generous gentleman like yourself, sir. Years ago this was. He had developed an attachment for a lady in 14F. Unfortunately, as sometimes happens, this lady was married. The gentleman and I worked out a similar arrangement, sir."

"Bless you and the gentleman," Kane said.

"That gentleman gave me blessing enough, sir. A most generous man."

The pharmacy had pretensions. It called itself a chemist's shop in the British fashion and featured displays of retorts and alembics and various colored apothecary jars.

Kane bought a manicure kit and asked that it not be wrapped. Under the plastic blister were a number of emery boards and three orange sticks for manipulating cuticles. One end of the stick was spade shaped, the other pencil sharp. Bahoud held the orange stick in his palm with two inches protruding between his thumb and forefinger. It was a clumsy instrument compared to his icepick, but it would serve. The wood was firm and the point was sharp. Using one of the emery boards as a file, he made the point even sharper as he took up his position by the window and waited.

The door was partially open when he arrived at 34B, and Becker walked in when the voice beckoned. He found Myra sitting at her word processor, a pretty young woman framed by her window and with the sun forming a nimbus around her.

"You said you're with the FBI?" she asked.

"Special Agent John Becker." He approached and showed her his badge and identification. She made no attempt to rise.

Becker noticed the withered arm held close to her side but did not look at it.

"Please sit down," she said, gesturing with her good arm. There was something very composed, almost regal in her movements. Rehearsed, Becker thought. She is playing a role. And she is very nervous, although she hides it well.

When he sat upon the overstuffed sofa with the pattern of huge English roses, he noticed her twisted leg, tucked carefully behind the normal one. Almost hidden, but not quite. Again he did not look directly at it, and this time he realized how often she must have noticed the stares not made, the glances averted.

"I can't imagine what I can do for you," said Myra.

She is not just tense, Becker thought. Not just composed. She looks braced. As if she is trying to prepare herself for what is coming.

"Do you know a man named John Henley?" he asked.

Her surprise was genuine, he was sure of that. Whatever she had braced herself for, it was not Henley. What had she anticipated he was here for?

"Mr. Henley? I'm sorry if I hesitated, but I never think of him by his first name. The John threw me. Of course I know Mr. Henley. He's a client."

"Have you seen him recently?"

"Yesterday. He brought me his script."

Myra tapped a neat pile of pages on her desk.

"He wanted it right away," she said. "I'm surprised he hasn't come by yet . . . But of course that's why you're here, isn't it?"

"What is?"

"Whatever has kept him from coming by to get his script. He's in trouble of some kind."

"What kind of trouble would you expect that to be?"

"Mr. Henley? I wouldn't expect him to be in trouble at all."

Becker had noticed the telescope as soon as he entered the room. He stood now and moved toward it.

"That's a beautiful instrument," he said. "Are you an astronomer?"

"Sort of an amateur. Just a dabbler, really."

Becker bent to the eyepiece. "May I?"

"What kind of trouble is he in?" she asked.

"Have you been able to see the new supernova?"

"That's in the Southern Hemisphere," Myra said. "I couldn't possibly see it from here. Actually, there is far too much light in New York City to be able to see much of anything very well."

Becker fiddled slightly with the focus. The United Nations plaza sprang sharply into view.

"Are you a United Nations fancier?" he asked.

"No. Why? . . . Oh, is that where it's pointing?"

Becker looked at her closely, smiling, waiting. There were times when no questions were necessary.

"I must have moved it without realizing," she said and she blushed slightly.

Now what is that all about, Becker wondered. What memory have I touched upon, and why does she feel it necessary to cover up?

"Mr. Henley has been murdered," he said abruptly.

Her face fell with a genuine shock that could not have been feigned.

"Oh, my God!"

She began to cry.

"I'm sorry," Becker said. "I shouldn't have done that so abruptly. I didn't realize he meant that much to you."

"He doesn't," she said. "Or I didn't know he did. He was a nice man. He tried to be nice to me."

She began to weep again and Becker gave her all the time she needed to compose herself.

"Why would anyone murder Mr. Henley?" she asked at length.

"We have no idea. You may have been the last person to see him alive. I thought perhaps you could tell me something about his mental condition at the time."

"Is that why you came to see me?"

Becker fixed her eyes with his own and smiled very slightly.

"Why did you think I came, Ms. Goldsmith?"

"What do you mean? I had no idea."

"I thought perhaps you did have an idea. I got the impression that you knew at first exactly why I had come. You looked resigned, almost."

"How could I possibly have known about Mr. Henley?"

"I don't think you did. You thought I was here for some other reason. What was it?"

Myra tried to laugh, but it came out high and forced. "I really have not the slightest idea what you're talking about."

"Are you aware that it's a federal crime to lie to an agent of the FBI?"

Myra paused. "No, I didn't know that."

"It is."

"But I'm not lying anyway. What could I be lying about?"

"Do you live alone?" Becker asked, and there it was, the fractional hesitation, the flash of concern behind the eyes.

"No," she said. "My brother lives with me."

"What is his name?"

"Howard Goldsmith. He's never even met Mr. Henley."

"Are you sure?"

"Of course I'm sure."

Very defensive, Becker thought. Why? He gave her more silence to fill.

"Howard is capable of some stupid things, but he would never kill someone ..."

Her voice trailed off as she thought about the killing at the mosque to which Howard had reacted so violently. But that could not have had anything to do with Mr. Henley. Becker's eyes on her made her very uncomfortable. His gaze was not unfriendly, but probing. She had the feeling he could see through her skin.

Something else, Becker thought. There is something else here. Something with the brother, perhaps more.

"What sort of stupid things is your brother capable of?"

Again the pause, the uncertainty. She's trying to assess what I know, what I don't know, what she has to admit to.

"It's just a figure of speech," she said, and Becker realized she had decided he knew nothing. "He's actually a very stable person. Very rational. He's not capable of hurting anyone."

"Everyone is capable, if the provocation is sufficient," Becker said.

"That's very cynical."

"I wish it were, Ms. Goldsmith. I would like to believe in people whose souls were so peaceful they would never hurt anyone. I can't. I've seen too many who found the cause that stirred them enough."

"My brother doesn't have a cause," she said. Too quickly, Becker thought. Again too defensively.

Becker studied her, keeping his eyes on her face. The fingers of her dwarfed hand stirred restlessly.

"Did you come here to ask about my brother or Mr. Henley?"

Becker did not answer. Let it come out, he thought. You want to tell me, whatever it is. I want to hear it. Let it come out.

"I think I have the right to ask you to leave," she said.

Becker stood. "You have that right," he said. "The police will be by to ask you some questions."

Not that they'll get anything, he thought. They'll want to know about Henley, and that's not what we're talking about, is it, Ms. Goldsmith?

"Isn't that what you've been doing?" she asked.

"No, Ms. Goldsmith," Becker said. "What I've been doing is studying you."

"Yes," she said. "Why?"

"Does anyone else live here?"

"Why?" she demanded.

Wrong answer, thought Becker. Yes. Or no. Not why.

He looked at her and waited. It had been a random question. The apartment was large, there was room for another. He might have asked anything. But it turned out he asked the right thing.

"No, of course not," she said.

And that's it, thought Becker. The first outright lie. The others were hedges, half truths. But this was a lie, and she wasn't at all good at it.

"Of course not? Why of course not? The place is big enough for more than two people."

"I merely meant that I would have told you if there was anyone else living here."

"Why would you tell me if I didn't ask?"

"You did ask, didn't you? You asked if I lived alone."

"So I did," said Becker.

He stood. There was no point in questioning her any further. She would lie freely now that she had crossed the line. He could trip her up or corner her, perhaps, but he knew he would learn no more than he already knew. There was something hidden, something about the brother, something about someone else. And there were quicker ways to find out what than grilling a defensive witness. She was within an inch of asking for a lawyer already, and once she did, there would be no progress.

"Thank you, Ms. Goldsmith."

"Is that it?"

"Oh, no, Ms. Goldsmith," Becker said. "That's not it at all." He handed her a card with his name and the Bureau's local phone number. "When you're ready to get to the rest of it, call me there."

"There is no rest of it. What are you talking about?"

"You can reach me any time, day or night," Becker said.

"I really have no idea what you're implying," Myra said. She was back in control now. Once more the imperious hostess. Bette Davis, local school teacher, slightly offended by this snooping, unwashed cop.

"Day or night," said Becker as he let himself out and closed the door.

*   *   *

The doorman was a much better liar, but then he had had a great deal of practice. And warning, Becker realized. Either that or just the perpetual wariness of his trade.

"No one at all, sir," O'Brien said merrily. "The Goldsmiths keep very much to themselves, you see. Miss Myra almost never goes out, you know. And Mr. Howard . . ." O'Brien shrugged.

"Has no friends," Becker said, finishing O'Brien's sentence for him.

"Not for me to say, sir. I'm sure he's very popular at work and all. He just doesn't have visitors."

Becker nodded as if accepting the man's version. There was an easy enough way to break O'Brien's saucy confidence, but it would require a trip to a private room somewhere away from his own baili-wick. Any witness was difficult to break down if he was on his home turf where he was comfortable and in command. All that O'Brien would require was enough threat and aggravation to overcome what-ever bribe he already had in his pocket and had reasonable expectation of receiving for his silence in the future. It was a job he could leave to Hatcher, who was very good at straightforward work. Sublety eluded him, but give him a straight line and a push and Hatcher could develop considerable momentum. Certainly more than enough to crack someone like the doorman.

O'Brien hurried into the street as Becker was leaving.

"Taxi for you, sir?"

"No, thank you," said Becker. O'Brien already had his hand in the air, waving.

Bahoud stepped into the street and quickly crossed to the other side where he could follow Becker unobtrusively. He took in the look of the man as best he could from fifty yards behind. He would have to get closer, eventually, but for a minute or two he was content to absorb what he could from a distance. There were things to be learned from how a man carried himself, how he moved, his grace, his athleticism.

When he thought he knew his man, Bahoud increased his pace to close the gap between them. He positioned the orange stick firmly in place in his palm, secured under his ring. While Becker paused for a red light, Bahoud crossed the street again to be directly behind him. Someone jostled Becker and he turned to look back. Bahoud saw

Becker's face from fifteen feet and his mind closed around it like a hand around a fly. I have you, Bahoud thought. Now take me somewhere with a little privacy. Just a little, just enough.

Becker stopped abruptly and backed up to admire a necktie in a shop-window display. He studied it just a moment before entering the shop to the accompaniment of a jingling bell. He explained to the salesman about the marvelous tie and was led to the window to point out the precise one. Becker's eyes never so much as flickered toward the street scene outside the window because he had seen all he needed when he turned to enter the store. He had become suspicious when dealing with the doorman, O'Brien, and was alerted still further by O'Brien's insistence on waving for a cab when no taxi had been in sight. He had not tried to pick up his pursuer for several blocks, allowing the man to build confidence that he was undetected. It was only when he sidled into the path of another pedestrian, allowing himself to be jostled and to turn in annoyance, that Becker saw the man, the one person within dozens of yards who did not so much as glance at this small street drama. Others might avoid Becker's eyes— as all prudent New Yorkers tended to treat one another—but they were at least marginally and fleetingly aware of the collision, of the potential for trouble or excitement. Only one man was studiously looking across the street.

Becker tried to recall the features of the Bahoud picture folded in his jacket pocket. The photo had been taken seventeen years ago. The man had put on weight, his hair style had changed, the features had matured. Even without looking at the photograph again, Becker knew he would not be able to identify his follower as Bahoud on the strength of that likeness. Nor could he say for certain that it was the same man he had seen getting into the cab nearly a block away from Solin's apartment. Not for certain. But then he did not have to be certain: he was not testifying in court. For his purposes, he was convinced enough. He knew in his gut it was Bahoud, and the bastard had just made a huge error.

Becker purchased the necktie and took his wallet from his pocket to get the cash.

"Look me straight in the face and don't look anywhere else at all," Becker said.

The clerk did as he was told, his eyes wide.

"Relax, though. I'm not going to rob you. Look down at my wallet now. That's an FBI badge. Do you see it? Smile and nod. Good, good. Put the tie in a bag and listen carefully. When I leave the store, call this number . . . " Becker put a card on the counter along with the bills. "Ask for Hatcher. Hatcher. Tell him I'm walking north on Madison from Forty-fifth Street and Bahoud is following. Do you have that?"

The clerk nodded dumbly.

"You can speak, just keep looking at me."

"You're walking north on Madison from Forty-fifth Street and Hood is following."

"Bahoud. Not Hood. Bahoud is following. And ask for Hatcher."

"Hatcher," the clerk repeated.

"And smile," Becker said. "You just made a sale."

Becker opened the shop door to the tingling of the bell and stepped back out on the street. He had no need to look further for Bahoud, no more glancing into reflective shop windows, no more doubling back, no pausing at streetlights to look around. He would just let Bahoud follow him to where he wanted to go. When it was time, Becker would turn around and greet him.

All right, Bahoud, he said to himself. Let's see how good you are. Becker's chest was tight with excitement.

Bahoud fell into step with Becker, starting half a block behind again and once more slowly narrowing the gap. When he was within ten feet, he would start to look for opportunities. He curled his fingers about the sharpened orange stick.

As he reached Forty-eighth Street Becker thought he recognized the first of the surveillance team as the man stepped into the pedestrian flow half a block ahead of Becker. By Forty-ninth Street he was sure the net was in place when he saw Karen Crist walking parallel to him across the street. He did not have to check behind him; he knew someone would be there as well, more than one agent very likely. With the net in place, all that remained was to lure his man into the trap, away from the crowds and all the potential confusion.

Becker turned left on Fiftieth Street, noting as he did that Hatcher was at a diagonal at the intersection, crossing, too. Hatcher scurried ahead, replacing Becker's first lead man. His waddle was more pronounced when he hurried. He looked like a duck with something snapping at its ass, Becker thought.

The crosstown street between Park and Madison was as near to being deserted as any street in midtown Manhattan ever gets at midday. Delivery trucks were double-parked in front of unmarked doorways with rolling steel shutters. A few pedestrians passed under the awnings of a couple of restaurants, but for Becker's purpose, the street was empty. A perfect place to spring the trap.

Bahoud took one look down the cross street and knew it was perfect. He had but to step beside his man, pull him between the parked cars where he would be sheltered on the outside by the bulk of the delivery van and front and back by automobiles. It was like a ready-made closet where the two of them would be alone for the few seconds Bahoud would need.

When Bahoud took his second look, he knew it was a trap. The man on the other side of the street, hurrying in a way men in suits seldom hurried, his feet splayed to the sides—Bahoud knew that man, he had seen that walk before, when the three men and the woman had rushed into Solin's building as Bahoud watched from under his cardboard on the sidewalk.

The waddling man stopped under a restaurant awning, glanced at the menu in the window, and then back, toward Bahoud, and Bahoud knew with certainty.

He timed his move perfectly, stepping into a cab as the light turned green. Turning to watch his wake he saw the reactions of the net that had surrounded him, the men behind him, the one in front, the woman across the street—he recognized her, now, too—and Becker as he sprinted back onto Madison from the cross street. Bahoud watched the man's face as he lost ground steadily in his race with the taxi. Bahoud grinned at him as the cab turned the corner and, for the second time in two days, left Bahoud's pursuer in the safe distance.

"That man ought to invest in a car," Bahoud said. The cabbie did not appear to understand, or care.

Bahoud got out of the taxi after five blocks, gave the cabbie too much money, and sent him to an address in the Bronx, ordering him to drive by way of Central Park. The pursuers might have the license number of the cab this time, Bahoud reasoned. If they sent out a bulletin to the police, the cab would be traveling much of the way through relatively cop-free territory in the park. By the time they caught up with the taxi, Bahoud would be safely back in Howard's apartment. If it still was safe. He would find out about that, too. He would have a little session with Myra and see just how much she could be trusted. Not that he had to trust anybody much longer. Two more hours. Two more hours.

21

Kane was back. Myra had longed for his return, she had sat there and yearned and burned, but now she was as nervous and shy as if their lovemaking had never happened. It was daylight, how would she look, how would he see her now?

Kane checked Howard's room, without speaking, saw he was not there, then turned to Myra and smiled. So much warmth. He was so glad to see her, she thought, to be alone with her. He felt as she did, she knew it.

"How was your day," he asked, crossing toward her.

"I missed you."

"Anything interesting happen?"

"It seemed so long without you." Was she saying too much, too soon? Would she frighten him off? Suddenly she had forgotten how to be coy, an art she thought she had mastered.

He leaned over her, supporting himself with his hands on the arms of her chair. He was so handsome, and when he smiled Myra felt her insides collapse.

"Anyone come to see you?" he asked.

She reached for him with her good arm, pulled his head closer. She sought his lips with hers, but he put his face past her, nuzzled her neck.

"Who came?" he asked. His mouth was at her ear, then his teeth. He bit her ear, a nip at first, then harder. Harder. She gasped in pain.

"Answer me," he said.

She was not aware he had really been asking questions.

"There was a man here," she said, puzzled. Was he jealous? Was that why he hurt her?

"Who?"

"He was with the FBI. He was asking me about Mr. Henley."
Kane was surprised. "Henley?"

"He's dead. He was killed."

He stood up straight, not looking at her for the moment. She touched his belt.

"Why was he asking you about Henley?"

"I don't know. I may have been the last one to see him alive."

"What did you tell him?"

"What could I tell him? I was very upset to hear about it. I liked Mr. Henley. I can't imagine why anyone would kill him. But I didn't know anything at all about his death."

He held out his hands for her. She started to rise, he gripped her under the arms and pulled her all the way up, then swept her into his arms and carried her to the sofa. He sat with her on his lap. He was so strong, Myra could have melted in his arms, she could have fainted.

Smiling at her, he asked, "Did he want anything else? This FBI man? Did he just ask about Henley?"

He toyed with the top button of her blouse. Her breath came with difficulty.

"He did want something else," she said. "I wasn't sure what it was, but he was implying something. At first I thought he knew about Howard."

Kane had opened her blouse and his hand, hot as coals, touched her flesh. His fingers slid along her ribs and around to her back.

"Knew what about Howard?"

How could he keep talking when they were like this, she wondered. She wanted to just grab him and tear at his clothes.

"About his organization. Your organization. The 'Brotherhood.' "

"What about it?"

He unsnapped her bra and his hand moved around to touch her breast. He cupped it with such tenderness. His fingers moved teasingly just below the nipple. She arched her back, trying to make contact with his fingers.

"I missed you so much," she whispered.

"What about Howard and the Brotherhood?" he asked. "How much does the FBI know?"

"He never mentioned it. I just thought he knew somehow. He seemed to be implying that he knew something. I knew Howard would get into trouble with it eventually . . . "

"What would get him into trouble?"

Myra wanted to tell him she loved him. She knew it was too soon, but she yearned to say it; she had never said it to a man. Why did he insist on this other conversation?

"The things you do. The thing at the mosque. A man died."

"Howard did it," he said.

She pulled back from him. She did not believe it. "Howard did it?"

He took her nipple between his fingers.

"Howard killed him. Howard is a killer."

"No!"

She tried to push him away, but he held her with his arm. He squeezed her nipple. It was too hard, it hurt.

"Yes," he said. "Howard has killed a man. He did it for the cause, he did it for the Brotherhood."

"I don't believe you."

"He is our leader," he said. He squeezed her nipple harder.

"That hurts," she told him.

His voice was very calm. "Did you tell the FBI man about me?"

"You're hurting me." He squeezed harder and twisted.

"Did you tell him about me?"

"No! Oh, that hurts! Stop!"

"Why didn't you tell him about me?"

It hurt so much Myra was starting to cry. She tried to push his hand away, but he was so strong and he only hurt her more.

"Why didn't you tell him about me?"

"Because I love you," she blurted out. She did not want to tell him that way. He released her nipple, but his fingers hovered there.

"Did he ask about me?"

She was so relieved the pain had stopped. She wanted to bury her head against him in gratitude.

"Did you hear what I said?" she asked in a whisper.

He put his lips to her breast and gently, so gently, kissed it.

"I heard you," he said.

She put her hand on the back of his neck. She wanted to hold him to her breast forever.

He straightened and took her nipple between his fingers again. She jerked involuntarily.

"Did he ask about me?" He squeezed.

"Not really," she said quickly.

He looked so calm, he must not realize what he was doing to her, she thought. But how could he not know? He was almost smiling and his voice was so patient.

"What do you mean, 'not really'? Did he ask about me?"

It hurt so much she could no longer look at him. She had to close her eyes to deal with the pain.

"He asked if anyone else lived here. I said no."

"Why?"

"I didn't want to tell him about you."

"Why?"

"I wanted to keep you here. I didn't want you to leave!"

He put his head to her breast again and laved her with his tongue. The pain was gone immediately. When he heard her sigh with delight he took her breast in hand again and she stiffened.

Suddenly Howard was in the apartment, Myra heard him enter. Kane heard him, too. He twisted slightly to look at him, but his hand stayed on Myra's breast.

"I want you out," Howard said.

Myra opened her eyes. Howard stood in front of them where they sat on the sofa. She realized how they must look to him, Myra on Kane's lap, his hand inside her blouse, on her breast. A parody of lovers. She didn't know what Howard made of the tears on her face, if he saw them at all.

"I can't leave," said Kane. "Sorry, Howard."

"I want you out, now," Howard said. His voice was shaking with his efforts to control it. "Today. Right now."

Kane smiled at him.

"Why is that, Howard? What's the rush?"

"Let go of her."

"She likes it. We're in love. Ask her."

Howard looked at Myra, his eyes large with horror. Was it the suggestion that she might enjoy a man that troubled him so, she wondered. Or the fact that she might love someone other than him? Did he think last night was rape?

He was waiting for an answer, as if everything depended on that. "We're in love," Kane had said. Not "she's in love." *We* are. Was the pain he had just given her a part of that love? A demonstration of it, or a result? What kind of experience was Myra in for? Whatever it was, she was not afraid of it. She knew she was not afraid of it. She was alive.

"We're in love," she said to Howard. He looked as if the very word disgusted him.

"You see, Howard?" said Kane. "She doesn't want me to leave. I don't want to leave. That makes it just you."

Howard pulled Assad's pistol from his pocket and pointed it at Kane. The gun wavered and jumped, he was so excited.

"This makes two," Howard said. "That's all I need. Now get your hands off her. Get them *off!*"

Kane moved very slowly as he shifted Myra off his lap.

"Howard," Myra said. She could hear the terror in her voice. She could think of nothing to say except his name.

"Howard."

"What's this all about, Howard?" Kane asked.

"Assad is dead."

"You knew that. You wanted it that way."

"He was alive when we left him!"

"Was he? Did you check?"

Kane got to his feet so slowly that Myra thought it looked almost like a joke. He was very calm, his voice without stress, but his eyes never left the gun.

"Howard," she said again. It was a plea.

"You went back," said Howard. The gun jerked as he spoke. "You went back and killed that man."

"Why me?"

"The rest of them don't have the guts."

"Why would I do that?"

"I don't know. But the police think we did it, they blame the Brotherhood."

"You're famous, Howard," said Kane. He was fully erect now, his hands were open and at shoulder height. "You always wanted to be famous and now you are."

"Not that way."

"What better way? He was PLO, remember?"

"Howard, please put the gun away," Myra said.

Howard looked at her with contempt. "You!" It was the worst epithet he could come up with.

Kane moved so quickly Myra couldn't follow him. His hand flashed out, froze the gun in Howard's hand, the other hand chopped against Howard's neck, and Howard plunged to the floor.

Myra gasped, or was it a scream? She couldn't tell for certain.

"Don't hurt him," she pleaded, and Kane looked at her quizzically.

"Why would I hurt him?" He examined the pistol that was now in his own hand. He seemed amused by it, as if it were a toy.

"Can you get up, Howard?" Kane asked.

Howard was on all fours, shaking his head back and forth. Kane took him under the arm and pulled him to his feet. The gun dangled casually in his hand.

"How you feeling?" Kane asked.

"Howard . . ." Again Myra could only say his name.

Howard said something that she could not understand. He sounded as if his tongue no longer worked.

"Get a little ice on that neck and you'll be all right," Kane said.

Myra was relieved to hear the solicitude in his voice. He cares for Howard, he cares for us both, she told herself.

"Give me the gun," Howard said, impossibly. He held out his hand for it.

Kane chuckled. "Well, now, Howard. I don't think so, not yet. You had me a little scared there. I think your sister was scared, too. You didn't want to scare her, did you?"

"I want you to go," Howard said. He didn't seem to understand that the situation had changed.

"You're right about that," Kane said. "It is time for me to leave. I can't stay if you want me gone."

"No," Myra said involuntarily. Leave? Leave now? She could not bear it.

Howard glared at her again. "Shut up," he said.

"I understand how you feel," Kane said. "If she were my sister, I'd probably feel the same way. But I want you to know, I feel very deeply about her, Howard."

"Get out."

"And I think she knows that, too."

Myra nodded in agreement. She did know that. He did love her, too. She didn't understand the pain, she didn't know what it meant to him, maybe he didn't realize how much it hurt, maybe he needed to hurt to love. She didn't know. She didn't care.

"But if you want me to go, then, of course, I will go immediately."

Myra realized she must have moaned because he put his hand on her head and patted her.

"So, go," said Howard.

"I'll need your help," said Kane. "I've got a trunk in the basement. I'll need to bring it up and pack."

"I don't remember a trunk," said Howard.

"I brought it in a couple of days ago. Did you think I was going to live in the same clothes every day? Can you give me a hand bringing it upstairs?"

Howard hesitated. Kane fiddled with the pistol and suddenly all of the bullets were in his hand. He put them in his pocket and handed the gun to Howard.

"No hard feelings. Okay?"

Howard stared at the gun in his hand as if he didn't know what it was or how it got there. Myra realized for the first time how desperate Howard must have been to use a gun. For her, was it for her sake? Oh, Howard, you don't understand at all.

"Will you give me a hand?" Kane asked. "Once we get the trunk I can be packed in ten minutes."

"All right," Howard said dully. They started toward the door together. Kane put his arm around Howard's shoulders.

"This is really just a misunderstanding, you know," Kane said.

Howard stopped at the door and turned back toward Myra. His lip was curled in a sneer.

"Cover yourself, for God's sake," he said.

Myra realized her breast was showing and she grabbed her blouse as the men went out the door.

They were back, carrying a steamer trunk between them, and Myra's fears were gone. She had dreaded what might happen between them once they were out of her sight, but now they were normal again, all the fury and frenzy of a few minutes ago subsumed into the concentration of two men doing a job together.

They carried the trunk into Kane's room. While they were gone, Myra got her crutches. Kane had still not seen her walk and she preferred that his first sight of her be on crutches where she had at least a semblance of grace.

She moved to the door of Kane's room to watch them. Kane had opened the trunk and removed a flat case of some kind, which he put on the bed. Myra saw a uniform in the trunk. He put that on the bed, too, then straightened and looked at the empty trunk as if well pleased with his work so far.

"Well, now," he said. "Ready to pack."

He looked at Myra standing in the door, and he smiled and winked. Her heart was filled with him.

He turned to Howard.

"Get in," he said to Howard. He was still smiling. "Get in the trunk."

"What?"

"Get in the trunk. There's room. Lie down, pull your legs up. You'll fit."

"No," said Howard, confused.

"Have I ever steered you wrong, Howard?" Kane asked. He laughed.

It was a joke! Myra laughed from relief and Kane heard and winked at her again. She should have realized he was joking.

Howard didn't seem to understand, he was still glowering at Kane.

"He's joking, Howard," Myra said.

Kane waggled a finger at her.

"No, no," he said. "No joke. Time to pop Howard in the trunk."

"Why?"

"For safekeeping," Kane said lightly. "He'll be safer there. In you go, Howard."

Howard looked at the trunk as if it were his open grave. He turned away and started toward the door, but he took no more than a step before he cried out and sank to his knees. Myra had barely seen Kane move, but whatever he did had hurt Howard badly. He was clutching his back.

"Get in, Howard."

"Don't hurt him," Myra begged.

"That's up to him," said Kane. "Get in the trunk, Howard."

Howard shook his head no.

"Please," Myra said. "He's afraid. Please."

"There's nothing to be afraid of. There's nothing *in* there, Howard. Take a look. Nothing in the trunk to hurt you."

Kane put his hand on the back of Howard's neck and did something. Howard's mouth opened in a silent scream. Myra could tell he could not yell because he was gasping with the pain, sucking for air.

"Lots of ways you can get hurt out *here,*" Kane said. "But nothing to hurt you in there."

Howard looked at the trunk, turned toward it.

"Oh, God, don't," Myra pleaded. She didn't know what was going to happen, but she was as fearful of it as Howard was.

"Shhh," Kane said to her. "It's all right."

"He doesn't want to," she said.

"I think he does now," said Kane. "You want to get in now, don't you, Howard?" Kane touched Howard's neck and Howard gasped. Myra remembered the strange mix of pain and pleasure that she felt when Kane held her breast.

Howard crawled into the trunk. Just before he lay down he looked at Myra. His eyes were sad and terrified. She had seen this look on his face when he was very young, when their mother locked him in the closet for some imagined transgression. He had not spoken then, either. Just cried out mutely to his sister with his eyes.

Kane spoke softly to Howard, but Myra could hear him.

"It's just for an hour, Howard. I have to do something, then I'll let you out, I promise. It's something you'll like, something good for the Brotherhood. I'll tell you all about it when it's time. Meanwhile, I don't want to hear a sound from you, do you understand? Remember, nothing can hurt you while you're in there, but outside, well . . . you know what can happen, don't you? And let me remind you, Howard, your sister is still out here with me. Do you know what I mean?"

"Yes," said Howard.

Kane turned to Myra. "Darling," he said, "get Howard a wooden spoon from the kitchen."

"A wooden spoon?"

"That's right, sweetheart," he said so calmly she felt like a small child. "Go on now, hurry. Howard's going to need it."

Myra hurried to the kitchen and returned with a wooden spoon. Howard was in the trunk, his legs pulled up to his chest in the fetal position. Tears and mucus ran down his face, but he was quiet. When he glanced at Myra his eyes were so big they looked as if they must burst. Kane bent over him with a pair of Howard's socks rolled into a ball. He took the spoon and put it in Howard's hand.

"Now when you feel like screaming, bite down on the spoon. Okay, Howard? Bite hard, because if I hear any noise from you I'll have to put this in your mouth." He held the sock ball delicately over Howard's face, grasping it between thumb and forefinger as if it were as fragile as a Christmas tree sphere.

He waited for a response from Howard. "Yes?"

Howard nodded. Kane opened his fingers and the sock ball fell onto Howard's chest.

"And if you try to get *out* . . . well, you won't do that, will you, Howard. I hope you don't try that. Your sister hopes very much that you don't try that. Do you understand me?"

Howard nodded again and small whimpers came from him with each shake of his head.

"Good. Shall I close the lid now, Howard?"

Howard squeezed his eyes shut. Kane lowered the lid and sat on it. He lowered the hasp over the locking staple and looked briefly about the room for a pin to secure it. Seeing nothing useful, he took the icepick from his rear pocket and slipped it through the staple.

"For safekeeping," he said, patting the trunk and grinning at his joke. If it was a joke, Myra thought.

"Why?" she asked, not expecting an answer anymore.

Kane tapped once atop the trunk. " 'sall right?"

Then he answered himself in a deep bass voice. "'sall right."

"A little joke my father taught me," said Kane. "Dad was a fun guy. He used to let me play Howard's part."

Kane looked up and fixed Myra with his gaze. She tried not to let her fear and confusion show.

"Well, now," he said. He knit his fingers together, put them over his knee, and leaned back. "What shall we do to amuse ourselves?"

They stood on the corner of the street, a small group of frustrated federal agents amid the endless and uncaring pedestrian flow of Lexington Avenue. The pursuit of Bahoud's cab had been frantic but brief, and ultimately futile, as Becker had known it would be. Three of the agents had noted the license number and the police had been notified, but Becker was almost certain they would not find the vehicle in time to do them any good. There was no chance whatsoever that Bahoud would still be in it.

"He's operating out of the Goldsmith apartment. He has to be." Becker rocked from side to side with unreleased energy. Hatcher viewed him warily. Becker in agitation was a state Hatcher had learned to be both rare and dangerous.

"Why?"

"First, I think Ms. Goldsmith was lying to me about something. Something I said had her very agitated."

"You do have that effect on people."

"The doorman was lying, too. I want you to pull him in and squeeze him."

Hatcher nodded, then glanced at one of the agents. The agent nodded back.

"Got it," said the agent.

"Second," Becker continued, "Bahoud picked me up sometime after I left the building. I don't think he was just hanging around in the neighborhood by coincidence."

"He's in the Goldsmith apartment! He has to be." Becker rocked from side to side with frustrated energy. Hatcher could not remember ever having seen him so excited.

"Why?"

"Because someone's there, I got that much from Ms. Goldsmith. Because Bahoud picked me up sometime after I left her building."

"He could have been following you all day," said Hatcher.

"Why? What would he gain by following me? Let me rephrase that. What has happened to other people he's followed in the last two days? He's killed them. Why? Because they were a threat to him. Why? Because they knew something, or he thought they knew something that would lead to him. What did I know that would lead to him? Nothing. What did he *think* I might know? If I had just come from talking to the woman in whose apartment he's staying, I might know anything. I might know everything. He couldn't be sure that Ms. Goldsmith didn't talk to me, and if she did, he didn't dare take the chance that I would act on whatever she told me. It also means he's close to the time when he's going to act. Very close."

"Why?"

"Because if he had three weeks to go and people were suspicious, he could just disappear and make another plan and reemerge where it was safe. But he's killing people because he doesn't have time to spare. He isn't hiding the bodies in New Jersey, he doesn't much care if we find out—although I don't think he imagined we'd find out as soon as we did—because he's going to do his job and get out of here before we can do anything about it. He's going to act soon, very soon, today or tomorrow. He wouldn't have taken the risk of coming after me on a midtown street if he wasn't very, very close."

Hatcher sniffed and studied the traffic pouring past them. "We don't know that he was actually coming *after* you, of course."

"We don't?"

"He might have just been tailing you."

"How close was he when he broke off?"

Hatcher cleared his throat.

"Twenty feet?" Karen offered.

Hatcher gave her a wintry smile. "Thank you," he said.

"You don't follow somebody from twenty feet, do you, Hatcher?"

"Not ordinarily."

"He wanted me, and he wanted me because he knew I was after him. He saw me at Solin's building, he saw me at Goldsmith's apartment. He wanted to get rid of me with such an urgency that he'd risk killing me out in the open in the middle of the day. He's primed and ready to go and he's going to go off very, very soon."

"It's not only his target who's in danger now," Karen interjected.

Hatcher looked at her as if she had made a rude noise.

"Who else?"

"If he thinks she told you anything about him, what is he going to do to Ms. Goldsmith?" Karen asked.

"She's right," Becker said.

"I'll need a warrant to get into the apartment," Hatcher said.

"That'll take a couple of hours, you idiot!"

Hatcher watched the tide of pedestrians flow around their little group on the sidewalk. The three other agents who had participated in the net stood a discreet few feet to the side, pretending not to eavesdrop. Hatcher knew they took delight in his confrontations with Becker.

"It's one thing to illegally enter the empty apartment of some low-life like Ike Solin," Hatcher said icily. "It's quite another to break into the apartment of someone like Ms. Goldsmith while there are witnesses. If I had any part of that I'd be back in Fingerprinting with Ms. Crist within a week."

"Christ, I wouldn't want you to make a wrong career move."

"That's not the point, of course."

"Of course not. The point is Bahoud is probably going to kill Arafat

within about an hour's time when he shows up at the U.N. And he
may well kill Ms. Goldsmith first, or after, or simultaneously. And
you're telling me it's a worse mark on your record to try to get into
her apartment to see if the bastard is in there than it is to let him go
ahead and kill her and whoever his target is.''

"That's very melodramatic, Becker, but that's not my position at
all. I'll get to work on the warrant immediately. It may be less than
two hours. We should be able to do it legally.''

"Fine. Work on the fucking warrant. Meanwhile, put these guys
outside the building so we can grab Bahoud going in. We don't need
a warrant for that. Do not, repeat, do not let them be seen. You can
do that, can't you, Hatcher?''

"I doubt very much that he'd go back to the apartment now. Why
would he?''

"Because of the view,'' Becker said. He turned to Karen. "You
can come with me or stay with them. Your choice.''

"Where are you going?'' Hatcher demanded.

"The smart thing is to stay with Hatcher,'' Becker said. "I'll understand if you do.''

"Do you need me?''

"I want to know where you're going,'' Hatcher insisted.

Becker looked at her for a moment, his eyes locked with hers.

"Go with your instincts,'' he said finally.

"Do you think I can help?''

Becker smiled at her but did not answer. He turned and started to
walk away. Hatcher caught him in a few strides and grabbed his arm.

"You listen to me,'' Hatcher hissed. "If you do anything illegal,
you'll ruin this case. You know that. You'll blow the case, we'll never
be able to prosecute.''

Becker pulled his arm away.

"That's the difference,'' Becker said. "You're still thinking it's a
case. I think it's time to catch the bastard.''

"Then just *catch* him,'' Hatcher said.

"What does that mean?''

"You know what it means. We both understand your history,
Becker. Just apprehend him, nothing more.''

Becker grabbed Hatcher by the throat and shoved him against the
iron siding of the building. There was a collective gasp from the tide
of pedestrians who swept a safe distance away from the violence.

"Apprehend this," Becker said. Hatcher gasped and clawed at Becker's hand.

The other agents formed a ring around the two men, but no one wanted to lay hands on Becker.

"I'm here to stop the bastard. You know that and I know you know it. McKinnon didn't drag me back into the Bureau to *apprehend* anybody, he brought me to *stop* him. And you're hoping like hell that I do it, aren't you, you hypocritical fuck? While you're dithering around with your warrant, you're hoping for all you're worth that I'll save your ass and go in and stop the murderous bastard for you."

Karen stepped forward and touched Becker's arm.

"John," she said softly.

Becker released Hatcher's throat, and Hatcher wheezed and struggled to keep the rage from his voice.

"It's not true," Hatcher finally managed to sputter.

"Isn't it? Show me."

"How?"

"Stop me."

Hatcher rubbed his neck, carefully avoiding the eyes of the other agents.

"Agent Becker, I order you to take no action whatsoever without my authority."

Becker grinned at him.

"Fine. Why didn't you say so?" He crossed his arms and leaned against the building.

"Well. Good. That's fine." Hatcher watched Becker uncomfortably. He had not expected it to work. He had not truly wanted it to work, which was Becker's point, and Hatcher hated him for having said it aloud.

Becker continued to grin at him, enjoying Hatcher's discomfort.

"I'll get on the phone and start the warrant process," Hatcher said. "The rest of you go to Goldsmith's apartment building and deploy yourselves. I don't think Bahoud is likely to show up, but if he does, apprehend him immediately."

"Anything you care to authorize me to do?" Becker asked.

"Well . . . Until I return, you'll be temporarily in charge. Use your discretion."

Becker barked laughter.

"I won't be gone long," Hatcher said.

"It won't take long," Becker said. "But then you know that."
Hatcher walked away with as much dignity as he could muster.

Walking hurriedly, Becker heard the trotting footsteps fall in line beside him.
"I want to help," Karen said.
Becker touched her shoulder. "I'm sorry," he said.
"For what?"
"For the pressure."
"It's all right."
"No. It wasn't fair. They are my demons to battle, not yours. I shouldn't have inflicted them on you."
"I just—I'm not qualified, John. I'm just not qualified to deal with them."
"I know," he said. "The only one qualified to deal with them is me." He glanced up at the building in front of him, searching for the window in Myra Goldsmith's apartment with the telescope trained on the U.N. plaza. "And I'd better start dealing fast."

22

Kane was at the telescope, peering into the city with great intensity. What did he see, Myra wondered. Was the reason for all this to be found in the lens of the telescope? Did her brother lie terrified in the cramped dark of the trunk because of something Kane sought on the far side of those finely ground lenses? Myra did not know how to phrase the question beyond asking "why?" That much she had done and he had not bothered to answer.

"Can I talk to him?" she asked. When their mother enclosed Howard in the closet Myra would lie outside, her lips next to the crack between floor and door, whispering support. She became his lifeline as surely as if her words carried in oxygen and food and water. He was frequently in the closet for some transgression against her, but Myra never wished him such treatment. There existed a bond between them that her mother could never see or comprehend. Their mutual abuse, petty and childish in its forms and strength, was a form of affection. As close as Howard could come to it; as much as Myra was prepared to expect. So when he was punished for mistreating her, she kept him alive in his claustrophobic dungeon. Her voice was his light in the darkness.

"He's fine," said Kane.

"I'll just talk to him," she said. "I won't let him out."

Kane turned from the telescope and looked at her. For a second there was no expression whatsoever on his face, his eyes were dead. Then he smiled and it was so sweet, so loving that she could almost imagine the events of the day had been a waking dream.

"I know you won't, sweetheart," he said. "None of us want him to get out. You saw how he kept getting hurt when he was out."

Myra was seated behind her computer. He cleared a space on her desk and cupped her face in his hand, then leaned down and kissed her. His lips were flutteringly soft, his touch so gentle. His hand caressed her neck, then moved slightly downward. Myra both dreaded and yearned for him to touch her. When he pulled away, his eyes gazed into hers, so soft and open that even then she wanted just to love him. The mysteries of his behavior she would solve, she would learn to live with, she would bring him out of. All was not yet lost, maybe nothing was lost. He did still care for her. She could see it in his eyes, in his every move.

"This must seem a little confusing to you," he said.

Myra nodded, afraid to say more. Confusion was so tame a word.

"It will all be clear to you in just a few minutes," he said. "There's really nothing to worry about, I promise."

She wanted so much to believe him.

"Why did you cut the phone?" she asked. After he put Howard in the trunk he had sliced the telephone line with the scissors.

"So we could be alone," he said. He grinned like a mischievous schoolboy. "The important thing is to not get caught up in details. The big picture will be clear soon enough."

He put the case from the trunk on her desk.

"Go to the sofa now, and stay there," he said. Myra grabbed her crutches and obediently crossed to the sofa.

"Can you walk without the crutches?" he asked.

Myra realized that for all their intimacy Kane knew virtually nothing about her.

"No," she said. She didn't know why she lied to him.

He studied her for a moment, as if assessing the truth of her statement, then he took the crutches from her and placed them next to the telescope. He seemed so far from her, all the way across the room, twenty feet between them. She wanted to be close to him, no matter what he was doing.

He opened the case, but from Myra's angle she could not see what was in it. Drawing out three short lengths of aluminum, he pulled on them and they extended into a tripod higher than the telescope. It looked almost like the legs of a surveyor's instrument, Myra thought. He put the tripod next to the telescope, then tried to open the window. There had been no fresh air in the apartment for years. Their mother feared the city air and the grime and soot it left upon her furniture. The apartment had been air-conditioned since Myra could remember.

Kane banged at the window frame with the palm of his hand, then tugged, then banged again. He stepped to the kitchen and returned with a hammer, which he used to hit the frame some more.

His face turned red and the tendons in his neck stood out as he strained to open the window. Finally he gave up, turned to Myra, and shrugged.

"Nothing left to do," he said. He picked up the hammer again as if displaying it to her. "May I?" he asked, grinning.

Myra did not understand what he wanted, nor why he asked her permission, but she nodded assent. He smashed the window with the hammer, then meticulously knocked out the shards that remained in the frame until every trace of glass was onto the floor or the city street below.

"A job worth doing is a job well done," he said, chuckling. He was enjoying himself immensely.

A breeze entered and stirred the air in the room. Myra smelled the city for the first time in months. The noise was loud and she heard a rushing sound that took her a moment to identify. It was the wind which was always strong at this height.

Kane had returned to the case and she watched in horror as piece by piece he assembled a rifle. She made a noise and he looked across the room at her.

"It's not the way it looks," he said. "It will be fine, you'll see, sweetheart."

Myra realized at last that his kisses and endearments were just calming gestures that one made to placate an animal headed for the butcher's ax.

He is going to kill us, she thought. Perhaps someone else first, then Howard, then her.

Becker and Karen rode the elevator to the thirty-third floor and stopped, one floor down from the Goldsmith apartment.

"I don't want him to step out of his apartment and see somebody hanging around the elevator," Becker explained. "He'll probably kill now at the slightest provocation, his time has run out. If I'm right and he's going after Arafat when he arrives at the U.N., he'll have to do it"—he glanced at his watch—"within half an hour. He won't have time to ask questions or to wonder. He'll just kill anything that looks dangerous. Do you understand?"

"Yes," she said, hoping her nerves didn't show.

"He may not be there. Hatcher may be right, he probably isn't there. But all you do is find out. If you see him, leave immediately. Understand me? Immediately. Don't get close to him, don't let him get within arm's length. Do you understand?"

"Yes."

"I mean it, Karen. Absolutely. If you see him, if you even hear him, get out of there immediately. Don't think you can handle him, don't think you can outwit him, don't think you have to balls it out or that it means you're a coward or anything else. Just get out and get down here to me."

"I am an agent, John. I do know how to defend myself."

"This is not about your abilities. This guy is far beyond what they taught you at the academy, and you will hesitate. That's natural. You're not him, you're not like him, you're nothing like him. You will hesitate, half a second, less, but that's all it will take because he will not hesitate at all. Is that clear?"

"Are you trying to scare me out of my wits?"

"You bet. I want you to be scared enough to do what I tell you. And don't think you can overcome your fear and handle him somehow. If you're scared at all, even the slightest bit, you will hesitate to act. That's what fear does to you."

Karen nodded. "You made your point. I will ascertain if he's in the apartment, I will not have contact with him, I will report to you immediately."

"Ascertain? You've been around Hatcher too long already."

"Should we get on with it?" she said.

He held her arm. "You don't have to do it at all," he said.

"You can't," she said. "He knows you and she knows you, too. You'd never get the door open."

"We can wait for Hatcher," he said.

Karen touched his cheek. "Let's go," she said. "I want to get it over with."

The doorbell rang like a scream. Myra gasped and turned toward it, but Kane was already at her side.

"Who is it?" he demanded of her, as if she could see through the door. His voice was now an iron whisper.

"I don't know. No one was announced from downstairs. It must be a neighbor."

"Do they just come over?" he asked suspiciously.

"Sometimes," she lied again. They almost never did. There were several neighbors on this floor Myra had never even seen. "They borrow things."

The bell rang again, insistently.

"Get rid of them," he whispered. "I'll be in the room with Howard. Do you understand?"

Understand? No, nothing, none of it, she thought. She was in a nightmare without signposts. But she recognized Kane's threat clearly enough.

"Yes," she said.

He glanced at his watch. The doorbell once more. Whoever it was, they were not going away.

"Get rid of them immediately," he said.

"My crutches," she said. Myra had started to move without them, but stopped herself before he noticed. She thought.

Kane crossed the room rapidly and put the crutches in her hand. His lips were against her ear, but there was nothing sensuous about it now.

"If you leave, Howard will be gone before you come back," he said.

"I know," she said. Then Kane was gone, and Myra was at the door.

When Myra opened the door it was as if she had created a wind tunnel and the outside air raced through the broken window and into the hallway. It ruffled the hair of the young woman who stood there.

"Hi," the woman said, bright and perky. "I'm Karen Crist, I just moved into 34K, down the hall there? They haven't installed my phone yet, and the thing is I have a kind of a crisis with my cat. She's throwing up and I need to find a vet right away."

"Your cat?" Myra said dully. The woman was not quite registering in her mind. She pictured Kane standing on the other side of the closed door, the rifle in his hand.

"I wouldn't bother you, but I'm so worried for Squeaky," the woman said. "I won't take but a minute, I promise." She was leaning forward, looking past Myra into the apartment. The wind surged again, and Myra heard papers on her desk flutter in the draft.

"I didn't realize you could open the windows in this building," the woman said. She could see that much, Myra thought. She could see

across the room to the window, but she could not see mother's bedroom from there. She could not *be seen* from there. Myra realized
suddenly that she herself could not be seen, either. She had the opened
hallway door between herself and her mother's room. It was but a
step to be into the hall, to be free. How fast could she get help? Not
fast enough. Not nearly fast enough.

"Are you all right?" the woman asked Myra. "You don't look
well . . . Is everything all right?"

How could Myra tell her? How could she alert her now without
letting Kane know? He was surely listening to everything—but he
could not see her, Myra thought. Hoped. And if she were wrong?

"I'm fine," Myra said aloud. She tried to signal with her eyes, but
the woman was looking again at the window, peering past her.

"It looks like you've broken the window," Karen said. "Do you
need help cleaning it up?"

Suddenly the woman was sweeping past Myra, into the apartment,
moving toward the window.

"Please!" Myra said. "The telephone doesn't work. It's out of
order."

Karen was already to the window. She glanced out, then kneeled
to pick up pieces of glass.

From behind the door of the bedroom, Bahoud could see her
through the crack where the hinges met the frame, her face neatly
positioned in the slim vertical slice of light. Pretty, Bahoud thought.
And very nearly dead.

"Please," Myra said again, crossing hurriedly toward Karen. "I'm
sorry about your cat, I really am, but I can't help you, I can't help
you at all."

"That's all right," said Karen, rising with a handful of glass.
"Maybe I can help you." She held the glass toward Myra, seeking
direction for where to put it as her eyes roamed the room.

One of the bedroom doors was not quite closed. Karen took one
step in that direction. Myra grabbed Karen's arm with a strength that
surprised her.

"I don't need help," Myra said firmly. "I am perfectly capable of
dealing with this. I'm sure you don't mean to be insulting, but I am
not as helpless as I look."

With a dexterity that Karen would not have guessed at from a woman on crutches, Myra moved her swiftly toward the door, gripping her arm firmly the whole time.

"I'm sorry," Karen said. "I didn't realize . . ."

"No, people don't." Myra propelled her into the hall. "I'm sorry about your cat, but I can't help you and I'm not really up for visitors right now. Maybe another time. When you're settled in."

Karen started to speak again but the door was already closed in her face. Alone in the hall, her audacity sunk in on her. If Bahoud had been behind the bedroom door, if Myra had not stopped her, what would she have done? Was Becker right in thinking that she was no match for Bahoud? Was she really ready to find out? She had not hesitated to step toward the door, she realized with some pride. She had been ready to do it. And it was only then, when the awareness hit her that she had unhesitatingly and unquestioningly stepped toward potential danger that she began to tremble.

She paused just long enough to control her body before hurrying downstairs to Becker. Halfway there she realized that she had seen the tripod set up in front of the window, and what it had to be for.

Myra closed the door on the young woman and returned immediately to the sofa and dutifully sat again.

Kane was at her side almost at once. He stared down at her, trying to read her face. Myra struggled to smile, knowing she looked frightened, but then fear was justified. She knew that what she must not betray in her face was hope. Kane scoured her with his eyes, stripping away the veils of her deception. She feared that in any second he would know that she had tried to betray him but failed. And then? He meant to kill her. Myra realized that with a certainty. He had the rifle to kill someone. Could he allow her to watch and leave her alive? He would kill his target, and then Howard and Myra. It was only her docility that had kept her alive thus far, she thought. Or his amusement.

But he did not read her betrayal in her face. A thing like that was not so easy to detect, after all. She had not read the perfidy in his face, had she? When he lay atop her and thrust himself into her, did she discern the monster? No, she saw only the lover. And now he saw only the helpless, pliable cripple, Myra thought bitterly.

He took the crutches and the rifle and returned to the window, ignoring her. After a moment he stepped into Howard's room, then immediately out again with some cloth that he dropped onto the desk.

Myra was disgusted with herself, filled with self-loathing. And she had thought she loved this beast. Even as he had tortured and tormented her she had excused him. And now he had left her alive only because she was so harmless. I am not worth worrying about, she thought.

Myra felt her self-repulsion turn slowly to rage.

23

Becker was waiting impatiently by the stairwell when Karen came into the hallway of the thirty-third floor. He wanted to go after Bahoud, she realized. She could read it in his face. There was a difference between urgency and need. It was urgent to stop Bahoud in time. But what she saw on Becker's face was need.

"Did you see him?" Becker demanded.

"No . . ."

"What?"

She hesitated.

"What, Karen?" He gripped her elbows, willing the words out of her.

"I didn't see him . . ."

"But what?"

"But he's there," she said.

He released her, his face awash with triumph and desire.

"Wait for help," she said, knowing he wouldn't. He was already sprinting up the stairs.

Kane fixed the rifle on the tripod and focused the scope. A distorted sea of bodies clarified and separated and Kane could see faces and features. He looked through the telescope and things became still clearer. He would use the telescope for verification to make sure he had identified his target precisely. The scope on the rifle was not sharp enough to count the fillings in his teeth, but it was good enough to fix him for death.

The United Nations Plaza was aswirl with people as delegations arrived in a precisely choreographed order of protocol and politics. Limousines pulled up and disgorged their passengers. Bodyguards and Secret Service men alike swarmed around the dignitaries and escorted them into the building while uniformed police cordoned off the spectators. Kane didn't need to see them to imagine the detectives working the crowd, the security men of all nations scanning the surrounding buildings.

Kane shared a secret with every one of the guardians below. It was all but impossible to provide real security from a determined assassin. There was no such thing as true protection under any but the most cloistered of circumstances, and outdoors, in New York, it was an outright impossibility. The imposing display of protectors was just that, a display, a bluff to discourage the uncommitted and a show for the consumption of the world press. There could as easily be a hundred rifles aimed at as many heads of state right this minute.

There was a movement behind him and Kane turned to see Myra shifting her position on the sofa. She looked at him meekly.

"Everything will be clear to you in about a minute," he said, watching the limousine that had just pulled to the curb. "We'll have a nice long talk and I'll explain it all. You'll be pleased, I promise." She was a sheep, Kane thought to himself. Not in bed where she showed an avidity that held promise, but otherwise as spineless as her brother.

"Who is it?" she asked timidly. "Can you tell me?"

"An enemy of the Brotherhood," Kane said. "Howard's worst enemy."

"Howard is his own worst enemy," she said.

He laughed. She had her brother assessed properly, but still she was wrong. I am his worst enemy, he thought, as he will find out as soon as I pull this trigger and can turn my attention to him.

A king emerged from the car below. Kane turned the telescope on the next automobile in line. He recognized the flag waving on the bumper.

The doorbell rang. Bahoud hesitated for just a second, deciding. His target would be in view in thirty seconds. He could dispose of the person at the door in ten. What he could not do was fire two shots and have someone standing in the hall to hear it. His escape would be jeopardized and when it came down to it, his escape was more essential than his mission. This was not a labor of love, after all.

Bahoud wheeled the desk chair to the sofa and tossed Myra onto it, then kicked the chair into the middle of the room. He grabbed the clothing he had brought from Howard's room and strode to the door with Howard's pistol in hand. He could not afford to fire a shot in the hall, but he was certain he would not have to.

Becker saw two things simultaneously and together they were just enough to make him hesitate. When the door swung open, he saw Myra Goldsmith in the middle of the room, her hands up in alarm, and coming around the door, his head slightly lowered as if caught in mid-prayer, a man wearing a yarmulke and a prayer shawl.

The half second of confusion in Becker's mind was all that Bahoud needed. He swung the pistol as he stepped around the door. Becker had already recovered, but it was too late. His arm flew up to ward off the blow, but the pistol was already past his defenses and it hit him on the side of the head. As Becker sunk to his knees, the pistol struck him again, this time at the base of his skull. Becker fell forward on his face and didn't move.

Bahoud was back at the telescope immediately. The familiar black and white checked kaffiyeh emerged from the limousine. Bahoud switched to the rifle scope and found his target as the man turned and looked back at the photographers and spectators. The unshaven face filled the scope, the cross-hairs centered on the bridge of his nose.

There was a scuffling, scraping sound behind Bahoud, coming very fast.

She was faster and lower than Kane expected, and when he turned she was already under his swinging arm. She hit him head down, smashing her skull into his groin. He was off balance because he was turning and he crashed backwards, grasping at the telescope for support. The windowsill caught his thighs and his upper body flew through the opening.

Myra pushed and pushed but his hands had caught the sides of the window and were holding with great strength. His head and torso were hanging in the air, thirty-four stories above New York, but his legs were still in the apartment and he strained to pull himself back in. She pushed with her head and shoulders against his torso but it was leaning away from her now and hard to get a purchase against. With her good arm she reached up and clawed at his hand, trying to pry away his fingers. He was too strong so she reached for his leg and tried to lift it, to lever him out.

She could see one of his hands straining to reach the hammer that he had used to break the window. He was so strong. Myra knew she was losing. The hammer was on the side of her baby arm, she could not reach it. There was nothing she could do except strain harder and watch as she saw his fingers scrabble for control of the hammer, then secure it, then lift it and swing it toward her head.

Bahoud aimed the rifle once more but the target was gone now, as he had known he must be, safe within the U.N. building. He left the rifle where it was. It was no use to him now, nothing was of use to him now except time. He needed time to get away. The agent would not be alone. Bahoud needed a minute headstart, maybe less. The woman's strength had startled him. He had had no idea, and he felt enraged at his own stupidity. He was so certain he had her under control, so positive that she could do nothing to stop him, *would* do nothing to stop him, the docile, love-struck little cripple. And she had damned near killed him. She had lied to him about not being able to walk without her crutches. That was what surprised him most, that she had had the presence of mind to lie to him. Not able to walk? She had fairly flown across the room. If he had the time, he would go back and give her what she deserved, but there was no time to spare now, none at all. He yanked on the plumber's uniform and tossed the yarmulke and shawl on the floor as he hurried toward the door.

As he punched the elevator button he told himself to stay calm. He knew how long it could take for the elevator to reach him. He had plenty of time, plenty of time.

There was a woman in the elevator when it arrived.

A plumber got on the elevator and looked quizzically at Karen. There were no stops higher than the thirty-fourth floor lighted on the panel.

"Getting out?" he asked, holding the door open.

"I thought it was going down," she said.

"It is now," he said, releasing the door.

The plumber held her in his gaze, refusing to look away, a slight smile playing on his lips.

It's him, her mind screamed. Do it now. Do it now! Becker had warned her about the fear, how it would make her hesitate, and she knew he was right even as she gripped her purse against her body, willing herself frantically to reach for the gun inside. Then she realized that if this plumber was Bahoud, then Becker had failed. Was he dead?

The plumber's eyes flickered from her face momentarily as he punched the button for the seventeenth floor.

Now! Karen screamed at herself. Do it!

She reached for the purse and something metallic hit her on the nose. Karen fought back, struggling as best she could to do what she had been taught, but the plumber had her hand immobilized in his grip and the metallic blow stuck again. She heard her nose break, felt the gush of blood. She kicked out but he was already at her side, beyond reach of her feet, then behind her, his forearm across her throat. She tried to dig her elbow backwards into him, but he had her pressed against the side of the car, immobilizing her.

She couldn't breathe, the blood from her nose flooded into her mouth as she gasped for air. She continued to struggle to get her hand on the gun. If she could fire it, anywhere, even into the floor, it might loosen his grip in reaction and it would alert others.

His forearm had shifted to her carotid artery. She knew she had only seconds left. She struck back with her free arm again, wrenching it from the wall, clawing for his groin. She heard him gasp, but his grip did not loosen, and her brain, starved for oxygen, shut down. She went black and did not hear the elevator door slide open, did not feel her body hit the floor as he tossed her into the hallway of the seventeenth floor.

Bahoud straightened his uniform as the door closed. The bitch had managed to scratch his face a bit with her flailings and for just a second he had thought she was going to rip his balls off, but worst of all, she had cost him time. Not much, not too much, he was sure.

The door closed and the elevator sank rapidly toward the basement.

When the car stopped at the lobby, Bahoud had composed himself. Three business-suited men rushed into the elevator, and one of them jabbed at the button for the thirty-fourth floor, then cursed under his breath as the doors closed and the cage headed down to the basement, completing its computerized course. Bahoud could tell they were federal agents without even looking at them.

He did not look back as he stepped into the basement, even though he could feel the eyes of one of them on his back. The overheated one was jabbing the floor button again as if his urgency could somehow rush the methodical machine. The doors eased shut at last with a hydraulic sigh and Bahoud was alone. He knew how long it would take them to get to the thirty-fourth floor and he could imagine their frustration en route. On the way down as he passed a floor he had pushed its button so that anyone ascending would have to stop at practically every floor. He would have ample time, no need to hurry.

He slipped the lock on the storeroom and retrieved the flashlight from under the drapes.

"Hey."

Bahoud wheeled to see the assistant superintendent standing in the doorway.

"What you doing?"

Bahoud smiled as he straightened to his full height. "You startled me," he said.

"What you doing in here?"

"Some kid on the twelfth stuffed a doll down the toilet. Can you believe that? Best I can figure, it's stuck in the main elbow just before the sewer outlet. I got to get it out."

"This look like a pipe room to you?"

"I was looking for the entrance to the subbasement," Bahoud said. He walked toward the super, smiling the while.

"You going to use tools?"

"Pardon me?"

"You going to use tools or you going to open the pipe with your bare hands?"

Bahoud held his palms up, the flashlight in his right hand. He looked at them speculatively as if gauging their effectiveness while he took one more step. He stopped, three feet from the super, still studying his hands.

"Why, you think they're not enough?" he said.

The super started to answer when Bahoud hit him with the flashlight, ramming the base into his temple. His jaw was still working as he sank to his knees, but no sounds came out. Bahoud stepped around him, but the super grabbed his leg and held with surprising strength. Bahoud threw his arms out to keep his balance, and the flashlight fell to the floor. Righting himself, Bahoud turned to the super, who was clinging to his pant leg, his mouth still working even though his eyes were rolled up into his head.

It took longer to find the flashlight than it did to dispatch the superintendent. Bahoud retrieved it from where it had rolled under a collapsible golf cart. He did not bother to hide the super's body. All that mattered now was time and the super's resistance had cost him some.

Bahoud slipped into the subbasement and felt the cool, clammy air slide onto his skin like a film of oil. He was sweating—adrenaline, he realized—and the temperature felt twenty degrees colder than when he had walked the route for practice. It reminded him fleetingly of the dungeon in Bulgaria.

He had to push the flashlight button three times before the beam flickered on unsteadily and Bahoud cursed himself for using it as a weapon. It was stupid. Uncharacteristicly stupid. He had made two mistakes in the space of a few minutes. First he had misjudged the woman and her abilities to resist him. Then the way he had dealt with the super. However, the flashlight would see him through well enough. He needed its light for less than three minutes now, and if necessary he could make his way without it.

Bahoud was halfway toward the doorway separating the buildings when he heard the noise behind him. He turned and immediately doused the light. The subbasement door burst open and a form leapt through, a moving shadow silhouetted momentarily against the background light of the basement. The shadow slipped to one side and the door banged closed, its metallic clang reverberating through the cavernous subbasement.

For the first time, Bahoud became aware of the acoustics of the place. It was as if he were walking inside a drum, a hollow pocket in which every sound was magnified. There was nothing in the empty space of the subbasements to absorb the sounds, no carpet, no wood, no furniture. Nothing but metal and concrete. And two men.

Pitch black. Twenty feet below ground level in a hole gouged from Manhattan bedrock. Bahoud was not frightened; he had all the advantages. He had a light which he could use when he needed it. He had Howard's pistol tucked in his belt inside the overalls. He knew where he was and where he was going and possessed at least some familiarity with his surroundings. His pursuer probably had a weapon. Bahoud had to assume he did, but no light and no mental map of where he was. Bahoud was not frightened in the least, but he was excited. This could even be fun. It was the kind of situation they liked to throw at candidates at the Master Camp.

Bahoud held his breath and listened. Nothing. His pursuer was lis-

tening for him. And then Bahoud realized he had one serious drawback to his situation. He *had* to move and his adversary did not. Time
was against him. If one man could follow him, others could be behind
him. Eventually, if he stayed frozen here in this stalemate, even the
New York City cops could put up a net that would be difficult for
him to elude. He *had* to move, so the trick was to put that to his
advantage.

He knelt to remove his shoes and was alarmed at the amount of
noise that made. The sound of cloth rustling against his skin was
magnified in the silence of the subbasement. He held the flashlight in
his mouth as he unlaced his shoes, his ears straining to hear beyond
the seeming cacophony of his own motions.

No sound from his pursuer yet. Bahoud imagined him, still
crouched in the dark in the same position in which he hit the floor.
That was good, that was very disciplined. But it couldn't last. When
the pursuer was fully oriented, when he locked in on Bahoud's location, he would have to come. And when he did, Bahoud would kill
him. He would wait for the sound, fix the target with the flashlight,
and drop him with a single shot.

There was no way to get at the pistol in his belt without undoing
the zipper on the uniform. He took it one notch at a time and was
surprised that it was as quiet as it was. He could hear it himself, just
as he could hear his own breathing, but he doubted that his pursuer
could. The gun, too, made some noise as he slowly drew it from his
belt, but not much. Not enough for the other man to use. Bahoud had
still heard no sound from the direction of his pursuer. He decided to
walk slowly backwards toward the wall. He estimated he had been
within thirty paces of the wall when the man burst into the room.
Bahoud would walk backwards for twenty-five paces, keeping both
the light and the gun pointed toward the place he knew the man to
be. When he got close enough to the wall he would feel for it with
one hand and grope his way to the doorway if he had to. But he was
certain the man would make a move before then.

He began to walk backward, pausing at each step, easing his weight
carefully, toe to heel. There was nothing he could do about the rustle
of the uniform, but it was very faint. He doubted now that the other
man could hear it. His perception of the noise level had been temporarily skewed by the peril of the situation, but now Bahoud realized
he was moving stealthily, quiet as a cat.

* * *

Becker was astounded at the noise the man made. He might as well have been wearing bells and sounding sirens. Becker heard him remove his shoes, heard him stand again, heard him pull something from his clothes—a weapon, most likely; perhaps his favorite icepick—heard him start to walk.

The walking motion was slow but rhythmic. Step, step, pause to listen, step, step. Becker timed his own steps to match Bahoud's, but he doubled their size, moving forward with giant strides, gaining on his target with every step.

As he leapt through the doorway, Becker had seen the subbasement in a flash, as if lit by a strobe light. If they continued at their current pace, Becker should be almost upon him by time Bahoud reached the far wall.

Bahoud took his twenty-fifth step backwards and stopped, listening. He put the flashlight in his mouth and reached behind him with his free hand, feeling for the wall. The room was so silent he could hear the bones in his wrist click as he moved his hand up and down.

A sound.

Bahoud yanked his hand back, grabbed the flashlight from his mouth, and held it at arm's length. The pistol was stretched forward beside it, both of them pointing in the direction of the sound. Bahoud had heard it, startlingly close to hand, a subdued gasp like a sharp intake of breath. Unmistakably human, frighteningly near. How had he gotten so close?

He trained both gun and flashlight at the spot. If the man was this close, Bahoud might get only one chance. He had to coordinate the flashlight with the gun, giving himself but a fraction to find his man and fire. The light would make Bahoud a perfect target and he must turn it off immediately and move as soon as he squeezed the trigger. If the man returned fire, his muzzle blast would give away his position. If he didn't, if Bahoud hit him, there would be noise enough to give him away so Bahoud could finish him off.

Becker estimated himself to be within fifteen feet of the wall when suddenly the terror hit him with such a rush that he gasped. His body burst into a sweat and his heart raced within his chest. It was like leaping from wakefulness into a nightmare, the same nightmare that haunted Becker night after night, a dream of unnamed horror in the dark. It was a dream not of normal fright but of dread, for in the dream there was no monster stalking him but himself. In the nightmare, Becker became the horror, transforming from within into the cause of dread, into the nightmare himself. He was his own worst fear and the awareness had tormented him with increasing intensity for years. Becker did not just fear the dark, he sensed within it the inevitability of his own destiny.

Now there was no time to fight the horror, no light to snap on, no body in bed beside him to cling to. He would conquer the sweat-drenched chill of dread or be killed, and it would happen now. Bahoud could hardly have missed the gasp. He would be searching for Becker with his weapon. Becker clenched his jaw, trying to keep his teeth still. His chest heaved involuntarily, still gasping for oxygen, but Becker opened his mouth as wide as he could and took in the air in shallow, truncated breaths that frustrated the racking sighs his body cried out for. There was nothing he could do about his heart, which now threatened to leap through his sternum.

He knew he was still too loud. He knew it was a matter of seconds before Bahoud zeroed in on him, but the terror of his own imagination still held him prisoner and he was unable to move.

Bahoud heard the sounds like the panting of something tiny, the gasping breaths of mice. But it was close and it was lethal and it wasn't mice. He moved the gun and flashlight a few inches to his left. He pushed the button of the flashlight.

It did not move. The button was stuck, knocked out of alignment during Bahoud's fight with the super. Bahoud pressed the button again, shook the flashlight, pressed a third time. The light came on. Much too late.

Becker was still crouched, arrested by terror, when the light flashed on and the shot rang out. Becker heard the bullet whine over his shoulder a split second before the blast of the gun filled the room with its deafening, reverberating roar.

All was light for a fraction of a second as the muzzle flash lit both men as brightly as lightning in the pitch black room. Becker saw Bahoud moving before the light on his retina burned and burned again with the same image like the stuck frame of a film. Although blinded and disoriented by the spectacle that was fixed in his eyes, Becker was shocked from terror to simple animal fear by the gunblast. Instinctively, he leaped into the darkness and rolled. When his shoulder hit the wall he rose to his feet—a different man. In the instinctual moment of saving his life, he stopped fighting the terror and gave in to it, opened himself to the dread, and became the thing he feared. The gasping, shaking, sweating man was altered in a pump of the heart to the man he feared he would become. He was no longer the boy who was tormented in the dark, but the very spirit of the man who had done the tormenting.

Bahoud fired and moved immediately as he had planned, but even as he took his first step he knew he had missed. He heard a scuffling sound behind him where he thought the wall to be and he fired again. The bullet ricocheted with a scream, then again and again as it caromed off pipes and concrete in the closed room. Bahoud heard it slam against the floor just in front of him, then off the wall only feet from his head before it finally ended its journey. The weapon was useless to him, he realized. He could as easily shoot himself as his enemy with the bullet cascading about like a marble in a box.

There was no point in subtlety now. He jammed the gun into his belt as he stepped rapidly toward the wall, one hand in front of him like a blind man. He found the orange stick in his pocket and readied it between his fingers as his free hand touched the cinder block of the partition. He moved quickly, crablike, to his left until his hand came to the empty space of the doorway. He would step through, crouch on the other side, and kill his pursuer as he came through the door. There was no other way for Becker to follow him. It would all be over in seconds.

Bahoud stepped through the door and knew he had made a terrible mistake. He felt the presence of the other man waiting for him like an animal in a cave. He could almost see the teeth bared in a parody of a grin, hear the bubble of laughter and rage rise in Becker's chest.

Before he felt the first blow or heard a sound, Bahoud was aware of Becker's presence by the heat, the overwhelming sense of heat.

Bahoud lashed out blindly but hit nothing. He wheeled and flailed an arm behind him but again touched nothing but air. He knew the man was there, his nerve endings screeched with awareness of the man's presence, but he could not find him. He sensed Becker standing very close, just out of reach, grinning at him.

Becker was on the floor, beneath Bahoud's waving arms. He listened to the movements, heard the scrape and shuffle of Bahoud's shoes, and when he knew exactly where his prey was, Becker rose, grabbing Bahoud's legs and lifting. Bahoud landed on his back, his head bouncing off the concrete floor. Even as he fell, Bahoud lashed out with his arms but again hit nothing. Lights flashed behind his eyes from the concussion with the floor, but he jabbed the air with the orange stick as he lay on his back. Still nothing.

Bahoud rolled to his stomach and felt the shoe collide with the side of his head. He was knocked to his side and he rolled, coming up again quickly, battling the dizziness. He expected to be hit immediately but nothing happened. As he listened to his own frightened breathing, he realized Becker was playing with him. He was being toyed with like a mouse in the grip of a cat, tossed, pinned, tossed again.

The next blow came to his right knee, an overwhelming sense of force but no immediate pain. The shock drove him backwards into the wall. He tried to turn to face the direction from which the blow had come, but he knew Becker had already moved. Bahoud stepped to one side and the knee gave out. He fell to the floor with a gasp.

The blow came to the back of his neck, driving his face into the concrete. The foot stayed on his neck for a moment, pressing down. Bahoud thought he heard a chuckle, brief and contemptuous, then the foot was gone. Bahoud reached out, cursing, and grabbed only air.

Bahoud knew he had to do something fast. Each attack left him further wounded, his strength draining rapidly. After a while the mouse was too hurt and shocked to even attempt escape and the cat did all of the work itself, tossing the mouse's body just to simulate motion, to keep the game alive.

The next attack came as Bahoud pushed himself to his feet. Even as the blow came from behind, smashing against his kidneys and filling his body with shooting pain, Bahoud realized it was his movements that brought the action. His tormentor could not see in the pitch black; it merely seemed that way. He was responding to Bahoud's noise, and Bahoud's only chance was to do the same.

He lay facedown where he had fallen, the bulk of the gun under his belt pressing into his stomach. He would have to use it now, he knew, even if it jeopardized his own safety. When he got up he would get the gun from under his uniform, but first he must lie absolutely still; he must pretend he was dead. Let the cat come to him, let the cat come close enough for one more torment. This mouse was not dead yet.

After waiting longer than his nerves could bear, Bahoud finally heard a sound, a foot moving in the space in front of him.

Bahoud came to his feet quickly, pushing off his good leg and diving forward into the utter blackness. His fingers touched cloth and he gripped it and pulled and suddenly he had his tormentor against him. Bahoud swung upwards with the orange stick and felt his arm blocked. A knee caught him in the chest, knuckles drove hard into his left bicep, temporarily paralyzing the arm. Bahoud gasped but kept fighting, coming in low this time with the orange stick, feeling it hit and stick in the man's thigh.

Becker grunted like an animal and gripped Bahoud's wrist, at the same time chopping hard at his neck with his other hand. Bahoud sank to the floor, felt the man's knee strike him in the face again, felt his own head fly back, smash into the concrete. Bahoud reached up with his left arm, clawed for Becker's eyes. Becker's full weight landed on Bahoud's chest and knocked the breath from him in a rush. His left hand fluttered toward Becker's face again, found his mouth.

Becker bit down on Bahoud's fingers and reached for his throat. He secured Bahoud's right hand with his knee, pinning it to the floor, then released his grip on Bahoud's wrist and with a grunt pulled the orange stick from his thigh.

Bahoud started to yell now from the agony in his fingers until the grip on his throat shut off his voice. With a final effort Bahoud arched his back and pushed violently with his good leg. He felt Becker being bucked off. He was on his hands and knees, free, breathing! He would make it. He lurched to his feet, yanked the gun from his belt, and fired blindly. In the muzzle flash he saw no one. Bahoud started to turn and the gun was wrenched from his hand and clattered to the floor. Becker's forearm was across his throat, Bahoud's legs were kicked from under him, he pitched onto his face.

The blow knocked him unconscious for a few seconds, and when Bahoud came to he felt the orange stick probing gently at his ear lobe.

"Is this the way?" a voice murmured. The voice was thick and slow as if crawling up through layers of tissue and time. "Is this the way you did Daddy?"

The orange stick touched the inside of his ear. Bahoud could feel Becker's breath on the back of his neck.

"Is this the way?"

When he heard the laughter, Bahoud began to scream.

EPILOGUE

Karen was surprised by all the visitors. Finney was easy enough because they were the same age and friends—of a sort—but the succession of agents who followed him were older and knew her only from their brief stint together in New York. They were stolid men, ill-at-ease in the hospital, unaccustomed to sympathy calls, even more uncomfortable in the presence of a pretty young woman, albeit a pretty woman with a bandage as big as her hand covering her broken nose. They had no knack for sick-room conversation, and Karen ended up entertaining them until they begged off for press of work. Although none of them said as much, she realized they were trying to congratulate her on her courage, on a job well done, perhaps on her very survival. The visits themselves were as close as they could come to praise, and she took them as such.

Hatcher was the worst because the courtesy call obviously pained him the most. He shot his cuffs and plucked at the crease in his trousers, then sat uneasily beside her bed for a full ten minutes before making his departure, looking the whole time like a man undergoing a proctological examination and determined to make the best of it.

McKinnon brought flowers, the only one to do so, as if his superior position made it permissible to admit that the visit was more than official business. The director was in a gallant mood but as his stay lengthened, Karen realized that the charm was born more of power and manipulation than sex and flirtation. In the beginning they were hard to distinguish.

"The good doctors tell me you'll be up and around soon," McKinnon said after a stretch of pleasantries. "I understand you'll be wanting a permanant transfer to Terrorism."

"I'm not sure, sir," Karen said, surprising herself with her frankness.

"I understood you to be rather keen on the idea."

"Yes, sir, I was. Very keen. But that was before this."

"Ah, well, you mustn't go by this experience. It doesn't usually go this way. You just happened to be working with Becker. Normally we're a fairly sedate little group." He smiled ironically. "You wouldn't be working with Becker again."

"No?"

"He's tranferred out again," McKinnon said.

"Oh," said Karen. She tried to keep the disappointment from her voice. "Where to?"

"Oh, somewhere in the maze of federal agencies. There are lots of people who have work for our boy . . . He recommended you very highly, my dear."

"Did he?"

"He says you have a nose for the work."

Karen laughed and gingerly touched the bandage across her face.

"I have a nose for something now," she said. "I'm not sure for what. Character work, maybe."

"Beauty is transient, Miss Crist. Character is forever. You'll be a better agent with a broken nose, you know. As you must have observed, a woman who is too pretty makes men uncomfortable and other women spiteful. No one really likes someone who is too good-looking, and it is an agent's job to be liked, or at least trusted."

"That is such a comfort to me, sir," Karen said ruefully.

"Age helps, too," he continued. "My best agents are plain and middle-aged."

Karen could not help laughing aloud.

McKinnon smiled painfully. "So you see you have your best years ahead of you . . . I trust you'll spend them with Terrorism."

When he left, Karen stared at the ceiling for a long time, trying to find in the stippled white plaster the shape of her future.

Myra swam in and out of the delirium caused by pain-killers and found it difficult to distinguish the reality from the dreams. There were men all around her, deeply attentive men who cared for her, for her health and well-being, and they wanted to talk to her. She could not always answer their questions, but she heard them, urging her, in their grave voices, to respond. Did she feel this, did she feel that, look into the light, look into their eyes, follow their fingers, give them her name, the date, tell them where she was.

She did not know where she was, which did not trouble her as much as not knowing where she had been. The last thing she could remember before this strange current state of oscillating consciousness was sitting in the middle of her living room while Kane peered through the telescope. She knew something had happened but had no memory of it and she *wanted* to remember it. She had done something, she knew that much; she had taken an action and she felt good about it, whatever it was. Good or ill, success or failure, she knew she had reached out from her emotional paralysis and done something. Taking a step in any direction from her center of immobility was progress and she would be pleased with that much alone, but she sensed it was more than that. She felt that she had done something good. She was aware of liking herself.

Sometimes the faces of the men that swam before her took on clearer shapes and she recognized them. Howard was there several times, holding her hand. Once she thought she saw him crying, but then later he was more cheerful. He was trying to tell her she would be all right. She understood that much, but she still had no idea what was wrong with her.

Once the face before her was one she had seen before. He was the man who had upset her when he questioned her about poor Mr. Henley; she could not recall his name. She had last seen him prone on the carpet just before she had done whatever it was she had done.

He didn't talk to her, didn't say anything at all, but he smiled at her and there was both warmth and concern in the smile. Howard said something and the man nodded approvingly. He reached out a hand and very gently touched her cheek, which so concentrated her focus that for the first time Myra became aware of the bandages that swathed her head. They did not alarm her.

The man rested the tips of his fingers on her flesh for a moment, still smiling at her, then she thought she saw him wink. Other men came later and Myra realized they were doctors and then still other men who were with the FBI, but it was the only time she saw the man who had touched her. She remembered the smile and the warmth of his fingers and the wink.

*   *   *

Becker was the last of the agents to visit Karen, coming on the day the bandages were removed from her face. She noticed he walked with a slight limp.

"Sorry I took so long," he said. "They had me hospitalized, too."

"For your leg?"

"For my head," he said. "They were shining lights in my ears to see what's creeping around in there."

"What did they find?"

"You're looking good," he said.

"Gee, thanks. You like the lumpy look, too, do you? McKinnon thinks it's a career enhancer."

"You're gorgeous," Becker said. "The nose just gives you . . ."

"Don't say character."

"It was never your beauty alone that I responded to."

"What was it you responded to, John? My potential, wasn't it? My ability to see things the way you do, to feel things the way you do? I don't have that, either."

"Maybe."

"I don't."

"Maybe you just don't want to recognize it."

"I don't have it. I'm not like you. You just wanted me to be. Needed me to be. I'm not the person you wanted."

Becker nodded slowly.

"I wish I could have been. I wish I could have helped more."

Becker continued to nod as if taking in a world of information.

"All right," he said finally. His voice was barely audible.

Karen was surprised that silence between them could feel so awkward. She thought they had gotten past that.

"Are you going to Terrorism?" Becker said at last.

"I don't know. It frightens me."

"You'll do well there."

"Why?"

Becker shrugged. "You just said you don't want to hear it."

Karen paused. "They tell me you got him," she said.

"Is that how they put it?"

"They said you killed him," she corrected.

"Yes," he said. "I did."

"They also tell me it was self-defense," Karen said.

"They always say that."

"Wasn't it?"

Becker studied the flowers McKinnon had left.

"Was it self-defense, John?"

"It was very dark," Becker said. His voice was thick.

"When the shrinks looked in your head, John, what did they see?...John?"

He grinned without humor. "A few loose wires."

"Can they reconnect them?"

His grin increased. She realized how similar cruelty could look to bitterness. "They don't want to reconnect them. They're just studying the design in hopes they can reproduce it in a few more agents."

They fell into silence again and after a time Becker rose to leave.

"Where will you go, John?"

"I don't know. There are lots of jobs for a man of my—talents."

"Couldn't you just stop?"

"Stop?"

"Get a job in private industry, become an instructor—there are lots of other things you could do. You don't have to keep doing this if it torments you."

"Just stop?"

"Couldn't you?"

Becker looked at her oddly, tilting his head to the side, studying her.

"Do you believe a man can change his nature?" he asked.

"Yes," Karen said. "They can, they do. If they want to badly enough."

"Ah," said Becker. "Do I want to?"

He kissed her softly, then left the room.